Rebecca Tope lives on a smallholding in Herefordshire, with a full complement of livestock, but manages to travel the world and enjoy civilisation from time to time as well. Most of her varied experiences and activities find their way into her books, sooner or later. She is also the author of the Cotswold Mysteries series featuring Thea Osborne.

www.rebeccatope.com

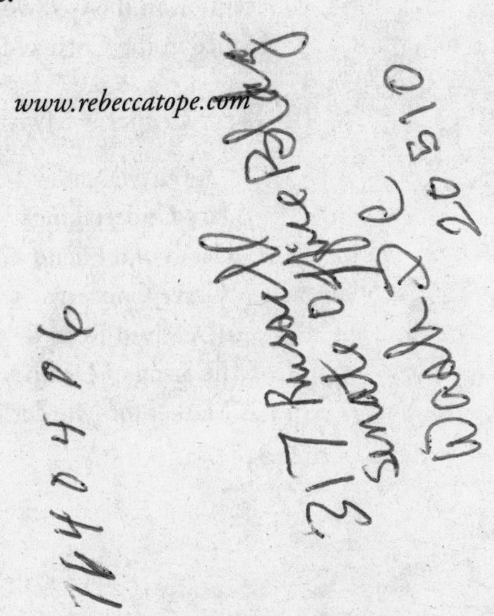

By Rebecca Tope

THE COTSWOLD MYSTERIES

A Cotswold Killing
A Cotswold Ordeal
Death in the Cotswolds
A Cotswold Mystery
Blood in the Cotswolds
Slaughter in the Cotswolds
Fear in the Cotswolds
A Grave in the Cotswolds
Deception in the Cotswolds
Malice in the Cotswolds

THE WEST COUNTRY MYSTERIES

A Dirty Death
Dark Undertakings
Death of a Friend
Grave Concerns
A Death to Record
The Sting of Death
A Market for Murder

A Death to Record

REBECCA TOPE

Allison & Busby Limited
13 Charlotte Mews
London W1T 4EJ
www.allisonandbusby.com

First published in Great Britain in 2001.
This paperback edition published by Allison & Busby in 2012.

All characters and events in this publication, other than those clearly in the public domain, are fictitious and any resemblance to actual persons, living or dead, is purely coincidental.

A CIP catalogue record for this book is available from the British Library.

10 9 8 7 6 5 4 3 2

ISBN 978-0-7490-4038-3

Typeset in 10.5/14.2 pt Sabon
by Allison & Busby Ltd.

The paper used for this Allison & Busby publication has been produced from trees that have been legally sourced from well-managed and credibly certified forests.

Printed and bound by
CPI Group (UK) Ltd, Croydon, CR0 4YY

For Sue
and for my beloved fellow writers,
whose support has been so greatly valued:
Julia, Martin, Jennifer, Gavrielle, Susan, Jeff,
Janet, Katherine, Mandy and Pearl.

AUTHOR'S NOTE

This book was written over the summer and autumn of 2000, when TB in cattle was the prevailing concern of West Country farmers. Since then, the cataclysm of foot and mouth disease has overtaken those same farmers. I don't think anybody anticipated this development, although in 2000 there was very much a mood of 'What next?'. My hope is that this story will serve to remind us that things were already bad before February 2001. And now, perhaps inevitably, with this 2012 reissue we are once again embroiled in the same arguments and dilemmas surrounding TB and the role of badgers.

PROLOGUE

The men approached the barn from every direction, climbing over gates, following age-old footpaths, in ones and twos, until fifteen of them crowded into the near-derelict building. Muffled in thick jackets and body warmers, there was a uniform colourlessness to them that would have made them difficult to recognise, even for someone who knew them. A shuffling schoolboy nervousness would have alerted anyone to the unorthodoxy of their activity.

The two dogs were snuffling eagerly. Men slapped them genially, encouraging their bloodlust. One of them was brought forward. 'Go to it, Brewster!' said a thin-faced man. 'Attaboy!' Brewster strained on his length of bale string, eyes fixed on the hessian sack five feet away. Something inside the sack was growling, thrashing to and fro.

Quickly, three or four men arranged a rough circle of musty hay bales in the middle of the small barn, leaving scant space for themselves between their ring and the walls. Fiercely cold air invaded the building through the many holes in the cob walls. It had once been a well-built store for fodder, nearly half a mile from the farmhouse. Now the house belonged to a computer programmer and the land was rented out to neighbours. Nobody used the barn any more. Except every second or third Sunday evening, these men who gathered for their illicit pleasures – and had done for years.

'Okay, mate. Let him out.' The sack was lugged into the middle of the makeshift ring and its mouth untied. Hastily the men retreated behind the bales and the dog was released from his string.

The two animals were of much the same size. Both bared their teeth aggressively, neither showing the slightest tremor of fear. The men had been unerring in their selection of natural enemies: two species programmed genetically to fight to the death.

Which they proceeded to do, taking twenty-five minutes from first to last. Before Brewster could become too exhausted, the second dog was released, shooting into the ring like a cannonball. There was only one outcome to be contemplated and fair play was never intended to be part of it. Now both dogs tore into the victim, sending it blindly snapping in two directions in a noble attempt to defend itself.

Open wounds poured blood; teeth clashed, claws flashed and sliced; an eye was lost, an underbelly ripped. They snarled and panted and spat bloody froth. And still they fought, seemingly oblivious to the frenzied encouragement from the men, who crouched scarlet-faced, rocking with the thrill of the fight. Together they moved, shoulder to shoulder, elbows out, fists clenched, in a rhythm that was visceral and universal. The rhythm of the war dance, the heartbeat and the sexual act.

As the wild animal from the sack finally sank defeated under the locked jaws of the dogs, the men exhaled as one. The long post-coital breath of release carried with it a weight of shameful anticlimax that had to be denied with grins and back slaps and promises that it wouldn't be long until the next time. Just give Brewster and Jasper time to get over their injuries.

CHAPTER ONE

The computer had packed up again. Gordon hovered impatiently as Deirdre struggled with it, tapping in vain on the unresponsive keys. 'You'll have to do it by hand,' he told her. 'I can't wait any longer. It's three already.'

Savagely, she slammed the laptop's lid down, making the farmer wince, and scooped up the two vivid orange boxes full of small plastic pots. 'All right, then,' she snapped. 'I'm ready.' Then she paused, and looked at him. 'Sorry,' she muttered. 'It's not your fault. Just me losing my temper again.'

He cocked his head in a curt sympathy. 'It was better before they started giving you those things,' he commented. 'Funny the way everything seemed better then.'

'Tell me about it,' she sighed. They indulged in a moment of nostalgic intimacy: two people nearing forty and feeling inescapably middle-aged. Five years ago, milk and beef prices had been high, computers in the milking parlour a distant possibility and bull calves a valuable source of income. 'Awful how quickly everything can change,' Deirdre added, after a few moments. 'Still shooting your calves?' She knew the answer already – she'd seen the pile of pathetic bodies out in the yard, waiting for the local hunt to collect them as food for the hounds.

He made an inarticulate sound of disgust and nodded. 'Only three or four stragglers left to calve now,' he said with relief. 'Worst thing I've ever had to do, telling Sean to shoot the poor little buggers.' He paused. 'Even worse than sending the TB-positive beasts for slaughter. BSE hardened us to that. At least with TB you know they're sick and liable to infect the others.'

Deirdre had heard it all before; not just from Gordon, but also from the majority of her farmers, forced to destroy newborns which until recently would have made good money as beef animals. Sometimes she had an image of farming as a dark underworld, full of suffering and despair, unceasing hard labour and wholesale betrayal. Even the media were beginning to take some notice as farms went out of business.

'It's a holocaust,' the farmers told each other, thinking of the thousands of incinerated animals, the brutal suicide levels amongst farmers, the generally uncaring attitudes of the population at large. Nobody thought it too strong a word to use, in the circumstances.

'What happened to number five-five-four?' Deirdre asked, running down his list of events in the herd since her last visit, and finding *dead* written against that particular animal. A strangled sound made her look up at him. His face was twisted with the pain of the memory and she wished she hadn't asked.

'She had a bad calving,' he said, looking away, his cheeks flushing.

'I remember her. The one with the curly topknot. One of your favourites, wasn't she?' She knew she was hurting him, forcing him to tell the story, but curiosity prevailed over sensitivity, as usual.

'We had to shoot her,' he said, pulling his top lip between his teeth and visibly biting down on it. The tears that filmed his eyes were not the result of the bite. 'The calf got stuck and she would have needed a caesarean.'

'Which costs two hundred quid these days,' she supplied, understandingly. Another story she'd heard more than once in the past few months.

'I didn't let her suffer for more than a few minutes,' he assured her grimly. 'Now, let's get started.'

The cows were crowding and jostling in the yard, their breath making clouds of vapour in the frosty air. Their winter coats made them look unkempt, an impression increased by the patches of drying dung on their sides and the swollen joints on many back legs. Wisps of straw clung to the muck, which extended to the soft area between the front legs, in some cases. Even to Deirdre's eye, they looked a mess. 'I see you've been economising on straw again,' she commented critically. Mucky udders were bad news for her – it took the dairyman long minutes of washing to get them clean enough to milk and she got home proportionately later.

'Long time till spring,' Gordon said shortly. 'Have to make it last.'

Deirdre knew she had no right to carp – Gordon was doing his best, and it was as frustrating for him to have to pick away the dung and get his hands chapped by the rapidly-cooling washing water as it was for her waiting for him to get on with the job.

He pressed the switch to start the motor. A

loud throbbing erupted, enhanced by whistles and hisses which were eliminated one by one as he closed valves and established a vacuum. Of their own accord, twelve rubber, plastic and aluminium clusters rose into the air, ready and waiting for the milk-heavy animals. The routine was unvaried, twice a day, year in, year out. Except on Recording Day, when Deirdre showed up and the herdsman had someone to talk to, and someone observing every move he made.

She watched him now, as she watched all the men she worked with. He was one of the more vigorous, fast-moving and focused. Unlike most, he worked with bare hands even in mid-winter, dipping them into a bucket of tepid water every now and then to clean them. He sported a matted woollen hat pulled over his ears and a grimy brown scarf crossed at his neck and tucked inside his ancient corduroy jacket. As protection against muck and other excretions, he wore a long grey rubber apron. Farmers' clothes were part of their camouflage, she'd long ago realised. Intelligent, efficient, courageous men disappeared into shapeless, colourless yokels when they donned their dairy garb. They became figures of fun in the public eye, sucking straws and scratching heads with grimy fingers. Deirdre knew better – she worked with a dozen or more of these men, glimpsing the complex individual beneath the camouflage as they made full use of her captive listening ear. The milk recording service monitored the quality and quantity of each cow's yield in a typical twenty-four-hour period, giving official confirmation for the farmer to use when completing dossiers on his herd, as well as laboratory analysis of the milk. With the inexorable escalation of farm paperwork, the job of a milk recorder had also expanded. Every event during the previous month had to be entered onto computer files: births, deaths, sales, purchases, inseminations, health problems, lactation details. Everything was assessed and quantified and used for predictions until it was all too easy to forget they were dealing with living creatures. Nobody but the most stubborn old-timers referred to the cows by name any more, and it was a rash herdsman who developed close favourites amongst his animals. 'Cull' was a word used so often that it had its own keystroke on the computer.

The milking got under way. Gordon tolerated very little dithering from the animals, whistling them in and slapping them if they stood awkwardly or moved too slowly. Deirdre had never seen him hit a cow hard enough to really hurt it – which was more than she could say for some of the men she encountered, including Gordon's own herdsman, who usually milked these cows. All the same, she suspected that Gordon was more self-controlled when she was watching him. She was dubious as to whether she ever saw the real man.

The herdsman, Sean O'Farrell, was employed by Gordon Hillcock, owner of the farm, to do the milking for five or six days each week, his time off forming a complex pattern that only he and his employer fully understood. It was fairly unusual for Gordon to be milking on Recording Day, but he generally joined Deirdre in the office for a ten-minute chat on her visits, and she met him now and then at markets or shows, or even in the local shops. She felt she knew the owner of Dunsworthy Farm nearly as well as she knew his herdsman.

She had been a milk recorder for five years, and it was axiomatic amongst farmers that Recording Day was a jinx. Something nearly always went wrong, either because of the need for additional equipment or because the cows objected to the stranger in their midst. Sometimes it seemed that any disaster waiting to happen would habitually choose Recording Day to make its move. Deirdre had grown accustomed to the sighs of half-suppressed reproach from the many different herdsmen and farmers she met, although none of them ever openly accused her of causing trouble. After all, they had opted to pay for her services – there was no compulsion.

Two lines of six cows lumbered into the tight herringbone rows on either side of the parlour. In a pit, three feet lower than the animals, the two people manoeuvred in a long-established routine. Gordon moved down each row, squirting a jet of water over the udders, from a nozzle hanging from the pipework overhead. Then he slowly worked back along the row, wiping a damp paper towel across each udder, pausing now and then to scrub a piece of dried dung from a teat or to inspect a suspiciously swollen quarter, before deftly swinging the unit of four simulated calves' mouths underneath the udder and one-two-three-four, applying them in turn to each teat. The rhythmic sucking, like that of babies in a well-organised Soviet nursery, brought pause and relief.

Gordon wiped his hands and glanced at Deirdre, waiting with her rack full of small pots slung comically around her neck. 'Bloody awful weather,' he commented idly. 'First frost of the year.'

The recorder merely nodded, waiting for more interesting conversation. When none came, she said, 'Sean's having a day off then, is he?'

Gordon hesitated, glancing along the double

row of cows before replying. 'He agreed to swap this afternoon and tomorrow morning, for Saturday. I want to . . . go somewhere at the weekend.'

She thought she knew where that 'somewhere' was, but said nothing. It ought to have surprised nobody that in that atmosphere of anxiety and frustration, farmers would feel compelled to fight back. In her awkward position as semi-spy with deeply ambiguous loyalties, Deirdre had learnt when to feign ignorance. So she gauged her reaction carefully and widened her eyes teasingly. 'Well, well, that sounds unusually amicable for you two.'

'It's no problem to him. Doesn't matter what day it is to Sean.' He spoke over his shoulder, as he moved to reapply a cluster that had fallen off one of the cows before she'd finished milking. Watching him retrieve it and patiently reconnect it to the cow, Deirdre prepared to go into action herself.

Moments later, one of the milking units detached itself from a cow and swung free, up and out, in an arc calculated to catch an unwary person full in the face. Deirdre adjusted her rack, felt in her top breast pocket for pencil and dipper, and went to work. Squinting at the flask adjacent to the cow, she read the calibrated figure indicating the milk yield and wrote it in indelible green on the white lid of the appropriate pot, already carrying a black number to correspond to that on the cow's rump. Then, with the manipulation of a sequence of switches and levers, involving the hissing of escaping air from the vacuum suction system, and several drops of milk trickling down her sleeve as well as into the dipper, she captured a few millilitres. This was poured into the pot, the lid raised and then pressed home with a practised flick of the left thumb. Finally, she kept one finger on the lever at the top of the flask until all remaining milk had drained away, leaving it ready for the next cow.

Thus was captured a record of the quantity and quality of Line Number 740's milk for that afternoon. The recorder would have to repeat this performance for all one hundred and four cows currently in milk – and then laboriously transfer the yields to printed sheets in the farm office. Normally, she would key them into the laptop – but the laptop was playing dead again. The same process would be duplicated in the morning.

Deirdre often wondered exactly what the men thought of her. They were usually friendly, glad to have someone to talk to for a change, and eager for the gossip she brought with her from her other farms. The chief topic of discussion these days was which farms had gone out of business since her last visit. Those hanging on would buy up the best of the dissolving herds at knockdown prices, and congratulate themselves on being amongst the survivors. Where once there had been friendly rivalry, there was now anxiety, grief and numbing shock, combined inevitably with *Schadenfreude* and self-righteous smugness – *I never thought 'e'd make a go of it, borrowing as heavily as 'e did.* Gordon Hillcock was the youngest farm owner in the district, by a decade or so. Farming was becoming an old man's pursuit, which in itself sounded a death knell in many people's ears.

Opportunities for conversation were brief. Gordon's pace increased as time went on, but his mood seemed to darken. Deirdre's own spirits were also far from sunny; since her computer had died on her, she was going to have to spend time she begrudged doing the job by hand afterwards. Gordon wouldn't get his computerised print-out, either, with an assessment of each animal's performance. But she didn't want to appear stand-offish. Maintaining good relations with the farmer was all part of the job.

'So you and Sean aren't cross with each other any more?' she prompted.

'What?' He turned to stare at her. 'What do you mean?'

'Well, last month you weren't speaking; you'd had some sort of fight. It probably seems a long time ago now.'

Visiting only once a month, her perception of the passage of time was inevitably very different from that of the men who performed this same task something like sixty times between her attendances. No wonder they couldn't remember what had been happening a month ago. And this time there'd been Christmas and New Year in between.

'We get along all right,' Gordon said curtly.

The slightest sceptical flicker of an eyebrow was her only response. For the past five years, to her certain knowledge, and probably much longer, Gordon and Sean had been antagonists. They would each regale her with stories of the misdeeds of the other, given the slightest encouragement. Mostly she tried to ignore their complaints, and avoid taking sides, but it was an uneven struggle. Sean was not an easy man to like and there had been instances where Deirdre had witnessed behaviour towards the animals that she regarded as needless cruelty. There was a tense atmosphere throughout Sean's milkings that was absent from Gordon's. She wondered whether the cows felt the same relief as she did, when the herdsman had a day off.

And Sean complained constantly. He was

underpaid; overworked; nobody understood what a trial his life was, with his sick wife and unpredictable daughter. Gordon had no idea how to manage a dairy herd – he thought he could survive the crisis in farming when everyone around him was going to the wall. Well, Sean could see the way it was going, and even Dunsworthy could go bust. He spoke in a monotonous nasal voice that jarred on Deirdre's nerves. She wanted to point out to him how lucky he was to have a job at all, how much worse off others were. She wanted him to shut up and get the job finished, so she could go home and forget about him for another month.

Gordon was altogether more restrained. 'Old Sean's been moaning at me again,' he would say, with a rueful grin. 'It's being so miserable that keeps him going.' But today he clearly didn't want to be reminded of the friction that existed between them. Perhaps he thought Deirdre was prying – after all, it was none of her business.

In the middle of one row, a cow began to defecate. Manure landed splashily, reaching Deirdre's shoulder and a considerable selection of surrounding machinery. Neither she nor Gordon reacted; it was a commonplace, not worth remarking. Despite stringent modern hygiene regulations, dried muck clung to almost every nook and cranny of the parlour, where metal and rubber piping ran along every wall, at all angles, carrying cattle cake, milk, compressed air, water. Splatters of dung reached high up the walls, their age apparent by the coating of dust or cobweb. Gordon and Sean were alike in being no cleanliness fanatics, although one or two of the farms that Deirdre visited could be so described. Yet the Dunsworthy cell count levels, indicating the presence of mastitis-producing organisms, were acceptably average; and besides, Gordon insisted, a bit of muck was healthy. It maintained good levels of immunity in the animals.

'How's Heather?' she managed to enquire, half an hour into the milking, as she always did, however busy she might be. Deirdre never ceased to be intrigued by the herdsman's wife and her mysterious malaise.

'Much the same,' he shrugged. 'Says it hurts in at least twenty different places. What can you do?'

'It boggles my mind,' she admitted. Heather, at much her own age, had succumbed to ME: the yuppy flu, chronic fatigue syndrome, or Malingering Extraordinary, as Deirdre secretly called it. Her own brisk health was the measure by which she judged others and no amount of persuasion from more sympathetic souls could convince her that some people simply found life too much to deal with. Her own husband had reproached her for her heartlessness, many a time, when she'd forced a fevered child to go to school or impatiently dismissed a friend's claim to be unwell.

But Heather O'Farrell bothered her in particular. Married to Sean for eighteen years or more, with one daughter, Heather now lived an invisible existence in one of the farm cottages: a sort of ghost suffering endlessly but quietly. There had apparently been a time, years ago, when she'd take a turn at the milking two or three times a month, but not any more. Sean had talked to Deirdre about it over the years, with an air of puzzled acceptance. 'Can't be helped,' he'd said, a thousand times. 'Just have to get on with it. I doubt we'd know what to do with ourselves now, if she suddenly got better,' he'd said on one of Deirdre's recent visits. Deirdre's fingers had positively itched with the desire to go and shake the woman into a resumption of normal life. She'd been surprised at her own strong feelings – the *anger.* Why she should so resent the invalid she herself couldn't begin to understand.

The unit detaching from the last cow in the left-hand line obliged Gordon to embark on another sequence of actions. Opening the front gate, chivvying those animals out, closing the gate, opening the one at the back, and whistling in another batch of willing milkers. Deirdre mentally ticked off another six. Only fifty-six to go.

The routine continued for almost two hours, with occasional interruptions for quick washing-down with a high pressure hose. Then Gordon muttered something about having to bring in five cows from the adjacent barn. 'They're this month's convalescents,' he grinned ruefully. 'Three lame, one bad calving and one victim of bullying.'

He waited for the reaction. 'Bullying?' Deirdre obligingly enquired.

'It's a new heifer, and the others have taken against her. I've no idea why. She's a poor little thing, and I took pity on her. She's much happier with the halt and the lame.'

He slid open a door at one side of the parlour, leading into an adjacent building, and went to collect his special cases. Deirdre tinkered with her pots, turning them so the numbers were all the right way up, waiting for the first lame cow to appear, thinking vaguely about how sweet Gordon could be, coddling his shy new heifer, like a bigger boy befriending a new child in the playground, unable to cope with the rough and tumble.

But instead of bringing the expected cows, Gordon returned alone, his face white. She stared at him, uncomprehending, waiting for him to speak. If she thought anything, it was that a cow must have trodden heavily on his foot, or crushed him in some way. When he simply stood there, leaning oddly against the door frame, she asked, 'What on earth's the matter?'

'Come and see,' he said, his voice scarcely audible over the milking machine.

At Redstone Farm, barely a mile away, Lilah Beardon and her mother Miranda were drinking tea beside a log fire. Lilah sighed contentedly. 'Isn't it marvellous without the cows!' she rejoiced. 'I really thought I'd miss them – but I don't. I can still feel how frozen my feet used to get, and how they'd slip about on the ice in the yard.'

'Should have done it years ago,' her mother agreed.

'I wish Daddy was here. He'd approve, I know he would. He'd kick himself that he hadn't thought of it ages ago.'

'No, he wouldn't.' Miranda shook her head. 'Things weren't so bad then. He was proud of his cows. And he'd say we were wasting a good farm.'

It was a conversation they'd had before, and one that never reached a resolution. Neither woman cared enough to pursue it to the point of serious disagreement. They lived on a farm almost denuded of animals, Miranda working for a local estate agent and Lilah attending a college twenty-five miles away to pursue a three-year course in horticulture. Plants were much less stressful than animals, she'd discovered.

'Are you going over to Gordon's this evening?' Miranda asked.

Lilah shook her head. 'It's too cold. And he's milking this afternoon, which means he'll be in a foul mood. I keep telling him he should pack it in like we have, but he's got too much invested in it – not just money, either. He really cares about his cows. We were never in the same league as he is. We were *dinosaurs*, compared to him.'

'I think you're mad to take up with a farmer,' Miranda said flatly. 'Stark raving mad. And Gordon Hillcock is absolutely the last person I would ever have imagined you with. Those red cheeks – that neck.' She shuddered exaggeratedly. 'I'll never understand what you see in him.'

Lilah took the rudeness calmly. 'You don't know him. He's quite different from the way he looks.'

'If you marry him, you'll be back to square

one. He'll have you out there with frozen feet, two days after the honeymoon.'

'No he won't. I'll make it very clear that I'm not his unpaid herdswoman. I don't like Friesians, anyway. Great clumsy things.'

Miranda turned to look at her daughter, without speaking. Lilah knew the look. It was a kind of impressed disapproval, which never seemed to diminish, three months after Lilah had jilted her former fiancé in favour of Gordon Hillcock. She was mildly impressed herself, at this strange, mad deed. Poor Den, to whom she would have been married by now, had wept and shouted and accused, to no avail. She was in thrall to Gordon, sixteen years older than her, a bachelor living with his mother and sister, a balding, rosy-cheeked, Devon-accented farmer, who had never been anywhere or done anything. It made no sense to anyone else, and the all-too-obvious explanation, of which Lilah herself was acutely aware, was not something she could put into words. Perhaps if she'd had a close girlfriend or sister she might have managed it. But how could you tell your mother or former boyfriend that you'd walk a thousand miles over hot coals for the things this man could make you feel?

Deirdre went to the phone in the office and pressed the nine key three times. She kept glancing back towards the door leading into the barn, but there was no sign of Gordon.

'Emergency. Which service do you require?' came the unemotional voice.

'Police, please. A man has been killed. We're at Dunsworthy Farm, between South Lew and Fellaton Cross.' Her voice faltered. How much of the story were you supposed to tell?

The woman asked for her name and phone number, and a quick account of what seemed to have happened. 'I'll notify the police and ambulance service,' she said calmly. Deirdre wanted to insist that there was no need for an ambulance, but she kept quiet. The whole process felt oddly irrelevant: bits of bureaucracy that couldn't be of the slightest help to the wretched Sean now. Much more urgent was the problem of Gordon. But Deirdre didn't think she could say anything about her last sighting of him, as he crouched in the straw, one knee in a heap of manure, sobbing like a small child.

After Gordon's unexpected reappearance in the parlour, Deirdre had slowly climbed the steps out of the well in the parlour and gone through the doorway. Gordon stood aside for her. 'Over there,' he said, indicating with his chin. 'See?'

There was something in a corner. All the

cows were standing as far away as possible. The barn was dark, the floor covered in a generous layer of fresh straw, which was disturbed around the thing in the corner, so it lay partly on bare earthen floor. Deirdre moved closer.

'It's a man!' she said.

Awkwardly, with her rack swinging out from her chest, she moved to bend over the figure and felt his cheek with the back of her hand. 'He's not completely cold, but I think he's dead,' she said, turning to look hard at Gordon, who hung back, leaving it to her. She took no more action. Time seemed to be suspended, paralysed. She took in the farmer's bulging eyes, the bared teeth against white knuckles. The sight of Gordon in such a state had done more to churn her stomach and quiver her bowels than did the body at her feet, in those first few seconds.

'It's Sean,' she had announced superfluously. 'But what on earth's he doing in here?' She frowned her puzzlement at the farmer.

Gordon hadn't moved. 'I can't look,' he muttered.

By contrast, Deirdre couldn't tear her eyes away. Growing accustomed to the poor light, she could now see more of what lay at her feet. The dead man wore a grubby jumper, full of snags and holes, with a quilted body warmer over it.

He had a woollen scarf around his neck and thick corduroy trousers. Dark blood streaked all these garments, and was smeared generously over the floor.

She looked back again at Gordon. 'The cows couldn't have done it, could they?' She stood up straighter, inspecting the animals. 'None of them's got horns. Jesus, Gordon, don't just stand there!' She heard the shrillness rising in her own voice. 'We'll have to phone – police, ambulance, all that.'

'Bit late for an ambulance,' Gordon said, the words emerging on a strange, bitter laugh. Deirdre steadied herself and squatted down closer to Sean's body, wondering whether she'd been too quick to assume him dead. But nobody with that strangely inexpressive and cold face could be alive. With those wounds, any flicker of life would have put all its efforts into some manifestation of pain and terror. The absence of either was enough proof that death had already occurred.

Growing up on a farm herself, she had seen sights as bad before – sheep torn apart by bloodthirsty dogs, or with their eyes pecked out while still alive; blood and muck and agony. She noted that it really wasn't so different when the victim was human. Especially when it was Sean O'Farrell, whose death was not something she was going to grieve over.

She nudged the body gently with her boot. It felt wooden, unyielding. She said, 'He's dead, Gordon.' A crazy thought entered her head, bringing a grim smile to her lips: *The Recording Day Jinx strikes again.*

Gordon appeared unaware of her inappropriate expression. 'Yes,' he breathed, in response to her words. 'Yes, I know.'

CHAPTER TWO

Detective Sergeant Den Cooper was flipping through the local paper, a mug of coffee at his elbow, while the call made its way through all the usual channels until it reached Okehampton Police Station. It was almost time to knock off and go home. Nothing much was happening; everyone was too exhausted by the New Year celebrations to carry out any felonies. They were ten days into the new year – the new century – and he was still waiting to feel optimistic, benign, newborn and all the other things that Prince Charles and the Archbishop of Canterbury said he should feel. The weather was depressing, he had a cold, his girlfriend had dumped him and he hated his job. Life was not merely proceeding exactly as it had done before; it was worse. He couldn't think of a single thing to look forward to. Even his twenty-seventh birthday at the end of the month was unlikely to bring any reason for rejoicing.

'Cooper?' It was Danny Hemsley, the new Detective Inspector. 'Den?' he amended, with a cheerful grin. 'Are you busy?'

Den flapped the paper and glanced at the tepid coffee. 'As you see,' he said.

'Something for you, then. Take Young Mike with you. Dead body on a farm. We've got the police doctor on his way, but you ought to be there first.'

Something stirred in Den's breast. Fear, excitement, memories. 'Which farm?' he asked.

'Hmmm.' Danny consulted the scrap of paper in his hand. 'Dunsworthy, looks like. Woman called Deirdre Watson. It doesn't say who's dead. Maybe it's her.' He shook his head. 'Usual balls-up.'

'*Dunsworthy!* That's Hillcock's place. Who the hell is Deirdre Watson?'

'Search me,' Danny shrugged. 'That's for you to go and find out.'

'But—' Den looked at the other man helplessly. Nobody at the station knew about Lilah's betrayal, beyond the fact that she'd called off the wedding and he wasn't seeing her any more.

He ought to try and explain the situation, now, right at the outset, before driving to Dunsworthy. He opened his mouth, to say, *That's where my girlfriend's new bloke lives. Are you sure you want me involved in this? Might there not be a conflict of interest somewhere along the line?*

But he didn't. If Gordon Hillcock was dead, it would feel like a friendly Fate lending a hand. It would make Den feel better. But it wouldn't affect his work. There was also the unavoidable fact that there was really nobody else. Sergeant Phil Bennett was off sick and likely to be for some time, after breaking his ankle. Already under-staffed, the DI had little alternative to sending Den out on this particular call.

And it wouldn't be a problem, Den insisted to himself. He would do all he could to discover how and why the victim had died. But who was Deirdre Watson? At least three families lived at Dunsworthy. Den guessed she must be a wife or girlfriend of an employee.

'Okay,' he said, getting up slowly. Standing, he was a clear four inches taller than Danny, himself almost six feet. 'Where's Young Mike?'

'Waiting by the front desk. Nobody can say that boy's not keen.'

Although he'd never been to this particular example, Den was familiar enough with the general layout of farms of the same type to make enlightened guesses as to the inhabitants of the three homes on the Dunsworthy farmstead. Close to the road, two semi-detached, low-level cottages came into view first. They had been built for farm workers a century or so earlier, and were still occupied by farm employees. Four hundred yards further up the rutted drive, the main farmhouse, inhabited by Gordon Hillcock and his family, sat squarely surrounded by a motley assembly of modern steel-and-concrete farm buildings, as well as older barns and sheds. The cow sheds were huge and extensive, providing cover for the entire animal stock. A round food hopper, containing cattle cake, stood outside the milking parlour and bulk tank room. A muddy yard, dotted with glittering patches that turned out to be frozen puddles, offered ample parking space, despite already containing a tractor, battered Land Rover, a mud-spattered Peugeot, an ambulance and a very disturbing heap of dead black-and-white calves, caught in the police car's headlights. Young Mike yelped when he caught sight of them.

'Good God! There's been a massacre here.'

'Not really,' said Den. 'They shoot the bulls at birth. Not worth trying to sell them these days. Remember all that hoo-ha at Shoreham?'

'Live exports, yeah.'

'Well, now the calves get shot instead of exported.'

'Hmm,' was Young Mike's confused response.

Den dragged his thoughts from conversations with Lilah on this and other agricultural subjects. He'd learnt more from her than he realised, in the years they'd been together.

'Poor little buggers,' Mike murmured. Indeed the calves looked pathetic enough, their long, thin legs outstretched, the sweet faces, marked with the vivid monochrome patches, staring sightlessly across the yard. From somewhere behind the complex of buildings, the distant, wavering cry of a surviving calf could be heard.

Two men stood beside the ambulance. Den got out of the car quickly and walked up to them. 'Not one for you, then?' he queried.

One of the men shook his head. 'You could say that,' he confirmed. 'You'll be calling out the whole team on this one, I reckon. And after that, you'll want the undertakers. We'll be out of your way now.'

Den let them go without further discussion. A woman came out of the door beside the food hopper, clearly waiting for them. 'Come on, then,' muttered Den. 'Let's see what's what.'

'It's this way,' she told them, glancing from face to face. She was of above average height, sturdy, wearing a navy blue protective outfit, with large wellington boots. Her hair, a pleasing chestnut colour, was dragged back into a tight knot, and there were splashes of muck across one shoulder. There was a hardness around the eyes and an impression that she seldom smiled. Her accent was barely perceptibly Devon.

'Are you Deirdre Watson?' Den asked her. 'Do you live here?'

'I'm the milk recorder,' she said, as if this explained everything. For Den, it mostly did.

'Recording Day, is it?' he asked, with a nod. Another agricultural mystery that Lilah had long ago explained to him.

It was dim inside the barn, even with the light on. Den fished in his pocket for a torch as Deirdre pointed out to them the relevant corner, keeping a safe distance, somehow understanding that she ought not to further disturb the scene. *Is it him?* Den was bursting to ask her. *Is it that swine Hillcock?* He'd know the answer soon enough.

Eagerly, he played the torch beam across the body, taking in the blood, the huddled stiffness. He could see the disturbed straw, the signs of frenzied movement. The hands were clutched to a wound in the abdominal region, and Den understood that there had been great pain in this dying. The hair was lank, greasy and plentiful. The neck was scrawny, under the grubby scarf. Narrow shoulders, narrower hips. A lean cheek and a long jaw. It was definitely not Gordon Hillcock lying there. 'Who is he?' he asked resignedly. 'And who found him?'

'Sean O'Farrell,' the woman told him. 'The herdsman. He lives in one of the cottages where you turn in off the road. And Gordon found him, when he came to collect the cows.'

He isn't going to live there any more, thought Den to himself. 'Has he got any family?'

'Wife and daughter. We haven't told them yet. I didn't like to leave him . . . and Gordon—' She threw a quick glance towards the milking parlour, where the motor was still running, providing a constant background throb to the proceedings.

'Yes – Gordon.' Den forced the name through his lips. 'Where's he, then?'

'He had to finish the milking. We were on the last five, when we came in here and found Sean. He thought he might as well finish them off.'

'It's taken us twenty minutes to get here,' Den calculated. 'Surely they're finished by now?'

'He's washing down. There's forty minutes' work still to do after the last unit's off.' She spoke woodenly, not looking at the figure on the floor. 'He was upset,' she added.

'He shouldn't be disturbing the scene,' Den said. 'Everything should be left just as it was.'

'We haven't moved anything in here,' she told

him defensively. 'The parlour's got nothing to do with it.'

Den let it go. She was right, anyway: a farm was one of the hardest places on which to conduct any kind of forensic examination. Work tended to go on however much you insisted things be left untouched. This was not his first experience of the destruction of evidence by water or trampling or newly-deposited manure.

Thinking quickly, he tried to sort out what had to be done. The witnesses were supposed to be kept separate, though what good that would do, he couldn't quite see. If they'd wanted to prepare a story free from contradictions, they'd had plenty of time to do so. He looked at Mike. 'You go and stay with Mr Hillcock, while I make sure nothing gets disturbed here. Don't ask him any questions. Just . . .'

'I know what to do,' Mike said, with an air of injury.

Outside, the lights of an approaching car flickered through the open door beside the huge steel bulk milk tank that squatted in its own anteroom between the milking parlour and the outside yard. 'That'll be the doc,' Den said. He faced the woman again; she was waiting for him just inside the door into the milking parlour. 'Who did you say found him?'

'Gordon,' she repeated. 'He came to collect

the cows that were in here. I don't know where he's put them, now they've been milked,' she added distractedly.

'Well, they can't come back in here,' Den decreed. 'There'll be a Scene of Crime team, forensic people. I don't think we can call this a natural death, can we?' He looked at her closely in the weak light, his question rhetorical, but none the less serious for all that.

She seemed to be considering the matter in some depth, her eyes veiled and turned away from him. 'Perhaps he had some sort of accident?' she offered.

Den raised an eyebrow. 'No sign of the cause of his injuries,' he observed, sweeping the shadowy, straw-covered floor with a sharp eye. 'It must have been something pretty substantial, by the look of it. Not just a rusty nail.' The barn was lighter at the further end and he directed his gaze at a second door set into the thick cob wall. Treading a delicate path along the inside walls, he made his way to the door and examined a dark smudge on it, at slightly lower than shoulder height. He had expected to find muck, but his finger found the substance to be slightly sticky, viscous. 'Blood,' he concluded, in a mutter. He extracted a thin plastic glove from his pocket and put it on his right hand before opening the door. It was operated by means of a wooden latch that could be worked from either side, thanks to a hole cut in the stout timber. It opened inwards, swinging easily. A gentle push was enough to close it again, the latch sliding over the grooved wooden catch.

Den continued with his hypotheses, silently working them out. The man must have leant against the wall and the blood pumped out onto the door. Arterial bleeding.

He turned his attention to the floor. 'Left quite a trail,' he noted. 'The attack could have happened outside, and then he dragged himself in here before he died. This door would have latched shut again if he'd leant on it.'

'So—' prompted Deirdre, with a pointed look towards the yard, where a car door was now slamming.

'Won't be long now,' Den assured her. 'Would you be kind enough to stay where I can see you for a few more minutes? I'll have some questions for you when I've got the doctor organised.'

Deirdre raised her eyebrows at something in his tone. 'You know him, do you? Gordon, I mean.'

Den narrowed his eyes at her and cocked his head. 'What makes you ask that?'

'I can see it on your face.'

Den sighed. Clever women irritated him. This one was only here by a freak of the calendar. He wasn't in the mood to play games with her. 'Yes, I know him,' he said tersely.

Then he made swift use of his phone, while indicating the scene to the doctor. The persistent throb of the milking machine, at first an irritant, had acquired a faintly sedative influence. Den was surprised at how calm he felt. He was thorough, and stuck as closely as was reasonable to the book of rules. Some officers might have given more thought to the possibility of a vicious killer lurking in the dark outbuildings, ready to attack again, but Den felt no anxieties in that direction. Outside could wait. A team would arrive shortly with powerful lights and protective clothes, to pore as best they could over mucky cowsheds and frozen yards. Meanwhile, there were questions to be asked. He needed details of times, places, movements. Sitting Deirdre Watson down in the untidy office, he rapidly, almost impatiently, ascertained these basics from her. Behind him, in the milking parlour itself, something much more important was waiting for him.

At last, he told Deirdre he had finished with her. Then, sliding the door tightly closed behind him, he went back to join Young Mike – and Gordon Hillcock.

'Mike!' he shouted, above the machine noise. 'Can you go down to the cottages and tell Mrs

O'Farrell what's happened? Stay with her until I get there, okay?'

'What . . . now?'

'Yes, now. Stay with her, but don't question her. I'll have a word with Mr Hillcock and wait for the cavalry to show up. I might be a while.'

Gordon Hillcock was standing in the well of his milking parlour, his back to the barn, a powerful pressure hose in his hand. Water gushed from it. At first, Den was bemused that Mike had not tried to stop him – it was theoretically possible that he was washing away vital evidence. But he could see, after a glance at Hillcock's face, that intervention would not have been easy. While Den watched him, he did not vary the direction of the jet by a millimetre, and by the look of that particular corner of the parlour wall, it had never been so clean before.

'Mr Hillcock?' Den called. 'Could I have a word with you?'

Slowly Gordon turned the nozzle to arrest the flow of water. He looked over his shoulder at Den. His face was streaked with grey marks and his eyes were red and ringed with hollows that made him look monstrous in the harsh light of the parlour. 'You saw him, then?' he said gruffly.

Den met his gaze. There was horror there, yes, and a dash of fear. But there was also a stillness that looked like resignation, acceptance of judgement. A slope to the shoulders, a forward tilt to the head that looked to Den like nothing in the world more than guilt. Den felt a wicked inner *whoop* of triumph. This was even better than if Hillcock had been the victim. For some unknown reason, the man facing him had murdered his herdsman: it was clearly written on his face. And Den was to be the arresting officer. *Oh, sweet revenge*, a small voice sang inside him.

CHAPTER THREE

'There's something going on out there,' Claudia called as another vehicle drove into the yard, its headlights sending slanting beams across the living room ceiling. 'Mary! Are you there?'

Mary appeared in the doorway, her hands covered in flour. 'What?' she said.

'The yard's full of cars and men talking in little groups. Something must have happened. Has Gordon been in?'

Mary went to the window. 'I don't think so. Not that he'd bother to come and tell us what's going on. Gosh, yes, you're right! Three strange cars, as far as I can see. One of them's behind the wall; it looks more like a van than a car. How odd. And there's a man with a torch.'

Claudia was comfortably settled in a deep armchair, with a file of notes balanced on her lap. A cat perched on her shoulder. 'Maybe you should pop out and see what's up,' she suggested to her daughter. 'I'd go, but I can't really move.'

'*I* can't go. I'm halfway through making a pie with those Bramleys. If it's something important, Gordon'll come in and tell us.'

'But – *three* cars,' Claudia said. 'It's not just the vet, is it? It's cold and dark out there – hardly a moment for a visitation from the Ministry.'

'It's probably nothing for us to worry about. If it is, we'll find out soon enough.'

'Oh, drat.' Claudia plucked at the sleeping cat. 'I can't just sit here not knowing. It makes us seem so *peripheral*, like Victorian womenfolk quietly getting on with things in the house while the world falls apart outside. There might be some awful crisis with the cows. Your father would have just shouted for us until we put in an appearance.'

'He would.' Mary pulled a face. 'I still hear him sometimes, expecting us to drop everything and run to his service. Gordon's a big improvement in that respect.'

'Well, I'm going to have a look. Sorry, Kitty, this hurts me as much as it does you.' She plonked the cat onto the floor and laid her paperwork on a stool close to her chair.

'I hope they don't want me,' said Mary. 'It's freezing out there and my boots have got a hole in them. And one of those cars looks like the recorder's, now I come to think of it. Probably it's just two vets, come from different directions. He'll have phoned them from the office. Though why he would call *two* . . .'

'Oh, well, I'm up now,' said Claudia. 'You get back to your apple pie, and I'll nip out and see what I can discover.'

Mary shrugged, but didn't go back to the kitchen. She watched her mother open the front door, kicking a crumpled rug out of the way and pausing to rummage for a pair of boots in the covered porch beyond the door. Curiosity flickered, but no more than that. Farmyard crises were common enough for her not to be worried. Innocent explanations abounded – and if it was something serious, she was in no great hurry to know what it was.

'Have you anything to say to me?' Den asked again, as he faced Gordon. 'There's a police doctor here now. We'll let him do his part and then we'll take statements. I'm afraid the running of your farm is likely to be disrupted. We'll need to check any possible weapons that might be on the premises.'

'Weapons?' Gordon stirred a little, a small

frown creasing his brow. 'What sort of weapons?'

'Firearms, for example, sir,' said Den formally.

'You think he was *shot*?'

'It can't be ruled out, sir,' Den replied, feeling somehow wrong-footed. Gordon said nothing more, but merely shook his head dumbly and began slowly coiling the thick rubber hose onto a metal hook beside him. The milk recorder's pots were still spread over the rickety wooden table in one corner of the milking parlour. 'Mr Hillcock,' Den said loudly. 'Will you come with me, please?'

Den tried to muster his thoughts. Was there already enough suspicion against Hillcock to warrant taking him in for questioning? The recorder woman had been at the scene as well, of course; her input was going to be crucial. Her calmness was unusual. And there was the family to deal with yet. The first hours after finding a murdered body were the most vital, as he'd been told a hundred times.

He led Hillcock through the tank room, glancing at Deirdre Watson, who was still standing in the office, perhaps not wanting to miss the excitement. 'Could you turn the machine off?' he asked Gordon. Obligingly, the farmer went to a corner of the tank room and stooped over an oily-looking contraption on the floor. A second later, there was blessed silence. The world seemed reborn in that moment. A kind of normality settled over the proceedings, as Den tried to maintain his close observation of the two key witnesses.

'The cows need to be bedded down,' Gordon said woodenly. 'Am I allowed to go and shut them in for the night?'

'How long will it take?' Den asked him.

'Well . . .' Gordon glanced at his half-washed parlour. 'I haven't finished in here, either. I need another half an hour or so to get it all done.'

'Okay,' Den decided, after a moment's thought. Strictly speaking, the man ought not to be left unsupervised, but Den could see no valid reason for putting a watch over him at this stage. If he'd wanted to run away, he'd surely have done it by now. 'But don't do any more washing down. Just see that the cows are all right for the night. Don't go into the barn, either. Wait here in the office until Constable Smithson comes back, or the SOCO chaps arrive. I'll meet you at the house in a little while.'

He glanced at his watch: nearly seven o'clock already. He turned back to Deirdre. 'You can go home now. Leave your name and address on here—' he tapped a piece of paper on the table, 'and somebody will call and interview you tomorrow. Phone number as well, of course.'

'But I have to be here again tomorrow morning,' she said with a distracted air. 'For the recording. Can I fetch my pots? I'm nowhere near finished up yet.'

Gordon coughed. 'You'd better be here,' he said. 'God knows what'll happen now. We might need this month's recording figures.'

Deirdre's vehement reaction took Den by surprise. 'Gordon!' she said. 'It won't come to anything like that.'

'You've lost me,' Den interrupted.

'He's thinking he might have to sell the herd,' she explained swiftly.

Den shook his head. You had to hand it to farmers, they certainly kept their minds on the job at all times.

For a few minutes the yard was a jumble of manoeuvring vehicles. Deirdre left and more police personnel arrived. Den wondered again if he should keep an eye on Hillcock; after all, the man was out in the dark somewhere with any number of unpleasant implements available to him. He could go berserk and attack the police officers, or even turn a scythe on himself. Until this moment, Den had successfully suppressed all thoughts of Lilah and this man together. He had kept his mind firmly and professionally on the matter in hand. But no longer. By some incomprehensible trick, Gordon Hillcock had stolen his – Den's – fiancée from under his very nose, and Den hated him for it. He wanted to go out and grab the man and throw him into the smallest, smelliest prison he could find.

But common sense prevailed and reminded him that he was going to have to tread very carefully. He went back to the barn, now filling rapidly. 'Any idea of the time of death?' he asked the doctor, who was peeling off rubber gloves and showing every sign of having completed his examination for the time being.

'Not more than six and not less than three, three and a half, hours ago,' he said. 'As far as I can tell for now.' He consulted a thermometer which had been on the floor beside the body. 'It's relatively warm in here, compared to outside. That'll have to be factored in. I'd say it must have been between two and three-thirty this afternoon.' Den made a careful note. Deirdre had already told him that the milking had started just after three, at which point she had been on the farm for an hour. The body had been found at five-thirty.

The police doctor rubbed his nose with a stubby thumb. 'Interesting scene for a killing,' he remarked. 'My granddad had a farm. Funny how the smells can be so evocative – that silage! Takes me right back to being ten again. And by the way, I think you can exclude any thought of firearm injuries. Something sharp, is my first impression. But you know the routine, Cooper. Wait for the PM, okay?'

'Looks like he took a while to die,' Den persisted.

The doctor shook his head. 'Writhed about a bit, is all we can say for sure. And that can happen in two or three seconds. Muscular spasms and so forth. The damage is mainly to the abdominal region – that tends to be fairly painful. Well, I've done all I can for now. Has someone been on to the undertaker's? They'll have to open the mortuary at Exeter for us.'

'PM tomorrow?' asked Den, knowing there was little chance of the pathologist turning out for a post-mortem in the evening, murder or not.

'It'll keep till then,' the doctor shrugged.

Den found his way down to the O'Farrells' cottage by car, not from any lazy reluctance to walk but because he needed his headlights to illuminate the way. It was a distance of perhaps four hundred yards from the main farm buildings. The track was rutted and curved round in a tight bend; he rattled over a cattle grid just before reaching the houses. The sky was deeply black and he wondered how Young Mike had managed to find his way.

Both cottages had lights coming from their front windows; Den had no way of knowing which one belonged to Mrs O'Farrell. He examined what he could see of the two dwellings.

The further one seemed to be less well kept; its modest patch of garden appeared to be home to various pieces of defunct equipment. In the shadows he could see two bikes on their sides; an aluminium ladder missing some rungs; a metal bucket without a bottom and other bits of scrap metal. By comparison the nearer cottage boasted a tidy winter garden and no clutter. None of this, however, told him which was the house he sought. Was Mrs O'Farrell a slut or a paragon? Had Sean been a slob or Mr Pernickety? As he dithered, the door of the nearer house opened.

'Den?' came Young Mike's voice. 'Are you out there?'

'How's it going?' Den answered him. 'It's bloody dark out here. Couldn't tell which house it was.'

'Tell me about it. I fell in a ditch walking down here.'

'Glad I brought the car then. Have you got Mrs O'Farrell in there?'

'She's in the living room. I told her you'd want a word.' They were speaking in low tones and Den was conscious of anxiety building inside him. Confronting a new widow was never easy.

Mike led the way through a short passage to a warm room, where Den found a huddled woman looking so white she was almost green. She sat in a large, well-upholstered armchair beside an open log fire. 'Good evening, madam,' Den said tentatively. 'I'm really sorry we've had to give you such bad news.'

'I'm never going to manage without Sean,' she bleated, her voice high and quavery. She looked at Den piteously. 'How am I going to manage?'

'Mrs O'Farrell isn't very well,' Mike explained. 'And her daughter's away for the night. She isn't sure she'll be able to cope by herself.'

'Perhaps the people next door . . . ?' Den suggested. 'Otherwise we can contact Social Services for you. Although . . .' He knew from experience there wasn't a chance in a million that anyone would be provided at this time of night, just to sit with a relatively young woman who didn't look too sick to fend for herself. 'The best thing would be to contact your daughter and ask her to come home. How far away is she? She needs to be told about her father anyway.'

'She's in Tavistock, at her boyfriend's house. But she can't come back by herself. She's only fifteen. Her father would have to fetch her.' Hearing her own words, the woman clapped a hand over her mouth. Den noted the vigour of the gesture.

'Well, I'm sure we can work something out,' he said briskly. 'But for now, would you just answer a few routine questions for me?' He didn't give her time to respond, but quickly produced his notepad and pencil. 'First, your full name, please.'

'Heather Elizabeth O'Farrell.'

'And your husband's full name and age.'

The strategy worked as it almost always did. 'Sean James O'Farrell,' she said promptly. 'He was thirty-eight on Christmas Eve.'

Den took her full postal address and phone number, before asking, 'And when did you last see him today?'

'After dinner. He made me some soup and scrambled eggs and then went back to see to something in the yard.'

Yet again, Den had cause to be thankful for his time with Lilah. How many policemen would be so *au fait* with the jargon? *The yard* meant not just a single piece of ground surrounded by buildings, but the entire complex of farm structures – which, on Dunsworthy, stretched to close to half an acre of covered barns, sheds, pens, all connected by a byzantine arrangement of gates and fences. 'What time was that?' he asked.

'Two o'clock.'

'You're sure you can be that precise?'

'Oh yes. He only takes the hour for lunch. Exactly one till two. Gordon's very particular about time-keeping.'

'And was there anything unusual about

today? What sort of mood was Sean in?'

She faltered at this deviation from the recounting of hard fact. 'Well, he wasn't doing the milking, even though it should have been one of his days. Gordon asked him to swap shifts so he could go to some meeting or other in Okehampton. That's quite unusual. And Sean couldn't just take the time off and go somewhere because there were still things he had to do. He wasn't that bothered about it for himself, but he didn't like it on principle. Being messed about just for some whim on the part of the boss.' Den could hear the quotation marks and assumed that Sean had probably used those very words. He felt the familiar handicapping sense of ignorance at the outset of any murder inquiry: he didn't know what Sean O'Farrell had been like, how he got on with Hillcock, what was important in his life. So much to discover, and probably little of it directly relevant. But he squared his shoulders and breathed deep. He had to press on.

'So you were worried when he didn't come back? If he wasn't milking, wouldn't you have expected him to be home for at least part of the afternoon?'

She sighed. 'To be honest with you, I was asleep. And even if I'd been awake, I wouldn't have worried. I'd have thought he might have been held up with a cow calving or something. There's always plenty to do on a farm.'

'So the time-keeping isn't always so precise?' Den said.

She blinked up at him. 'It is at dinner time,' she insisted petulantly. 'And Sean knows I depend on him for almost everything these days. He wouldn't have left me alone for long. This young man arrived before I really missed Sean. He woke me up.'

'You were asleep here? In the chair?'

'That's right. It's cold upstairs when the weather's like this.'

'How long had you been sleeping?'

'Oh, I don't know.' The impatience was mixed with self-pity. 'Since about half past three or four, I suppose.'

'The fire had almost gone out,' Mike offered. 'I built it up again for the lady.'

'Very kind of you,' Den remarked. 'It's certainly pretty warm in here now.' He glanced around and noticed as well as the blazing fire, a free-standing gas heater behind her chair, going full pelt. No wonder the room was so stifling. He decided not to make any further notes for now. There was still the matter of who, if anyone, was to sit with the widow, to support her in her shock and grief.

'Would you like us to find your daughter and

bring her home?' he suggested. 'She ought to be back as soon as possible, in the circumstances.'

The woman shuddered. 'No, no. God, I can't cope with her throwing tantrums at a time like this! Let her alone for tonight. You can go and get her in the morning. I'll give you the address. Although . . .' A new, disturbing thought seemed to have struck her.

'Yes?'

'There's her animals. Normally, when she's out, Sean does them for her.'

'Animals?'

'She keeps some . . . pets . . . outside. A sort of amateur rescue shelter in the back garden.' Mrs O'Farrell frowned.

'And they need to be fed?'

She nodded. 'There's a bag of pellets and some hay in the back scullery.'

'I'm afraid you might have to do it yourself,' he told her, trying to keep the severity out of his voice.

She threw him a look of pure amazement. 'Me?' she squawked. 'But I *never* do it.'

Mike stepped forward. 'Let me,' he offered. 'Is it rabbits – that sort of thing?'

The new widow had shifted into uncooperative mode. 'All sorts of things,' she mumbled, shrinking down in her chair. Den felt a great urge to shake her, force her onto her feet, urge her to take some sort of control of her own life.

'Come on, then,' he snapped, angry with Mike for volunteering and himself for being so churlish.

Outside, the land sloped downhill, a half-acre plot littered with ramshackle hutches. They had a torch each – one from the police car and one from the O'Farrell scullery. It looked like a miniature shanty town. A copse was a dark mass at the bottom of the hill. Den played his torch over the area in astonishment.

'She must spend most of her time coping with all this,' he said.

'Quite a responsibility,' Mike agreed. 'Let's see what we've got.'

'We can't feed everything,' Den decided. 'Must be eight or ten cages here. God knows what's lurking inside them.'

'Just a scattering to keep them going,' Mike insisted, already filling a metal bowl with small brown food pellets. 'Looks like it's mostly rabbits and guinea pigs.'

Den left him to it. Mike moved from cage to cage, aiming his torch through the netting, trying to locate food bowls. One of the boxy constructions had a long netting run attached to it. Den could see movement inside. 'What's that?' he called.

'A badger!' came Mike's enthralled reply. 'Seems to have a bad leg – it's limping.'

'Do badgers eat rabbit food?'

'Shouldn't think so. I think they eat mice, or slugs. I don't know.'

'Rabbits, probably,' said Den grimly. 'Well, they'll have to make do for now. We should get a move on. Hillcock's waiting.'

They went back indoors to report that the animals would be fine until morning. But instead of thanking them, Heather O'Farrell just sank her chin lower onto her chest. Her face was pale and soft, like that of a much older woman; although not lined, it seemed to sag downwards, an impression strengthened by her hair, which was straight and long and colourless. If the daughter was only fifteen, and the husband thirty-eight, Den supposed she must be something under forty, yet she looked like a woman in her late fifties. In fact, she observed, she looked at least as old as his own mother.

'How about asking someone from next door to come and sit with you?'

She shook her head. 'Mary Hillcock,' she said waveringly. 'I think Mary might be kind enough . . .'

'She's up at the big house, is she?' Den remembered a sister accompanying Gordon to one or two village events that he'd attended in his younger days. And once more, he remembered Hillcock waiting for further questioning and probable retribution. The thought revived Den and he came close to rubbing his hands together in anticipation. 'Okay, then,' he said briskly, 'we'll ask her if she'll come down. Thank you for your time. We hope you'll soon get better. I'm afraid we'll have to come back tomorrow for further questions. The Coroner's Officer, Mr Newcombe, will contact you, too. And . . . we're both very sorry about what's happened.'

She nodded unresponsively and let them make their way unaccompanied out of the room. At the last minute, Den heard her murmur, 'I won't *ever* get better, you know,' before he left.

Outside, Mike let out a long breath. 'I thought you were never coming,' he said. 'She was sending me round the twist in there.'

'What's wrong with her? Did you find out?'

Mike shook his head. 'No idea,' he said. 'But you can't help feeling sorry for her husband, can you?'

Den drove carefully back up to the farmhouse, where the scattered cars of the forensics people had been joined by a discreet undertaker's vehicle. The body was being loaded onto a shelf at the back when Den and Mike arrived.

'Now, you find Hillcock while I go and talk to the family,' Den said, with ill-concealed relish.

* * *

The big house had windows looking over the farmyard, as well as down towards the road and the workers' cottages. Lights were on in most of the ground floor rooms, and as he approached, Den could see through the uncurtained windows to the domestic scene inside. To the left of the front door was a large living room, lined with bookcases and illuminated by three standard lamps. A woman sat sideways-on to the window, in a comfortable-looking armchair, writing on a thick pad perched on her lap. Den wondered at this – surely she must be aware that something untoward was taking place in the yard just outside? To look at her, anyone would think it was just an ordinary winter's evening.

Curiosity aroused, Den moved to peer through the window on the other side of the door. It revealed a kitchen cum dining room, cluttered on every surface with saucepans, mugs and assorted paraphernalia, with a dense forest of pot-grown plants along the windowsill. It took a moment to locate the human being in the room. A youngish woman stood at the sink halfway along the right-hand wall, washing up. *That must be Mary*, thought Den, although he didn't really recognise her.

He didn't want Young Mike to hear anything these women might say about his ex-girlfriend. He gestured at two cars still parked in the yard, one of which was being approached by a young woman from forensics. 'When you've found Hillcock and brought him to the house, I bet she'd give you a lift back to the station, if you ask nicely.'

Mike dithered uncertainly. 'Are you going to take Mr Hillcock in for questioning?'

'What would you do, in my place?' Den asked him, really wanting to know.

'Well,' Mike reacted nervously, as if being tested. 'It . . . er . . . looks as if he's been around the yard all afternoon, which makes him a key witness, if nothing else. He does seem a bit . . . unstable. We've got to take him in.'

'That leaves them with nobody to do the milking in the morning,' Den reminded his junior.

Mike shrugged as if this was a minor detail. *Townie*, thought Den. But he was disproportionately relieved to have Mike endorse his own inclinations. It wouldn't be *responsible* to leave Hillcock at large, given what had happened. The timing was unfortunate, but that couldn't be helped. 'Right then,' he said. 'Off you go. I'll be okay. I'll fetch Hillcock; you needn't wait.'

The forensics girl was already in her car and looked ready to drive off. Mike sighed. 'Sorry, Sarge, but I don't think I should leave you on your own. What if Hillcock plays up in the car? It wouldn't look very good, would it? I'll stay.'

With an uncomfortable cocktail of emotions, Den nodded. 'You're probably right,' he admitted. 'That's our man, look. Over in the tank room.'

Gordon was clearly waiting for them with some impatience. He had taken off the rubber apron. 'First, make him account for his guns – there's sure to be at least one around the place. The doctor said O'Farrell wasn't shot, but we can't be too careful. Then get him to give you that thing he was wearing.' Mike nodded cooperatively. 'Take him upstairs and make him change. Bag up everything he takes off. Quick as you can, okay?'

Alone, Den knocked on the farmhouse door. It was answered by the younger woman, who looked anxious. 'What on *earth* is going on out there? My mother went out to ask, and some officious idiot told her to stay in the house. We do *live* here, you know.'

'I know. I'm very sorry for all the disturbance. I'm afraid I can't tell you anything for another few minutes. Mr Hillcock will be coming in very shortly and we'll speak to you then.'

She looked up into his face and he tried to analyse her expression. She was pale and frowning, but he could detect no real fear. *Nobody she loves is under threat*, he concluded. *Not yet, anyway.* It sounded as if her mother was just the same, as if she'd meekly withdrawn to the house when asked to, content to wait for explanations. There was no sense of urgency to these women. 'I'm assuming you are Mr Hillcock's sister Mary,' Den said. 'Is that your mother in the living room?'

'That's right. She decided that if we were confined to quarters, she may as well get on with some work until officialdom condescended to enlighten us.'

Mike and Hillcock arrived quickly, Mike carrying the rubber apron in an evidence bag and Gordon pushing ahead, striding into the passageway and making straight for the stairs. His sister put out a hand to stop him. 'Gordon?' she said. 'What happened? What were all those cars doing in the yard?'

'Sean's dead,' he told her briefly. 'I found him in the barn. These are the police. But I suppose you know that already. You've missed all the excitement – the body was taken away ten minutes ago.' He stood rooted to the floor of the hallway, breathing heavily. To Den, he seemed bovine, a bullock waiting for the next incomprehensible move from the humans around him.

'What?' Mary said with a bemused frown. 'What are you talking about?'

Den studied her, aware of having taken almost no notice of her on their previous brief encounters. In her early thirties, with the same round cheeks as her brother, but none of his high colour, she gave a similar impression of rootedness, like a piece of large furniture. Her hair was light brown, cut very short, but still betraying a persistent curl. She wore a sloppy jumper, which came well down her thighs, with narrow leggings underneath. It partly concealed her generous girth, but not entirely. Mary Hillcock was a big woman, of a shape once greatly admired, but currently dismissed as *overweight*. Den was sorry for her.

'What's going on?' came a voice from the doorway. The woman from the living room stood there, tall and stern. She resembled neither Gordon nor Mary; Den would have labelled her as a visitor, rather than a blood relative, if he didn't know better.

'Mother,' said Gordon dully.

'I'm afraid there's been a fatality,' Den told her. 'Sean O'Farrell died some time this afternoon.'

'But . . . what happened to him?' The woman darted wide-eyed looks from one face to another.

'We believe he was attacked,' said Den carefully, wanting to pre-empt any suggestion of suicide. 'Could I ask you both where you were between two and four this afternoon?'

'We were at work,' said Mary promptly. 'We came home together, arriving just after five-thirty.'

'Do you work at the same place?'

Mary shook her head. 'I teach in Okehampton

and my mother's a counsellor in North Devon. Barnstaple, to be exact.'

Den frowned. 'So how come you share a car?'

'She comes home via Okehampton and collects me. It saves petrol.'

Den wrote it all down in his notebook. It gave him some satisfaction to inform them, 'Mr Hillcock will be coming with us now, to assist us with our enquiries. My colleague and I have been speaking with Mrs O'Farrell. She did ask whether Mary might be able to go and sit with her this evening. She's all alone and apparently she isn't well . . .'

'You're *arresting* Gordon?' the older woman interrupted, incredulity bursting from every pore.

'No, no,' said Den. 'He isn't under arrest. But—'

'I hope you can get him back in time for the morning milking,' said the mother grimly. 'It'll be chaos otherwise.'

Den wondered why one of these women couldn't stand in. He was reminded of Lilah's mother, who could no more have milked a herd of cows than masterminded a military campaign. Maybe his former girlfriend had found Dunsworthy more of a home from home than he'd imagined.

'We'll ask Lilah,' said Gordon, flatly, unnervingly. 'I'll have to phone her anyway. That's assuming I won't be allowed home again tonight?' He directed an unfocused gaze at Den. His words came slowly, as if fighting to the surface through layers of tightly-packed emotion. Den noticed the man's hands were shaking, despite the clenched fists, bunched against his legs. Hearing Lilah's name issuing from Hillcock's lips gave Den a deeply painful moment; the casual proprietary tone was scarcely bearable.

'Gordon,' his mother began, making a small movement towards him, which was quickly arrested. 'I can phone Lilah for you – ask her to come and do the milking tomorrow. And what else can we do?' She pulled at her hair, dislodging a clasp that held it tidily at the back of her head. It was an oddly disturbing gesture. Den watched the tresses slowly tumble down her neck and shoulder, making her look girlish and vulnerable. It seemed quite impossible that she could be old enough to have produced Gordon. At the moment, she looked ten years younger than him.

Hillcock sighed raggedly. 'I don't know,' he said.

'It must have been an accident,' Mary put in decisively, as if the words could make it true.

Nobody responded. Den felt a sudden desire to let her hold on to her delusion for a little while. The facts were blatant enough to survive a little blurring on this first evening.

But there were things to be done. 'Mike.' Den nudged the constable and tilted his chin at the stairs, running up from the far end of the hallway. Gordon sighed again. 'They want me to change out of these things,' he explained, in reply to his mother's questioning look.

'You haven't had your tea,' Mary said. 'We kept it warm for you. You'll be hungry.'

'I don't want it,' said her brother, and headed for the stairs.

Den squared his shoulders. 'Constable Smithson will go with you and collect up everything you were wearing this afternoon. We'll need it for forensic analysis.' Gordon shrugged as Young Mike followed him upstairs.

Gordon's mother was not what Den had expected at all. A long, straight back, slender neck and skin that managed to suggest a recent afternoon in summer sunshine, rather than early January pallor. Her hair was a natural-looking light brown, and the only lines were those you'd expect in a woman just over forty, though she had to be in her middle or late fifties. A pair of reading glasses hung on a chain round her neck, and she wore a richly patterned woolly jumper over a pair of winter-weight trousers. The house, he had noticed, was not particularly well heated. She struck him as possessing great strength. A subtle confidence; an expectation of being listened to.

But perhaps he'd only got that impression from the information that she was a counsellor – a position that sounded authoritative, even though he didn't know precisely what it meant – nor how to spell it. Was she a dignitary on the Council with a 'c', or a purveyor of counsel, with an 's'? She didn't look like a widow, although Den knew that Gordon's father had died some years earlier. She betrayed none of that slight air of cautious hesitancy, that unspoken loss of trust in a world that could remove the husband once depended upon. As one of Den's aunts had memorably remarked, on the day of her husband's funeral, 'Even if you never liked him much, you're bound to miss him.' Feeling effectively widowed himself these days, Den thought he could understand loss as well as anybody now.

'Are you the only two people who live here, apart from Mr Hillcock?' he asked, as the silence threatened to become uncomfortable.

'There's Granny as well,' Mary told him. 'She's virtually bedridden. She has a room upstairs.'

He asked for their full names and details of where they could be contacted, filling a few lines of his notebook with the answers. Mary gave her name as Mary Cecilia Fordyce. Den raised an eyebrow. She grasped his meaning instantly. 'I'm divorced,' she said. 'The marriage only lasted a year and then I came back to live here.'

'How long ago was that?'

'Ten years,' she said tiredly. 'But I suppose Fordyce is still technically my name. I never bothered to change it back to Hillcock, though most people seem to use it when they refer to me.'

'And are you the owner of this property?' Den asked Claudia.

'No, my husband left it all to Gordon. Mary was married at the time of his death, and he – wrongly, as it turned out – assumed she wouldn't be interested in a share. But since her divorce she's been treated as an equal here. We've made sure she doesn't feel excluded – haven't we, darling?' Den watched for Mary's reaction, which came in the form of a smile that looked to him more like resentment than gratitude.

'You two were out this afternoon, but the old lady was here, I presume?' he asked. 'Could I have a quick word with her, do you think?'

Claudia and her daughter exchanged a glance which looked to Den like shocked amusement. 'I hardly think . . .' Claudia began.

'She isn't . . . I mean . . . she's fit to be questioned, is she?' What he wanted to ask was: *Has she got all her marbles?*

'She'll talk to you all right,' Claudia smiled. 'She'll be only too pleased, I'm sure. I was just wondering how long you've got.'

Mary joined in with a smile of her own and

Den felt he was somehow being teased. Was the poor old girl really so lonely and neglected that she'd keep a policeman chatting all night?

'How old is she?' he asked.

'A hundred and one,' said Mary, with obvious satisfaction. He frowned, not certain he could believe her.

'She's my husband's mother,' Claudia explained. 'Lived here all her life.'

'Bright as a button,' Mary supplied. 'But you have to let her tell you things in her own time. Quite honestly, I'd recommend you come back tomorrow. She isn't going anywhere.'

Except maybe to her Maker, thought Den. Every morning's awakening must seem like a minor miracle at that age. He wondered whether he could delegate the questioning of Gordon Hillcock's granny to Mike, or one of the others. Maybe one of the female officers would make a better job of it. This was threatening to turn into a serious case involving the whole team, unless there was a quick confession from Hillcock. 'Yes, I think we can leave her for the time being,' he agreed coolly.

Claudia began to talk more freely, in an apparent effort to sound forthcoming and helpful. Den had met this behaviour before – women in particular, unnerved by the presence of the police, could babble on unceasingly. 'I'm sure you're aware of how very bad times are for farmers at the moment,' she said, her face pushed forward earnestly, the loose hank of hair swinging untidily. 'The milk price has dropped shockingly and there's nothing we can do with the bull calves except shoot them. Sheep and pigs are just as hopeless. We're surviving on Mary's salary at the moment, with a bit of help from me. Not that I earn very much. The farm's rather a part-time commitment for both of us, I'm afraid. I suppose Sean was shot?' she concluded abruptly, looking Den right in the eye.

He found himself wanting to keep her on his side. 'We can't say anything about the cause of death until after the post-mortem,' he explained. 'Our men are searching the premises for evidence at the moment.'

'Poor things. It's freezing out there.' Her voice was warmer than her expression, with the usual hint of Devon accent overlaid with Grammar School diction. She clearly wasn't stupid, even though she had apparently married and had her first child while still significantly short of twenty. What did she think of Lilah? he wondered. How on earth was a third woman – fourth, if you counted the granny – going to fit into this household? His resentment against Gordon stirred again. What was he playing at, surrounding himself with all these women like some sort of feudal lord?

It was as if Claudia Hillcock had heard his thoughts and decided to cut through any further prevarication. 'Do I know you?' she asked suddenly. 'Are you local?'

'I've lived near Okehampton all my life,' he told her. 'You might have seen me a few times.'

'I have,' she remembered. 'With Lilah, last year. You're the policeman she used to go out with.'

It felt like an accusation. The stab of guilt was ridiculous, but he felt it just the same. He grinned weakly and nodded. 'Small world,' he mumbled.

'What?' Mary put in thoughtfully. 'I *knew* I'd seen you somewhere. It must have been at some village thing with Lilah. But surely . . . won't that affect your judgement? I mean, I shouldn't think you're very fond of Gordon, after what happened. If you're going to be investigating this . . . incident, how can we be sure you'll be fair about it?' Two pairs of female eyes scrutinised him boldly. Then Mary put a hand over her mouth, as if astonished at her own temerity. Claudia fiddled nervously with an earlobe.

Den paused, unsure how to reply. Police training nudged him towards a stiff adherence to protocol and a brief deflection of their anxieties. But compassion for their situation forced him to take a more human line. 'I'll tell my superior the whole story,' he assured them. 'It'll be up to him whether I'm kept on the case or not. Whatever my involvement might be, we'll make a full and fair investigation.' He watched their faces as he spoke, seeing denial, anger, fear – but not the violent indignation that might have been expected if the idea of Gordon as a murderer had been truly unacceptable to them. They knew the man, and already Den believed they knew him to be capable of murder.

CHAPTER FOUR

It began to feel as if he was never going to get away. Den's need to acquire early reactions and essential facts, as well as taking care of the pastoral aspects, was inevitably time-consuming. He'd been a fool to think he could manage it alone, without Mike to assist. The close avoidance of an error of judgement made him uneasy – what else might he be overlooking or dodging?

'Now what are we going to do about Mrs O'Farrell?' He tried for a friendly smile at Mary. 'Can I leave it that you'll see she's all right?'

Mary's nostrils flared in a quickly-suppressed distaste, but she nodded cooperatively.

'And . . . would you mind explaining just what

it is that's wrong with her? She seems to be some sort of invalid.'

'Invalid?' Mary repeated, with a glance at her mother. 'Yes, I suppose you could say that. She's got ME – or chronic fatigue syndrome as they want us to call it. It's the most bizarre illness. Absolutely nothing to see physically; doctors can't find anything wrong. But she says she hurts all over, and every time she does more than walk from one room to another, she gets terribly weak. It's been like that for six years now. She almost never leaves the house any more.'

'I see,' was all Den had time to say, before Young Mike and Gordon Hillcock made an entrance into the living room. Mike carried a second sealed bag, bulging with what Den assumed to be Hillcock's newly-removed clothes. Both men looked awkward and Den wondered whether Mike had insisted on staying in the room while Gordon changed. 'We'll need your boots as well,' he said.

'They're in the porch,' said the farmer. 'The big green ones.' Mike went to fetch them, fishing in his pocket for yet another sealable bag as he went.

Den followed him out. 'Did you find any guns?' he asked quietly.

'Just the one,' Mike nodded. 'It was stone cold. Forensics have bagged it, but I don't really see the point. Any fool could see the bloke wasn't shot.'

'At least it means nobody can use it from here on,' Den said. 'We'd better check the cottages as well. There's still the people next door to the O'Farrells. They need to be questioned.' He rubbed his head, thinking he should have called for the DI ages ago.

They went back into the house. 'We'll drive you down to Mrs O'Farrell's,' Den offered Mary. 'It's very dark out there – and cold.'

Mary seemed startled, but then resigned herself to the inevitable. 'Let me get my coat,' she said.

At the last moment, mother and son became visibly aware of the significance of what was happening. Gordon stopped dead as Claudia made a small sound, part moan, part gasp. He turned back to her, his eyes wide. 'Say goodnight to Granny for me,' he said urgently. 'But don't tell her . . .'

His mother twitched her head sideways, as if to dodge this unwelcome message. 'Darling—' she choked. 'You will be all right, won't you? I don't think . . .'

Gordon's eyelids came down slowly, as the urgency died out of his face. 'Don't worry, Ma. You won't have to visit me; they can't keep me there very long. It won't be like last time.'

Den's incautious sniff of amazement made them both smile. 'We don't mean he's been in *prison* before,' Claudia explained. 'Last time it was hospital. He was ill. And it was a very long time ago.'

In the car, which Mike was driving, Den asked briefly about the occupants of the second cottage, writing awkwardly on his knee while balancing the torch to shine on the paper, as Mary filled him in. Mike drove slowly, but it was barely two minutes before they pulled up outside the cottages. 'Ted Speedwell, tractor driver,' Mary told him. 'He lives there with his wife, Jilly. They'll be wondering what's going on.'

Den forced himself to look at Hillcock, twisting to peer into the shadows of the back seat. The engine was still running. 'I'd better have a quick word with them,' he decided, again acutely aware that he had embarked on a far larger investigation than he was capable of without more senior involvement. Here was a third man living on the estate; a man who also had access to all the billhooks and pitchforks and slicing, stabbing tools that lay to hand around a farm.

'You needn't worry about Ted,' Mary said, before she got out of the car. 'Much as I would like to throw suspicion onto somebody other than Gordon, even I would have to admit that Ted Speedwell would not hurt a fly.'

'Turn the engine off,' Den told Mike. 'I might be a while.'

First he went into the O'Farrell cottage with Mary and asked the lethargic Heather whether Sean had kept a gun. She pointed out a shotgun in a locked case in the hallway. 'The key's in that drawer,' she told him.

He extracted the weapon and returned to the car with it. 'This one's cold as well,' he reported back to Mike.

Then he headed for the further cottage. 'Don't be long – it's freezing out here,' Mike called after him.

The door was answered by a woman who threw it open with no sign of wariness. 'Mrs Speedwell?' Den asked.

'That's right,' she said in a rich Devon voice.

'Could I come in a minute? I'm Detective Sergeant Cooper. There's been some trouble here. You've probably been wondering what's going on.'

'I told Ted. I said, something's happened up in the yard, you better go and see what's to do, I said. But he had his boots off, and said 'twas too cold to be going out again for a bit of nosy-parkering. Mr Hillcock'd call if us were needed.' She burbled on as Den wiped his feet and ducked through the doorway, to follow her into the snug sitting room off the tiny hall.

'Here he be!' she announced, as if she'd produced her husband by some magic trick. Ted Speedwell was sitting in a deep, old armchair, a fluffy grey cat on his lap and a rheumy black labrador at his feet. 'Ted – 'tis the police come to tell us what's been goin' on.'

The man looked up at Den, squinting slightly, one hand on the arm of the chair, beginning to push down as he sought to lever himself out of it.

'I'm afraid there's been a fatality,' Den said quickly. 'That is, your neighbour, Mr O'Farrell, has died. We have reason to believe that his death was as a result of . . . violence against him.' Den cursed the clumsiness of his own words, kicking against the necessity not to say more than was strictly demonstrable as fact.

'You're telling us someone's killed *Sean*?' Mrs Speedwell demanded. 'Well, whoever would believe such a thing?' She seemed part angry, part thrilled by the news; her eyes bulged and she clasped her hands together under her chin. 'Ted! Did you hear that?'

'I heard,' the man confirmed, and slumped back again into the depths of his chair. Den examined him. A small man, wiry perhaps, but with little suggestion of any real strength. His head seemed over-large for his body, the grey hair thinning. He seemed to be nearing sixty, his wife a few years younger.

'I'm sorry to be a nuisance,' Den continued, 'but I'm afraid I'll have to ask you to fetch me the clothes you were wearing this afternoon. We'll need them for laboratory analysis, you see. And please show me any firearms you have in your possession.'

The Speedwells stared at him in utter bewilderment. Ted looked down at himself. 'But . . . these is them. I mean, I've still got 'em on. And us's never had no gun.'

The wife brayed a sudden horrified laugh. 'You think my Ted killed Sean O'Farrell?'

'At the moment we don't know what to think,' Den said stiltedly. 'But unless you can tell me that you were off the farm all afternoon, with witnesses to back you up, I'm afraid we'll have to include you in our investigations.'

Gently setting the cat onto the hearthrug, Ted finally struggled out of his chair. Den could see clear signs of an arthritic hip and a stiff shoulder, both on the same side. He took note of the garments and let the man limp upstairs to change out of them, without supervision. He could see no trace of blood or mud or muck on trousers or jacket, and with a faint sigh he asked Mrs Speedwell if he could quickly look through her unwashed laundry while they waited.

'Why'd you want to do that?' she asked, before comprehension dawned. 'Oh, I see now. You think he might have had Sean's blood on his trousers and put them in the wash. Come on, then,' she invited, her tone long-suffering.

She took him into a small scullery behind the kitchen, where an ancient twin-tub washing machine was tucked under a cream-coloured draining board. A red plastic basket contained items waiting to be washed. None of them could conceivably be construed as Ted's working clothes. While it was possible that incriminating garments could have been removed and disposed of since the attack on O'Farrell, Den had no jurisdiction to search for them. 'Thank you,' he said. 'You've been very helpful.'

'What about me?' she asked him. 'Don't you want to know where I've been all day?'

'I was coming to that,' he said severely.

'Good. Well, I was out at work. I'm a dinner lady at the little school, the one on the corner as you get onto the Tavistock road.'

Now why doesn't that surprise me? Den smiled to himself: Mrs Speedwell had to be the most typical dinner lady in the whole world. 'What time did you get home?' he asked her.

'Quarter to three,' she said. 'Had to wait for a lift, so I was a bit later than usual.'

Mindful of his colleague and their suspect freezing in the car, Den kept his visit short. As soon as Ted returned with the clothes, he bagged them up, labelled them, and made his departure. 'You'll be seeing me again in a day or two, I expect,' he warned them, as he left. 'Please don't leave the neighbourhood without informing us.' He handed them a card and left, fully aware of the disruption his visit had caused.

'Okay, Mike, hit the road, mate,' he said, slamming the car door.

They drove as fast as the twisting lanes with treacherous icy patches would allow. Den felt the presence of Lilah's new lover behind him like a gun trained on his spine. He felt queasy being in the same car as the man. Resist as he might, he couldn't evade the images of the two together. Lilah had been *his*. She had been his future wife; they had had special private jokes together, plans and dreams constructed jointly. He wondered whether the sensation of being dropped over a very high cliff would ever entirely go away. It still made no sense to him, even after three months. Some stupid cosmic mistake had occurred, and one day soon everything would come right again.

Perhaps that would be sooner than he had ever dared to hope. If Gordon Hillcock was in custody awaiting trail for murder, for instance, things might come right quite quickly. And if he was tried and found guilty and sentenced to fifteen years or so in prison, everything would come very right indeed.

Deirdre described the events at Dunsworthy to her husband over a late supper.

'More than I bargained for today,' she began. 'I was at Dunsworthy – you know, Gordon Hillcock's place.' Robin worked for a company selling gates and fences, and therefore had a working knowledge of most farms in the area.

'Mmm,' he answered, with his back to her. He'd had his own supper hours earlier, and was now tinkering unprofitably with a broken radio on one of the kitchen worktops. 'You're certainly very late. Did you have to help with a calving again?'

'Just the opposite, actually.' Her tone filtered through to him and he turned to face her.

'Something died?'

'Some*one*, as it happens. Sean – the herdsman. Gordon found his body while I was there. I called the police.'

'You're joking!' He stared at her in shock. 'What happened? Heart or something, I suppose?'

'Much more dramatic than that. He'd been attacked. Covered in blood. Been scrabbling about in the barn with some lame cows. It was horrible, Rob. And I was so cool and calm, I scared myself.'

'You're always like that,' he said distractedly, still trying to grasp what she was telling him. 'Like when Matthew fell off the swing and blacked out.' It was a famous family story and Deirdre smiled weakly. Robbie's attention was now fully on her. His questions continued, 'What do you mean, he'd been attacked?'

'It looked like he'd been stabbed. Or possibly shot, though the police didn't seem to think that. In his stomach. There was blood everywhere.'

'So you said.' He blinked and rubbed a hand over his bald patch. 'This is going to mean real trouble for Dunsworthy. Are you going back in the morning?'

She put her fork down, and laid both hands flat on the table. It was a gesture of sudden trepidation. 'I'll have to, I suppose,' she said. 'But I admit I don't fancy it, not if Gordon's milking. I don't know how I'll face him after the way he behaved this afternoon.'

'Why? What on earth did he do?'

She hesitated. 'He went to pieces, basically. Completely turned to jelly. It was me who had to phone the police and organise everything.'

Robin looked into her face reproachfully. 'He'd just found a body covered in blood,' he said. 'Isn't he entitled to go into shock? I know

I would. Not everybody's like you, remember. Shock does all sorts of weird things to people. I don't see why it should make you think worse of him.'

She shook her head. 'It wasn't just shock. He was – *horror-struck*. He didn't know what to do with himself.' She closed her eyes for a moment, before bursting out, 'I think he did it, Robin. I think Gordon killed Sean. I mean – he *must* have done it. There's no one else. And it fits with how he was and what he said. At first he was very white and sort of *ghastly*, but I think that was because he hadn't expected to find Sean in the barn. The policeman thinks he was attacked outside somewhere and staggered in there, pouring blood, and died in the straw. There was blood smeared on the door. They were talking about taking him in for questioning, when I left.'

Robin leant hard on both hands, facing her across the table. 'But you *like* Hillcock. Much more than you like – liked – Sean. Did you say all this to the police?'

She shook her head. 'They didn't really *ask* me. Not whether I thought he'd done it. But I expect they thought the same as me.'

'What a thing,' her husband murmured, shaking his head. 'Just shows, doesn't it – you never know what's going on behind closed doors.'

'Not closed doors exactly,' she corrected him.

'But out of sight, yes. It all feels so *unreal*. Anyway, if the police have got Gordon, I don't think they'll let him go. He did seem rather . . . unpredictable.'

'So he's not likely to be doing the milking in the morning, is he?' said Robin reasonably.

'But someone's got to.'

'They'll call an emergency relief person. In which case, you'll be very useful. But surely there are other people living there? I thought it was one of those places with three or four houses dotted about.'

'There's a tractor driver chap, Ted, who I hardly ever see. I don't think he's ever milked. And neither of the Hillcock women seem interested. And on top of everything else, my computer packed up on me. I've brought everything home so I can enter the weights on the parlour sheets. Bloody nuisance, that is. Not that Gordon's going to care about not getting his printout.' She frowned at her husband. There was such a lot she needed to tell him, to make him understand. Fortunately his attention was thoroughly caught, and he showed no sign of wanting to make his usual quick exit. 'Except,' she went on slowly, deliberately, 'he told me he wanted it done. Hinted he might have to sell up after this. At least that's what I took him to mean. It's no good – I'll have to go back and see what they've got organised.'

'I'd have thought you'd be desperate to go

back and find out what's happening,' he grinned feebly at her. 'Nosy cow like you.'

'Very funny,' she sniffed. 'It's not a joke, Rob. It was all a very nasty shock.' She stared down at her hands, which had begun to shake. 'Look!' she drew his attention to them. 'I'm shaking.'

'Delayed reaction. It was bound to catch up with you. Go and have a bath and get to bed early,' he advised. 'I really don't think you *should* go back tomorrow.' He scratched his head. 'Can't you ask Carol what to do?'

Carol was the Area Field Manager, to whom Deirdre was responsible. She tried to imagine what she would say in the phone call, and decided it was not a good idea to call her. Word would get out soon enough, and Deirdre would have time to hone her account of how it had been at the scene of a murder. She would gladly tell the story a hundred times, once she was good and ready. But for the moment, she preferred to keep her own counsel.

'I'm not phoning Carol tonight,' she decided. 'I'll just turn up as usual in the morning. They start at five-thirty, which isn't too bad. I'll just enter up these yields and then go to bed. Okay?'

Robin blinked at her, typically non-committal. Whatever Deirdre decided to do, there was nothing he could usefully say about it. She never asked for his permission, or even took much account of his preferences, when deciding on a course of action. He nodded. 'Okay,' he said. 'I'll try and be quiet when I come up. Is Sam in tonight?'

She winced, trying to suppress the surge of irritation at the question. She'd only been home half an hour, while Robin had been there since six. How should *she* know what Sam was doing? An eighteen-year-old daughter was very much a law unto itself, and Deirdre had given up trying to monitor her movements. 'I've no idea,' she said tightly.

The slamming of a car door outside answered the question for both of them. Their daughter had come home. A few moments later, the kitchen door opened, with a swirl of cold air, and a muffled figure appeared.

Nobody spoke, other than the usual murmur of greetings. Deirdre acknowledged the habitual loosening of tension at the knowledge that the girl was safely home, but made no attempt to speak. It was a mild surprise when Sam plonked herself down at the table, without removing coat or scarf. 'We found a dead otter on the road. Down by the river.'

Robin hissed an inarticulate gasp of sorrow, which Deirdre recognised as expressing a deeper grief than he had shown for Sean O'Farrell. 'Don't they hibernate in winter?' he asked with a frown.

'Not really,' Sam informed him. 'They still have to eat.'

'Did a car hit it?'

'We're not sure. Jeremy's taken it for examination. We think it's more likely they've been lamping again. Like the badgers last week.'

'Lamping *otters*?' Deirdre echoed. 'How horrible.'

Lamping was a growing practice, receiving media attention for the first time in history. It was a quick and easy way to kill wild animals – assuming you could find them to start with. Just shine a bright light in their faces and shoot them while they freeze in bewilderment. Not very sporting, by any reckoning – merely an effective means of destruction, and one which drove conservationists to a frenzy.

'A lot of country people don't like otters any more than badgers,' said Robin.

'I know that, Dad,' Sam said, with exaggerated patience. 'What do you think the group's trying to do? We spend more time than anything else, talking to people, persuading them there's room for wild animals as well as farm stock. But it's all going crazy just now. It's total war out there. The cull's the final straw.'

'I'm very sorry about the otter,' Robin said placatingly. 'Now, your mother's had a nasty experience today, and she's going to bed. No loud telly, okay?'

Deirdre waited in vain for Sam to enquire about her nasty experience. After a minute she left the room to fetch her boxes of pots from the car, wondering whether Robin would tell Sam the story. She filled in the yields in the small jumbled back room that they used for various hobbies, and then went up to bed.

When she got the recording job, she'd suggested she should sleep in a separate room because of the disruptive hours, but Robin wouldn't hear of it. To his credit, he had never complained at the alarm going off at three and four in the morning, twelve times a month. Less to his credit, he still hadn't mastered the technique necessary to get himself to bed two hours later than his wife, without waking her.

Robin did not tell his daughter about Sean O'Farrell's death. She didn't enquire, and he was unsure of how the narrative should be pitched. Deirdre had seemed upset, as anyone would, but he found himself wondering at certain aspects of the way she'd behaved. He'd watched her hands, as he often did, marvelling at their sinewy strength. They were her best feature, somehow revealing more of her character than her rather immobile face. Even before the milk recording job, she'd been deft at anything practical – needlework, rug-making, gardening. She'd erected fences, tinkered with car engines. She was quick and sure in her movements, often reducing Robin to little more than a passive observer.

When she'd drawn his attention to the shaking, he'd already noticed it. And also that her hands had been perfectly steady only seconds before.

In the Dunsworthy cottages, Sean O'Farrell's death was naturally the sole topic of conversation. Mary Hillcock listened patiently while Heather O'Farrell bemoaned her fate in a repetitive litany of self-pitying complaints. At least, Mary made a show of patience, which belied her real feelings. Although Heather showed no sign of wondering who had killed Sean – which was bizarre in itself – Mary's head was throbbing with the inescapable impression that it had been her brother's work.

'We'll have to leave here, won't we?' Heather was saying. 'How long have we got, do you think? Mary, will you ask Gordon to give us until the summer? Where will we go? I'm never going to be able to work, not like this. And Abigail – she's got her GCSEs next year. I can't make her change schools now.' The questions piled up without pause for an answer, the voice tinny and jarring on Mary's ear.

'I'm sure everything's going to be all right,' she said, her tone brusque in spite of herself. She got up to put another log on the fire. 'You're covered by the law, anyway. We can't just throw you out into the cold, even if we wanted to.'

'Not *you,*' Heather protested, eyes widening. 'I don't mean you, Mary. Everybody knows that Gordon runs the farm and you've got your own work. I hardly even think of you as one of the Hillcocks.'

'Thanks,' said Mary, unable to ignore the irony. She wanted to thrust her face into Heather's and scream *What about me? What about my mother? If Gordon's sent to prison, what are we supposed to do?* But she didn't. She lapsed into another silence and let Heather carry on moaning.

Next door, Ted and Jilly Speedwell were sitting side by side on their sagging old sofa, taking no notice of the television that was trying to interest them in the amusing antics of king penguins. 'Poor old Sean,' Jilly sighed, for the third time. 'Whoever would have thought it?'

Ted made no comment.

'The police had Gordon in the car with them,' she continued – another remark she had made several times already. 'So who's going to do the milking tomorrow? You?'

Ted shrugged. 'Haven't milked for eight, nine years,' he muttered. 'Not since the old man died.'

'I know what – they'll have phoned that girl,

Gordon's new girlfriend. She'll know how to do it. She comes from Redstone, where they had the Jerseys until a year or so ago.'

'Mmm,' said Ted.

'It'll be all round the district by tomorrow,' Jilly marvelled. 'And in the paper. Telly too, probably. Devon Farmer Charged With Murder. What'll happen to us, Ted? What'll happen to Dunsworthy?'

Ted closed his eyes. 'Who knows?' he said miserably. Jilly heard the fear in his voice, and gave him a sharp look.

'What? What's worrying you?'

'What d'you think?' he demanded, suddenly angry. 'Why'd they take my clothes like that? What if Gordon can prove he was somewhere else all afternoon? Who'll be main suspect, then?' He stared at her, a hunted look in his eyes.

Jilly reached over and patted his knee reassuringly. 'They must be thorough, my lover. They don't know anything about us, after all,' she said. 'They'll see soon enough that it could never have been you. Don't you go worrying about that.'

'You can't be sure,' he insisted, and she saw that he wasn't entirely easy with her ready dismissal of the idea, as if she'd demeaned him with her implication that he wasn't capable of killing. She smiled a little at the irrepressible male ego that felt the need to be judged up to the job, even when it was murder.

'So,' she continued, a little anxious now, 'where were 'ee this afternoon, then?'

'That's just it,' he said. 'I was mainly around the yard. The muck spreader needed a new tailboard and Sean helped me put it on – that was before dinner, and then we changed the filters on the tractor. After dinner we only saw each other for a minute, then he went off somewhere. Gordon had swapped the milking, see. It was an afternoon off for Sean, and he said he was going to make sure he spent it doing something he'd been wanting to for a long time.'

'Messing about with the muck spreader?'

'That was *before*. He only had the afternoon off. I haven't seen him since just after two.'

'But where *were* you?'

Ted worked his shoulders uneasily. 'Here and there. Cutting silage, filling up the hopper with cake. Mostly just messing about in the Dutch barn. It was cold and my hip was paining me.' He spoke with a trace of self-pity; he'd made no secret of his tendency to work at half-speed these days, especially in the winter months.

'So you just say you were away in the fields somewhere, you hear me? Did Gordon see you this afternoon?'

Ted shook his head. 'Doubt it. As far as I could tell, he went straight from the house to the office after dinner, and got talking with the recorder until they started milking.'

'As far as 'ee could tell?'

He frowned painfully. 'You know how 'tis up there; all those buildings, like a maze. You could have five people working there and they'd never see each other. If someone wanted to creep round unseen, it'd be easy. Gordon could have gone out of his back door, past the calf-pens, through the shippon and into the gathering yard without me or the recorder seeing him. The recorder always parks right outside the parlour, where you can't see anything that's going on. Even the old granny very likely wouldn't have caught sight of Gordon or Sean from her window, if they stayed in the far corner of the yard.'

Jilly felt her confidence ebbing. Who could trust the police to notice the obvious? If they discovered that Ted had been dodging in and out of the buildings and around the yard all afternoon, with nobody to vouch for what he'd been doing, things might get very unpleasant. 'Then you've got to say you were hedging or ditching or something, in one of the top fields – all afternoon,' she decreed.

He pulled away from her. 'Gordon did tell me I should have a look at the ditch along Top

Linhay. If I said that's where I'd been, he'd never doubt it.'

She nodded her satisfaction, before changing tack. 'And what about Eliot?'

Ted sank against the sofa cushions behind him. 'Why bring Eliot into it? He doesn't come to Dunsworthy any more.'

'Because someone, sooner or later, is sure to tell the police that Sean knew Eliot. Anything that happens to Sean is something to do with Eliot, you know that.'

Ted's eyes closed again. 'Then we'd best hope Eliot was at work all day,' he said.

CHAPTER FIVE

Dunsworthy farmyard at six next morning was an all-female arena. Lilah was on the tractor, scraping mucky straw from the cows' sleeping quarters, while the animals milled about in the gathering yard. Strands of police tape had been strung across a section of the yard, with the intention of safeguarding a spot where the previous evening's searches had found blood on the ground. The forensics team had stayed until almost midnight, with searchlights and photographers. It hadn't taken them more than an hour or so to find a likely murder weapon in the shape of a three-pronged garden fork, thrown down onto a pile of straw in a different barn from the one containing Sean's body. They had also found – with considerable good fortune – enough blood outside to identify the site of the actual attack.

By the time they left, a scenario had emerged that seemed to fit with their findings. Sean had been attacked with a fork in the gathering yard. This yard was bordered on two sides by the barn in which the body had been found and the milking parlour. Over a hundred cows had been through it subsequent to the attack on Sean, and it was liberally strewn with manure and mud. Nonetheless, a distinct trail of blood had been detected, leading from a featureless point in the yard to the door of the barn. The victim had dragged himself – or been dragged – the twelve yards of the trail, entered the barn and died there. The tape had been strung across that corner as a matter of routine, but the team had gathered just about all the samples and pictures they needed. Little more could be added to the accumulating hypothesis of what had happened until the pathologist made his report.

Lilah's mind had been in turmoil ever since Claudia had phoned her at eight-thirty the previous evening, telling her what had happened. It had taken a long time to absorb the facts and their implications. Bewilderment, panic and rage all flooded through her. 'How on *earth* could they think it was Gordon?' she demanded finally.

Claudia had sounded distant. 'Because he was on the spot, I suppose.'

'Have you arranged for a solicitor to be with him when he's questioned?'

'We haven't really got anybody. Don't they provide someone, if you ask?'

Lilah snorted. 'Only if they're forced to. We should find somebody who'll do a good job, not some bored junior from a rota.'

'It's a bit late . . .'

Lilah had another thought. 'Did they find a weapon? Do they know what was used?'

'I don't know. They wouldn't tell me, would they? They seemed interested in Gordon's gun. They're still out there now, with horrible bright lights, crawling all over the yard beside the parlour. It's all very disconcerting, like something you see on telly. I just hope you can manage the morning milking for us? It's rather a lot to ask, I know. But at least you won't be all on your own – the recorder's going to be there, Gordon says.'

'What?'

'The milk recorder. You know – that Watson woman. She was here all afternoon.'

'Was she? Well, that'll be fun for both of us.' Lilah tried to swallow the growing sense of dread, fending it off with flippancy. 'You can stop worrying about the cows, anyway,' she added. 'I'll be there.'

She wanted to finish the call and close her ears to any more of the dreadful story. But she knew she couldn't. 'Gordon didn't do it, did he?' she said softly. 'I mean – it surely must have been somebody else.'

'He was on the spot,' Claudia repeated. 'It isn't looking very good, if you think about it. Basically, it must come down to him or Ted.'

'But—' Lilah wanted to scream a denial. 'We can't *let* it be him,' she said desperately.

'We won't if we can help it,' Claudia assured her gently.

Two hours later, just as Lilah was going to bed, Claudia phoned again. 'One more thing,' she said in a tone that was unmistakably conspiratorial. 'Well, two, actually. The first is – I found a solicitor. Somebody Mary used to know. He says he'll sit with Gordon while they question him.'

'Good,' said Lilah listlessly. 'What's the second thing?'

'Well – they seem to be putting a lot of very flimsy-looking tape across one corner of the yard. I assume they've found something they think is evidence there. It really does look very flimsy. You'll see what I mean in the morning.'

Lilah felt a surge of affection for the woman. 'I'm sure I will,' she said, on a short laugh.

* * *

Deirdre Watson's headlights were visible before she turned off the road, and Lilah followed her progress from the tractor seat. Having made a reasonable job of cleaning out the cowshed, she should have switched off the tractor and got started on preparing the milking parlour for the first cows. Instead, she waited another minute, until the recorder's car was in the yard. Then, as Deirdre got out of the vehicle, Lilah revved the tractor and reversed it clumsily into the nearest strand of police tape. One or two cows standing close by trotted rapidly out of her way. The tape snapped and the tractor shot forward again, turning in an arc towards the clustered animals.

As Lilah had hoped, Deirdre appeared at the corner of the barn, peering through the metal-pole fence to see what was going on. It was impossible to speak over the noise of the tractor, but Lilah ventured a loud shout at the cows, designed to sound as if she wanted them to scatter out of her way. Then she brought the vehicle to a sudden shuddering halt, sending it skidding on a slippery patch of muck.

Bewildered cows did their best to dodge her, several of them crossing the line recently marked out by the now-broken tape. Lilah switched off the engine and jumped down from her seat, one hand to her mouth. 'Gosh! What have I done?' she cried in a high-pitched voice. 'That tractor's got a mind of its own. Lucky I didn't hit one of the cows, just then.' There was a moment of deep silence, before a cow coughed, and the faint bawl of a calf came from somewhere.

Deirdre stared at her. 'Are you the relief milker?' she asked.

'Sort of. I'm Lilah Beardon, Gordon's girlfriend. You're Mrs Watson, aren't you?'

'Deirdre – yes.'

'Well, look, you'll have to be my witness that this was all a stupid accident. The police are going to go bananas at me when they see what I've done. Cows trampling all over their evidence. Mind you, that tape was ludicrously flimsy. They'd probably have broken through it anyway. You'd think someone would have told them this was the gathering yard, wouldn't you?'

Deirdre gave a forced laugh, still bewildered by what she'd seen. 'They probably worked it out for themselves. I doubt if you've done anything too awful. Not after the cows trampled it all yesterday in any case. Do you think this is where Sean was attacked?'

'Well, they obviously think it's important. They'd taped off the area to include the barn door. Isn't that where Sean was found? I'm still very hazy about the details.'

Deirdre nodded. 'It's very strange coming back here again after yesterday. Doesn't seem a lot of point to it, really. But Gordon insisted.'

'Did he? Did they let you speak to him?'

'Not really. We were both together in the office for a few minutes with the policeman, and he made it clear he wanted the recording to go ahead as normal. Why – do you think they expected us to conspire together somehow?'

'They're supposed to keep witnesses separate,' Lilah said. 'Now, let's get this show on the road.'

Deirdre cast her eyes skywards for a second, in a moment of exasperation that Lilah found mildly offensive. 'That's what everybody says,' Deirdre explained. 'I must have heard it a hundred times, just before milking starts.'

Lilah couldn't see why this should be a problem, but she didn't say anything.

'Could you describe the policeman?' she asked, a few minutes later. She already knew what was coming. It had been one of her first panicky thoughts. But she hadn't checked it out until now.

'Very tall. A long face, mid-brown hair, blue eyes . . .'

'I thought so,' nodded Lilah.

Working with a woman always unsettled Deirdre. When she started the job, she had asked, 'Are there many herdswomen these days?'

'Very few,' her Field Manager had replied. 'They've got more sense.'

It was a memorable remark, but Deirdre didn't quite believe it. It had nothing to do with sense – it was something altogether more visceral. Docile in the face of exploitation, dependent and patient, the cows were necessary victims in the dairy industry. Something about this tension, this dubious morality, disturbed women very much more than it did men.

The demands of the milking and recording always kept conversation to a few brief snatches, much of it concerning the animals surrounding them. Lilah abandoned any attempt to feed them according to their yields, as was the usual routine; Deirdre assured her that none of them was on antibiotics and their milk therefore to be discarded. 'That's a relief,' Lilah said. 'Have you ever let antibiotic milk into the tank?'

'Once,' Deirdre admitted. 'I'm covered by insurance, but I never want it to happen again. You should have seen the herdsman's face.'

'It wasn't here?'

'No.'

Deirdre was noting down the yields directly onto the parlour sheets, risking them getting mucky or wet, to save time. Lilah was surprisingly quick, given that she had never milked these particular cows, nor any at all for over a year. When Deirdre commented, she smirked and said, 'Like riding a bicycle, I suppose.'

'A lot of them aren't giving as much as they should,' Deirdre noted. 'Must be because you're strange to them.'

'What *exactly* happened?' Lilah finally permitted herself to ask, as the recorder sealed her boxes and started to pack away her equipment. Deirdre told her the story in a tight, unemotional voice.

'Was Gordon terribly upset?' Lilah demanded abruptly. 'When he found Sean, I mean.'

'Shocked,' Deirdre told her judiciously.

'There you are then! He wouldn't have been so shocked if he'd killed him!' Something childish and pathetic appealed to Deirdre's mother instinct. This girl was very young – much too young to get drawn into the mess that was unfolding on Dunsworthy Farm. Her salvation, if it was to exist at all, probably lay in coming from a farm background herself. She'd have that robustness in the face of disaster somewhere inside her, the harsh experience of pain and helplessness and cold and trouble that they all shared, and which marked them out from the rest of mankind. Even policemen, Deirdre realised, though they might not accept the distinction.

Outside it was very slowly getting lighter. An unfriendly east wind had sprung up since the milking had started and a few hard spatters of icy cold rain were starting to blow in on the gusts.

If by nothing else, the two women were united in a desire to get on to more important business. And for then both, the next item on their agenda was an interview with Den Cooper, Detective Sergeant.

Lilah watched the recorder drive away, standing at the door to the tank room, thoughtfully nibbling at a chapped lower lip. The weather was not conducive to standing for long in the open air, however, and she retreated to the parlour, where the usual quagmire greeted her. She'd have to do at least a token washing-down – cleaning the clusters and scraping muck from the stalls.

The sliding door into the adjoining barn had been sealed shut with rather more efficiency than the taped-off area outside, and she was curious to see what was inside. The building boasted no windows and she'd already observed that the outer door was similarly barricaded. The blue tape brought with it a stabbing reminder of the events on her own farm, more than three years earlier. She remembered the way the tape made your own home seem alien, and your own daily activities suspicious and open to misinterpretation. She shivered on Gordon's behalf, and her own. In her mind's eye, Gordon's face floated, his full lips forming a teasing half-smile, his eyes slicing through all the normal defences between any two people, so that he could see clearly into her furthest depths. Gordon made her feel *known*, in every cell of her body. He knew *her,* what she wanted, what she thought. He knew, and he approved, and he acted on his knowledge.

Whatever – *whoever* – was trying to take Gordon away from her now, was in for a great surprise. Because there was *no way* that Lilah was going to let him go. The merest glimpse of the idea made her feel as if all her skin had been peeled off and a vicious blast of cold air directed onto her naked nerve endings. What did it matter that the wretched Sean O'Farrell had been killed, anyway? He had been a shifty sort of character, always slinking away around a corner of a barn or calf-pen, never stopping for a proper conversation, never looking her in the eye. For all she knew, he deserved to be killed. There was no pang of sympathy in her for the murdered man. Every ounce of Lilah's sympathy was reserved exclusively for herself and Gordon.

The word *murder* felt wrong, as well. Ordinary concepts like birth, work, cold, exhaustion, sickness and death – all slipped askew somehow in the context of a farm. A farm was a closed secret community, out of public sight, struggling with eternal verities against the capricious elements, even in these days of heated tractor cabs and ubiquitous lighting. Life on a farm might not be as cold and dark as it used to be, but it was still just as elemental. Lilah had seen the brutality, the sudden loss of control in the face of pain, frustration and towering rage. If a cow accidentally trapped your hand between a gate and a wall, you either reflexively hit back, punching or kicking the animal, or you grimaced ruefully, cradling the afflicted hand and muttering something that accepted the beast's ignorance and innocence. 'Didn't do it on purpose,' or 'Can't expect her to understand.' Lilah's father had been in the former group, frightening and distressing her at times with his violence.

Gordon Hillcock was the other sort. He was not vengeful against unthinking animals, nor enough of a fool to believe that animals hurt you deliberately. Lilah had seen very little of him in a social context, but he appeared to attract goodwill and fraternity from his neighbouring farmers. He raged only against the government, the supermarkets, the Ministry that had failed for thirty years to effectively address the perennial problem of TB in West Country dairy herds – just like any farmer. He worried about his finances, and the idiotic fact that it cost him more to produce milk than the dairies paid him for it.

Of course Gordon had not killed Sean, she repeated to herself, a protective mantra of common sense and hope, as she ushered the cows back into their shed, promising them that Ted Speedwell would be along soon with their breakfast. Or if he *had*, another little voice persisted, then it would have been accidental, or self-defence. In any case, the police were never going to be able to prove anything. They were never going to find evidence sufficient to prosecute him amongst the muck and confusion of Dunsworthy. On this first day, that was all she cared about: that nobody was going to take Gordon away from her. Whether or not he had killed Sean O'Farrell was scarcely relevant to her, this morning. She wasn't ever going to ask him; she wasn't even going to think about it. Anything Gordon did was okay with her. She *loved* him, didn't she? And love was all you needed.

Den was attending the post-mortem on Sean O'Farrell, which started at eight-thirty that morning. The pathologist dictated his findings as he went on, noticing, as always, details that should have been obvious but weren't, to a less skilled eye. 'Slightly built adult male, aged late thirties, early forties. Reasonably well nourished . . . upper front incisor chipped . . . evidence of earlier injury on and around right ear.' Here the man paused for closer inspection. 'Ragged wound on top and back of ear, extending to skin beneath the hairline. Possibly caused by . . . um . . . clawing or biting. No indication of suturing. I estimate the injury was sustained up to a year ago and left to heal without intervention.' Den edged closer, peering at the ear in question. A crooked silvery line ran out of the hair across the back of the ear and up to the top of it. The normally smooth curve had been badly damaged, leaving a split of at least half an inch. 'Dog bite?' he suggested.

'Possibly,' grunted the pathologist. 'Quickest way to find out'll be to ask his family. Must have made quite a mess when it happened. Ears bleed profusely, as you probably know.'

Den stepped back again and let the man continue with his observations. 'Hands calloused, skin around fingernails ingrained with oil . . . chilblains on both feet . . . scarring on left knee suggesting surgery at some time. Deceased probably walked with a mild limp as a result. Flexion will have been compromised.'

Poor chap, Den thought. Torn ear, stiff knee, broken tooth, callouses: Sean was beginning to sound like a peasant from the Middle Ages, not a modern man with all the services of the National Health at his disposal. And they still hadn't got to what had killed him.

That came ten minutes later, as the scalpel and the saw were brought into play. The mutterings of the pathologist accelerated as he described the damage. 'Let's see,' he began counting under his breath, 'six puncture wounds, arranged in two rows of three. One row at the level of the thorax . . .' he turned to the diagram on an adjacent table and carefully marked the position of three wounds, '. . . and the second row across the abdomen . . .' and he marked another three. Den stared at the diagram, wondering what could have produced such an odd pattern. The pathologist was ahead of him. 'The lower three wounds are more ragged and more shallow, suggesting the victim resisted. They are very similar in size, depth and angle. The upper row penetrated to a greater depth and are less ragged, suggesting greater force and less resistance. As an early hypothesis, I would suggest the murder weapon was a three-pronged metal implement of some kind. Something used in the deceased's place of work, most likely.'

'Can you comment on the degree of force needed to cause this amount of damage?' Den asked, trying to visualise the scene.

'Depends on the angle of penetration. No great force at all if the victim was already on his back. Some farm implements have heavy handles. Its own weight would possibly be enough to break the skin and penetrate a few millimetres. Even a fairly slight person leaning on it could drive it in to this depth. But if he was standing up, it would have to be a much more violent action, by a much stronger individual.'

'Right,' said Den thoughtfully. 'Well, I'll be off now. Lots to do.' He had hoped all along that he could skip the part where all the vital organs were removed and weighed; it always made his own insides contract with an irrational sympathy. 'I'll catch up with the final report later on.'

Nobody replied. The Coroner's Officer was making his own notes, and the mortuary assistant was washing away the seepage of body fluids as they threatened to obscure the pathologist's work. A young trainee was standing mutely at the foot of the slab, jaw clenched, one hand flat against her stomach. Den had given her a few encouraging smiles at the outset, but then forgotten her as the findings became more interesting. Besides, he knew from personal experience there wasn't anything he could do to assuage her queasiness.

He drove the twenty miles back to the station as fast as he dared. Hemsley would be impatient to get on with the interviews, and there was a great deal Den wanted to tell him. The Superintendent would be expecting a briefing before lunch, too.

But first Den wanted to see for himself the detailed findings of the forensic teams from the previous evening. According to Mark Newcombe, the Coroner's Officer, the team had been there till midnight, rigging up lights and literally crawling all over the yard looking for evidence. But even before the body had been found, the entire herd of cows had walked over the whole yard. 'It's a miracle they found anything,' Newcombe had remarked. 'But it looks as if they managed to find the spot where the bloke was attacked. Too much blood even for a herd of cows to obliterate. They'll be back again this morning for another look in daylight.'

As expected, Den found a well-established file in the station office, containing a list of work so far accomplished. Most notes contained a footnote: *Further examination by daylight required.* As well as the samples and photos from the gathering yard, the forensics team had also examined the outer yard, between the farmhouse and the outbuildings. Evidence of no fewer than seven distinct sets of tyre marks had been identified, all of which had apparently visited Dunsworthy over the past forty-eight hours – since the last rainfall, which had helpfully provided a new layer of mud which then froze lightly, keeping tyre marks nice and crisp.

They had also discovered what was almost certainly the murder weapon. Den smiled grimly to himself: it exactly fitted the pathologist's description of what they should look for. He wondered, inconsequentially, if they should return the two shotguns they'd taken the previous evening. It would be difficult to argue now that they were in any way pertinent to the investigation. At any rate, he smugly told himself, if things went the way he hoped, it would all be sewn up by bedtime. If Hillcock's clothes revealed traces of O'Farrell's blood and if Speedwell's did not, Den thought they'd have more than enough to launch a prosecution against Hillcock.

But perhaps he was being unduly precipitate. There were still a host of unanswered questions. If Hillcock had dragged his victim into the barn, why was he then so horrified at its discovery? Had it been simply good acting, for the benefit of Deirdre Watson and the police? Deirdre Watson didn't look like someone who'd be easily fooled. And if Sean had dragged himself into the barn, why would he do that? Why hide away like that, instead of trying to reach the big house and summon help? Had he staggered away in terror of further assault? Perhaps he hadn't understood how severe his injuries were. After all, his arms and legs still presumably worked at that point, and his head was undamaged. It hadn't looked as if any bones were broken. Perhaps he'd been so terrified – or even enraged – that the pain was secondary to the fear or his desire to hit back.

The geography of the farm buildings was extremely complicated, and Den had difficulty in remembering how they all connected up. Could the barn have been a short cut of some sort? To a telephone in the office perhaps, or a first aid box.

That struck him as a highly persuasive theory, and he made a note of it.

And where had the murderer gone, though, immediately after the attack was over? Had he waited to see what his victim would do, or had he flung down his weapon and run in the opposite direction, hoping to establish some sort of alibi for himself? Had he been cool and calculating, or distraught at what he'd done?

Danny Hemsley swept into the room as if there wasn't a second to spare, his head thrust forward on his thick neck. 'Cooper!' he shot out. 'Where the hell have you been? We've got a million things to do this morning. Forensics have hardly scratched the surface yet, and you know what farms are like – shit all over everything.' He eyed the open file. 'Reading the exercise in minimalism they've produced so far, eh?'

Den leant against the desk, taking his weight on his knuckles. 'Looks okay to me,' he said. 'Chap's attacked in the yard and staggers, or is dragged, bleeding into the barn, where he dies. And the pathologist says it was done with a farm or garden implement with three prongs, which is exactly what they've found.'

'I know. They phoned. There was no need for you to be at the PM. Wasting time when you could have been questioning the Dunsworthy people.'

Den didn't try to argue. Hemsley's habit was to panic at the outset of an investigation, to want everything done at once, full reports submitted before breakfast. Den had printed out his own lengthy findings from the hours following the first summons to Dunsworthy, and left them on the DI's desk the previous evening, before finally getting home at nine-thirty. His own conscience was crystal clear where reports were concerned. 'Is Hillcock still here?' he asked.

'Too right he is. Not a happy badger, either.' Den and the others had long ago given up trying to decide whether Danny knew the difference between badgers and bunnies or whether he just thought he was being funny. 'He says he did not kill his herdsman, and that he can't provide any witnesses to where he was between one-fifteen and three-fifteen p.m. Full stop.'

'He only needs to account for the hour between two and three,' Den said. 'O'Farrell was alive at two, his wife saw him – and the Watson woman arrived just after three and was chatting to him before they started the milking.'

Hemsley nodded impatiently. 'Whatever. He says he had lunch alone in his house, having taken a sandwich and some fruit up to the old granny at one o'clock. The milk recorder got there about half past two and he had a quick word with her in the yard before she went into the office to number her pots, or whatever she does. Then he went back indoors where he did some paperwork. He says he made a phone call to a Mr Harold Spear, a neighbouring farmer who was concerned about a hole in their shared hedge. The call lasted five minutes max, and involved some disagreement about hunting. Mr Hillcock thinks the hole was made by the hunt, of which he disapproves. He would quite like to ban them from his land, but has not done so up to now. This has been confirmed by Mr Spear, who seems to be a very helpful gentleman.' The Detective Inspector looked up from the notes he had been consulting. 'On the face of it, Hillcock has to be the main suspect. But there is this Speedwell bloke as well. His clothes have gone to forensics, but Mike had a quick look at them and says they seem clean.'

'I thought so, too,' said Den. 'And he's quite a frail old chap.'

'He's still in the frame,' Danny said sternly. 'Never mind frail, the man's a farmworker, chucking great hay bales about and turning grown sheep upside down.'

Den suppressed a sarcastic snort at the image this conjured. Hemsley pressed on. 'And there seems to be a number of women and youngsters about. Plus, we can't rule out somebody visiting while Hillcock was in the house, and doing the deed out in the yard. I'll talk to him one more time, and then we'll have to let him go.'

Den pushed himself upright and cleared his throat. 'There's something I should tell you,' he began. 'I should have told you last night, but there wasn't really a chance – and besides, I don't honestly think it's relevant. But . . . the thing is, Gordon Hillcock is my ex-girlfriend's new bloke. I hardly know him. It's just one of those horrible coincidences. Lilah's going to be very upset, of course. She's been around violent death before and this'll bring it all back to her.' He twisted his hands together, giving his worries full play. 'I don't really know what it'll do to her.'

'Obviously, this is *relevant*,' Danny interrupted, in the tone he'd come to adopt since his promotion. Briskly professional more or less described it, with a dash of impatience at other people's slow-wittedness.

Den looked up at him and chewed his lip. The DI's mind was obviously working at full speed, his eyes darting restlessly from one point in the room to another.

'It means we'll be vulnerable to a defence argument that you lacked objectivity in the pursuit of O'Farrell's killer. It means, Cooper, that I really ought to take you off the case, from this moment on.'

Den opened his mouth to speak. Then he

realised he didn't actually care very much if Danny carried out his threat. Anyone else would come to exactly the same conclusions as he had done – and the case would assuredly arrive at the same eventual outcome, anyway. In some ways, it would be a relief to be free of it and let someone else get their hands covered in muck.

'But I can't really do that,' Danny went on. 'We need your statements from yesterday and I have a feeling it would cause more of a stink if you were taken off now than if you carried on with squeaky-clean integrity. It'd look as if we didn't trust you. As it is, we'll have to be completely upfront about it – try and make it work in our favour. No one else is going to have your background knowledge, for a start. You've always been the one we sent on the farm jobs – and it'd look funny if we changed our usual practice now.' He tapped his teeth for a moment, before adding, 'And anyway, there isn't anybody of your rank to replace you, with Phil off sick. So that's the way we'll have to play it. You'll listen to everything anybody has to say with a completely open mind. You'll scour the countryside for mental patients let loose into the community; you'll investigate O'Farrell's life, in case there's something in his past that would make him vulnerable to attack. You'll get to know everyone living at Dunsworthy, find out what they do all day, what they think, what star sign they are. Sorry, mate – that's the way this game has to be played. Your only hope for a rest between now and Valentine's Day is if Hillcock comes out with a confession, backed up with motive and evidence. On the positive side, I'd say that isn't totally beyond the realms of possibility. Otherwise, it's grindstone time.'

'Right, sir,' said Den gloomily. He couldn't fault the logic, however strong his sense of injustice might be.

CHAPTER SIX

When questioned again that morning, with Den present, Hillcock had sighed and slowly shaken his head. 'I don't remember anything more than I've told you already.' He said it over and over again. The solicitor, summoned by Gordon's mother, sat motionless and impassive throughout.

'Please try, sir,' DI Hemsley had persisted. 'It is very important, as I'm sure you'll realise. Shall we go back a bit? When did you last see Sean O'Farrell alive?'

'About ten-thirty yesterday morning.'

'And how would you describe his frame of mind?'

'He was all right. A bit grumpy at the change.'

'Grumpy? Change?'

'I told you – I'd asked him to swap that afternoon's milking with me. I'd do Tuesday if he did Saturday. I had plans for the weekend. It made him grumpy – though hardly more than usual. You wouldn't call Sean a cheerful man at the best of times.'

Den took note of Hillcock's pallor after a night at the police station. He didn't suppose he'd managed much sleep. But his manner was calm and relatively cooperative; he didn't seem frightened or defensive. Den looked at Gordon's hands, clasped loosely in his lap, just visible over the edge of the table, as the DI continued his questions. Had they wielded a heavy fork and thrust it twice into another man's body? Den had seen the hands of murderers before, had even suffered unpleasant dreams about them, but he knew better than to suppose that he could identify guilt from them. Gordon had short fingers and square palms. The joints were pronounced, the nails clean. None of the oil that Sean O'Farrell had had ingrained into his skin and nails could be found on Hillcock. Did the farmer leave the unpleasant jobs to his employees, while he contented himself with paperwork and an occasional stroll along his hedgerows?

Hemsley appeared to have run out of questions, giving the solicitor an opening to push out his chin and demand that his client be permitted to leave. With a sigh, the DI nodded. 'We would ask that you remain in the vicinity for the next few days,' he said. 'Detective Sergeant Cooper will be interviewing the Speedwell family this morning, and there will be further forensic examination of the yards and buildings. Please ensure that nobody goes into the barn where the body was found until we give you the all clear.'

Gordon snorted slightly, but said nothing. Then, in a sudden rush, all four men got to their feet and skirmished briefly at the door before leaving the room in single file.

Den and Danny exchanged a few more words before going their separate ways. 'Mrs O'Farrell says that Sean went back up to the yard after lunch – at two o'clock,' Hemsley observed. 'If Hillcock was there too, why does he say he never saw him?'

'It's a complicated collection of buildings,' Den explained. 'They could easily have missed each other.'

The Inspector put his hands together, pressing a fingertip into a spot beneath is chin. 'When did Speedwell last see O'Farrell?'

'I don't think I asked him,' Den flipped through his report and shook his head. 'But it looks bad for Hillcock, eh?' he couldn't resist blurting.

'No alibi for that forty minutes, inconsistencies, opportunity . . .'

'And not a morsel of proof,' Hemsley reminded him. 'Early days, my friend. And a mind so open, I could get the Millennium Dome into it. Understood?'

'Yes, sir.' Den let a short silence elapse, cementing his serious intent, before continuing, 'I said I'd go and interview the milk recorder woman this morning. Mrs Watson. She's got a lot of background information – knew both men and how they behaved towards each other.'

'And she was there,' the Inspector said. 'That's the most important thing about her. What's she like physically?'

Den didn't pretend to misunderstand. 'Quite sturdy,' he acknowledged.

'I thought she might be. And she was there alone, unobserved, for the best part of an hour. What's more, she was oddly calm and collected when you arrived, according to your report. You follow my drift, I'm sure.'

'Yes, sir.'

'So, I'd expect you to see her again today. But don't leave Speedwell for long. I need to know all you can find out about him. Cross your fingers there's prints on that fork and O'Farrell's blood on someone's clothes. Should get results on all that later today – at least the blood groups. You and Mike did a good job last night, you know. Very thorough.'

'Thanks,' Den nodded. Despite Hemsley's earlier impatience, Den was aware that neither of them had any sense that this was a complex mystery to be solved. Such murders were, after all, the exception. Far more common was the red-handed, smoking-gun scenario, where the stunned perpetrator was taken in for questioning, charged, remanded, tried, sentenced, in the slow, jerky style of the legal system, and all was well with the world again within the year.

As he walked into the reception area, intending to collect the keys to a pool car, Den came face to face with Lilah. The shock was none the less for knowing her involvement with Dunsworthy. He looked down at her familiar features and all the old feelings returned, like a tsunami. He had to clench both fists rigidly at his sides to prevent himself from wrapping his arms around her.

'Hi,' he said warily.

'Don't you *hi* me,' she snarled. 'I know what you're doing. I've come to demand you release Gordon this minute. You know as well as I do this isn't about him – it's your revenge for me dumping you!' She spoke shrilly and at least three police officers heard every word.

Den hovered between anger and embarrassment. The former took momentary precedence and he clamped one hand tightly onto her shoulder, turning her towards the outer door. 'Come with me,' he ordered. 'We'll talk about this outside.'

She resisted at first, but when his grip only tightened, went with him, a mulish expression on her face. Outside, he backed her against the rough stone wall of the building and leant his face close to hers. 'Listen to me,' he said softly. 'I've told the DI all about the situation at Dunsworthy. There's nothing you can accuse me of that will cut any ice with him. There isn't going to be the least little bit of prejudice in this investigation. Because of you, in fact, it's going to have to be the most thorough for a long time. If your Gordon *is* guilty, by the time I've finished, it's hardly going to be worth the defence's time showing up at the trial. But they will. If he pleads not guilty he'll have every chance to defend himself. And what's more, he's just been told he's free to go home, having helped us with our enquiries. Everything's been done by the book, so you'd better just sit back and let the law take its course. If ever there was a fair investigation and trial, this is going to be it.'

She wrenched herself free, eyes blazing back at him. 'Fair!' she spat. 'When you've already got a completely closed mind about Gordon? Don't make me laugh. Let me tell you this, once and for all – Gordon did not kill that man. Gordon would never, ever do a thing like that. He simply isn't capable of it.' Tears filled her eyes and she dashed them away impatiently. 'This has ruined everything,' she complained with alarming bitterness. 'And you talk about fairness! If anything was ever unfair, it must be this. Why can't I just get on with a nice normal life for once?'

Den's anger was ebbing slowly, leaving space for the pity that had been edging in as he listened to her. 'Since when was life fair?' he asked gently. 'But I know you've had a raw deal and I'm sorry. You didn't deserve this.'

'Don't be *nice* to me, for God's sake!' she said. 'We're enemies over this, Den. If you're going to try to prove that Gordon's a murderer, that makes you my adversary, and I'll do everything I can to stop you. Someone else killed Sean O'Farrell and I'm going to find out who!'

The pathology report was faxed through to Detective Inspector Hemsley, giving the actual cause of death as exsanguination from a ruptured aorta, resulting from a puncture wound. There was also severe damage to liver and spleen caused by two of the six wounds discovered on the body. The fatal wound was one of the upper row, although such was the damage to the other organs that it was probable that death would have resulted from them even without the injury to the aorta. The most acute pain would have come from the lower injuries. It was estimated that death would have occurred barely one minute after the attack, but that it would have been feasible for the victim to walk or even run a short distance within that time, despite substantial loss of blood from several of the wounds.

'Nasty,' said Danny, on the mobile to Den to relay the salient points of the report. 'But mercifully quick.'

'A minute probably seems a long time if you're in agony,' Den replied, trying not to imagine how it would feel to die in a barn with only five lame cows for company.

'Where are you, by the way?' Hemsley asked. 'We're going to have to keep close tabs on you today. Don't go wandering off on some tangent without calling in first.'

'I've just pulled up outside Mrs Watson's house. I'll be with her for about an hour, I would think. Then I'll go to Dunsworthy and speak to Ted Speedwell. I also told Mrs O'Farrell we'd want to speak to her again. And there's the old granny at the big house who's the only other person we know for sure was around the place when the killing happened. Someone ought to see her.'

'There's no need for you to do it all yourself.

Young Mike's looking for something to do. I'll send him over to talk to the granny now. Then he can meet you at the cottages at . . . say, eleven or just after?'

Den felt his usual reluctance to share an investigation. Although he was happy to solicit opinions and suggestions from colleagues at the briefing meetings, be believed the actual interviews with witnesses were most effectively done by the same person. This had been the main reason why the DI hadn't pulled him off the case, he assumed. Nobody else would now be able to interpret those early, often subliminal, impressions, as well as Den could. So, in essence, Den Cooper was now the central investigating officer in the Dunsworthy case. The connections and contradictions, the nuances and nervousness, all created a picture that would never come together if different people tried to assemble it. But he supposed Granny Hillcock could be delegated more readily than anyone else.

'Okay,' he conceded.

'Right,' Danny snapped back. 'As soon as we have an ID for the fingerprints on the fork, I'll phone it through. It might affect how you approach the Speedwell chap.'

'If they're his, then it might,' Den agreed with scant enthusiasm, thinking of Lilah and how triumphant she'd be if that turned out to be the case. Thinking, too, that it wouldn't actually comprise hard evidence. Speedwell worked on the farm – it might be his fork. On its own, such a finding wouldn't incriminate him.

Den could see Deirdre Watson standing in the open doorway of her house, watching him, wondering, no doubt, why he hadn't yet got out of the car. 'I'd better go now,' he said and disconnected the phone.

Deirdre Watson lived in a good-sized stone house, which must have once been at the centre of a farm. In the upheavals of recent decades, it seemed that the land had been sold off and most of the outbuildings demolished, leaving only a half-acre garden and a couple of sheds.

'You got the message that I'd be coming, then?' he asked.

She nodded. 'Good of you to warn me,' she said warily. 'Come on in.'

As he settled in her warm kitchen, he had to force himself to attend to the matter in hand, while looking around the room for any distraction that might offer itself. Why did he feel as if the forthcoming interview was no more than a formality? The explanation was obvious, he realised. These interviews were merely designed to pre-empt any challenge to his objectivity. He was already convinced that Gordon Hillcock had killed his herdsman. He knew from the man's demeanour, and from something even less tangible. Forget Ted Speedwell and Deirdre Watson and any assorted hypothetical ramblers or nutters – sitting here now, Den could *taste* his certainty.

But he had to keep his mind open. He had to satisfy Hemsley that all the stones had been overturned. He declined the woman's offer of coffee and sat up straighter, notebook open in front of him.

'How long had you known Sean O'Farrell?' he began.

'Five years. Since I started recording at Dunsworthy.'

'How did you feel about him?'

She sat at an angle to him, so they faced each other across a corner of the big pine table. Her face seemed flushed, her breathing a trifle shallow.

'He was all right,' she said, briefly meeting Den's eye. 'Efficient. Reliable.'

'Did you ever meet him outside the farm? What do you know of his personal life?'

'I would guess I've seen him three times in five years, off the farm. And then only to say a quick hello. I know he has an invalid wife and a daughter. He seems to have belonged to some sort of farming action group, as well. They meet at a pub somewhere. He talked about it a couple of times, while he was milking.'

'Action group?' Den echoed, writing the words in the notebook.

'I don't know what it's about, really. They all seem to be farm employees, worried about the way things are going in the dairy industry. Everybody's concerned, of course. To put it mildly. It's a permanent state and lots of them have decided to do something. Just as BSE's out of the way, we've got TB to worry about. It's just one awful thing after another. From what Sean said, it's mainly TB they're bothered about at the moment. There've been a lot of reactors in the latest round of tests.'

'On Dunsworthy as well?'

'Bound to be – or so Gordon seems to think. It's too soon to say for sure – the second test is due this week. Sean was full of it last month, but it wasn't mentioned yesterday. Dunsworthy's in a non-culling area, you see, though it's only a mile away from the experimental area. Lots of people think the diseased badgers will just shift over here and spread TB even more than it is already.'

'You'll have to explain some of that to me.'

'Surely you know about the Ministry tests? They divide the whole county into areas, and cull all the badgers in one area, while leaving them alone – protecting them, in fact – in another. Then, if the culled areas become free of TB, they'll assume the disease is carried by badgers and act accordingly. The trouble is, some farmers are already convinced of the link and if they're in a non-culling area, they don't like it. And there are studies that suggest that culling only *increases* the spread of TB. The whole process is viewed with contempt, quite frankly. The Ministry don't help, either, by being so secretive about it. You can never get a straight answer out of them.'

'Seems a daft sort of set-up to me,' Den agreed.

'Try explaining that to them,' she sighed.

'So, what was Sean's line on all this? And Hillcock's?'

'Sean automatically despised anything the Government did, on principle. He just wanted farmers to be left alone to get on with the job. Not very realistic, to say the least.'

'And Hillcock?'

She tightened her lips and stared at the table in front of her for a moment. 'Gordon's more complicated,' she said. 'More intelligent, too.'

'Would you say they disagreed a lot?'

She laughed. 'All the time. I think it was the only way they could communicate, through an everlasting argument. It was quite entertaining at times.'

'Did you ever see it get nasty?'

She shook her head. 'I very seldom saw them together,' she explained. 'Just for a couple of minutes in the morning sometimes, at the end of milking. Sean disobeyed most of Gordon's orders – or he said he did.'

'And got away with it?' Den was struggling to get the picture.

Deirdre heaved a sigh. 'Remember I only saw them once a month. Usually it was Sean doing the milking, so I very rarely got Gordon's side of the story. And he was much less forthcoming, anyway. You need to understand what it's like. Milking's a lonely business, so they mostly take the opportunity of talking their heads off when it's recording. A lot of what they say is rubbish – just letting off steam to someone they think is uninvolved, impartial. From the things he said to me, I'd put Sean down as sullen, resentful and worried about his job. Most of the herdsmen are the same around here.'

'And the farm owners?'

'They're worried too. Money is running down the drain and most of them have given themselves a cut-off date. If things aren't better by then, they'll have to sell up. Dairying isn't financially viable these days.'

Den had been aware of the crisis in the industry, as had everyone living in rural areas. 'And that wouldn't make for a very relaxed atmosphere,' he suggested. 'Have you been expecting Dunsworthy to go out of milk?'

She shook her head again. 'Not this year.

Although I have often been surprised by farmers packing it in, with almost no warning. If they have got TB, there'll be compensation, and they can buy in new cows from the south-east, where things are even worse commercially and animals are going for a low price. And they have nothing like the same levels of TB. I must admit, I see Gordon as one of the survivors.'

'So would you say there'd been anything new or different at Dunsworthy recently? Any change in either Hillcock or O'Farrell?'

She pondered over the question. 'Not that I can think of,' she said at last.

Den also pondered, thinking about the body on the mortuary slab, the damage to it, both old and new, the sense he'd picked up of someone neglected, unloved. 'What was he like to work with?' he asked, tapping his pencil against *efficient, reliable*, the words she'd used about Sean, knowing they couldn't be taken as positively as they seemed on the page.

'Look,' she began, betraying some agitation, 'the way different herdsmen treat their cows is fundamental. Not one of them is sentimental about it, but there are those who are gentle by nature, and nearly as bovine as their animals. Even they will hit out, or shout, and to anyone from a town, it might look cruel. Especially these days, when the world's gone so soft. But Sean wasn't bovine. He wasn't patient, either, not really. You never knew where you were with him, that was his trouble. The cows didn't know, either. One minute he'd be gentling them and crooning to them, and the next he'd be laying into a heifer for trying to kick him. I've seen him do real damage. His fists were like iron.' Pain crossed her face and she put a hand to her side; Den became alarmed at the implication.

'He didn't hit *you*, did he?'

She shook her head vigorously. 'Of course he didn't. But when he punched a cow in the ribs, in some crazy way I felt it myself. It's very *intense* in the milking parlour, you know. You're enclosed with the man and the animals, as if the world outside didn't exist. Everything's heightened – you feel every little thing. It's difficult to describe. But Sean was not my favourite man to work with, by a long way.'

Den made more jottings, finally feeling that the picture of Sean O'Farrell was coming into focus. But it was still full of contradictions. 'And yet he seems to have been such a good husband to his sick wife.'

Deirdre sighed, as if in relief. 'That was easy,' she said. 'She's been like that for years now. So long as he kept her happy and listened to her moaning, he didn't need to worry about her. And it made him look good – just as you say. I think he lived his real life well away from Heather and the cottage. It sounds daft, and it took me years to understand it myself, but her illness was really quite liberating for him.'

'Are you saying he had other women?' Den felt a new twinge of alarm at the thought of outraged husbands.

'Oh, no, I don't think so,' she said hurriedly. 'Nothing as obvious as that. But he had a lot of empty time. That's probably why he took up with the protest group.'

They were silent for a moment. Den examined her more closely: a substantial woman, tall, with wide shoulders and generous hips, her hair carelessly gathered back in a wide rubber band, she seemed to have herself well under control. There was some kind of invisible layer around her, something protective that kept her at a slight remove from events going on around her. Her features were masklike – there were no lines on her face, neither from laughter nor frowns. She moved her hands more than her mouth or eyes.

It was clear to Den that she didn't really care that Sean O'Farrell was dead, or, probably, that Gordon Hillcock might be charged for murder. She was detached, taking the role of observer, and Den found this both useful and unsettling.

'Let me just run through the timings again,'

he said. 'Did Hillcock leave the parlour at all, during the milking?'

'Definitely not for long enough to commit a murder,' said Deirdre dryly.

'Would you have seen Sean in the gathering yard when you parked your car – what was that? Two o'clock? – if he'd been lying there?'

'It was ten past two, I should think. I can't be exact to the last minute. And no, I never go wandering around the yards. They're always muddy or slippery, apart from anything else. The gathering yard is at the far end of the barn where we found him. You'll have worked that out, of course. I wouldn't have any reason to go in the barn or the yard.'

Den thought quickly, and jotted *No need to conceal the body?* on his pad. It was a point he had not yet discussed with the DI. He pressed the point with Deirdre. 'Not even if you were looking for Hillcock to ask him something?'

She paused. 'Well, then I might,' she conceded. 'In fact, I did walk round there this morning, when I heard the tractor. I wanted to know who was doing the milking – if Gordon had come home.'

'So who was it?'

'Lilah Beardon – Gordon's girlfriend.'

Den kept his face expressionless. 'Was she on the tractor?'

'She was scraping down. Rather beyond the call of duty, if you ask me.'

Den let a small silence draw a line under that subject. 'Did you see Mr Hillcock when you arrived yesterday afternoon?'

She nodded. 'He popped his head round the office door, to say hello, just for a few seconds.'

'And did you see which way he went after that?'

'No.'

'What was his mood like yesterday?'

'A bit tense. On edge. I wasn't in the best of moods myself, so I just thought we'd both struck a bad day. It was cold, and we were keeping our heads down and getting on with it. My computer died, which was an extra annoyance. But, really, everything's an endurance test this time of year.'

'Did he say anything about Sean?'

'Nothing much. Just about him having an unexpected afternoon off because Gordon had swapped the days. And I asked after Heather.'

'Did you get a response?'

'Not really. I was just making conversation. I don't think Gordon has anything to do with her if he can help it.'

'You arrived just after two p.m. and the milking started at three, but Hillcock was with you from two-forty – is that right?'

She nodded doubtfully. 'He was in and out

of the parlour, fixing up the special equipment I need for catching milk samples. He wasn't *with* me, exactly. I had more trouble numbering my pots accurately, because of the computer. Do you want me to explain the whole procedure?'

'No, thanks. When did you last see Sean O'Farrell alive?'

'Last month, of course. The December recording.'

'So, just to go over it again – nothing unusual happened during the time between your arrival on the farm and the start of milking?'

'Only my bloody computer packing up.' She stared balefully at the offending machine, where it sat recharging at one end of the table. 'It used to do that a lot, but I thought I'd got it sorted out. I think there's a loose connection in the cable, so it doesn't charge up when I think it does.'

Den remained uninterested in the computer. In the pause that followed he inspected the big farmhouse kitchen they were sitting in. Generously warmed by a big old Aga, it was obviously the favoured haunt of two cats, curled on the cushions of a wooden settle under the window. A stack of magazines and newspapers cluttered one end of the big table, and a substantial amount of washing-up seemed to have been waiting for attention since at least the previous day. They both seemed to realise simultaneously that the interview was effectively over.

It was time he left, but the image of the body in the mortuary once again floated in front of his eyes. He tapped his pencil against his teeth. 'Do you know what happened to his ear?'

'Pardon?'

'Sean O'Farrell – something had torn his ear half off, not so long ago.'

'Oh yes,' she responded readily. 'That was Fergus, Gordon's Alsation. He was a rescue dog and his temper was always a bit unpredictable. He was okay with me – I'm very good with dogs. But Sean couldn't get anywhere with him. He took it quite personally, I think – the fact that Fergus would let me pet him, but not Sean. I wasn't there when it happened, but they both told me the story. Two different versions, of course, but I gather the dog went for him one day last summer. Got hold of his ear and wouldn't let go. Made quite a mess, but it healed up perfectly all right. Everyone said Gordon should have the dog put down, but he wouldn't.'

'Did Sean report it?'

Deirdre shook her head. 'Gordon told him he'd give him the sack if he got the dog in trouble.'

'Where's Fergus now?'

She looked down at her hands, which were loosely interlocked. 'Dead,' she mumbled. 'I'm not entirely sure what happened, but Gordon said somebody poisoned him. It was horrible, apparently – he took all day to die.'

'And nobody put him out of his misery?' Den was incredulous.

'Apparently not.'

'But they shoot all those calves. It would have been easy to do.'

She smiled bleakly. 'Gordon loved the dog. I guess he hoped it would get better. It's not everyone who can shoot their own dog, you know. And Gordon's soft in his way.'

'So who poisoned him?'

'I hate to think anyone did it deliberately. Farmers put poison down for vermin now and then, and there's all kinds of stuff about the place that could have done it. Gordon wouldn't pay for a post-mortem to find out exactly what it was. He had run up a massive vet's bill as it was, and wasn't keen to let it go any higher.' She swallowed visibly. 'Though I suppose I should tell you that Sean made a poor show of hiding his relief that Fergus was out of the way.'

'Oh?'

'I can't say more than that. I'd be guessing if I said Sean had anything to do with the poisoning. I don't suppose anybody knows for sure.'

But it would give us a motive, mused Den silently. 'When did all this happen?'

'August, September – thereabouts. I asked Gordon where the dog was when I met him in the yard, and he choked out the story.'

Den scribbled busily in his notebook. Then he glanced at his watch, to discover he had twelve minutes to finish his interview and meet Young Mike at Dunsworthy.

'I'll have to go in a minute,' he said. 'I think we've covered everything for now. Thank you – you've been very helpful.'

Her smile held something of complacency in it, he thought, and remembered his irritation towards her show of cleverness the previous day. He had an impression of a woman who felt she'd acquitted herself well and could award herself a gold star accordingly. He reminded himself that she had been at the scene of a murder, with more than enough means and opportunity, and possibly motive, once the whole story was known. Certainly she hadn't liked Sean very much.

'I'll need to see your clothes,' he said suddenly. 'The ones you were wearing yesterday afternoon.'

'My recording suit, you mean? Too late, I've washed them. They're hanging on the line outside. I always do them as soon as I get in from a morning milking.'

Den suppressed a sigh. 'What did you have on underneath? I assume you don't put on the protective suit until just before the milking starts?'

She plucked at the jumper she was wearing. 'This,' she said, 'and my black jeans. They're in the wash as well.'

'Actually in the machine?'

'No – the laundry basket.'

Den brusquely asked her to go and fetch them. At least, he thought unhappily, he'd have something for forensics to examine.

It was more difficult to leave than he had anticipated. At the final moment, a last question occurred to him. 'Exactly how long have you known Gordon Hillcock?'

For the first time, a flush suffused her cheeks. 'Thirty-five years,' she said, with a girlish giggle. 'We were at primary and secondary school together.'

'And after that?'

'Oh, well, after that I married Robin and Gordon never seemed capable of settling down, and . . .' she tailed off.

'Are you telling me you were in a relationship at one time?'

The flush deepened and she shook her head slowly. 'No-o-o,' she said and paused. 'No,' she said again more decisively. 'We were never in a relationship.'

The phone rang again as he got into the car. 'Den?' came Hemsley's voice, 'just thought I'd tell you –

the most recent fingerprints on the fork belonged to Sean O'Farrell. Looks as if he grabbed hold of it as he was being attacked. We've also got another set, both hands, including palm prints. They match Ted Speedwell's.'

'That'll be because it's his fork, that he uses every day for chucking silage about,' Den said.

'Very likely,' said Hemsley neutrally.

CHAPTER SEVEN

Young Mike was hovering outside the Speedwells' cottage when Den arrived a few minutes past the appointed time.

'How'd you get on?' Den asked him.

'Well, I went with WDC Nugent to collect the daughter – Abigail – from Tavistock this morning and we told her what had happened to her dad. She's in the house now with her mother. Nugent took the car, so I've got to stick with you from now on.'

'How was she? The girl, I mean.'

'Very flat. Didn't react much at all. She's at the age where they just talk in grunts. Didn't even get anywhere when I told her I'd fed her animals.'

'Oh?'

'Seemed to scare her, if anything.'

'She maybe thinks she needs a licence or something,' Den surmised vaguely. 'I'll have to speak to her later on. How did it go with the old granny?'

Mike's face, with its big, mobile features, expressed a mixture of emotions: amusement, frustration, bewilderment. 'Could barely understand a word she said,' he admitted.

'Why? Is she foreign?' Den was confused.

'She might as well be. The thickest Devon accent I have ever heard. Plus she's got no teeth, so she mumbles. I didn't think there were any people left who talked like that. Oh, and cows are all male, to hear her talk. They should put her on telly – she's the last of her kind, I shouldn't wonder.'

'So how much did you get out of her about yesterday?'

'Not a lot. She was in her room, in a big old chair she's got up there, watching the racing all afternoon. She thinks she fell asleep for a bit. Can't be sure what won the three-thirty, but she knows she was awake for the two races before that.'

'Did you ask her about family history? How Gordon gets on with his mother and sister?'

Mike grinned. 'There was quite a lot under

that heading, but it wasn't easy to follow. Gordon was a very difficult baby, born "afore his time" and his mother not yet twenty. His granny had a lot of the rearing of him, and he's very much her favourite. Something about him being sickly on and off for years. She seems disappointed in him these days. Says Mary's been a "gude little maid" but she's given up all hope of ever being a great-grandma.'

Den winced and struggled to breathe past the tightness that was suddenly in his chest. 'So this is her entire family? Gordon's father was her only child?'

'As far as I know, yes. Nobody else was mentioned.'

'What did she think of Sean?'

'Didn't seem too clear who I was talking about,' Mike said. 'She obviously doesn't go outside much – if at all. She's got a bad leg, very swollen up. Started talking about somebody called Wilf, who can do anything with a cow. Magic hands, he do 'ave, an if'n a cow be bad, Wilf can do wonders for 'e. I have a feeling Wilf was on the scene about the time Gordon was born.'

'O . . . kay,' said Den, making it a long, drawn-out expression of ironic summary. 'It doesn't sound as if *she'll* be called to the witness box.'

Mike laughed. 'I can see it now,' he said.

'So what's happening about the Speedwells?'

'There's nobody at home. Mr Hillcock's back, of course, doing something important with a cow's rear end. Ted Speedwell's driving a tractor . . .' He cocked his head to listen for a moment. 'Yes, you can hear it. I told him we'd want to talk to him, and he just nodded.'

'How was his manner? Did he seem worried or scared?'

'I only spoke to him for a minute. He didn't say anything. He did look a bit scared, I suppose. But maybe he thinks he's going to be murdered next.'

'Maybe he does,' Den agreed. 'Well, time we had a word with him. Do we go to him, or is he coming to us?'

Mike looked at his watch. 'I told him we'd like to see him at about eleven-thirty. It's that now. We'll probably have to go and find him. I got the impression that the farm work comes well before anything we might want.'

It wasn't so much the painful rush of memories that Den found so disturbing, as the unpredictability of their onset. For a minute, he experienced total recall of the early days of the investigation into the murders on Lilah's family's farm, when the burden of milking had weighed heavily on the girl and her young brother and Den had found himself stumbling in Lilah's wake, trying to catch a word with her between innumerable vital farm tasks. It was disabling, as he stood there in the bleak January chill, recalling the rawness of the farming life, the completely different rules that pertained in this world.

'Yeah,' he breathed. 'That's about the way of it. We'd better go and look for him, then.'

Ted Speedwell was forking up stray clumps of silage when they found him. Gradually the system for feeding the cows became clear to Den, as he assessed the scene. A long row of aluminium troughs lay beside a double row of metal railings. From the positioning of yards and gates, it would seem that the cows lined up behind the railings and pushed their heads through to eat from the troughs. A reasonably tidy operation, but some silage spilled out in the process and lay beyond the reach of the animals. Ted was carefully collecting it and putting it back in the now-empty trough.

The fork he was using was a narrow, two-pronged pitchfork, which appeared to be causing him some difficulty. A quantity of silage fell off repeatedly, and the police officers could hear him muttering crossly about it.

'That isn't the fork you usually use, is it?' Den asked him as they approached.

'No, 'taint. You fellers 'ave tooken my normal one,' he replied.

'And where is that one usually kept? The normal one, I mean?'

Ted nodded vaguely towards the silage pit. 'Round there someplace,' he mumbled.

'Where anybody could lay their hands on it?'

The man shrugged and nodded. *Obviously*, he seemed to be saying.

Den took a moment to examine Ted Speedwell in the cooler light of day, supplementing the impressions he'd gleaned the previous evening. There was something gnomish about him. He wore a woolly hat pulled down over his ears, and strong leather boots, not the rubber wellingtons that most farm workers adopted. His face was small and pinched; the features clustered together gave him a defensive look. His stained and gappy teeth appeared to be reaching the end of their useful life.

'How long have you worked here?' Den asked him.

'Thirty-five years, must be. Since I left school.'

'You knew Mr Hillcock's father, then?'

'Aye.'

'Where were you yesterday, between one and four o'clock?'

Speedwell turned his attention back to the silage, speaking over his shoulder. 'Ditching,' he muttered, and then seemed to think more detail was required. 'That is, had dinner till two, then up Top Linhay to clear out bottom ditch. Got n'self filled up with dashles and muck o' that sort. Next time 'e rains, 'twill run over, see?'

Den blinked and carefully avoided Young Mike's eye. Granny Hillcock might not be quite the last of her kind, after all.

'What time did you finish?'

'Near four. When 'twere too dark to go on. Days be short just now,' he added, as if this was a piece of information they'd be glad of.

'Did you go home then? Did you come back into the yard?'

'Went for some tea. I starts at half-seven of a morning, cutting out the silage. Eight-hour day takes me to half-three. Never used to count it, in the old man's time, but now we all get to clock-watching.' He shook his head at the folly of modern life. 'Din't come near the yard, no. The boss can shift for n'self then.'

'Even when it's Recording Day?'

Ted gave a blank look. 'Makes no odds to me,' he said.

'So when did you last see Sean?'

'Yesterday mornin',' came the prompt reply. 'Before dinner. He was having the milking off yesterday. Proper vexed 'e were about that. I said to 'e, "You be daft to let 'un do it." But—' He stopped abruptly at the sound of approaching footsteps. Gordon Hillcock appeared from a small side barn, carrying a plastic bucket.

He paused at the sight of the three men – a rather contrived show of surprise, it seemed to Den. He must have heard their voices from where he was, if not the actual words.

There was something about the appearance of the man who'd so recently been held overnight in a police cell, now strolling around his farm as if nothing had happened. For a moment it seemed that the death of Sean O'Farrell was a mere dream, or an event that had happened a long time ago. The strands of blue police tape cordoning off one part of the yard had been broken and trodden into the muck and mud of the yard, he noted; now they just looked irrelevant. In Den's opinion they *were* irrelevant. Any minute traces of forensic evidence still undiscovered after the previous evening's searches were almost certainly lost for ever, beneath the countless bovine feet and the comings and goings of Ted's tractor.

'Excuse us, sir,' said Den formally. 'We are conducting an interview with Mr Speedwell which we would prefer to be in confidence. If we're in your way here, perhaps there's somewhere private we can use?'

Gordon Hillcock spread his free arm in a generous arc. 'Take your pick,' he said, indicating two or three buildings and doorways. 'Office over there, as you'll remember. Straw barn – that's quite cosy. You'll let me know when I can use the barn next to the parlour again, won't you? My lame cows aren't at all happy where they are.'

His tone was clipped, his head held high. Den understood the struggle to recapture the dignity that had been lost in the events of the past eighteen hours or so. *I am not a criminal*, was the subtext. *I will not become your prisoner again.*

And Den's unspoken reply, as he smiled thinly and said, 'All in due course, Mr Hillcock,' was *Oh yes, you will, matey, if I have anything to do with it.*

'Perhaps we'll go into the office,' he said to Mike and Ted. 'Just for one or two more questions, if that's convenient?'

They settled themselves awkwardly into the small space, and Den prompted the little farm worker to continue where he'd left off. 'Sean wasn't happy about the change to the rota? And you were telling him to make a stand. What did Sean say to that?'

'Nothing, really. What's to be said, when it comes down to it? Precious little work any more for the likes of us; we stick it, like it or not.' He looked nervous and spoke in a low mutter. The realisation that Gordon might have heard what he'd been saying outside appeared to worry him. Den cursed himself for embarking on a sensitive conversation in such a public spot.

'You're saying that you and Sean have both been unhappy working here?' Den tried to clarify the point.

'Tidn' all the boss's fault,' Ted said. 'Same all over, nowadays. All runnin' downhill into the shit.'

The image was graphic, and Den took a moment to savour it.

'But Mr Hillcock and Sean didn't always get on together, did they?' Den prompted.

Ted Speedwell looked sideways at the floor, indicating an unwillingness to commit himself on that point. Den squared his shoulders. 'Mr Speedwell, I shouldn't need to remind you that we're here to investigate a vicious murder. Mr O'Farrell died here, just a few yards away, after a violent attack. What do you have to say about that?'

The little man looked up and met Den's look full on. 'I say, more fool he. I say, 'e 'ad it comin' to 'im. I never met a man in my whole life more provoking than Sean O'Farrell. But I'll tell you another thing – 'ee won't find no blood from

Sean on any of they clothes 'ee took last night. I can tell 'ee that for nothing.'

Den exchanged a long, thoughtful look with Young Mike before speaking. 'So – who did he provoke, Mr Speedwell? Who would you say killed him here yesterday?'

'Why,' the man's eyes widened, 'how would I know that?'

Den and Mike walked back towards the car, comparing impressions. '*Dashles?*' Mike queried.

'Thistles, I think.'

'Ah. So what d'you reckon?'

Den glanced over his shoulder. 'Reckon we're nearly there,' he said.

'But Speedwell hasn't got an alibi. How do we know it wasn't him?'

'Good question,' said Den, feeling irrepressibly cheerful. Mike went back for another look at the assumed scene of the killing while Den called in his report to Danny. 'I've seen Ted Speedwell, sir,' he began. 'His wife isn't due back from work till two. Mike's had a chat with the granny. Any idea how we should use the time till two?'

'Hillcock's there, is he?'

'He is, yes. Business as usual, as far as I can see.'

'What about your girlfriend? Is she lending a hand?'

'Ex-girlfriend, sir,' said Den stiffly. 'No sign of her at present. She's got her studies, you see . . .'

'Right, right. Well, keep clear of her if you can. It's only going to complicate matters if you start going at each other's throats.'

'So where to now, sir?' Den repeated, ignoring the coded reference to that morning's encounter with Lilah.

'I suggest another word with the widow – and what's happening with the daughter? Has she been tracked down?'

'Yes, sir. She was driven home this morning. She's with her mum now, having a day off school.'

'Go and see them. Keep it shortish, then treat yourself to a bit of lunch. Go back just after two. Talk to Mrs Speedwell when she gets home. I take it the Hillcock women are both out?'

'Hang on, sir.' Den leant out of the car and called to Mike. 'There's only the granny in the big house, right?'

Mike nodded. 'Right,' he said, and began to walk back across the yard. From his thoughtful expression, Den suspected something was bothering him.

'As you say, sir. They're both out,' Den told Hemsley.

'Then play it by ear after you've seen the widow. Oh – and Cooper?'

'Yes, sir?'

'Forensics tell me they've found blood on Hillcock's clothes. Not a lot, mind. But they're analysing it now. It'll only take a little while to make a preliminary comparison with O'Farrell's. An exact match'll take longer, of course. But if it's a totally different blood group, we'll have to think again.'

It wasn't exactly excitement that Den felt – more a sense of closing in on his quarry; another potential avenue of escape sealed off. He had no doubt that the blood would be of the same group as Sean O'Farrell's. 'Come on,' he said to Mike. 'We've got to go back to the cottages. Might as well walk. Time to have a proper talk with the wife and daughter.'

They walked down the farm track without speaking. Den was becoming increasingly impressed with Young Mike's ability to remain quiet when appropriate; for the moment his own thoughts were more than enough to occupy him. He was struck by the way nobody seemed particularly upset at Sean's death. Nobody behaved as if they thought it was unduly horrific, or even unexpected. Deirdre Watson, Ted Speedwell, Hillcock's wife and sister – they had all seemed almost unmoved by what had happened to the herdsman. They had all behaved with a peculiar kind of resignation.

Only Lilah, probably because she was

new to Dunsworthy, as well as because of her involvement with Gordon, had shown any real emotion. And that had been rage against Den and fear for what might happen to Gordon. Even she showed no feeling towards Sean O'Farrell.

He decided to run his theory past Mike. 'Notice something odd?' he began.

'I was just going to say . . .' came the ready response. 'We're not assuming that only a man could have done it, are we?'

'Well, there's the Watson woman. She has to be in the frame.'

Mike spoke with animation. 'Right! Because I think a woman could have done it. Say she pushed him over first, and then jabbed the fork into him while he was lying flat on his back. That wouldn't take too much strength, would it? Not through the fleshy parts of the body, anyway.'

'Hmm,' said Den slowly, remembering what the pathologist had told him. 'Did you have anybody in mind, apart from Mrs Watson?'

'Young Abigail's a strong girl. You'll see for yourself in a minute.'

'So I will,' agreed Den. 'Actually, that wasn't what I meant by "something odd". Doesn't it strike you that nobody's particularly sorry that the man's dead? I mean – he obviously died in agony, but we've yet to come across anybody who's shown much pity for him.'

Mike sucked his teeth for a few seconds. 'Maybe we just haven't spoken to the right people yet,' he suggested.

They waited on the doorstep of the O'Farrell cottage for a full minute before the door was opened to them. A round-faced teenage girl stood before them, holding the edge of the door defensively, head turned away as she shouted back along the passage to the living room. 'Okay, Mother – I've opened it now.' There was resentment and impatience in her tone. She stepped out of the way of the men without looking at them. Den noticed smudges on her cheeks and traces of eyeliner around her eyes, apparently left over from the day before. She looked tired and hungover.

'Me again, Abigail,' said Mike amiably. 'This is Detective Sergeant Cooper. He'll probably let you call him Den.'

'Nng,' said the girl without a flicker of a smile.

Not waiting for direction or invitation, Den led the way to the living room where Heather O'Farrell, invalid, wore a thick, all-enveloping dressing-gown, a rug over her knees for good measure. She looked like the inmate of a nursing home. She sat almost exactly as she had the previous evening, huddled in the big armchair. Abigail flopped down on the couch and started picking at her fingernails, oblivious of where the policemen might want to sit. Mike opted to share the couch with her and Den collected an upright dining chair from a far corner of the room and carried it closer, to complete the little circle round the hearth. There was a frowsty smell, far from unpleasant, suggesting self-indulgent winter days of childhood, snuggled in bed for a long lie-in while Mum cooked lunch downstairs. Except there were no cooking aromas in this house.

Abigail sniffed noisily from time to time, while Den began his questions. 'I hope we're not intruding,' he smiled, routinely. 'We'll try not to take long.'

The woman nodded patiently at him. 'That's all right,' she said. 'I'll do what I can to help.' She spoke breathily, as if making a noble effort in the face of great constraints. Den felt like a brute for forcing her to cooperate.

'Thank you,' he nodded. 'We have the basics, of course, from last night. What we're hoping for now is a bit of background – trying to get the wider picture, if you like. For example, if Sean was having the afternoon off yesterday, what would you have expected him to be doing with his time?'

She frowned and fixed her large moist eyes on his face. 'Didn't I tell you about that yesterday?' she said weakly. 'If I'd thought about it, I'd have assumed he was cutting logs – we needed more. Gordon lets him have as much dead wood as he likes from the copse. Though I think he said he was going back to the yard. I don't think I bothered much about where he was. I was asleep. I *told* you.' The petulance and self-pity were almost tangible. Den heard Abigail emit a small sigh.

'Did he say he was cutting up logs?'

She frowned irritably. 'I don't know. He might have done. I can't remember anything exactly, after such a dreadful shock.' She put a hand to her throat, in an attitude so stereotypical Den almost laughed. This woman was a throwback to some Victorian age where no one was surprised if a lady went into a decline and spent her short life languishing on a chaise longue. There was definitely something farcical in the situation. Then he reproached himself for his lack of sympathy. For all he knew, the woman was genuinely ill, perhaps with some rare condition the doctors couldn't identify. It certainly wasn't for him to make snap judgements about other people's health.

He turned to Abigail. 'Were you here at all yesterday?'

'In the morning, yeah. I got the bus to school and went straight to my friend's house in Tavistock afterwards. I stayed the night there.' She suddenly glared fiercely at her mother. 'Nobody even bothered to tell me what was going on here! My dad lying in the muck, and me fetched from school by the police, and missing some really important lessons. Why didn't anybody tell me yesterday?'

'That was mostly our fault,' said Den ruefully. 'We decided it was better to leave you in peace until this morning. Sorry if we did the wrong thing. You'd have missed the lessons anyway,' he added, with a firm look. 'There's no way you'd have gone to school today.'

Abigail sniffed again. 'Now *she* says I can't see him.' She exploded into fury, punching the cushion beside her. 'I *can* see him, can't I? When my mate's gran died, they let her go and visit and leave a note in the coffin.'

'Nobody can see him until all the examinations have been done,' Den explained calmly. 'But after that, there's no reason—' he glanced at Heather and modified what he'd been going to say, '—your dad will go to the undertaker's and they'll be able to talk to you about what's best.'

'When'll that be? I want to see him *now*. Last I saw him, he was perfectly all right, and now you blokes come along and say he's *dead* . . .' She lapsed back into silence, as if her allocation of words had come to an end. Her mother made an exasperated clicking sound with her tongue.

'You'll have to do as they tell you,' she said with something close to complacency. Den badly wanted not to be seen to be on her side.

'When was that, then?' he asked Abigail. 'When you last saw him?'

'Monday night.'

'What time?'

'Around ten. Bedtime in this house.' She grimaced mockingly. The frown deepened and Den could see the battle against tears. 'I never said goodbye.'

Here, then, at last was someone who was grieved at O'Farrell's passing. He looked in fading hope at the mother. 'I'm terribly sorry,' he said feebly.

Abigail got up with a single movement and made for the door, one hand over her face. All three adults let her go without a word. Den observed how solid she was: her shoulders broad and well-muscled under her sweatshirt, large hips and strong-looking legs. Mike was right – she was a robust young thing; but Den had the greatest difficulty in imagining her driving a fork into her father's body.

'What were Sean's hobbies?' he asked the

widow, after a few moments. 'What did he do in his spare time?' He remembered Deirdre Watson's suggestion of a separate life, lived by Sean O'Farrell well away from his family.

'What do you mean?' Heather seemed to have been wandering in a world of her own since before her daughter's departure from the room.

'Fishing? Darts? Horse riding? Bird watching?' Den suggested. 'Anything like that?'

'He had mates,' she said. 'They go shooting together sometimes. Rabbits, pigeons, mainly. Didn't get much spare time, working here.'

'What can you tell us about the incident where the dog attacked him?' Den dropped the question without warning.

Heather stared at him. 'Dog?' she echoed foolishly.

Den spread his hands and smiled apologetically. 'It sounded nasty,' he prompted. 'Mr Hillcock's animal – an Alsation, I understand.'

'Oh, that,' she dismissed. 'That was his own fault. It mended clean enough.' She paused. 'Abby was upset about it, though. Heard the poor thing howling when it died, and got herself in a real state over it. Soft about animals, is Abby.' She cocked her head towards the area behind the house, where the little menagerie was.

Den stuck to his point. 'Who do you think poisoned the dog?'

Heather sighed. 'Good thing Abby isn't here – she wouldn't even let us talk about it. If anyone even *mentions* the name Fergus, she gets in a strop. She goes on all the time about badger baiters and that stuff – it's her age. They're all up in arms about animals, these days.'

'Do you think Sean might have poisoned the dog?'

She worked her shoulders minimally. 'He might have done,' she admitted.

Den said nothing. Mike caught his eye, conveying a question; Den remembered that he hadn't been told about Fergus.

'Let's just make sure we've covered everything,' he resumed. 'Sean was here for the lunch hour, but not for the rest of the day. Even though it was an unscheduled afternoon off, he still stuck to his usual hour's break and was then outside somewhere. Have I got that right?'

Heather nodded. 'Sounds funny, put like that,' she realised. 'But that was his habit. He didn't like to hang about in the house, at least not when the weather's dry. He'd make sure I was all right first, of course.' Her lip began to quiver ominously and Den understood that they'd been lucky to have had twenty minutes free from tears. He felt a pang of alarmed sympathy for Abigail. Was she going to be sucked into replacing her father as reliable provider of soup, tea and firewood?

'So you never really knew what he was doing? You didn't go out with him on his days off?' What he wanted to know was: *What do you do all day, cooped up here with your mysterious illness?*

'Not very often,' Mrs O'Farrell confirmed. 'He talked a bit about the farm, of course. He was very committed to the cows. He takes them to shows in the summer, you know. *Took*, I mean,' she added pathetically.

Den thought he understood how it had been. She was far too self-absorbed to waste much attention on the activities of her husband or daughter. So long as she was warm and fed, she wasn't going to let herself fret. Like a big lazy cat, he thought, or a pampered sheep. But what had been in it for the devoted Sean? Some idea of martyrdom, he supposed, remembering Deirdre Watson's comments.

On the face of it, Sean O'Farrell sounded almost inhumanly patient and conscientious – but only towards his wife and daughter. To everyone else he was a sullen or provoking individual. Den had seen it before, of course. Men who showed one side of themselves to their family and something completely different to the outside world. It was almost a commonplace. Except, he suddenly realised, that it was generally the other way around. Most men presented themselves as polite and charming to their neighbours and workmates, whilst wreaking havoc at home. Street angel, house devil. Sean O'Farrell turned that on its head.

CHAPTER EIGHT

Lilah arrived at Dunsworthy just as Den and Mike were leaving the O'Farrell women to their grief and heading for lunch at a local hostelry. She had been to a morning lecture at college, the first of the new term, and thus not to be lightly missed, but she had sat through it unheeding, turning over and over in her mind all the reasons why Gordon could not possibly have murdered Sean, and what she might be able to do about it.

The drive back had gone as unnoticed as the lecture, the car somehow managing to get her from college to farm without any conscious effort on Lilah's part. She wanted to join Gordon in the house, when he went in to get himself and Granny some lunch. If she got the timing right, there'd be half an hour for sex before he went out again to get on with the jobs. Sex with Gordon was Lilah's highest priority, and had been for the past three months. She kept wondering when the novelty would wear off, when they could settle into something less frenzied and more ordinary. She kept hoping it wouldn't be for a long time yet.

The sight of Den turning out into the road, as she reached the entrance, jolted her into the here and now. She noticed, as she always had, how his head reached right to the car roof, so he had to tilt it forward. She remembered, while irritably trying to quell the memory, how this had always amused her. His height had been a source of wonder to her, and an odd kind of pride. She had never succeeded in forgetting how concerned and kind he'd been when her father had died, how she'd sheltered in his protective tallness, and how he'd been injured in the process of catching the killer. The only way she could deal with it now was to stoke up her anger with him. Originally, anger at his naked suffering for the past three months; but now, a gratifying and much more righteous rage at what he was doing to Gordon.

She reminded herself of the awful things Den had said about Gordon when she'd first told him he'd been displaced. *That old womaniser!* he'd shouted. *You'd better watch yourself, then. He'll give you some foul disease if you're not careful.* That had been the one she'd been unable to ignore. Nobody of her age, even in the remoter reaches of Devonshire, could entirely dismiss the threat of HIV. Mustering her courage, she'd murmured her worries to Gordon, who had smiled in the sweetest way and assured her there was no need to worry. He'd padded over to his big oak bureau, and produced a piece of paper that gave a negative blood test result, dated six months earlier.

'Just as if I'd known you'd ask,' he'd laughed at her. 'I've been having routine tests like this for quite a while now. And—' he'd look at her with complete openness, 'I haven't slept with anyone else since this was done.'

She refused to meet Den's eye, as their cars passed within inches of each other. Looking straight ahead, she bounced her Astra through the puddle at the farm entrance and sped up the farm track. *Bugger Den Cooper*, she repeated to herself, five or six times.

Gordon was washing his boots under the tap outside the back door when she found him. 'Perfect timing,' she boasted. 'What's for lunch?'

He looked her full in the face, without smiling. His eyes were more shadowed than usual, and there were lines she hadn't seen before around his mouth. 'Wrong,' he said lightly, but with the controlled anger just audible. 'Perfect timing would have been if you'd got here half an hour ago, and had something waiting on the table for me.'

'Ha!' she responded, choosing not to notice that he was serious. 'You should be so lucky. After I did the milking for you, too!' She moved towards him, tucking her hands under the fleecy jacket he wore. 'Anyone would think you weren't pleased to see me.'

He kissed her lingeringly on the forehead, working his lips against her skin. A slight moan told her she'd achieved her goal; the power of her effect on him was intoxicating. Her own body was responding, too, the familiar throb building up.

'Never mind lunch,' she whispered, nestling into his chest, feeling his heat under the rough layers of clothes. 'First things first.'

There was a greed to their lovemaking that had been completely new to her. A confusing sense that they could have as much as they wanted, and yet never really have enough. All her previous experience now seemed prim and miserly: snatched nights with Den in their first year together, with his job and her farm responsibilities distracting them. It had very quickly become routine, secondary to the plans they kept making and the discussions of daytime matters. With

Gordon, there was much less conversation and much more direct bodily contact. There were never any plans, no references to the future.

She hadn't known it was possible to be so aroused. She felt perpetually on the edge of orgasm whenever Gordon was in sight. He had taught her an infinity of practices, which she felt frightened and foolish not to have discovered before. Frightened, especially, at the knowledge that, if she'd stayed with Den, she might never have discovered this secret world. Gordon used parts of their bodies she had never previously imagined could be given a sexual role. He rubbed her armpits hard with his nose, he massaged her inner thighs with his heel. Introducing her to sensations she might have gone to her grave never having known.

From the start, he had demanded that she avoid all contraception. 'I won't make you pregnant,' he'd promised. 'I'll make sure of that. You have to trust me. That's why I have those tests – so you needn't worry about infections.'

This had been a shock initially, and for a few minutes she had to fight down the panic that came with it. 'But why can't we use condoms?' she'd asked him. 'What difference does it make?'

He'd given a self-conscious little smile, and shrugged. 'It's a thing with me,' he said. 'I like sex to be unimpeded.'

'But the Pill . . .'

'Is very bad for you,' he'd reproved her. 'And it damps down your responses. You'll have to believe me – it's much better my way.'

And he'd been right. At twenty-five, Lilah's body was screaming to reproduce in any case, and the danger of knowing he could lapse from his promise and ejaculate inside her sent her insane with irrational excitement she didn't even try to control. She found herself employing all kinds of tricks to make him do just that, and many times believed he had. It didn't seem possible that he could last so long, driving her to frenzy, and still withdraw in time to come all over her belly, thrilling her with his final abandonment of control. It made her feel powerful, that he could be so helpless, if only for these few final seconds.

She was impressed, this lunchtime, that he could perform at all, after a night in police custody and with the threat of arrest hanging over him. But the sex was not as abandoned as on some previous occasions, and there was a moment when she was sure he wasn't going to pull away – a long, hovering, crescendo of a moment, when his eyes met hers and she saw him almost decide to stay where he was. She flinched involuntarily, and he withdrew, flopping onto her with a groan.

She was increasingly aware that Gordon was predominantly a physical being. He went through his daily routines, he read farming magazines and completed endless government forms, he balanced his accounts and instructed his employees – and all the time he was only half alive, until he took his clothes off and became his true self. Lilah felt she'd been handed a uniquely precious gift, that she had discovered the elixir of life, the secret of true bliss. The idea that all this might be snatched away from her was unendurable. She would fight to the death to prevent it from happening.

Because Lilah had already – silently but definitely – made a number of assumptions about the future. She would marry Gordon and move into the house, living with him and his mother and sister – and grandmother. She would have babies with him, but that wouldn't impede their sex life. Nothing could do that. She'd help on the farm, and use her horticultural skills to augment their income, diversifying into fruit and vegetables, where a substantial sum could still be made. Her mother could sell Redstone, and move to a house in town, where she'd settle down and be quite happy. Farm prices were rocky, but at worst there'd be some hundreds of thousands of pounds in equity after such a sale. Roddy would make his own way in life – Miranda could keep it all and indulge whatever whims she liked. To Lilah it had all seemed so obvious, so easy. Until yesterday.

The two of them stumbled shakily down the stairs again at ten to two, Gordon muttering about keeping Granny waiting for her lunch, surprised she hadn't started ringing the bell or banging her stick by now. Lilah spread Flora on slices of granary bread while Gordon shaved thin slivers of cheese onto a plate, and then cut two tomatoes carefully into slices almost as thin as the cheese. 'Just how she likes it,' he boasted. 'Plenty of black pepper, and it'll be perfect.' Lilah watched his big square hands deftly arrange the filling in the sandwich and smiled. Gordon's affection for his granny was one of the things she found most sweet about him.

'What are we having?' she asked. 'More of the same?'

He shrugged. 'Whatever you like. There's some leftovers at the back of the fridge. One of Mary's crumbles, and a wodge of cottage pie. I never had any supper last night, so they kept it for me to have today.'

'We'd have to heat it up, and there isn't time. I'll just do a couple more sandwiches, shall I?'

But Gordon had gone, carrying a small tray with Granny's sandwiches and a glass of orange juice on it. He appeared five minutes later, and picked up the conversation as if there'd been no interruption. 'Fergus used to love cottage pie,' he said, scratching an eyebrow absently. 'I always tried to save him a bit.'

'Fergus? Oh – the dog.' She spoke carelessly, still savouring the recent lovemaking, still tingling, hot in some places and cold, almost raw, in others.

'He was a dog in a million.' The intensity of his tone made her freeze. She worried that she'd been flippant, dismissive of something important to him.

'Oh, I *know*,' she said with deliberate sincerity. 'We had a dog just before Daddy died – Lydwina, of all dopey names. She got kicked to death by a heifer. It was terrible. I've never seen Roddy so upset.'

'I remember your dad. A lot of people thought he was a bit round the twist. Calling a dog Lydwina can't have helped his reputation.'

'He was just unusual,' she said loyally. 'Didn't want to be seen as a thick Devon farmer. Actually it worked very well, as a name. You can sort of sing it when you're calling.'

'Sean killed Fergus, you know,' Gordon said quietly. 'Poisoned him.'

Lilah's blood stood still. She could feel veins of ice forming deep inside her. 'What?'

'At least, I thought he did,' the farmer amended. 'He denied it. Said he'd never do such a thing. But Fergus attacked him, ripped his ear half off – I wouldn't blame him really.' He spoke in a dull voice, as if it really didn't matter.

'Wouldn't you?' she queried. 'It might be a good idea to try and keep that story quiet, though. I mean, the police . . .'

'They'll see the scar. They'll ask what happened. Heather'll tell them, if no one else does.'

'Gordon—' She finished cutting up the sandwiches, and put the knife down. But she didn't go to him, remaining out of arm's reach.

'What?' He leant over the breakfast bar and helped himself to a sandwich. 'I hope you're not going to ask me whether I killed Sean?'

'No. Of course not. I know you didn't. Obviously you didn't.'

'But it isn't obvious, is it?' he demanded, staring into her face, the aftermath of their lovemaking still in his eyes, on his lips. 'What's obvious is that I had ample opportunity, a whole farm full of means, and maybe a motive as well. Revenge for Fergus. Everybody knows how much I loved him, how proud I was of what he'd turned out like. He went everywhere with me. He could read my mind.'

Lilah became aware of an unexpected emotion rising from somewhere in her chest. *Jealousy!* She realised. *I'm jealous of a dead dog!* Out of nowhere – or so she supposed – came the suspicion that she had been a mere replacement for Fergus. A playmate, a companion who would feed Gordon's ego, be something to be proud of.

He laughed, still watching her face. 'I can read you like a book,' he chuckled. 'Every thought is plain on your face. Don't worry, little girl – I never got round to fucking my dog.'

It was a sluice of cold water and she almost drowned in it. She floundered like a swimmer out of her depth, at the glimpse of the person she had taken up with. He was so . . . unknowable. She felt so young and naïve in comparison to him. She was insubstantial and ignorant, inexperienced and ingenuous. He had seen and done dark things, he could make jokes about bestiality and murder. But much worse than all this, she suspected that he regarded her as nothing more than a sexual plaything.

Well, she'd show him. Forcing a smile, she picked up one of the sandwiches, as casually as she could. 'I never thought you did,' she said, with her mouth full. 'I shouldn't think you were ever that desperate. And – well – it's not as if it was a *female* dog, is it?'

Gordon put up one hand in an odd kind of salute, and said nothing. The gesture said, *Well done, kiddo. Good to see you've got some gumption.*

Too right I have, she silently responded. She knew now what she had to do. Her bridges were well and truly burnt – there was no going back.

And Gordon had thrown her a challenge she couldn't ignore: *Take me as I am, face up to the person I might turn out to be, and you won't be sorry.* It was like that terrible moment, poised at the pinnacle of the highest of all rollercoasters, knowing pure terror as it tips you over into the abyss. Knowing that when it's all over, you'll be proud and thrilled and relieved.

'We're going to prove you didn't kill Sean,' she said with sudden force. 'We're going to make sure there's never going to be a case against you. It won't even come to trial.'

'Thank Christ for that,' he smiled. 'I was hoping that's what you'd say.'

Deirdre had another farm to record that afternoon. One of her earliest ones, starting at two-thirty in the afternoon and three-thirty in the morning. Perversely, it was one of her favourites, even in the winter. The cows were friendly and relaxed, and the calf-pen adjacent to the office, so she could watch their antics as she filled in the events of the previous month. And, unlike Dunsworthy, Streamside Farm was lavish with straw, ensuing that the animals were clean and their legs undamaged.

She arrived promptly at one-thirty, allowing a full hour for the laborious paperwork necessitated by burgeoning quantities of government regulations.

The Streamside herd boasted one hundred and eighty cows, the majority of them scheduled to calve in the autumn. This meant that there were sixty-five 'services', by five different bulls, to be documented. Fast as she was, it comprised an onerous and irritating job. Miraculously, the laptop seemed to have recovered from its vapours of the previous day, and submissively absorbed all the data without a single recalcitrant *beep*.

The milking parlour was far from being in the first flush of youth, with six stalls on either side, and scarcely space in the well between for two people to move in without knocking into each other. Deirdre was well accustomed to the intimacy this involved, and she and Tom had long ago ceased to laugh and apologise every time they collided. She was skilful in anticipating his next move, and managed, most of the time, to stay out of his way. But the meters from which she obtained her samples were at floor level, so she had to bend or squat to reach them. More than once, Tom found himself bumping backsides with her, as he worked on the opposite row of cows.

They talked idly about the weather, caught up with how Christmas and the excesses of the new year had treated them, and only then cautiously sidled up to the subject of the events at Dunsworthy.

'You heard, then,' Deirdre said, knowing full

well the answer. The bulk tanker driver, assorted reps, even the postman, would all have spread the news in the time-honoured fashion. *What price the Internet?* Deirdre thought to herself. *It's never going to improve on this!*

'Heard you were there at the time,' he grinned back at her. Tom was fifty-five, energetic, unworried even in the face of his industry's darkest hour. Murder on a nearby farm wasn't going to throw him into any sort of a spin.

'That's right,' she said, giving nothing away.

'Nobody's saying just how it happened,' he prompted her. 'Percy Fielding said he heard Sean'd been trampled by one of the cows. Have they still got that great Simmental bull?'

She shook her head. 'I think he's got that a bit wrong,' she said. There were three more hours of milking still to go – plenty of time to feed him the story, little by little. Plenty of time to select exactly which details she was going to share with him. The image of Gordon's contorted face, the things that had gone unsaid between him and her – those were definitely to be edited out.

Much later, Tom paused after attaching a row of clusters, and summarised. 'So poor old Sean was definitely murdered? Some people were saying it was most likely suicide. Plenty of farmers topping themselves these days. And Sean was a miserable sod a lot of the time. It could have been that. But didn't they take Gordon in for questioning?'

She nodded.

'So they must think he did it? Right?'

Deirdre wouldn't commit herself on that point. 'Who knows what they think?' she said, before embarking on another row of sample retrieval.

As often happened, conversation gained momentum at the very end of the milking. Having checked that all her pots were filled, and that everything tallied, Deirdre watched Tom release the final row of cows. 'How well did you know Sean?' she asked him, as they enjoyed a moment of satisfaction at another milking accomplished.

He met her gaze. 'Can't say he was my closest friend – nor anything like it. Saw him in the pub now and then at dinnertime.'

'What, the Limediggers?'

'No, no. The Bells, in West Tavy. You must know that's where they get together.'

'Seems a bit of a way to go for lunch.' It was often good policy to pretend to a greater ignorance than was genuine. If the police started to investigate the herdsmen's 'protest group', she didn't want it supposed by local farmworkers that they'd learnt about it from her.

'It's where we all go on a Thursday, when we can get away,' Tom elaborated. ''Specially in winter.' Something in his manner alerted her; he seemed to be half-regretting being drawn into this conversation.

'You make it sound like a meeting of Freemasons,' she said lightly. 'What do you all talk about?'

'This'n'that. It's good to get off the farm for an hour or two. I only go once in a blue moon, myself. It's mostly herdsmen – not the farmers. Makes me feel a bit out of place, to be honest.'

'And this was something Sean went to regularly, was it?'

'One of the keenest, so they say.' Deirdre recognised the impulse to talk that most of the men she worked with suffered from. 'Sean was a bit of a weirdo,' he went on, with a grimace that showed he knew he shouldn't say such a thing about a dead man. 'Always thinking up some new subject that he thought we should chew over. Some of the chaps thought he was a pain in the backside, to be honest. And there was something . . .' He paused, eyeing her uneasily. 'I oughtn't to speak ill of him, now. He didn't deserve what happened to him – whatever it was.'

'That's true. But I didn't find him an easy man to like either,' she encouraged. 'He looked as if he had a lot of secrets. And that wife of his – I never thought he could be quite such a saint as he made himself out to be, where she was concerned.'

Tom spluttered at that. 'Saint! No way. You're right about the secrets, too. We none of us know the half of it, but there've been rumours.'

'Oh?'

His glance slid away, unease plainly increasing. 'Well, the usual sort of stuff. Badgers, mainly.'

'What? Badger baiting?' She widened her eyes at him. 'Sean? Not just lamping – you mean real baiting, with dogs and everything?'

'Sshh,' he warned her, although there was nobody around to hear. 'It's only a rumour. I've never heard anything definite. But Fred Page has got that Staffordshire bull terrier, which always seems to have some sort of injury – and Sean was very matey with Fred. We all like to pretend it doesn't happen, but we know it does. Cock fighting, as well. Not that I mind that particularly – bloody things'll fight to the death whether people set them up to it or not. But the badger thing's different altogether. Sick.' His face puckered at the thought.

'Yes,' Deirdre agreed distractedly. 'Well, he's dead now, anyway.'

'Yeah,' Tom agreed. 'And it'll be hard to find anybody that's sorry.'

'Right – time we got some lunch,' Den announced, as he and Young Mike emerged from the O'Farrell cottage. 'Know any good places round here?'

Mike considered. 'There's the Limediggers, couple of miles away. My dad used to go there once in a while. Probably changed hands and been grocklised by now, but I reckon it's the nearest.'

'Right then.' Den was in no mood to argue.

The Limediggers Free House stood flush with the road, space for cars carved out of an adjacent field and a sad-looking garden on a sloping bank behind it, boasting three or four picnic-style tables. Not exactly *grocklised*, but enough to tempt a scatter of hungry passing tourists in the season. Den expected to find it empty at one-thirty on a January Wednesday.

He was wrong. Inside, there was one large bar, with high-backed antique seats, many of them turned to face a massive log fire. At the back of the room tables were set up for meals; all of them were in use. There was a babble of voices, a clatter of cutlery and the welcoming scent of woodsmoke. It was also very warm. *Thank God for plain clothes*, thought Den, peeling off his thick jacket almost at once.

But the plain clothes failed to serve their pretended purpose. It was quickly evident that most of the people present knew just who he and Mike were. Den's height, and the fact that he'd grown up in Okehampton and gone to the local school, made him a familiar figure.

The landlady was slim and nervy. She rushed up and down the bar trying to anticipate orders almost before they were out of people's mouths. If they hesitated between ham and cheddar cheese sandwiches, she jittered impatiently on the spot. She looked to be about forty-five, and was clearly determined to appear at least ten years younger. When Den approached her, she frowned up at him. 'If you want food, you'll have to order it now. The kitchen closes at two.'

'We'll have two stilton ploughmans,' he said briskly. 'And two pints of Bass. Okay?'

'Fine,' she shot back at him, glancing automatically along the bar to check for any incipient queues. Nobody showed the slightest sign of needing her services.

'Does Gordon Hillcock drink here?' he asked the woman, as she set the pints down in front of him. Mike had taken up a position on one of the high-backed seats, and was gazing dreamily into the blazing logs.

'From Dunsworthy?' she made a show of asking, although Den knew she'd been anticipating the question. He nodded. 'Now and then,' she admitted. 'He and his family generally come here for their supper on a Thursday.'

'Every week?'

She nodded carelessly.

'What about Sean O'Farrell? Did he drink here?'

The woman laughed. 'That'll be the day.' She glanced at a group of young drinkers ranged along a wooden bench. 'Six Bells lot, he was. Wouldn't go down too well if he'd 'a shown his face here.'

Den examined the group: three boys and two girls, leaning in together, talking intently. 'Who are they?' he asked. 'Students?'

'One or two might be. Couple of them work at the Nature Conservancy. They're an animal rights group.'

Den looked more closely, but failed to recognise any of the youngsters, in spite of the clue. He'd been involved with animal rights people before – hunt protesters specifically – and this group was evidently something different.

'So why wouldn't they get along with O'Farrell?' he asked the impatient landlady.

'Why ask me?' she demanded, casting worried looks around the bar. 'It's got nothing to do with me.'

'Just answer the question,' he told her fiercely. 'You know full well who I am. This is a murder inquiry, in case you didn't realise. Do you want me to formally take you in for questioning? I think you'd find that a lot more embarrassing.'

She tossed her head, refusing to be intimidated. 'Well, it's no secret,' she said defiantly. 'Sean O'Farrell had it in for badgers. He didn't like this limited cull business – said they should all be shot, for giving his cows TB. Shouted his mouth off about it everywhere he went.'

Den nodded his thanks, and left it at that. He knew when he'd pushed someone to the limit.

Mike was waiting for him close to the roaring log fire, and Den took the beer over. 'I'm just going to have a chat with that little lot,' he said, tilting his head towards the five young people. 'Won't be long.'

There was no room for him to sit down, so he leant over one end of the bench, an arm stretched along its width to support him. 'Hiya,' he said affably. 'I'm Detective Sergeant Den Cooper, in case you're wondering. Mind if I have a quick word?'

Nearest him was a girl in her late teens, with a thick knitted scarf hanging loose around her neck. Something about her seemed familiar. She looked up at him enquiringly, her broad face showing no trace of suspicion or wariness. Next to her sat a stocky youth, bundled into a navy fleece jacket; he showed more signs of anxiety. 'It'd help if I could just have your names,' Den added in a quiet voice.

'What for?' demanded the youth. The whole row was now staring at him in silence.

Den squatted down, and kept his face blank. 'You've probably heard that there was a fatality at Dunsworthy yesterday?'

Various expressions of ignorance came from all five. The girl nearest him seemed seriously alarmed. '*Dunsworthy?*' she repeated. 'My mum goes there. I think she was there yesterday – yes, I'm sure she was.'

'Who's your mum?'

'Watson. Deirdre Watson.' *Aha*, thought Den. Hence the familiar face. She had her mother's hair and jawline, and direct gaze.

'Sam?' the boy at the other end of the row called her. 'What's he talking about?'

'You honestly don't know?' Den found it hard to believe them. 'Everybody else here seems to have heard all about it.' He swept the bar with his gaze, noticing that nobody would meet his eye.

'We're too busy for gossip,' said the girl righteously. 'We're having a meeting.'

'This isn't gossip. This is a friendly chat, made in the course of our enquiries. The fact is, Sean O'Farrell, the Dunsworthy herdsman, died yesterday. If you watch the local telly, or read the *Morning News* tomorrow, you'll hear all about it, I shouldn't wonder. How many of you knew him?'

'O'Farrell?' said the girl in the middle of the row. 'We don't like him.'

The childish simplicity of the statement seemed to annoy her friends. 'Susie!' two of them reproached her.

'Well, we don't. Everybody knows he's one of the enemy.'

'It's okay,' Den cut through the growing mutters flying between them. 'I know about the badgers. Look—' he stood up again, and produced his notebook. 'Just a quick list of names and addresses, and if it seems important, we'll maybe get back to you with a few more questions. And I'll leave you my number, so you can phone me if you think there's anything I ought to know. Right?'

One by one they recited their details, their tones varying from an eagerness to please (Susie Marchand) to a noticeable sullenness (Jeremy Page – the stocky lad next to Sam Watson). The remaining two identified themselves as Paul Tyler and Gary Champion, who seemed the oldest by some years. Den ventured one step further. 'Have any of you any connections with Dunsworthy?'

Those on both sides of Gary Champion nudged him encouragingly. 'My kid brother's girlfriend lives there,' he admitted. 'Abigail O'Farrell. But I hadn't heard what'd happened to her dad,' he added earnestly. Den noted him as a slow learner, more comfortable around people younger than himself.

Den made another note, and closed his book. 'Sorry to disturb you,' he told them. 'You've been very helpful – thanks.'

As he walked away, he heard Susie Marchand say excitedly, 'Well, if Sean O'Farrell's *dead*—' before the others hushed her.

'It's nice in here, eh?' Mike commented peaceably, when Den went back to him. The ploughmans he'd ordered had arrived, and he tucked into his lunch with enthusiasm.

Sitting across the low table from them were two men in their seventies, a Jack Russell and a springer spaniel curled contentedly at their feet. It made a pleasing picture – the men could almost be in their own home, enjoying retirement and the sense of finally having all the time in the world. They stared at Den and Mike unashamedly while they ate their lunch. Finally one of them leant forward. 'You'll be the Cooper boy,' he said to Den. 'The one as got jilted by young Beardon maid. Best get it sorted now, though, and not when there's two or three kiddies in the picture.'

Whoever first spread the idea that only women were interested in gossip must have been a complete moron, Den decided, forcing himself not to recoil at the unexpected recognition.

'That your partner?' asked the other man, nodding towards Mike. 'Doesn't 'n get to ask any questions of his own?'

Den grinned, and shook his head. 'His job's to save me a place by the fire,' he said. 'And he assists me in putting together all the bits and pieces I pick up from helpful gentlemen like you.'

'Bad business at Dunsworthy,' the first one said, with an air of having considered and then dismissed the idea of teasing Den for a bit longer. He had thick grey hair and a low brow; his eyes peered out from under an overhang of untidy thatch. His friend was bigger and wore a greasy-looking cap. Both had straight backs, and the stiff movements suggestive of bad hips. Both faces carried weathered wrinkles around the eyes, and deeply-carved grooves between nose and mouth. The one with the cap had a canyon between his eyes deep enough to lose yourself in. How many decades of frowning must it have taken to form such a feature? Den wondered. And yet he looked an amiable fellow in every other respect.

'You know the Hillcocks?'

'Oh, aye,' they both smiled. 'Everybody knows the Hillcocks. Last June – no, tell a lie, June before that – they gave a party for old Hilda's century, in the village hall. Still going strong, they say – though no one ever sees her any more. Dare say your Beardon lass gets a glimpse now and then.' The old man twinkled at Den, but not unkindly.

'What about Sean O'Farrell?'

'Herdsman that got n'self killed.' The two men nodded, all trace of amusement suddenly wiped away. 'Not a thing to joke about. Don't get many murders in these parts – leastways . . .' Den could see them remembering the events surrounding Lilah's family, three years earlier, and the unsavoury killing of a young Quaker since then.

'You're right,' he assured them. 'Only two or three a year at most.'

'Reckon you must get a bit out of practice,' the man with the cap observed, deadpan. Den found that, despite the personal remarks, he was rather enjoying himself. He sipped his beer appreciatively, and glanced at Mike; the young detective constable raised his tankard amicably.

Den returned to his informants. 'So you knew Sean, did you?'

Both men regarded him steadily. 'Can't say we saw a lot of him,' said the low-browed one.

'Wouldn't have come here, anyhow,' said the other. 'Drank at the Bells, over to West Tavy. That's the farm workers' meeting place. Quite a club they've got going, so they say.'

Den swigged more Bass, and nodded. 'So I've been hearing,' he agreed. 'I bet you two're thankful to be out of farming, things being the way they are. Though Hillcock seems to be doing well enough.'

'He's lucky there's no loan on Dunsworthy. 'Tis that makes the difference. And he's not only reliant on milk, like some. Though it's bad all round this time – never seen it like this before. Hillcocks'll come through, all the same. Leastways, 'e *would* have done, without this business.'

'Oh?'

'Hillcock lands himself in gaol, that'll knock 'em right back. Can't see poor old Speedwell running the place.' Both men laughed. 'Dare say your girlfriend's going to find herself taking charge – if she sticks around.' Den watched as the same penny dropped as had dropped with Claudia Hillcock, and Lilah herself. 'Come to think of it, you'd be well pleased then, shouldn't wonder. Chances are she might go back to you, if her new bloke turns out to be a murderer.'

Den struggled to maintain his composure, and looked down at the empty plates on the table. 'Can't stay here all day,' he announced heartily. 'Ready, Mike?'

Mike took the hint, and wiped a hand across his mouth. Together they got to their feet. 'Thanks for the chat,' Den said to the old men, who showed every sign of being settled for the afternoon.

They nodded to him in unison, and the one with the cap raised a gnarled hand in a friendly salute. He had a twinkle in his eye that Den found disconcerting. Perhaps by that age everything was amusing, laid on for your personal entertainment.

CHAPTER NINE

'What did those kids have to tell you?' Mike asked, as they got back into the car. Den didn't reply; he was too preoccupied with wondering whether everyone in West Devon knew about him and Lilah, and whether or not they thought he ought to be working on the Dunsworthy case. There'd been no hint of disapproval from the two old men – wry amusement and idle curiosity seemed to be their only reactions. But was it possible that locals trusted the police to be entirely objective, in the circumstances? The implication was that Hillcock was so self-evidently guilty that it scarcely mattered who conducted the investigation. Or was that mere wishful thinking?

Belatedly he answered Mike. 'Sounds as if we

should have gone to the Bells at West Tavy for our lunch,' he remarked. 'D'you know it?'

Mike shook his head. 'Off the beaten track, that is. You wonder how places like that ever keep going.'

In the car, Den invited Mike's observations. 'Funny sort of atmosphere,' the constable responded. 'I was listening in to that group the other side of the fire from us. The usual stuff about how farming's going down the tubes. How their wives and daughters are bringing in more money than they are – women running the whole place these days, one of them said. They're all pretty miserable – even scared, from the sound of it. Not much hope for the future.'

Den nodded. 'Right,' he said. 'Do you think it makes any sense for us to connect what's happened at Dunsworthy with the things that're going on in farming? How would that work?'

Mike scratched his nose. 'Well, if Sean had asked his boss for more money, say, that might have been the final straw. Or if they'd had some major row about selling off the cows. Maybe Sean told Hillcock they'd never be viable.'

'Yeah,' said Den dubiously. 'But that would be more likely to work the other way around. If Hillcock told O'Farrell he was going out of milk, and didn't need a herdsman any more – then wouldn't Sean be the aggressor?'

'Maybe he was. Maybe he grabbed the fork first but Hillcock wrestled it off him and jabbed him with it in self-defence.'

'Yeah,' repeated Den. A gloom was rapidly descending on him, as he assessed his morning's work. 'We've got nowhere, basically,' he muttered. 'Not a thing that would stand up as evidence. The whole neighbourhood's taking it as read that Hillcock's the killer – and if we're not very careful, we'll never build a case against him. And I bet you the bugger knows it.'

'Should we call the DI and see if there's anything new from Forensics?' Mike had a knack for optimism that Den was only now beginning to appreciate. 'It's going to be down to them, basically, isn't it?'

'Okay.' Den reached for his phone and keyed in Danny's number; the Inspector answered on the second warble. Den gave a summary of the interviews with Heather and Abigail O'Farrell, and Ted Speedwell, plus the oddments they'd gleaned in the Limediggers, before asking, 'Any progress from Forensics?'

'Give them a chance,' Hemsley protested. 'You don't get results that fast.'

'No, but—'

'We've got all the pictures pinned up. Barn, yard, footprints, tyre tracks. Not that they're very exciting. Everything's overlaid with about a million cow footprints. And a muck scraping doo-dah got there before this morning's team could show up. Did you see what they'd done?'

Den tried to remember. 'The tapes were a bit messed up,' he offered.

'More than a bit. From what I hear, it's close to deliberately interfering with a criminal investigation. Someone drove a tractor over it.'

Den groaned inwardly. He thought he knew who that might have been. 'I don't suppose there'd have been anything left to see, anyway. The cows were all over the yard last night in any case.'

'Lucky for whoever it was, then,' the DI growled.

Den shivered at Lilah's narrow escape. He was in no doubt that she'd taken it into her head to make sure nothing would be found that could incriminate Hillcock any further. She knew about dirty farmyards and police investigations – and must have decided that they'd hardly prosecute a herd of cows for obstructing their enquiries. As scenes of crime went, a cow assembly yard must rate top for obliteration of evidence. But it had been a silly thing to do, all the same, and he felt a twist of irritation with her.

Hemsley was still on the line.

'It's not looking too promising, is it?' Den said. 'We've got no proof at all that it was Hillcock – and it's not easy to see how we're ever going to get any.'

'Give Forensics a chance. It's barely twenty-four hours. If we find O'Farrell's blood on Hillcock's clothes, then with a bit of fancy footwork on the angle of the fork, weight, height of the attacker – we're in with a chance. You don't think it was the Speedwell chap, then?'

'I don't think so, no. But at this rate it wouldn't be hard to put together a case against him as good as the one against Hillcock. It stinks, sir.'

'Calm down, Cooper. Some of that stuff you've got from the pub could do with a bit of processing. There might be something in there. Go and talk to the Speedwell wife – then the Hillcock women – you haven't even started on them yet, have you? Oh, and be there for this afternoon's milking. Check noise levels, and the way it all works.'

'Right.' Den was trying to work out the timetable. 'First Mrs Speedwell, then the milking – he starts about three – then the Hillcock women. They don't get back from work till nearly six. Do I keep Mike with me for all this?'

'Has he got wheels?'

'Nope.'

'Then leave him to do the Speedwell lady, and you go and shadow Hillcock. See what he does before milking starts. Where are the cows? Does he do it all on his own, or does someone else usually help? It was this time yesterday the deed was done. Just see what gets thrown up from watching the routine – okay?'

Den wasn't happy. The prospect of spending more than a minute in the company of Lilah's new lover was horrible. 'Yes, sir,' he managed.

Claudia Hillcock was so distracted that she could barely pretend to be listening to the wretched woman who sat facing her. The counselling room was small, with the blandest of furnishings: modern, upright chairs, a low table useful for the occasional drawing of geneagrams or arrangements of coins, in one of Claudia's favourite symbolic games.

'He just won't *listen* to me,' the woman was complaining. 'Every time I start to speak, he leaves the room. What am I supposed to do about that?'

'You might have to accept that he's afraid to hear what you have to say.'

'He's not afraid – he's bored. That's what he says. That he can't be bothered to stay and listen because it's always the same old thing.'

'And is it?'

'Well . . .' The client stopped; Claudia hoped she was genuinely trying to answer the question. The brief silence gave her thoughts an opportunity to return yet again to the topic of Gordon and the murdered Sean.

The antipathy between the two men had been building up for years. Claudia had listened to supper-time tirades from her son scores of times. Sean had ignored an instruction; Sean had been overfeeding some of the poor milkers; Sean had ordered the wrong semen from the AI place; Sean had sent the whole herd through the footbath three times in one week, which anyone could see was sheer madness, as well as very cruel.

'Then sack him, why don't you?' she'd asked, many a time. 'Get someone else, who'll do things your way. God knows, there's plenty of herdsmen out there looking for a job.'

'I can't,' Gordon always sighed. 'Not after all these years. And what about Heather?' In his twenties, Gordon had been rampant, working his way through every nubile female for miles around, including the pretty young wife of the herdsman. Sean had been nerveless and – even then – disaffected, and Heather must have been impossible to resist. Claudia had turned a blind eye: something she had always been skilled at doing. There had been several incidents over the years where she had badly failed her family.

During her training as a counsellor, some of this had inevitably been revived, and much of her residual guilt expunged. Her supervisor was a deeply wise woman, who had gentled Claudia through the initial wracking self-recriminations, at the same time forcing her to confront the aspects of her nature that she preferred to avoid. Claudia had emerged reborn, changed – at least in her own eyes – almost out of recognition. The relationship she had now with Gordon was as good as anyone could expect. They gave each other plenty of space, with Mary as a useful buffer between them.

Her experience after three years as a counsellor was that every family had secrets. There had been times, in the counselling room, when wives had disclosed the true parentage of their children, that she had wanted to say: *But this is a commonplace. Why, I could tell you a story of my own* – but she never did.

Not that Gordon ever showed the slightest hint of claiming Abigail for his own. When Granny started her accustomed rant about great-grandchildren, Claudia never caught a flicker in her son's eyes. When Abigail was involved with a group of Year Nines at school who'd been identified as running a not-so-amateur racket, cheating younger children out of their pocket money, and Sean had been distraught about it, Gordon had seemed merely amused. But Claudia believed she knew better than to take his feelings at face value. She believed that Gordon himself stuck with Sean as his herdsman because he wanted the girl where he could see her.

Which, of course, gave rise to some strange logic if Gordon had suddenly flipped and killed his herdsman. Heather and Abigail would have to leave – the cottage would be needed for a new man. Nobody would expect the Hillcocks to extend charity to the point of letting them stay. And if Gordon had killed Sean, then Claudia and Mary would have to rally round to defend him – that much went without saying. Except that she didn't know how to do that, and the search for an answer to this problem was the main cause of her inattention to the wretched client before her.

'He told me yesterday that he wouldn't care if I *did* leave him,' the client was mewing pathetically. 'Ever since I started coming here, and trying to talk to him about things, he's just got colder and more uncaring. It really isn't going the way I wanted it to.'

'You wanted me to show you how to change him,' Claudia returned. 'You thought I'd explain him to you, and you could just go home and make everything all right. Don't you remember I said at the start that it doesn't work like that?'

The woman frowned and pushed out her lower lip. She looked for all the world like a mutinous three-year-old. 'Yes, but . . .' she began.

'It's hard, Celia, I know. If we could have had Steve here as well, it might have been clearer – but the fact that he won't come is a message in itself, do you see? He isn't interested in sharing his feelings with you. I think you have to accept that. What you have to do now is to decide whether or not you choose to remain in a marriage that's conducted on that basis.'

'But . . . what should I decide? I never thought it would come to this. It didn't cross my mind not to stay married.'

'Nobody's saying there's a right or wrong answer. It's what you – you, yourself – choose to do. Plenty of people live in that sort of marriage, quite contentedly. There's nothing wrong with it.' She was speaking automatically, words arising from one of the most fundamental tenets of her work. She had little hope that the client was hearing her. Sometimes she blamed her own profession for the idea that marriage should consist of total union, complete revelation of the contents of each heart and soul to the other. At other times she blamed the endless magazine stories, films, soap operas, novels that built up a picture of relationships as something that went beyond fantasy into realms of utter impossibility.

'So I should give up then, should I? Stop talking to him altogether? That's probably what he'd like.'

Claudia sighed. 'You could try saying less. Leave a vacuum and you might be surprised at what happens.'

'You think I nag him, don't you?'

I'm damn sure you do, thought Claudia. She shook her head. 'I think you're very anxious to get him to listen to you. It's not a nice feeling to be ignored, after all. But he might be hearing a cracked record. It might help if you assume he *has* heard you, but he doesn't know how to reply.' Claudia felt like a cracked record herself; she'd said all this for several sessions now. If she could just concentrate a bit more, she might be able to think up a few practical strategies the woman could try – but that always felt manipulative if she only had one half of the couple in front of her. The chances of doing any real good were not high without the wretched Steve in the room as well.

The big clock above the woman's head showed only five minutes to go. The relief was like a drink of cool water. Claudia picked up the diary on the corner of the low table. 'I'm not sure about you, but it seems to me that we've done nearly everything we can. We agreed six sessions, I think? What would you say to just having one more – cutting it down to five?'

She knew what the reaction would be; the petulant lip pushed out again. 'I don't feel as if we've got anywhere, really. Steve isn't the least bit different from how he was at the start.'

Claudia gritted her teeth. How nice it would

be to possess the magical powers that clients so often invested you with. 'Well, let's give it one more week, okay? Try to keep in mind what we've been saying this afternoon. Give some serious thought to what's good in your marriage, what you like about Steve, and what sort of circumstances produce the sort of behaviour you're happy with. Keep on trying to avoid doing the things that you know lead to problems. Think about what you say to him – listen to yourself.'

The lip quivered. 'You upset me, saying that about choosing whether to stay in the marriage. I never wanted to separate. That would be *terrible*.'

'There you are then. That's a tremendous thing to have realised. Just knowing that will give you more strength to help put things right.' God, she sounded revoltingly *bracing*, to her own ears. It wouldn't matter if she thought the client understood a word she was saying, but it was her own failure that she couldn't find the language to get her message across. She knew she couldn't bear more than another hour of this futile exercise.

'Next week, same time. Okay?'

She didn't wait to hear whether or not it was okay. Standing up, she ushered the woman out of the room and down the corridor. Leaving her at the top of the stairs, Claudia dived into the office for a word with Janice on reception before there could be any more discussion.

'Phew!' she sighed, as they heard the front door bang shut. 'I'm getting too old for this job.'

'Rubbish,' laughed Janice. 'You're the best of the whole lot, and you know it.'

It was plain that Janice had heard nothing about the Dunsworthy happenings. It was worth the thirty-five mile journey to North Devon just to be amongst people who knew virtually nothing about her home area. But it had a price, too. She felt isolated, anxious about her son.

Anxious . . . What an inadequate word to describe what was going on inside her. When that tall young police sergeant had appeared with Gordon last night, she had at first suspected nothing of what was about to happen. She had been almost criminally slow to understand; to grasp the full implications of what was happening before her very eyes. She had even gone to bed while the high-powered searchlights were still playing on the yard, men in protective suits crawling through the muck looking for evidence that she fervently hoped they wouldn't find. What, after all, could there be, after a hundred cows had trampled over the spot? Some blood – just enough to show where Sean had been attacked – and very little else. But she'd been pathetically pleased with her hint to Lilah that a bit of accidental damage to the police tape might not come amiss.

Lilah had understood immediately, and cooperated magnificently, as Claudia had noticed on her way out that morning. But now it didn't seem such a clever idea, after all. Forensic evidence these days could be found on the point of a pin, on the merest wisp of fluff from a pocket, couldn't it? All Lilah had done was to antagonise the police, in all probability.

It was time to go home. She and Mary shared a car, carefully planning their journeys to make this possible. Mary would be waiting at her school to be collected. There was something both irritating and comforting about having to pick up a grown daughter from school and take her home. It was as if nothing had changed in the last twenty years or more. They would usually chat amicably in the car, telling stories of their day. This afternoon, of course, they would have only one topic to talk about.

Lilah drove back to Redstone at half past two, leaving Gordon to get on with the afternoon milking. Ted Speedwell followed his usual routine, moving the big lightweight gates behind the assembled cows, to channel them back into their cubicles after they'd been milked. It was his only contribution – and he made sure he was out of the way before the actual milking started.

Den's car was in the yard, as Lilah reversed hers out of the parking area beside the house. The sight of it mangled her emotions even further; her entire body felt stuffed with marshmallow. Her hands shook on the steering wheel. How long would the police hang about, asking the same questions, searching over and over for some speck of evidence that would incriminate Gordon?

She tried to think intelligently. There must be the seeds of a plan somewhere, if only she could find them and set them germinating. On the assumption that Gordon was innocent, the obvious task was to identify who else might possibly be the killer. Ted Speedwell? Why not?

She tried to think of anything incriminating in Ted's behaviour or conversation in the brief exchange she'd had with him that morning. He hadn't seemed sorry about Sean's death. He'd been more upset at the disappearance of his fork – which, according to the official receipt left by the police in Gordon's office, had been taken for forensic examination. 'That fork's the only thing that gets up the silage proper,' he'd complained. ''Twill be a mess, trying to use that darned pitchfork instead.'

If it was Ted's fork that had been used to kill Sean – wasn't that in itself suspicious? Not really, she had to admit. He habitually left it lying around where anyone could pick it up. And the image of the peaceable, ageing tractor driver committing such a sudden act of violence was an unconvincing one. Even if she could find a way of shifting police attention to Ted, she knew she wouldn't be able to make a plausible case for the prosecution. Not even to save Gordon. There must be someone else . . .

There was. The milk recorder, Deirdre Watson, who'd known Sean and his unsavoury ways from years of milking alongside him. She'd been there when Sean died; she'd more or less shared in the discovery of the body. She'd seemed uncannily calm; she'd returned to the farm that morning, when most people would be far too traumatised to contemplate such a thing. Lilah thought hard, and productively. Yes, there might well be something there that she could work with.

She knew how Den's mind worked – how he tried to see the best in people, and fought against the temptation to jump to conclusions. Her attack on him that morning hadn't been very fair, she now admitted to herself. However furious she might be that he was involved in the murder investigation, she couldn't seriously accuse him of letting prejudice affect his judgement. He'd told Danny Hemsley the full story – and if Danny was keeping him on the case, it could only be that everything would be squeaky-clean, every step of the way.

Even now, when his personal feelings were so intimately involved, Lilah believed he'd go carefully and take heed of anything that might implicate another suspect. She knew a great deal about the realities of police work, too: the odd mixture of insane levels of thoroughness on the one hand, and a tendency to a profound intellectual laziness on the other. Combined with an inability to get to grips with anyone not fitting one of their stereotypes, this left them vulnerable to manipulation. Or so she hoped.

Motive – that was where the focus of attention would be from here on. They had their murder weapon; they knew, more or less, who had had the opportunity to attack Sean at that particular time. What they didn't know was *why*. And the power of that question never relaxed its hold.

'What on earth's going on?' her mother demanded when she got home. 'Everyone's talking about your Gordon being arrested for murder. Is this to do with that phone call you got last night from Claudia?'

Lilah nodded. 'She asked me not to say anything to you. They haven't actually arrested Gordon, though. They took him for questioning and kept him all night, but he's home again now. Of course, without Sean, he's got to do all the milking.'

'So it is Sean that's been killed?'

'That's right.'

Miranda sat down heavily. 'Shit, Li. Not again. How the hell do you manage it?'

Lilah gave a bitter laugh. 'At least I know the ropes by now. Serves me right for taking up with a policeman.'

'Except I thought you'd dumped the policeman precisely because you didn't want any more to do with death and drama and all that stuff.'

'Can't escape my fate, apparently.'

'So did Gordon kill the man? Why would he do that?'

'Of course he didn't!' Lilah flashed back hotly. 'There's absolutely no evidence against him.'

'Den's not on the case, is he?'

Lilah nodded ruefully. 'Main investigating officer.'

Miranda blew out her cheeks with surprise. 'No prizes for guessing who he'd like to pin it on. Fancy letting *him* take it on!'

'I don't think there's anyone else,' Lilah realised. 'They've had some budget cuts this winter, and Phil's smashed leg won't have mended yet.'

'Poor old Den,' murmured Miranda. 'But it doesn't seem fair.' She sighed, drifting off the subject, as she often did. 'But jealous souls will not be answer'd so.'

'What?' Lilah wanted to shake her impossible mother, who never seemed to offer the sort of support and advice she wanted.

'It's *Othello*.'

'It's always *Othello*. Your English teacher has a lot to answer for.'

'Den likes it, as well. Remember? We used to quote bits at each other. All those lovely lines. "She will sing the savageness out of a bear".' She drew breath to throw other random quotes at her daughter, but Lilah interrupted.

'That's enough Shakespeare,' she said firmly. 'I'm not in the mood.'

'Sean O'Farrell's the badger baiting bloke, isn't he?' Miranda spoke casually, her back to Lilah as she started to remove shopping from a carrier bag.

'*What?*'

'I don't know who told me. Hetty or Sylvia, or someone. I imagine he goes in for lamping them, too. But I suppose that's not exciting enough for his sort. I remember – it was Hetty. She was in the Post Office, muttering about it. Somebody saw Sean with a shovel late one night, and said something to somebody else – I don't know – it's all nods and winks round here. But O'Farrell's name is always the first anyone thinks of. Or Fred Page, of course. Because he's got that dog.'

'I haven't heard a word about any of this.'

'Well, people don't talk in front of you, do they? At least not when you were engaged to Den.'

'But surely nobody approves of badger baiting?' There were times when Lilah felt disablingly young, with the world still hopelessly difficult to comprehend.

Miranda sighed, evidently feeling something similar about her daughter. 'It's not a matter of approval. They know it goes on. And it's their own sons and brothers doing it. And they're all convinced that badgers spread TB. They don't want the stigma of a police prosecution, do they?'

'Well, if Sean O'Farrell was involved in it, he *deserved* to be killed. He should have been ripped to pieces, like one of the poor badgers.'

'I don't suppose he was murdered for being into badger baiting,' Miranda smiled. 'Even the keenest animal rights activist isn't likely to have gone that far.'

'Hmmm,' said Lilah, narrowing her eyes, and suddenly feeling quite a lot better. 'I wonder.'

Den had as unpleasant a time observing the afternoon milking as he'd expected. Gordon ignored him completely, having asked the detective to stand on the steps leading out of the sunken area, and to be as quiet as he could. 'They've had enough upset for one week,' he said.

'Christ knows what sort of a job Lilah made of them this morning.'

Den clenched his fist, conscious of an urge to thrust it violently towards the mouth of this man who could utter her name so naturally. There was no sign in the man's eyes that he knew how Den was feeling – which, oddly, made it easier to relax and concentrate on the matter in hand, after the first awkward minutes.

He acknowledged with a stab of surprise that he had never once helped Lilah with the milking at Redstone, so he had never before witnessed the routine. In spite of himself he was absorbed by it.

It was less cold than he expected. The cows themselves provided a barrier between the parlour and the wintry gusts from the gathering yard. At first, he breathed shallow, cautious breaths, afraid of the olfactory onslaught. But as his nostrils detected no more than a sweetish whiff of what he supposed was silage on the animals' breath, he relaxed. Even the smell of a fresh deposit of dung close by, from a cow on its way out of the parlour, was not nearly as obnoxious as he'd expected. As the minutes dragged by, he found his thoughts wandering to the cows themselves.

The way they were positioned for milking, the only part visible was the backside and udder, except for the first one in each row. Without exception, each time a new row arrived the first cow noticed Den, paused, and turned a watchful eye on him, before slotting herself into her stall and setting about eating the cattle cake provided. The others followed suit, reassured by their leader's behaviour.

Den found himself involuntarily identifying with the creatures and their routine. It was clear that some were much more resigned to the process than others. Some hung back, and seemed to have a tension about them as the cluster was applied to the heavy udder.

There was an unmistakable sympathy between Hillcock and his beasts. The farmer moved amongst them easily, responding to interruptions or delays with equanimity. There was a sense of a shared goal between the man and the cows: they all wanted the milk taken from the udders. The patient, unemotional face of the front cow was always the same. Having finished the food in the hopper, she would simply stand there, moving minutely in time to the sucking rhythm of the milking machine, in no hurry for it to finish, perhaps permitting the illusion that her own calf was sucking the milk, perhaps not caring what it was that eased the tightness of her udder.

For the first time in his life, Den wondered how it was to be a cow on a modern dairy farm. He tried to persuade himself that there were worse existences – that they were mostly healthy and free from pain. But he couldn't ignore the obscenely huge udders on some of them, the swellings on the joints of their back legs. And he couldn't forget the carnage of the BSE experience, with death coming to whole herds *en masse*, a waste beyond calculation, mostly conducted in too much of a hurry to care about precision in handling the stun gun. He had no illusions about the certain fate of every one of these cows. Almost none of them would die a death free from fear and horror. Those who did would drop down dead in the yard from some injury or illness that would almost certainly involve a degree of suffering.

His head hurt with the brutal knowledge of what was done every day to livestock such as these. They were living, breathing, feeling beings, and he was suddenly not at all sure it was right to drink their milk or eat their bodies.

He watched Gordon reach out to pick a piece of straw from the flank of a cow. It was lightly attached by a bit of dry manure, so he had to pull it slightly. The cow's hide rippled with the sensation, which could hardly have been more than the briefest tug on a few hairs. Hardly more than a fly walking on her. The obvious sensitivity made Den's own skin quiver in sympathy.

The moment passed and he hardened his resolve. Where would it lead if he allowed himself to start empathising with farm animals? Donkeys in Greece, dogs in China, bulls in Spain and live exports all across the world – wherever there were animals, they were exploited. It was the way things were – and it was definitely not part of his job to start letting it get to him.

Forcing his attention yet again onto the man rather than his animals, he tried to make an objective assessment of Gordon Hillcock, without allowing the thought of Lilah to intrude. He resolved to be friendly: *The robb'd that smiles steals something from the thief*, he reminded himself. It had always been a pleasing thought.

Hillcock manifested self-confidence. There was nothing to indicate that this was a killer, seen barely twenty-four hours after taking another man's life. But Den knew how people could conceal their own guilt from themselves as well as others. He had seen bereaved parents appear at news conferences to appeal for public help in catching the killer of their own child – only to turn out to be guilty of the crime. Hillcock was following an everyday routine, every move for which was familiar to him. He wasn't being asked to explain himself, or to demonstrate his innocence. It would be more surprising if he suddenly did or said something that would incriminate him.

Den made a big show of writing down every move, with timings. Gordon left the parlour three times, and Den forced himself to ask him exactly what he'd been doing, on each occasion.

'Checking the tank isn't overflowing. Making sure the gates are right for them to go back into their stalls. Having a piss.' He was gone for less than a minute, two minutes, and ninety seconds respectively. If this was typical, there was clearly no opportunity to commit a murder during milking. And Den had a strong suspicion that the piss would not normally require a removal from the parlour. If the cows could do it all over the floor, he saw no reason why the man shouldn't, if he was sure of being unobserved.

'Does it take longer to milk them when it's Recording Day?' he asked, when the ordeal was finally over and the last cows had been released.

Gordon nodded.

'How much longer?'

'Ten, fifteen minutes. Longer to set it all up, too. Have to put sixteen meters up.'

'How long does that take?'

'Ten, fifteen minutes,' he said again.

'When did you do it yesterday?'

'Around one-thirty.'

'Before Mrs Watson arrived?'

Gordon nodded again.

Den wrote it all down, but he knew there were glaring gaps. In his mind's ear, he could hear Gordon's defence lawyer making a mockery of their case. *Nobody to say whether or not Mr Hillcock was in the yard at the relevant time . . . The nature of the buildings could easily conceal . . . Why, why, why . . . Is this the likely behaviour . . .* Phrases designed to throw doubt and confusion into the minds of a jury, to highlight the complexity of a modern farm and the numerous comings and goings that could take place unobserved. Den gritted his teeth and avoided Hillcock's complacent gaze.

CHAPTER TEN

'I have to interview your relatives,' Den announced, when the milking was well and truly finished. 'Including a quick word with your grandmother,' he said, on a sudden whim; the brief flash of alarm on the farmer's face was profoundly encouraging. 'I know my colleague spoke to her this morning, but I have one or two further questions for her.'

'She's a very old lady,' Gordon objected. 'Surely she has a right not to be brought into all this? I doubt she even knows who Sean O'Farrell is, for heaven's sake.'

'I won't upset her, I assure you. Your sister led me to believe she'd be quite glad to have someone to talk to.'

'Did she now,' Gordon snorted dismissively.

Den had noticed one lighted window on the upstairs floor of the farmhouse, the previous evening, as he and Mike had driven away from Dunsworthy with Mary and Gordon in the back. A corner room looking out obliquely over the gathering yard where Sean had been found. Something told him that the Hillcock family would not be inclined to leave lights on in empty rooms. It was probable, then, that this was Granny's room – and what more likely than that the old lady would spend her afternoons sitting by the window, looking for anything unusual that might be going on outside? Young Mike had gleaned very little from her, beyond the fact that she had indeed been sitting near the window, but Den hoped this was only because he hadn't asked the right questions.

'I'll be out here for another half-hour at least,' Gordon told him. 'My mother and sister'll be home by now. Why don't you go and make a start? They'll be grateful you haven't disrupted them at work, I'm sure.'

Den hesitated, trying to assess Hillcock's tone. It was cooperative, even considerate. It was obvious that he habitually gave some thought to other people's needs as well as his own. His handling of his cows had been deft, gentle, compassionate. And yet to Den it all felt like a façade – as if Hillcock's real thoughts and feelings were happening somewhere else; somewhere much deeper and darker.

The ramifications of the situation were beginning to snag at Den's smouldering and instinctive dislike of Hillcock. There was Lilah, and the acute awareness that they had shared intimate knowledge of her body. There was the shadow of Sean's dead body in the adjacent building. And there was the looming, threatening void that was Hillcock's future. It wasn't possible that the man was unafraid. Den could feel it himself, somewhere just below his stomach – a sharp acid turbulence, when he thought of how it must be inside Gordon Hillcock.

Dunsworthy farmhouse was solidly built, with large square rooms, high ceilings and quarry-tiled floors throughout much of the downstairs rooms. The house had been designed for airiness and space, with a dairy, pantry and generous kitchen. Some of its original furniture was still in place – a great oak dresser, a set of straight-backed chairs and a strange piece comprising nine drawers, kept in the former dairy for the storage of all kinds of assorted oddments. Claudia's mother-in-law had introduced an Aga, and Claudia herself, in her first weeks at the farm, had bought a handsome oak table to replace a rickety predecessor. The living room was well filled with three unmatching armchairs, a large sofa and a big mahogany writing desk. An old carpet was almost invisible under a varied collection of handmade rugs, mostly the work of Gordon's grandmother.

There was another large ground-floor room, which the family rather eerily referred to as Daddy's Room. In it were two glass-fronted cases containing the best china; a filing cabinet used by Mary for her school paperwork; and a large polished walnut writing desk.

Den had assimilated some of this information on his first visit to the house, an hour or so after the discovery of Sean O'Farrell's body. He had described it to himself as comfortable, well-kept, unpretentious, traditional. There had been few shocks or surprises – no unclean corners or signs of unusually messy indoor animals. He had in his line of duty encountered pet lambs, incontinent puppies and even a Vietnamese potbellied pig, all making free with every downstairs room in a succession of houses. Nothing so uncouth met his gaze here. Dunsworthy was not obviously a farmhouse at all.

It had been dark for well over an hour already, and the sky was bright with stars. A sliver of new moon was rising over the fields, and the air was biting. Twenty-four hours ago he had just arrived here, summoned to a sudden death, holding himself in a state of suspension until he knew whether it was Gordon Hillcock who'd got himself killed. What a lot could happen in a day, he sighed.

'More questions for you, I'm afraid,' he said, when Mary opened the front door to his knock.

She looked as if there were a number of questions she'd like to ask *him*, but she couldn't quite find the words. After all, what could she say? *Are you any nearer to proving my brother's a murderer?* wouldn't have been acceptable, in the circumstances.

The two Hillcock women had changed dramatically from his previous encounter with them. Claudia was unsmiling, monosyllabic, subtly hostile; Mary looked tired and anxious. 'What happens now?' she asked. 'With Sean, I mean? I said I'd drop in on Heather again this evening. When will she be able to go and see the body?'

'That's a matter for the Coroner's Officer,' Den told her. 'And the undertaker. It'll be a few days yet, I would think. It's good of you to be so concerned about her.'

'The woman's ill, for heaven's sake. What else would you expect me to do?' Den glanced at the mother, sitting stiffly beside the kitchen table, a large glass of white wine close to her hand. The bottle, already half-empty, stood nearby.

'I'd like a few more words with you both, as well as with Mrs Hillcock senior,' he said firmly. 'Perhaps I should start with the old lady? I won't keep her long, but there are one or two things I'd like to clarify.'

'Have you been here all afternoon?' Claudia asked suddenly.

Den nodded. 'I wanted to see what went on during a typical milking.'

'My God! Three hours of uninterrupted tedium, I should think. I don't suppose Gordon was very chatty either.'

Den retained his dignity with only minor effort. 'It's surprising how fast the time passes,' he smiled. 'Now would one of you kindly show me up to the old lady's room? And then I'm afraid I'll have to speak to each of you separately, for half an hour or so.'

Mary unlatched a door opening onto a staircase that turned and turned again, so that Den had to look back and check that he still had his bearings. The room they went into was the first on the left, as they moved along a short landing. Yes, it would be the one over the downstairs living room – the one to the left of the front door. The corner room, where he'd seen the light.

The old lady was in bed, sitting up against a pile of pillows, a large fluffy cat snuggled against her side. The bed was facing the window, but some distance from it; Den doubted that she would be able to see much activity outside from where she was. But, more promisingly, there was a Parker Knoll armchair closer to the window, with a good-sized round oak table beside it. A jigsaw was laid out, half-finished, alongside a pile of thick books that he thought might be photograph or stamp albums. A good-sized television occupied another corner, visible from either bed or chair; it was switched off. The room was far from overheated, which Den found surprising.

Mary moved to close the velvet curtains across the window. 'Chilly this evening, Granny,' she said. 'Shall I get you an extra blanket?'

The old woman shook her head vigorously. 'Can't abide to be too hot,' she said firmly.

Mary smiled. 'It's the secret of her long life,' she told Den. 'Isn't it, Granny?'

'Not 'ealthy to be too hot,' came the confirmation.

A pair of dark brown eyes stared keenly at him from beneath straggling white eyebrows, as he stood awkwardly in the middle of the room, the ceiling only a few inches above his head. Her hands lay on the covers, brown and bent and mottled. She was shrunken and fleshless, but an energy radiating from her filled the room. ''Oo be thiccy?' she demanded, her voice high and reedy.

Den noticed that she appeared to have no teeth at all; it plainly affected her speech, giving her words a lisping fuzziness that was rather endearing.

'This is one of the policemen I told you about this morning,' Mary said. 'One of the men got killed yesterday – remember? They're asking a lot of questions about it.'

Granny Hillcock narrowed her eyes, and looked shiftily from one side of the room to the other. Apparently Mary knew the significance of this. 'It's all right, Granny. You probably don't remember.'

'One of my colleagues came up this morning to speak to you,' Den ventured. 'Your grandson brought him up, about coffee time.'

'She doesn't drink coffee,' Mary interrupted. 'You'll just muddle her saying that.'

'Do it be zupper time?' the old woman asked.

'Another half an hour. Gordon's not in yet,' Mary said. 'I'll go and get it ready, and you can talk to the man.'

Den let Mary go with a sense of helplessness. 'Mrs Hillcock—' he began, approaching to within a foot of her and speaking much louder than normal.

'I can yere 'ee,' she interrupted. 'I idn deaf.'

'Do you sit over there in the afternoons? Where you can see out of the window?'

She nodded, frowning slightly. 'That be my chair. Can't bide in bed all day.'

'Quite right,' he smiled. 'So do you watch Gordon out there working?'

A repeat of the eye movements, darting to left and right like the evasive glance of an uncooperative child. It was a disturbing trick. 'What should I watch 'un vurr?' she said slowly.

'Oh, I don't know. For interest. Do you know Sean O'Farrell? The herdsman. The one who does most of the milking?'

She tucked her chin down tightly into her neck. 'They cows is proper mucky,' she observed. 'Dan'l'd have zummat to zay bout that.'

Den found some encouragement in this; she obviously did glance outside now and then. 'Is that Sean's fault, would you say?'

'Nasty sod,' she spat suddenly. Den couldn't suppress a smile. 'What be 'ee laughin' at?' she demanded. 'Dog got un. I zaw it. Screamin' fit to bust, and Gordon just standin' there. Serve 'un right, the boy zed. 'Twill end in trouble, I thunk – zee if I weren't right, eh?'

She fixed him with a look of such intelligence that it took his breath away. A deep, limpid glance, completely at odds with her previous demeanour as a confused old woman. 'Was he teasing the dog, then?' he asked her.

'Made it vair mazed with teasing,' she confirmed. 'Nasty sod.'

'Well, yesterday, somebody killed him,' Den

said slowly. 'Out there in the yard.' He walked to the window, pulled back the curtain and looked down. The corner where the worst of the bloodstains had been found was lit up by one of the high-wattage outside lights. 'You can see it from here.'

'I zeed 'un teasing the dog,' she repeated.

'That was a long time ago,' he told her. 'What about yesterday?'

''Tiz all the zame to me,' she grinned. 'But tid'n our Gordon you be wanting. Us'd never get by wi'out the boy. You leave 'un be. They be going vur to make me a great-granma, ifn 'ee leaves 'un be.' A smile was followed by a sudden frown, as if she'd remembered a disconcerting truth that gave the lie to her words.

It took a second for the import to make itself clear to Den. When it did, he clenched his jaw tight enough to crack his molars. The effort brought a stinging suggestion of tears to the place behind his eyes, as he remembered that Mike had reported a similar remark.

'Well,' he said. 'I think that's all for now. I'm sorry if I've disturbed you.'

She raised one hand briefly, in a queenly gesture of dismissal. 'Nasty sod,' she muttered, and Den hoped it was still Sean O'Farrell she was alluding to.

* * *

Mary Hillcock sat comfortably on the big old sofa in the sitting room, facing Den as he took the most formal chair in the room, balancing his notebook on one knee. He began by superfluously verifying her name and age, and her whereabouts on Tuesday afternoon. She answered him steadily, unsmiling, watching unblinking as he wrote down her replies. Her manner seemed to be everything he could ask for in a witness – concerned, attentive, thoughtful. Why then, he wondered, did he get a strong sense that he couldn't trust her?

'I'd like to get a bit of background,' he said. 'I understand the farm's been in the family a long time?'

'I was born here,' she nodded. 'So was Gordon. My father was about twelve, I think, when his parents moved here. It was during the war – they came from Hampshire.'

'And is there a mortgage on the property?'

She shook her head. 'Daddy paid it off about five years before he died. It must be worth around fifteen hundred times what they paid for it. Frightening, really.'

Den blinked. From the sound of it, someone had done the calculation quite recently. He supposed a farm of Dunsworthy's size – two hundred acres or so – would have fetched about five thousand pounds in the 1940s. Possibly less.

Now they were thinking in terms of £750,000, if the sums were right. He agreed with Mary – the idea really was frightening.

'But nobody's doing too well in farming these days?' he suggested.

'Too right,' she nodded emphatically. 'It's only me and Mum that's keeping it all going, at the moment. It's very hard for poor Gordon, working such long hours, and not even breaking even most months. They've just put the price of cattle cake up again, you know, at the same time as milk prices are dropping. It's a complete scandal.'

She spoke placidly, like somebody repeating words that had become so familiar they'd lost much of their meaning.

'Could you tell me anything about the other families living here? The Speedwells and O'Farrells? How long have they been with you?'

She pursed her lips. 'The O'Farrells came at the same time as my grandparents. Ted and Jilly came quite a bit after that. You'd have to ask them the precise dates.'

'The Speedwells have a son, is that right? Did he grow up here?'

She smiled. 'Eliot, yes. He's only a couple of years younger than me. We were playmates when we were little. I don't see him much any more, though. He's got himself a job at the pasty factory.

Some managerial role. He was good friends with Sean,' she added.

'Oh?' Den thought she looked sorry that she'd disclosed this snippet. He wondered whether he'd ever disentangle all the relationships that had been forged between three families over the course of generations.

'Well, they grew up together,' she said vaguely. 'Eliot worked here until he was about twenty-two, and then he went into the Army. That surprised everybody, I must say. He didn't last long – I think they threw him out, actually. I never found out why. I was going through my own bad patch at the time, and never heard the full story.'

Den made a firm note. People didn't get thrown out of the Army for nothing.

'Now – Sean O'Farrell,' he said, watching her face. Very little changed, apart from a small frown and a subtle hardening of her features. 'How did you feel about him?'

'I didn't like him much. He seemed unduly brutal with the cows. No worse than a lot of others, I dare say, but these days it isn't necessary. I don't know why he always had to go for the stick or the fist when they'd do what he wanted much more easily if he just whistled at them and let them take their time.'

'I thought you didn't get involved with the cows?'

'I don't now. That's partly because I couldn't bear to see how he treated them.'

'But didn't your brother object? They're his cows, after all.'

Her frown deepened. 'Gordon mostly managed not to notice,' she said in a low voice, as if worried that her brother could somehow hear her. 'It's a bit of a family trait, that.'

Den scratched his head, just above one ear, with his pencil. He took a deep breath. 'So what else is going unnoticed?'

Mary swallowed. 'Well, I don't suppose it matters much,' she said, with a quick shake of her head, 'and it's probably going to sound a bit peculiar. I was thinking of something that happened a long time ago. It really isn't a bit relevant.'

'Shouldn't you let me be the judge of that?'

She made a face, as if chewing on the dilemma. 'I spoke without thinking,' she said. 'I was remembering the way my mother used to ignore anything bad that might be going on. She's not like that now. I suppose I meant Gordon had taken after her, in some way.'

'I see,' said Den. He did, up to a point. 'So your brother knew Sean ill-treated the cows, but preferred to let it go unchallenged?'

'Something like that,' she agreed. 'But you have to understand that men on farms are a law unto themselves. I had to grow up with that as a given. I could tell you terrible stories of suffering, exploited animals – none of them particularly unusual. You have to get used to it, steel yourself. But I seem to have got softer as I get older, and I really can't cope with it any more.'

'How much did you see of O'Farrell, on a daily basis?'

'Practically nothing. Last summer, getting the hay in, we all lent a hand for a weekend – and quite honestly, since then, I don't suppose I've exchanged more than ten words with him.'

'But you didn't like him. I've got that right, haven't I?' It seemed important that he should hear her say the actual words once more.

She rubbed the back of one hand with the fingers of the other. 'No,' she admitted. 'I didn't like him.'

In a rather awkward piece of choreography, Mary was replaced by Claudia, who sat straight-backed on the edge of the sofa, hands clasped in her lap. She seemed to Den oddly prim, despite her youthful looks and casual clothes. She had obviously recovered from the shock of the previous evening and come to grips with the situation. This Claudia Hillcock was a lot more incisive after twenty-four hours in which to consider her son's position.

He opened with the same questions – name, age, nature of her employment. When she told him she was fifty-seven, he raised his eyebrows with a surprise he couldn't conceal.

'That's right,' she anticipated. 'I was only eighteen when Gordon was born. And a useless mother I was, too.'

'How old was your husband?'

'Thirty-three.'

'And Mrs Hillcock upstairs is his mother, I think you said last night?'

'Yes. Norman would be well into his seventies now if he'd been alive.'

'She mentioned a Daniel – who would that be?'

Claudia smiled ruefully. 'Her husband; my father-in-law. He died thirty-four years ago – a week before Mary was born, as it happens. Granny does tend to live in the past these days. It's normal for someone of her age.'

'And Gordon was born here?'

'He was actually *born* in Plymouth. But we were living here at the time, yes.'

'How well did you know Sean O'Farrell? I mean – did you work alongside him on the farm at any stage?'

She frowned, in much the same way as her daughter had done. 'Well, on and off, over the years. When my husband was ill, I lent a hand outside, but I've never done the milking. It's an odd question – how well did I know him. He's been here all his life, working with my husband and son. In that sense, I know him very well. But we hardly had a single meaningful conversation in all that time. I shouted at him once or twice, when I caught him tormenting the animals, but I was warned off that.'

'Warned off? Who by?'

'Norman and Gordon both told me I was out of order, that Sean was a good herdsman – just a bit primitive in his methods. All I could see was that the cows were scared of him. And with good reason. It was very unpleasant to watch him working with them. And yet he always got good yields out of them, which I suppose is the main thing these days.'

'Last night – I did get the impression that you were not entirely surprised by what had happened.'

She looked hard at the floor beside her feet, her eyes flickering in rapid thought. 'Did you? I can't think what gave you that impression. I was absolutely stunned – that's the truth of it.'

'That's understandable,' Den responded.

'I do admit I'd been furious with Gordon yesterday morning,' she said. 'That might account for any apparent coolness between us, perhaps. But mostly, I'm sure it was pure shock.'

‘Why were you furious with him?’

‘Oh – he was insisting on going out on Saturday – to a political meeting. They’re talking about staging some sort of protest, marching to Westminster with a flock of sheep, that sort of thing.’

‘And you don’t approve?’

‘I think there are better ways of making a point.’

‘What about Sean? Would he have wanted to be involved in the protest?’

Claudia snorted derisively. ‘I don’t think Gordon would give him the option. Although he has been getting political lately. Gordon found out about his little group at the Six Bells – and didn’t like it.’

‘Oh?’

She tossed her head. ‘It seems they’d got very worked up about the badger cull, and wanted to take some sort of direct action. Gordon said it was muddying the waters, when they needed to be focused and united. Sean hadn’t the brains to follow anything through for long. Nor the passion. He didn’t care enough to be seriously involved.’

‘So – what did he care about? What might have got him excited?’

She cocked her head on one side, eyebrows lifted as she contemplated the question. ‘I’ve no idea,' she admitted, a few moments later. 'I've always thought him rather – well, *nerveless* is the word I use. *Bloodless* might be better.'

Den remembered what her work was. Presumably counsellors used that sort of label routinely.

'His wife appears to have no complaints against him,' he said. 'Does that mean he had no vices? Drink? Gambling?'

She laced her fingers together loosely, and let them lie in her lap – a gesture suggesting she'd given up any attempt to find answers to these questions. 'You're making me realise I hardly knew Sean at all,' she said. 'How funny.'

'If I may say so – you don't seem in the least upset by his death,' Den commented dryly.

'I won't miss him,' she conceded, candidly. 'But I am very upset to think that Gordon might be in trouble because of the wretched man.' She drew in a breath to say more, and then checked herself. Den look at her questioningly, but she remained silent.

'Mrs O'Farrell's illness,' he remembered. 'Can you tell me anything about that?'

Claudia sat up straight. She was on familiar territory now. 'Heather has ME, as I expect you know. She's had it for six years. Before that, she was physically quite fit.'

Den could hear another hidden message beneath the simple words.

'Physically?' he picked up.

'Right.' A degree of admiration gleamed in her eyes. 'She was never entirely healthy in other respects. Socially maladroit, extremely dependent on Sean to protect her from the outside world. He rescued her from a highly unpleasant father, and brought her here, where he thought she'd feel safe. You never saw such a shy little thing as she was then. But she did improve dramatically, in those early years. Made a reasonable job of mothering Abby when she was little, and got on with her life, in her own somewhat limited way.'

'And you were all friends – you three women?' Den asked. 'Four, with Mrs Speedwell, of course.'

'Five, with Granny,' Claudia reminded him. 'You couldn't say we were friends, exactly,' she went on. 'Class divisions run deep. Heather has scarcely read a book, or even been outside Devon. We've never had anything to talk about. She takes little interest in the farm – and neither do I, to be honest. But I like her well enough. I'm sympathetic towards her illness, and professionally quite frustrated that I've never been of the least assistance to her in overcoming it. Jilly Speedwell's a good gossip, and more or less my own age. She and I drive into town now and then, and find plenty to chat about in the car. Jilly's got more about her, anyway, having her job to keep her mind active, and a wise way with her. She comes out with some wonderful remarks sometimes.'

'I'm sorry – I diverted you from the ME. What's your opinion on that? I know there's a lot of disagreement amongst doctors.'

Claudia made a self-mocking face, shaking her head as if in warning. 'You'll wish you never got me started on that subject,' she said. 'But if you really want to know – I'm convinced that it's a hysterical reaction to the way she lives. That's not to say it isn't real. She is genuinely ill – it just isn't a physical illness. As I said, Heather has never really felt comfortable in public situations. With Abigail growing up, and Sean's income being fairly limited, it was reasonable to expect her to find some sort of job. That's one factor to bear in mind. There are others, that I don't think we need to go into. Suffice it to say that she's a classic example. Being an invalid has solved a number of problems for her – and the human mind is extremely clever at solving problems. A hundred years ago, she would have had "nervous trouble" or been one of Freud's hysterical females. But please don't make the common mistake of assuming that a psychosomatic illness isn't real. She hurts every bit as much as someone with sciatica or arthritis, or anything else.'

'But,' Den interrupted, 'couldn't it be that Freud's patients had a form of ME, as well, but it hadn't been properly identified then?'

'Absolutely not,' Claudia said. 'This is a new form of the same old syndrome. There's an epidemic of ME at the moment – though I detect a definite lessening, now we're in a new century. A lot of it stems from a general anxiety about social change and the unpredictable future.'

Den scratched his ear with the pencil. 'Okay,' he said. 'I get the idea. So, as far as you know, it wasn't that Mrs O'Farrell had some specific shock six years ago? There's nothing you can pinpoint as sparking off the illness?'

Claudia shook her head, and Den could feel the interview's impetus slowing down. He'd had a long day, and needed to go somewhere quiet for a drink and a think.

'You work as a counsellor,' he switched subjects abruptly. 'Did you train for that?'

'I counsel for Relate – couples, mainly. The training takes two or three years. I got the taste for study years ago, and that came as the last in a whole succession of courses.'

'You managed to fit it all in with the farm and having children?'

She gave him one of her rueful smiles. 'Didn't I say? Granny Hillcock did most of the child rearing for me. Gordon was much more hers than mine when he was little. I rather lost interest, to be honest. I went back to college at nineteen and did a degree. My husband was very good about it – he seemed quite proud of me, actually.'

'So how long have you been counselling?' he asked.

'Three years, just about.'

'It must teach you a lot about human nature.'

She nodded. 'It's shown me what people are capable of,' she said, a little grimly.

'Good or bad?'

'Bad, mostly. People can be incredibly cruel to each other. Compared to the mental cruelty that I've witnessed, skewering somebody in the stomach with a fork doesn't seem quite as dreadful as you might think.'

With a sigh, he closed his notebook. 'Thank you very much for your time,' he said formally. 'You've been most helpful.'

As he left, Mary went with him to the door. 'I hope you've got all the answers you needed,' she said, with a backward glance at the kitchen. She half closed the door behind her and they moved out into the porch, a wide covered area beyond the front door. 'Actually – there are one or two things I could tell you about the milk recorder, if you're interested,' she murmured hesitantly.

'Oh?'

'For one thing, she got involved in a complaint

against Sean, when she first started coming here. She claimed he was being cruel to some of the cows, and wrote a formal letter to Gordon about it. It caused rather a stink for a bit. Gordon had to go to some trouble to placate her. She was threatening to take it further, you see.'

Den resisted an urge to downplay this new snippet. 'Take it further? What would that involve?'

She paused to think. 'I'm not sure, now you ask.'

'The RSPCA?'

'Oh no. Nobody in farming has any time for them. Probably the Recording people she works for. Really, Sergeant, I don't know who she'd have gone to.'

'What did Gordon do?'

She shrugged. 'As I said before, we didn't much like Sean's ways of doing things either. But Gordon stuck up for him.'

'Must have been awkward, though. Isn't it surprising that Mrs Watson went on doing the recording here?'

'Don't ask me. I imagine they didn't have anyone else in the area. She does virtually all the farms around here, as far as I know. It all settled down again, and we heard no more on the subject. But, after what's happened, you ought to know about it – don't you think?'

'Any information's useful,' Den assured her. 'It all helps to build up the complete picture. And what was the other thing?'

'Pardon?'

'You said, "for one thing". That implied there was something else you could tell me.'

'Oh. Well – just that Deirdre Watson – or Deirdre Dawe as she was – always had a crush on Gordon, from when they were at school. He never really responded, but they went out together a few times when they were about nineteen. I remember teasing him about it. She was never much to look at – and she had awful spots. She's improved a lot with age, funnily enough. But she always makes a point of watching out for him when she's here, even if he's not doing the milking. I saw her last summer, when she didn't know I was there. Well – the look on her face!'

'Tell me,' Den prompted.

'It was quite obvious that she's still carrying a torch for him.'

As he walked to his car, he caught sight of Gordon Hillcock emerging from the bulk tank room. The man's broad chest gave him a powerful look in the shadowy light. His silhouette seemed a collection of chunky rectangular shapes – even his head seemed boxy, set squarely on his shoulders. He walked heavily, doubtless weary from the long day's work after a night with very little sleep. Den tried not to notice the lack of spring in the man's step. The last thing he wanted was to feel any pity for the man who'd stolen his girlfriend; the man who had surely murdered his herdsman.

CHAPTER ELEVEN

With a strong sense of having put in a satisfactory day's work, Den drove back to the station hoping to catch Hemsley. But it was seven-fifteen when he got there and the Inspector had gone. There was, however, a new page of forensic findings on Den's desk, with a post-it sticker from Danny: *Thought this might interest you.*

> *Analysis of deceased's clothing: traces of oil, animal manure, blood (human and animal), animal hairs (various), organic matter (soil, fermented grass, corn husks). Blood types and hairs currently undergoing laboratory examination.*

Analysis of Mr Gordon Hillcock's clothing, namely rubber apron, trousers, shirt, woollen jersey, rubber wellington boots: traces of organic matter (similar to above), animal manure, animal blood, animal hairs (very small quantity). No human blood found.

Den scowled angrily at the page in his hand. *No human blood* on Hillcock's clothes? Then he shrugged his worries away. So he had managed to avoid getting Sean's blood on himself – or washed it off. The apron and boots would receive a thorough cleaning in the milking parlour anyway. Little surprise, in fact, that there was nothing to be found. But this lack of hard evidence was a blow, for all that.

He went back to the first paragraph, pulling a face at the long list of substances found on O'Farrell's clothes. What were all those animals he'd been in such close contact with? The answer came swiftly: his daughter's collection of pets. Sean sometimes fed them – did he also take them out and handle them? Did he, to quote Mary Hillcock – *torment* them?

There was also a report of Mike's interview with Jilly Speedwell. In summary, it read, *Didn't have much to do with O'Farrell. Sometimes did a bit of shopping for him. Out from 10.45 to 2.45 on Tuesday. Numerous witnesses to confirm this.*

Den put the files back on his desk and left the office. Almost the whole building was in darkness. Any emergencies during the night would go through the Control office miles away, and be passed on to the night staff in the few stations that stayed open around the clock. But Den's team was now investigating a murder and time meant little. Danny, Mike, Jane or Den could be summoned day or night, as well as a few uniformed officers who could be attached to them for routine legwork. The trick was to catch some sleep when the chance arose, and now he intended to do just that.

Deirdre and Robin Watson spent the early evening together, trying to decide whether and when to have a summer holiday. 'I have to tell Carol what I'm doing,' she said, as she did every year.

'Five months' notice is more than enough, if you ask me,' replied her husband. 'Anything can happen between now and June.'

Deirdre was forced to agree. At least three of her farms had made warning noises about going out of milk and another three were threatening to stop having their herds recorded. It was, as Robin said, quite possible that she'd have a lot less work by June.

'Are we taking the kids with us?' she asked.

'Let's not,' he grinned boyishly at her. 'They make me feel old. Sam's got plans to go to Glastonbury this year, anyway.'

Deirdre moaned, and Robin made it worse by telling her more of their daughter's doings. 'She's got very involved in the animal rights stuff. It's the new boyfriend. They were trying to disrupt the Lamerton hunt last weekend.'

Deirdre moaned again. 'That's all we need. I hope nobody connects her with me. Most of my farmers are in favour of the hunt – more than ever, now it's under threat. I'll never live it down if they find out my daughter's sabotaging.'

'Not to mention badgers,' Robin carried on. 'I found a leaflet that must have fallen out of her schoolbag. I pretended not to see it.'

'Coward. Who's the boyfriend, anyway?' She had long ago come to terms with the way her husband and daughter exchanged confidences that she only ever learnt secondhand. She knew Robin would eventually tell her anything important.

'He's called Jeremy Page. Lives near Tavistock. He's twenty-two and works for that computer place on the Horrabridge road. Sounds quite bright.'

'Not related to Fred Page, I hope.'

'Who?'

'Fred Page. Farmer from hell. Not much better than a gypsy.'

'Ah – the one with muck up to the eyeballs and cows that cringe at the sight of him?'

'That's the one. I pray every night that he'll give up milk, but there's no sign of it so far. How long has this new romance been going on?'

'Started at the Millennium party. Early days. All I've got is a name and a job.'

'Well, I don't think I could bear it if he's related to Fred.'

Lilah spent half an hour that evening on the phone, ostensibly catching up with old friends. 'Hilary? Hi, it's me, Lilah . . . I know . . . time just flies. You heard about me and Den? . . . Yeah, well . . . Look, I was driving past your place at the weekend and saw Samantha Watson coming out of your gate with a boy that looked like that weird Jeremy, son of Fred Page, the one who was in the paper because he was at the anti-hunt protest at the weekend. I didn't know you knew him . . . Oh, right. Everybody's somebody's cousin round here, I should have guessed. So they're together now, are they? . . . I know . . . You can't really blame the son for what his dad gets up to, but I can't see Sam's mum being impressed. She records for the Pages, I think . . . Gosh, your *uncle*? . . . Sorry . . . no, not really, it's just something my mother said about Sean and badgers and Fred Page. I wanted to check it out, that's all . . . okay then, see you around.'

'Hi, Tamsin. I was just chatting to Hilary . . . you know, Hilary Spencer. Lives near Chillaton. Anyway, I thought of you for some reason while we were chatting. I've got loads of catching up to do . . . Are you still going out with Davy Champion? And your sister – is she with Gorgeous Gary? *What?* But she's only fifteen, isn't she? . . . Did you hear about her dad? . . . yeah . . . Well, it's all quite gruesome, obviously . . . I guess you know I'm with Gordon Hillcock now . . . right . . . so Abby's with Gary now, is she? Who'd have thought it? Did you dump Davy or did he dump you, or shouldn't I ask? . . . Sorry. I've really been out of things. . . . How about Eliot Speedwell? Didn't you fancy him a while ago? I know . . . he's over thirty, so what. Gordon's thirty-nine, actually . . . You're joking, surely. He was in the *Army*! Well, that would explain why he's never had a girlfriend. What a waste! . . . okay, Tams, better go. Keep in touch, right?'

She put the phone down thoughtfully, letting her fingers do a cheery little dance on the receiver. 'Nothing like networking,' she muttered to herself.

There was one further call to be made before the project was complete, made necessary by the startling suggestion that Eliot Speedwell was gay and had been seen in a gay bar in Plymouth.

Practised at helping Den think through some of his detective puzzles, she knew the incalculable value of making connections. And she had seen Eliot a time or two at Dunsworthy before Christmas. He had been with Sean O'Farrell, walking close to him, smiling and laughing. It had meant nothing to her at the time, but now the implication cascaded around her head like a flock of pigeons.

Focus, she adjured herself. *Remember the plan*. The next step was relatively simple.

Thursday dawned wet and raw. Den's spirits felt very much in tune with the weather as he looked out of the window at seven-thirty. Despite a good sleep and a bowl of porridge, he was not happy. Some time during the night he had dreamt of Lilah. She had been shouting at him with hate in her eyes, having caught him carrying Sean's blood-soaked body and accusing him of planting evidence to incriminate Gordon Hillcock. In some way, this had struck Den as an entirely justified accusation, even though he had been intending only to take Sean to the mortuary. When he put the body down his arms and chest had been covered with tufts of red and black animal hair, sticky globs of blood arranged in neat lines across his body. '*See!*' Lilah had shrieked at him, pointing a wavering finger at him. 'What sort of evidence do you call *that*?'

For a few minutes afterwards, Den had lain awake, wondering whether there might be a clue in the dream, something that had only registered in his unconscious mind. But if there was, he couldn't see it. Now, in the grey January daylight, the nightmare seemed as irrational and meaningless as dreams usually did.

He wasn't sure what the day would bring by way of work. He'd interviewed all the main players at least once, and found little or nothing to divert him from his original assumption: that Gordon Hillcock had killed Sean O'Farrell. If they were to follow the usual routine, then the next step was to discover more about the victim: his friendships, his moral values, past experiences, future plans. Compared to previous murder investigations, Den knew he had a much more hazy image of the dead man than was usual. A hard worker, a committed husband and father, and yet nobody so far had claimed to like him. Although nothing had been said, Den wondered whether Sean could have been mentally disturbed. Prone to tormenting animals, argumentative, stubborn, tolerated but apparently disliked by local people, and seemingly a man who hadn't properly known how to look after himself – it all suggested a certain social frailty.

It was axiomatic that there would be undercurrents and connections yet to discover. The Hillcocks and the O'Farrells had been at Dunsworthy for generations; the Speedwells went back a way, too. The younger generation all went to the same school and conducted an endless dance of couplehood, changing partners regularly. They were all strands in a big net that Den knew he would have to disentangle if he was to understand why Sean had died.

There were certain tenets that he'd imbibed with his early training, which he knew better than to ignore. *Motivation for murder very often goes back a long way*, for example. That one seemed of primary importance in this inquiry.

Never assume that married couples are faithful or children legitimate. Experience had already taught him this as a firm maxim to keep in mind.

The oddest things acquire major significance for people. Not just money, but politics, status, self-image, religious belief. People could kill someone for offending them, or making them look stupid. 'O, I have lost my reputation, I have lost the immortal part of myself, and what remains is bestial.' *Exactly*, thought Den. In a tight-knit rural community, loss of face could be worse than losing property or money. If you risked becoming a laughing stock, you might well kill to avert such a fate.

Doggedly, he set off for work, walking the quarter-mile from home to police station. Shortly before Lilah left him, they'd been making definite plans to move into a new house during the coming spring. For a week or so after their separation, Den had wanted to get away quickly, to escape the memories and the aborted dreams. But he hadn't been able to do it. He found he wasn't capable of making the decision by himself. He kept expecting to discover that the whole thing was a silly mistake and Lilah would come back one day, grinning sheepishly. What if he moved to somewhere she didn't like? Easier and safer to stay where he was for a few more months.

There was little sign of a buzzing murder investigation at the police station. A phone was ringing and a printer chuntering in the first office he passed, but no sign of tension or urgency in the general atmosphere. As murder investigations went, this one was attracting very little excitement. Everyone knew that the chances of a successful prosecution depended largely on forensic findings. The case against Hillcock might be circumstantially strong, but would never be enough without something concrete to back it up.

Danny was in his office, on the phone. 'The Super,' he mouthed at Den. He jotted something on a pad. 'Very much so, sir. I think that's absolutely right.' After another few phrases of unconditional concurrence, he rang off.

'He says we should concentrate more on motive,' he told Den. 'Give Forensics time to get all their results together, and hope we arrive at a coherent picture between us.'

'It's *got* to be him,' Den insisted, half sitting on the desk. 'The only other man on the place is Ted Speedwell and he's a little mouse of a chap.'

'Could have been a woman. I've been reading the pathology report again. There's one theory that the victim could have been pushed over and attacked while on his back. Wouldn't take much force to do the damage, then. Think how easy it is to drive a fork into your own foot. With gravity on your side, anyone of any normal strength could have done it.'

'A kid?'

'Teenager, anyway, yes. Can't rule anybody out, as far as I can see.'

'Please don't tell me it could have been a hundred-and-one-year-old granny.'

Danny grinned. 'I think we can safely eliminate her.'

'What about O'Farrell's wife? She's pretty fragile.'

Danny shrugged. 'We should get a medical opinion on her. She was on the spot, and—'

'I know,' Den interrupted. 'The vast majority

of murders are committed by someone in the family. But everyone at Dunsworthy is part of a big extended family, effectively. They've all lived there for decades.'

The Inspector made two fists and knocked them gently together as he mustered his thoughts. 'You're saying O'Farrell and Hillcock were like brothers?'

'Not quite,' Den corrected. 'None of the Hillcocks are acting as if they've lost a brother or a son. As far as I can see, the only person who cares a hoot about him is his daughter, young Abigail.'

'People to interview, Cooper,' said Hemsley, pushing himself up from his seat. 'Neighbours, relatives. Get the big picture.'

Den forced himself to relax and let Hemsley take charge. His own uncomfortable position was making him edgy, waiting for accusations that might never come. There were bound to be suspicions that he was too close to the people involved, but this was rural Devon, where Den had lived all his life, and if he were always to avoid cases involving people he knew, he'd be condemned for ever to some dull ghetto of farm subsidy swindles. In an ideal world, with infinite resources and total integrity, doubtless he would be taken off the case. As it was, the Devon Constabulary had little choice but to use him for the work he did best. Either that, or insist he transfer to another force altogether, somewhere else in the country.

It took Danny five minutes to round up Mike and DC Jane Nugent. Den spent the time rereading the entire forensic report. Eventally they adjourned to the larger briefing room and settled themselves into the square plastic-seated chairs.

The Inspector gave a brief summary of his exchange with Den and then recounted all the salient points of the investigation. 'I've made a few enquiries myself,' he revealed. 'And I can tell you that there's a chap called Fred Page, unpopular local farmer. Keeps some very nasty dogs. There've been complaints. One individual, by the name of Brewster, has a reputation all of his own. Kills cats for fun, apparently. The significance of this is that Fred Page and Sean O'Farrell were mates, by all accounts. So keep an eye out for anything there. Cruelty to animals is a big issue these days. It might sound over-dramatic, but it's a viable motive for killing.'

'Are you suggesting anything in particular, sir?' asked Young Mike.

'No speculation, Smithson. Just keep it in mind, okay?'

Mike nodded.

'Cooper and I were going over the pathology

and forensic reports, and we think there's a chance the attack could have come from a woman or even a sturdy youngster.'

'Do you mean Mrs Watson?' Mike demanded.

'Among others. Would you describe Mrs Watson's manner on Tuesday for us again, lad? Just to refresh our memories.'

Mike gulped. 'She was very much in control. No signs of shock. She called the death in, initially, and she gathered up all her pots and papers very efficiently. Didn't drop a single thing.'

'That's good, Constable. Very well observed,' said the DI.

'And she did have the opportunity,' added Mike, more boldly. 'If Hillcock was in the house, or doing something in a cowshed, she could have gone out into the yard and attacked O'Farrell before they started milking.'

Den could not quite stifle the gurgle of protest that rose up in his throat. 'Sorry, sir,' he said meekly. 'I just don't see it, that's all. I do agree it's theoretically possible,' he added dutifully.

'It's on file that Mrs Watson and Gordon Hillcock have known each other most of their lives. That makes her interesting.'

'You mean . . .' Mike bounced irrepressibly, 'O'Farrell might have seen them together and threatened to tell her old man?'

'I mean, Smithson, that if and when it comes

to establishing a motive, the lady's feelings for Mr Hillcock might just turn out to be significant,' Hemsley said firmly. 'Meanwhile, I repeat – we're a long way from closure here. It could still be just about anyone.'

'Except Granny Hillcock,' Den muttered. Only Mike laughed.

'Sir,' put in Nugent, 'nobody's said anything about concealing the body, have they?' She looked round the room invitingly. Nobody replied. 'I mean, why didn't the killer try to hide the body?'

'Cooper?' Hemsley invited.

'Several possibilities, sir. That little barn might have seemed like a reasonable hiding place, in the short term. Even the gathering yard is out of sight from most directions. Full of cows, in poor light, the body wouldn't have been seen if it was left out there. We don't know whether O'Farrell got himself into the barn, or if the killer dragged him there. Forensics think, on balance, that he got there by himself. His back showed none of the abrasions you might get from dragging.'

'Very thorough, Cooper,' said Hemsley carelessly. 'Now, it's this milk recorder woman that interests me, as I might already have suggested. She's been to that farm every month for five years. She's seen those two men having their disagreements. I dare say she took sides, and I wouldn't expect it to be O'Farrell's.'

'We know she preferred Hillcock,' said Den. 'Is that suspicious, sir?'

'I didn't say it was suspicious. I'm just saying it's interesting.' Without waiting for further comment, he moved towards the door, still talking, not looking at any of them. 'Another bit of gossip I gleaned yesterday – Hillcock's reputation with women. They might not all approve of him, but they're bloody attracted to him. Most of them drool at the mention of his name. I doubt if the Watson woman is any exception. Sorry, Cooper, I know this is sensitive for you, but you'll confirm the point, I think.'

Den gave a neutral nod.

'So, that's enough for one morning. Keep at it, and keep each other posted – as well as me.'

Den stood up. He'd keep at it all right, even though he knew it was all for nothing. Hillcock had killed O'Farrell. It was blindingly, screamingly obvious.

CHAPTER TWELVE

Den spent a frustrating afternoon on Thursday. He caught the Inspector early, knowing there'd be little new material to talk about, but eager to make a good impression and to provide further proof that he wasn't pursuing a vendetta against Hillcock.

He began by returning to the topic of the morning meeting. 'If O'Farrell was on his back, how did he manage to get up and into the barn where they found him? Assuming he wasn't dragged. Surely he'd be too badly hurt to get there himself?'

Danny rubbed the back of his thick neck. 'Not necessarily; haven't we been over this? There was a period – a minute or two – between the rupture of the aorta and loss of consciousness.'

'I wonder,' Den mused, 'whether the attacker thought he'd done much less damage than he actually had? Then, if O'Farrell was actually getting up again, seeming not too badly hurt, whoever-it-was left him in the yard, thinking he'd get home and call a doctor or something.'

The two detectives fell silent for a moment, trying to work out the permutations consistent with the forensic report. 'And what was he doing there, anyway, if it was his afternoon off?' Hemsley added.

'Apparently he didn't properly regard it as an afternoon off. It was just that Hillcock had swapped milkings. Mrs O'Farrell said she assumed there were things he had to do around the yard.'

'What things?' demanded Hemsley.

'I don't know,' Den admitted. 'She suggested he might have been chopping logs, but we found no evidence of that.'

'And why did he make for that barn? Why not go to the house for help?'

'Ah,' said Den triumphantly, 'I think I worked that one out. There's a phone in the farm office and the quickest way to reach it would be through that barn. It has a door that opens onto the milking parlour and from there it's only a few feet to the office. I'll have to draw it for you,' he smiled, noting Hemsley's frown.

'I'll take your word for it. So he staggers into the barn, closes the door behind him, and collapses into the straw. All just a few feet from where the recorder was working in the office before milking started. Wouldn't she have heard him?'

'Thick cob walls round the barn, sir,' Den offered. 'And he might have been too far gone by then to cry out.'

The Inspector scratched one ear. 'Hypothetical, of course, but it sounds all right to me,' he concluded. 'Now, have we finished?'

'There is something else,' said Den conscientiously. 'Mary Hillcock told me Mrs Watson put in a complaint about O'Farrell's treatment of his cows. I should have mentioned it during the briefing.'

'When?'

'Nearly five years ago. She'd only recently started as the recorder at Dunsworthy.'

Hemsley considered. 'Suggests there'd have been animosity between them, but he'd have been the one with the grievance, not her. And it's too long ago, surely, for us to worry about?'

'That's what I thought,' Den nodded.

'Look, there'll be another briefing in a little while. We'll sort out exactly where everybody was on Tuesday afternoon and how convincingly they can prove it. In effect, the Watson woman and Hillcock are covering for each other, aren't they? They're the only two people we know for sure were on the spot at the time in question. And there's some sort of history between them.'

Den didn't respond. It was Hemsley's habit to keep going over old ground and Den had learnt not to encourage him. He was already suffering from a strong sense of stuckness, which was not helped by the DI's repetitions. Neither did he much like his superior's growing interest in Deirdre Watson. He waited quietly for whatever might come next.

'You spent yesterday afternoon in the milking parlour with Gordon Hillcock – how was it?'

'Uncomfortable,' Den admitted. 'Claustrophobic.'

'As I expected,' Danny nodded. 'Intimate, even? Just the two of you enclosed by all those cows, and the noise and everything getting dark outside. Am I right?'

Den stared at him. 'Exactly right. How did you know?'

The DI shrugged. 'I've got an uncle who runs a herd of Jerseys. Used to spend a week or two there most summers.' He matched Den's stare with one of his own. 'And this woman – is she attractive? She's no great age, I see.'

Den wanted to shout, *But Hillcock is screwing Lilah – not the milk recorder! This is nothing to do with it!* 'She's nothing special. A bit on the heavy side,' he said. 'I really don't think . . .'

'You're probably right. But we should take a look, all the same.'

Den shuddered. 'I can't believe a woman would have done it,' he muttered.

'You mean you don't *want* to believe it,' Danny corrected him. 'But I promise you, it's a possibility. Especially if she thought her own life depended on it.'

'Self-defence?' Here was another angle that Den had scarcely considered. 'But there was no other weapon. Nothing Sean might have used to hurt anyone.'

'Other than the fork,' Danny reminded him. 'With Sean's fingerprints on it. We don't know whether he had it first and the other person snatched it off him. Or he had something else, and the killer took it away with them, for disposal where no one would find it.'

Den was careful to appear open-minded; he pursed his lips and nodded slightly. 'Could be,' he said. It sounded like a flight of fancy to him.

'So – we meet in the briefing room at nine-thirty tomorrow – okay? We'll sift through the alibis and get Mike and Jane to check them all. If nothing else emerges, I suggest you go for another nice long chat with your milk recorder friend.'

Den knew better than to protest at the implication.

* * *

Deirdre reached home five minutes late, to find her daughter standing impatiently on the path up to the house. She was hugging herself in the hopelessly inadequate garment she used for a coat, and dancing on the spot. Before Deirdre could fully stop, Sam had run to the car and jumped in.

'For God's sake, Mum. I'll be late for third lesson,' was all she said.

'Too bad,' Deirdre snapped back. 'I warned you I couldn't be certain of getting back in time.'

'Well, I'm not going to freeze to death waiting for the bus. It's been late every day this term.'

'So they won't be surprised if you're late again today, will they?'

Sam grunted something inarticulate, and Deirdre left a few minutes' silence before trying again. 'I hear you've got a new boyfriend.'

'*Boyfriend*,' the girl sneered. 'He's not my *boyfriend*.'

'Well, whatever he is, I'm interested to know about him. Jeremy something, right?'

'Right. And before you say anything, yes, he is related to Fred Page. That's his dad, as it happens.'

'Bloody hell, Sam.' Deirdre couldn't stop herself. 'That man's a monster. He's deranged. You should see the way he is with cows.'

'Well, Jeremy's not like that. Not at all. He's

with us in the protest group, if you must know. He was the first to give a cheer when we heard Sean O'Farrell's been killed. Oh yes – and thanks for keeping me informed,' she added sarcastically. 'I felt a right idiot yesterday when the police had to tell me about it.'

'What? When?'

'We were in the Limediggers at dinner time.'

'For Christ's sake – you're meant to be at *school*, not trekking round the countryside to sit in pubs. How did you get there?'

'In Jez's car, if you must know. And I didn't miss any lessons. Never mind that – why didn't you tell me about it?'

'I didn't really feel up to it. It would have brought it all back and I was trying to put it out of my mind. Anyway, what were you saying about raising a cheer about Sean?'

'Keep up, Mum. Fred Page and Sean O'Farrell are the main anti-badger blokes. *Were*, I should say. They've been lamping them for months now.'

'Nasty,' was all Deirdre would allow herself to say to that. But her thoughts were galloping. 'I hope Jeremy's not getting himself into trouble – or you, come to that.'

The girl didn't bother to respond. Deirdre chewed her lower lip. 'Did the police ask for your names?' she said, after a short silence.

'They did, yeah. It was the tall chap – the

one Lilah Beardon used to be engaged to. You probably don't know Lilah Beardon. She's got a brother, Roddy, in the year above me. He left last summer.'

'I know her now – she did the milking yesterday morning when I was there.'

'Small world,' said Sam drily. 'Pity the poor police people, trying to work it all out. They ought to ask you to help them. I bet you know all the farmers and their rotten little secrets, don't you?'

Deirdre ignored the challenge, putting her foot down for the last mile into town. She was hungry, thirsty and irritable. She had no reason for going into town and the round trip was going to take forty minutes at least. 'Tomorrow you can jolly well get the bus,' she said, as she drew up at the school gate. 'Or get your precious Jeremy to ferry you around.'

'Thanks, Ma, I love you too,' said the girl, as she slammed the door.

Mary Hillcock slumped dramatically into one of the sagging chairs in the staff room at the start of the mid-morning break. 'Coffee,' she begged. 'Someone fetch me a coffee. I've just been asked by Peter Stevens, arch-wit of Year Eight, whether they're going to hang my brother or put him in the electric chair!'

Nobody moved to get the requested coffee. The room was hot and stuffy, the heating in the whole school turned well up against the January chill. Except the chill had given way to something much milder, while the heating persisted relentlessly in driving up the temperature. Five other teachers were present. They all exchanged glances and raised eyebrows, but said nothing.

'Hey!' Mary protested. 'Is this a conspiracy? Guilt by association? Well, blow you, then.' She heaved herself up and went to the kettle on a shelf in the corner. There was enough hot water in it for half a mug of coffee and she contented herself with that, carrying the drink back to her chair.

'They haven't got any real case against Gordon, you know,' she continued, facing her silent accusers. 'You're all reacting to gossip, the same as the kids. Nobody knows what really did happen to Sean.'

'Except that he's dead,' said Teresa Franklin, the newest and youngest member of the staff. 'And not by accident.'

'Even that hasn't been demonstrated for certain,' Mary argued. 'Farms are full of dangerous implements—'

'Come off it,' put in Gillian Dee. 'You don't get police crawling all over your yard and putting up all that tape for an accident.' Gillian Dee's husband was the Unigate tanker driver, who'd done more than anyone to spread the news of events on Dunsworthy Farm.

Mary sighed. 'You're right, of course. But why take it out on me?' She glared at them all again. 'You're like a Wild West mob, looking for someone to lynch.'

'We just want justice,' Teresa mumbled. 'That's all.'

'And what would *justice* consist of, exactly?' Mary challenged her. The concerted hostility of her colleagues was unexpected and upsetting. Never inclined to submit herself to anything unpleasant, Mary was shaking with the effort of standing up for her brother. She had assumed the news of Sean's death would have got round in a couple of days, perhaps with the added angle of Gordon's being taken in for questioning. She'd also assumed that the general reaction would be one of concern, even sympathy, for Gordon's relatives. One assumption was right and the other badly wrong, she was now discovering.

'There's only one person under suspicion,' said Teresa.

'You mean Gordon? Well, why don't you have a nice chat about it to young Peter Stevens? Shall we hang my brother or put him in the electric chair?' Her voice was rising to a shrill note, close to breaking into tears. 'I never thought—'

she choked on the words. 'You don't even *know* Gordon, any of you. You're just letting gossip control you. The justice of the lynch mob,' she finished with a glare at Teresa.

'You don't understand,' Gillian Dee put in calmly. 'This is a school and we're under the scrutiny of the children and their parents. Any suggestion of something criminal or violent connected with a teacher gets blown up – maybe out of proportion, but if the children are asking you questions like the one you've just told us about, then that's a serious matter. Do you see? We have a duty to shield them from this sort of event – and here you are, large as life, apparently thinking everything can carry on as usual.'

'Of course it can carry on as usual,' said Mary, sitting up straighter. 'What else can we do?'

Nobody spoke, and Mary felt a chill of real apprehension wash through her. She swept the room with a worried glance. 'What? You want me to stay at home? Just because our herdsman's been killed? This is absolutely unreasonable, don't you see that?'

'It's for Rachael to say, of course,' Gillian pronounced. 'She's the Head; she'll have to do what she thinks best for the school.'

'If she tries to suspend me, I'll take it to arbitration,' Mary said emphatically. 'And there is *no way* she'd get away with it.' She slammed her mug down on the unsteady table beside her and stood up. For a moment she didn't move, standing tall, looking defiantly at each face in turn. It was several seconds before she was aware that her anger was not, after all, directed at her fellow teachers. The person she felt really furious with was Sean O'Farrell.

For Den it was turning into one of those scrappy, wasted days when nothing gets accomplished. He was sitting with Young Mike, going through lists of names, times, relationships, assessing where they most needed to turn their attention now.

'Local farmers?' Mike suggested. 'Any of them could have had a quarrel with O'Farrell. And what about the Speedwell son? You've put a query over him, look.'

Den murmured a half-hearted agreement. More than ever he felt these peripheral enquiries were just a waste of time and effort. If it hadn't been for his unfortunate connection to Hillcock, he was sure Danny would never have ordered such extensive investigations. But in spite of himself, his curiosity about Sean was growing. There was something bleak about the man, signalled by the lack of mourning over his death. Eliot Speedwell had been his friend, according to Mary Hillcock. Perhaps he at least would show some grief.

'He works at the pasty factory – I don't know what he does there,' Den mused. 'I don't like to tackle people at work – it only leads to gossip. And I don't know about you, but I'm planning on spending this evening at home with my feet up. There'll be weekend work on this, the way it's going. I vote we leave young Speedwell till then. Tomorrow evening, if Danny gets agitated, otherwise Saturday morning.'

Mike shrugged. 'You're the boss,' he said easily. 'So where to next?'

Den fingered his chin meditatively. 'I want to give Dunsworthy itself a rest. Let Hillcock think we're off on some other scent. It's not going to do any good just repeating the same questions.' He closed his mind to the deep reluctance he felt at the prospect of setting foot again on the farm, thereby risking another encounter with Lilah. He felt her presence all over Dunsworthy, even if he didn't meet her in the flesh.

'Has anyone run a check on sightings of strangers, vagrants, travellers, ramblers?' he asked. 'Weren't they sending out a couple of uniforms to sniff round for that sort of thing?'

'It'll be in the file,' Mike pointed out, nudging the collection of papers on the desk between them. Den flipped slowly through them all, right down to the bottom. His own notes comprised a substantial portion, but the forensic findings did their bit to pad it out.

'Can't see anything,' he concluded, sitting back slackly in the chair.

'Is this the second-day blues Nugent was talking about?' Mike asked him.

'What?'

'She says when there's a murder, everyone rushes round at fever pitch on the first day, taking statements, getting as much of the story as they can. It's all new territory then. But on the second day, it sometimes all seems to grind to a halt. Going over the same old ground for the third or fourth time, trying to pick up the inconsistencies. Compared to Day One, it all feels a bit futile.'

'That must be it,' Den agreed.

'So maybe we should try looking for inconsistencies?'

With a sigh, Den acquiesced. He fetched a large blank jotter pad from a shelf across the room, and took up his pen. 'Okay, let's start over again with the timings.' Together they listed the precise times of every movement as provided by the witnesses. Mike suddenly stabbed the pad forcefully with his forefinger.

'Surely it can't be credible that Hillcock never saw Sean at all, when he went back to the yard after his dinner? I know we asked him about it, and I know all that about the place being like a maze with all the buildings. Even so, unless the man was deliberately hiding from his boss, I can't see how they'd miss each other.'

Den sighed. 'It was only an hour or less. I think if Hillcock insists he never saw Sean, we can't hope to prove that he did. He says O'Farrell had his routines and was pretty much left to get on with them. Hillcock didn't keep tabs on him.'

'Can we go through the actual attack again?' Mike suggested doggedly. 'Now we've got all this forensic stuff.'

Den slumped. 'I already had a long talk with the DI about it. He agrees that it could conceivably have been someone relatively weak – a woman or a teenager, if Sean slipped onto his back. It was icy, remember, as well as mucky. It looks as if the bleeding was mainly from the first set of injuries, the lower ones.' He couldn't resist demonstrating his newfound medical knowledge. 'Although the aorta is the body's main artery and any rupture leads to extremely rapid loss of blood, it doesn't always spurt out of the body like it does from other arteries. The reason the upper set didn't bleed so much was that his circulation was already slowing down, from the first injuries, which would have been the more painful part.'

Mike looked confused. 'So?'

'So I visualise him writhing about after the

first jab, probably on the ground. Then the attacker drove the fork into him again, higher up and deeper in. And that was the killer blow.'

'And? How the hell did he then get up and reach the barn?'

'Sheer willpower, probably. His hands and legs weren't especially mucky, which suggests he walked, rather than crawled. It's not far.'

Mike seemed unconvinced. 'And the fork was found in one of the sheds running at an angle from the house?'

Den nodded. 'Just thrown down for anyone to find. Wooden handle, greasy and cracked. Speedwell and O'Farrell's finger and palm prints all over it. Nothing to link it with Hillcock.'

'He might have been wearing gloves. It was cold,' Mike said.

'True.'

'I wonder about young Abigail,' Mike went on. 'Don't ask me why, when it seems so daft. She was obviously upset about her dad. Although, in the car yesterday, she seemed different. She hardly said a word, just stared out of the window. I was surprised when we went back to the house and she was showing so much more feeling.'

'You think she was play-acting?'

'I think it's possible. For her mum's benefit, maybe.'

Den shook his head. 'She was just shocked, in the car. It's far too complicated to include her as a suspect. She'd have to have had some help with transport from Tavistock and back again. How could she do that without someone seeing her? We know she was at school that afternoon, anyway, so it absolutely doesn't work.'

'School finishes at three-thirty. She could have got a ride home and be there by four easily; do the deed and off again to Gary's house with nobody the wiser.'

'Except for the person who drove her. They'd have to be an accomplice. And four is too late.'

'Okay – so maybe she can drive and borrowed a car from somewhere earlier. She lives on a farm, around tractors and quad bikes and stuff. I bet she can work a motor, no trouble.'

Den nodded tightly. *Keep an open mind*, he told himself.

They ploughed on, going over the same reports again and then one more time. By then it was half past four and time to wind down for the day.

Lilah did not go to Dunsworthy that day. She had an essay to finish, and forced herself to spend the morning on it. Carefully drawing comparisons between the soil composition of nitrogen-saturated Devon fields, and that of subsistence-farmed southern India, she let a significant part of her mind address the task of rescuing Gordon from prosecution for murder.

The first small steps had been taken towards the execution of her plan, but there was much more to be done yet. Her three-year relationship with Den had given her invaluable knowledge that she now had every intention of exploiting for her own purposes. If she could just find a way of directing the police to the first link in the chain of reasoning that she wanted them to follow . . . a chain of reasoning that was so compelling, anyone noticing it was sure to believe it was true. If she could only be sure that they would listen to her, she would simply phone them and state her case. As it was, she'd have to be more devious.

Thinking about Den was only tenable if she focused on his failings: his habits and hesitancies, which had become so easy to predict. His anxiety to avoid hasty judgements, his inability to live for the moment: all qualities that led to a good policeman, no doubt, but not to a thrilling lover. *Thank goodness I escaped when I did*, she thought, for the thousandth time. Gordon was incomparably better in bed. *And I love him*, she silently shouted. She was in love, body and soul, for better or for worse. This stupid murder was a mere hiccup in their relationship; something sent to test them. And Lilah was growing increasingly sure she could direct the police to the real killer.

Mary Hillcock drove herself home that day, because Claudia was scheduled for the evening counselling session, as well as a case discussion with the rest of the Relate team. The car would get twenty minutes' rest before it was needed again – more, given the speed at which Mary was driving.

The day had not improved since the episode with Peter Stevens and the lack of sympathy in the staffroom. Having become sensitised to her role as sister to a murderer, it had seemed that everyone was watching her warily. *As if I'd caught something*, she thought. And although there had been no contact from the Head, and therefore no formal repetition of the suggestion that the school might be better off without her for a while, the idea continued to niggle.

It was her habit to drive fast when she was in a bad mood. How she had survived the months surrounding her separation and divorce from Mark Fordyce, she never knew. It had been summer at the time and only too often she had swerved recklessly in and out of streams of holiday traffic, completely impervious to horns and angry snarls.

She reached Dunsworthy with her anger still simmering and slammed out of the car, having left it untidily in the yard. The relentless throbbing of the milking machine told her that Gordon had started promptly, which further annoyed her – this time on her brother's behalf. Without Sean, he would have to do the work of herdsman in the inexorable twice-daily routine until someone could be found to replace the murdered man. Which alone, she thought defiantly, was sufficient proof that Gordon was innocent. He would never be such a fool as to kill the worker he depended on.

Her mother was nowhere to be seen, the house silent and dark. Granny would be upstairs, as always, but Mary's mood was not so dark that she was tempted to dump it on the old lady. Ten or fifteen years ago, that would have been the instinctive thing to do. Granny had always been there, ready to listen and click her teeth over her granddaughter's tales of treacherous friends or unkind teachers. She'd rummage in her deep old cake tin and come up with flapjack or rock cake as the universal panacea. 'No wonder Mary's getting so fat,' Claudia would say, if she caught them. 'Stuffing her full of cakes as you do.'

But Granny was too old now to be of much comfort. She was a marvel for her age, and could be wickedly funny at times, but it was no longer possible to get her to follow a logical narrative thread.

Mary and Gordon had both been stunned when their mother had announced her intention to apply for counsellor training. 'She's just about the last person I'd have thought would be any good at that,' Gordon had said to his sister, and Mary had agreed with him. But they'd been wrong. Claudia had become very much more balanced and confident as the training progressed. She had even admitted that she'd finally realised what a poor mother she'd been to them in the early years. 'It's probably too late to make up for it now,' she said. 'But at least I won't run away from problems like I used to.'

Mary and Gordon had been dubious, but it turned out that their mother had in fact become better company since then. She listened, sympathised, even offered constructive suggestions whenever difficulties arose. But many of the old habits persisted: and in this current crisis, Mary still could not summon the necessary trust in her mother to completely confide in her.

And anyway, where *was* Claudia? She was supposed to be leaving in fifteen minutes and there was no sign of her. 'Mum?' Mary called, investigating first the sitting room and then the rooms at the back of the house, known to the family as 'Daddy's Room' and 'The Dairy'. Neither was much used, though Gordon kept a lot of farm records in the former, and Claudia had adopted the latter as a study in which to write up her counselling notes, cool and damp though it was.

There was no answer. A flicker of anxiety made itself felt in Mary's stomach and she mounted the stairs in further pursuit. The most likely explanation was that Claudia was sitting with Granny, probably over a cup of tea. But there was no sound of voices coming from Granny's room. With her usual half-knock, Mary opened the door and peered in. Her grandmother was in the chair by the window, a standard lamp lit beside her. She was reading – or looking at the pictures – from a heavy book she often favoured. *A Young Person's Illustrated Treasure House*, produced in the 1880s, had somehow survived, along with its owner, and had now become a kind of Bible. Its aura was unmistakable, every picture and page imbued with familiarity and nostalgia. Mary could only guess at the memories and associations it conjured in the old lady's mind, but she always liked to see it in place on her lap.

'Have you seen Mum?' she asked, as Granny looked up.

The question was ill-considered. 'Mum?' Granny repeated. 'I haven't seen Mum for a long, long time.'

'Never mind then. Sorry I bothered you.' And she left quickly, going into her own room to change her clothes and to wonder again where Claudia might have got to.

A shout from outside made her jerk her head up, as she fastened the button on her cord trousers. A man's voice that could only be Gordon's was yelling inarticulately. Nobody seemed to be responding, so Mary, from age-old habit, went running downstairs to see what was required. She might not have been actively involved in the animals or the crops for some years now, but it was never going to be possible to ignore such a call when it came.

The nearer part of the yard was lit by the outside light on the corner of the house, and another pool of illumination lit the area around the milking parlour. In between were shadows and slippery mud. 'What's the matter?' she shouted from the doorway, unable to see anybody. She had grabbed a pair of boots from the front porch, where assorted footwear had accumulated for years, and was thrusting her feet into them.

'Mary!' came Claudia's high voice from the calf shed, down on Mary's right. 'Come here, will you?'

Mary obeyed. 'Where's Gordon?' she called, as she got closer to the shed. 'I heard him shouting. What's going on?'

The shed was partitioned into four small pens, each containing a young female calf, leaving a larger area for fodder, buckets, rolls of wire, tools – the normal paraphernalia that littered every farm building. Gordon was poking in a corner with a stick, swearing frustratedly, while his mother hovered behind him.

'It's a badger!' Claudia said shrilly. 'I saw it in the yard, and went to tell Gordon. He chased it in here.'

Gordon turned on her furiously. 'If it's come into the buildings, it must be diseased. If the cattle get anywhere near it, we're totally in the shit. Go and get my gun, will you? I'll have to shoot the bloody thing.' Then he clapped a furious hand to his head. 'Bugger it – the police have taken it,' he remembered.

'Your father's is still in the case under his desk,' Claudia said coolly. 'We forgot to tell them about that one. If you're really sure about this—'

'Yes, yes, fetch it,' he snapped to Mary.

'But . . . the milking . . .' Mary hesitated, the sound of the motor in the parlour still throbbing across the yard. 'You haven't finished, have you?'

'That can wait,' he blazed at her. 'Do as I tell you.' He jabbed his stick into the gap between a sturdy cast-iron beet chopper and a pile of paper sacks full of sand. The low growl of a creature in pain or distress was the response.

Mary lifted her chin. 'Just the gun, or a box of cartridges as well? And Ma – you're going to be late for work if you don't go in about two minutes.'

'Gun and cartridges,' Gordon grated, as Claudia squawked and started to leave the shed.

The women went into the house together, separating at the foot of the stairs. 'Ma?' Mary stopped her mother as a thought struck her. 'What were you doing out there in the first place?'

'What? Oh, I just wanted to have a talk with Gordon, and I knew he'd try to avoid me if I waited until he was in the house. So I decided to tackle him while he was milking and couldn't get away.'

'I see,' said Mary with a frown. 'Well, don't tell me about it now. And mind how you drive. I'd better help him finish off that wretched badger, poor thing. Except they're protected, aren't they? And surely they're not really such a threat to the cows? Do you think he knows what he's doing?'

'He went mad when he saw it, chasing it

across the yard and yelling his head off. Must be stress over the Sean business, I suppose. Normally, he'd be the first to give the thing the benefit of the doubt. He's not his normal self at all.'

The gun was kept unloaded in a wooden box in Daddy's Room. Cartridges were in a drawer of the desk. She had no doubt they'd all genuinely forgotten about it when the police asked about firearms. Gordon had his own newer one, never having cause to use Daddy's. Mary had been enthusiastic about shooting in her teens and had always taken on the job of cleaning the gun for her father. Handling it confidently, she went back to Gordon and his prey.

'Torch!' he ordered, as he loaded the shotgun. Mary hurried back yet again to the house, uncomplaining, her head full of partly-answered questions and slowly growing suspicions.

The badger died quickly, but not before giving a heart-stopping scream of rage and pain, the sound merging into the shattering explosion of the gunshot in the enclosed space. Gordon left it a moment and then thrust his hand into the gap and pulled out the bloodied body. 'Doesn't look old or diseased to me,' said Mary mildly. 'Seems rather a fine specimen.' The strong alien smell of the animal filled their nostrils, hinting at a secret other-world existence, disturbing and somehow shocking. Mary closed her mind to the way it had died.

Gordon threw it out into the yard, with an effort. It was a dense, heavy body. Then he handed her the gun. 'Time I got back to the cows,' he muttered.

CHAPTER THIRTEEN

Heather and Abigail O'Farrell cared no less than Lilah or Den about the solution to the mystery of who had killed their husband and father. But their need to know the truth was diluted by the change wrought on their daily lives. Abigail had ridden home on the school bus, for once, instead of hanging around in town and then cadging a lift from her boyfriend, surprising her mother by arriving at four-fifteen. She came in through the back door, having first visited her collection of animals and topped up their food and water pots.

'Fallen out with Gary?' Heather asked, looking up from her chair by the fire and displaying little curiosity.

'No,' said the girl with a scowl. 'Of course I haven't.'

'So how come you're so early?'

Abigail's shoulders drooped and she flung her schoolbag violently onto the sofa. 'I had to see to the animals. And I'm starving. Is there any food in the house?'

'Eggs. Jilly brought them for us. And a few other things. She went to Tesco on the way home from work.'

'Good for her. Is she going to do that every day?'

Heather shivered, a habitual reaction to difficult questions. Abigail knew better than to assume she was cold. 'Well?' she insisted. 'Is she?'

'I don't expect so,' managed her mother, in a little-girl voice.

'You'll have to do it then, won't you? You'll have to drive to the shop and buy food. Otherwise we'll starve. You'll have to cook it sometimes, as well, because I won't be here all the time. For a start, I'm going to Glastonbury this year. You and Dad both said I could.'

'That's not till June, Abby. I'll be back on my feet by then.'

'Are you sure? How many years is it now? I was ten – I know that much. So long ago that I've forgotten what it was like to have a normal mother. And now you've decided to get better at last, have you? Great! Pity Dad won't be here to see it, though.'

'I hate it as much as you do,' Heather said, her voice suddenly very much stronger. 'I often think you don't believe that. Do you think I'm just pretending to be so weak and tired all the time?'

'Who cares what I think?'

'There's just us now.' Heather's tone was decisive, different from her usual whine. 'We shouldn't be fighting. I will try to get better, honestly. And I won't stop you going away with your friends.' She began to get out of the chair. 'I'll even scramble those eggs for us – how about that!'

Abigail watched her mother stand up and fold the rug that had been over her knees. Her hands shook and she shuffled her feet like a woman of ninety. It was dreadful to see, but the girl forced herself to resist the urge to help. There were days when her mother's back hurt, sending sharp pains in all directions; days when she could hardly lift her arms to change her clothes; days when her head ached and her vision swam. But officially there was nothing actually the matter with her and hadn't been for so many ghastly years, during which Sean had done all the housework, shopping and cooking and endured the disbelieving quips and comments that his acquaintances were prone to make. Abigail had watched her father distance himself emotionally from the situation, going through the daily routines like an automaton. He seldom even looked at his wife or spoke to her intimately. His conversation centred on logistics – whether he could go shopping as well as work a full day; whether Abby would be home for the evening meal or whether he'd have to drive a twenty-mile round trip to collect her from Gary's. No wonder she stayed in Tavistock overnight as often as she dared. Gary's mum didn't mind, so long as they weren't too noisy. She ran an off-licence, which stayed open in the evening, making it easy to keep out of her way. But Abigail had realised that she wouldn't be able to do that any more. Dad wasn't there to feed her animals. If she didn't get home, they'd go hungry.

But on the bus journey home that day, it had not been the rabbits and guinea pigs and badger and birds she'd been thinking about. It had been her mother and how much she wanted to be held in those weak white arms and kept safe.

'Have they said when I can go and see him?' she asked without warning. 'I hope you didn't think I'd just stop asking, because I won't. Everybody at school says I should be able to see him.'

'You haven't been talking to them all about it, have you?' Heather turned stiffly to face the girl. 'How could you do that?'

'How could I *not*? They all know what's

happened, and it's sick to try and pretend it hasn't. He was my father, for God's sake. It's not just some horrible dream.'

'The teachers should have told your friends not to say anything,' Heather insisted. 'Getting you upset for no reason.'

'No *reason*?' She stared at her mother in disbelief.

'I meant . . .' bleated Heather feebly. 'I don't know . . .'

'Anyway, they all say they'll come to his funeral, if they can get the day off school.'

'They will not. I won't invite them. They didn't even know him.'

'They did! Gary and Emma and Natalie and Matthew Watson – they all knew him. And some of the others.'

Heather was in the kitchen by this time, talking over her shoulder as she leant exhaustedly against a worktop, drained by the unaccustomed effort. 'Matthew Watson? Who's he?'

'He's in Year Eleven. His mother's the milk recorder. He came here when Gordon did that farm walk. The whole Watson family came.'

'What – the woman who was here on Tuesday when it happened?'

'I suppose so, yes. And Matthew came here that day it snowed before Christmas. Dad drove him home. That's how most of them know him.'

‘As a taxi driver,’ Heather scoffed breathlessly.

‘If you like.’ Not waiting to see whether her mother was actually capable of scrambling eggs, Abigail snatched up her discarded bag and clomped doggedly up the stairs to her room. Although it was impossible to admit it to her mother, she had come home expecting to have to prepare the meal, as her father would have done, washing it all up afterwards; then stoking the fire, feeding the cats, taking out the rubbish: all the household jobs that Heather professed herself incapable of performing. How much of the work would the woman suddenly find herself able to do, after all these years?

Instead of laying out her books in preparation for homework, she slumped on the bed, leaning against the pillows and staring sightlessly at the darkness beyond her window. It was true that she’d talked to her schoolmates about her dad’s murder. It was weird for Heather to think she’d do anything else. But she hadn’t told her mother everything her friends had said.

Natalie had started it. Her dad knew Eliot Speedwell and had been talking about the Dunsworthy news over supper. ‘He says there’s always been trouble brewing there,’ Natalie had confided to Abigail. ‘Like a time bomb waiting to go off, he said. But he never thought it would be Mr O’Farrell who got himself killed. Says it must have been worse than he thought. Says you'd be well off out of it, and you and your mum should try and get a new place to live before anything else happens.'

Abigail had wrapped her arms around herself in the chilly playground. 'He's talking rubbish,' she'd maintained. 'We don't want to move somewhere else.'

'You'll have to, Abby. The house went with your dad's job. Besides, you'll need to live close to shops and stuff, with your mum in the state she is.'

At that point Emma Pearson had joined in. Emma lived on the other side of the school's catchment area and knew none of the individuals concerned. 'Aren't you *scared* to go on living there?' she enquired, eyes wide with melodrama. 'I mean – there's a *murderer* somewhere close by! And with these dark evenings – I'd be *petrified*.'

Abigail blinked. All she'd been able to think of so far, when she'd been able to think at all, was the absence of her father and the urgent need to get a glimpse of his body. She wanted to write him a letter, telling him the things she'd never been able to say, but every time she thought about that, she felt tears prickling behind her eyes, and had to stop. The idea that she had anything to fear came as a complete revelation.

'So . . .' Emma prompted. 'Who d'you think did it then?'

That was too much for Abby. The dreaded tears had forced themselves into view, not so much from grief for her father as from an overwhelming sense of being under attack. She had shrunk away from her so-called friends, turning her back on them and trudging with bowed head to the girls' toilets, the only refuge she could think of.

'What d'you have to say that for?' Natalie was demanding of Emma, as Abby left them. 'Tactless cow.'

'Well . . .' Abby heard Emma start to defend herself, before she was even out of earshot.

Sitting on the closed lavatory seat, head in her hands, she'd tried to collect her thoughts. Clearly everyone found the fact that Sean had been murdered irresistibly exciting. They didn't notice or care that he was just as dead as if he'd had cancer. He was dead at thirty-eight, which even at her age, she knew to be ridiculously young. People often lived fifty years longer than that. Her own great-grandfather had recently died at eighty-nine, and old Granny Hillcock was past a hundred.

But, unlike her mother, Abby wasn't worried about how they were going to manage, or where they were going to live. Abigail was worried, more than anything, that people were going to find out just what a wicked man her father had actually been.

The gunshot and simultaneous scream came clearly through the evening air. Abigail heard it from her bedroom and instantly knew what had happened. She flew downstairs.

'Did you hear that?' she yelled at her mother.

Heather was standing at the cooker, head cocked, eyes staring. She nodded.

'Bodgy must have got out,' Abby howled. 'I can't have latched his door properly when I fed him. They've shot him!' Tears were spattered on her cheeks.

'But—' Heather couldn't get the words out fast enough. Her daughter was already running up the farm drive.

Stumbling in the dark, Abigail focused on the lights of the yard and house. The sharp bend in the drive meant the buildings were closer than the distance she actually had to travel. By day, she would have cut across the pasture instead of staying on track. But there was a wire fence and a ditch, impossible to negotiate in the dark.

Finally she arrived, panting and desperate. The milking machine was the only sound. Whirling round, she saw the milked cows slowly making their way back to their stalls for the night, a light on as always in the old lady's window.

It was bewildering: surely that scream had rung out only seconds before? How could everything be so quiet and ordinary already? The light mounted on the corner of the milking parlour was illuminating part of the yard, and she moved to the brighter area. The black-and-white striped head suddenly seemed to fill the entire frame of her gaze. She couldn't see anything else, couldn't understand how she'd missed it till then. Lying a yard or two from the door of a smaller barn, was her precious pet. The blood on the grey chest told the story in an instant. She knelt on the cold mud and stroked the warm fur. The front feet were crossed appealingly, the snout extended, the glazed eyes open. In a moment of hope, she ran her hand down the long curve of the back, to find the crooked break on the hind leg that had given Bodgy his limp. The knob of misaligned bone confirmed his identity, and she wailed aloud her grief and rage.

There was only one person who could have shot him. Without conscious thought, she got up and headed for the milking parlour.

Gordon was applying a unit to the udder of a cow, his back to the steps on which Abigail stood. She picked up a plastic pot of teat disinfectant and threw it at him. It caught him squarely on the back of the head.

Gordon and Abigail had never before confronted each other in anger. She had always known him as affable but uninvolved: the boss man, powerful and remote, with his restless succession of girlfriends and deepening worried frown as the farming industry seemed set on collapsing on top of him. Sean had warned her not to let him find out about her animals – the badger in particular. Badgers were a universally sore point on every level, and Abby's insistence on keeping Bodgy as a pet had already caused innumerable arguments.

'If he shows *any* sign of sickness, he's got to go,' Sean told her. 'And you're *never* to let him into any of the fields. And if anybody asks you, I never said you could have him. I thought you'd just got a few rabbits and the jackdaw – right?'

She'd nodded a casual assent and carried on as before.

Now Gordon had found the badger and shot him. And he was glaring at her, his face glowing with shock, one hand to the back of his head. He went on staring, as if his eyes were telling him something impossible.

'You shot my badger!' she screamed at him before he could utter a word. 'You're a monster, a *murderer!* I hate you!' The words were much

too inadequate for what she was feeling. She jumped down the steps and hurled herself at him, fists flailing. The cows in their herringbone stalls shifted uneasily, unable to turn their heads to see what the noise was about.

Gordon grabbed her forearms in hands that felt like mechanical crushers. 'Stop it!' he ordered, his face an inch from hers. 'Behave yourself.' His eyes, glittering dangerously, stared into hers. They seemed to be spilling over with pain and anger and a near loss of control. She withdrew, pulling back against his grip, alarmed most of all by the naked suffering she could see in his face. Surely the missile hadn't hurt his head that much? She hoped it had, of course she did. It would serve him right. But she didn't like having to watch the consequences.

They stood there for a long moment. A unit detached itself from a cow, swinging out and missing Abigail's shoulder by half an inch; she flinched. Gordon relaxed his hold on her and took a deep, shuddering breath. 'Who said you could keep a pet badger?' he demanded. 'And how was I to know it was yours? Don't you have any idea how I feel about the creatures? I had ten reactors to the TB test this morning. Ten!' he shouted. 'They've all got to be destroyed, and it's all because of badgers.'

'Badgers don't give TB to cows,' she snarled

into his face. 'That's just stupid. I would have thought you'd have more sense than to believe that rubbish.'

'Oh and you know all about it, do you?'

'More than you do.' She shook with the passion of her certainty, and the thrill of telling Mr Hillcock, the boss, just what she thought.

But he didn't look as if he was listening. He seemed to be concentrating on something inside his own head, his eyes still fixed on hers, but flickering now. His mouth even twitched at the sides in a tiny smile that wasn't friendly or forgiving, but spoke of a connection that gave him pause.

'How was I to know it was yours?' he repeated, more quietly. 'How do we ever know what's ours?' he added, more obscurely. She knew then he'd regained mastery of himself; he wouldn't hurt her now. And she realised too that she no longer wanted to hurt him, either. The atmosphere had become too terribly sad for the trivia of fisticuffs. She pulled right away from him, and he let her go.

'I'll never forgive you,' she choked. 'I *loved* Bodgy. I rescued him from the road when a car hit him and broke his leg. I've had him for months.'

'Did your father know about it?'

'Of course he did.' She was defiant again, her chin jutting forward. 'And he told me not to tell you. You didn't know half of what went on down at the cottages.' She was taunting him, backing away up the steps out of the parlour well, knowing she was beyond his reach.

He lifted one arm, hand in a fist. 'Go away, little girl,' he shouted at her. 'Get out of my sight. I hope I never have to see you again.'

It was after nine that evening when Lilah drove quietly along the road to Dunsworthy and left her car on the grass verge before the farm entrance. She'd brought a torch with her and used it to negotiate the dark and treacherous way to the O'Farrells' cottage.

The girl, Abigail, opened the door to her, peering out through a gap of a few inches before slowly moving back to admit her. Cuddled against her chest was a rabbit, the browny-grey fur suggesting it was, or had been, wild. 'What d'you want?' she demanded. There were smudges on her face, betraying a recent bout of weeping.

'I came to see how you're getting on, that's all,' Lilah reassured her, in a voice deliberately sweet and chirpy. Abigail stroked the rabbit and said nothing. Lilah tried a more serious tack. 'My dad was murdered a few years ago, you know,' she confided. 'I've got some idea of how you must be feeling.'

'I don't *think* so,' snapped the girl. 'Not after what's happened here today.'

Lilah's blood congealed. Surely nobody else had been killed? It was her own terrible experience that murders tended not to come singly.

'What?'

Abigail scowled at her. 'Your precious boyfriend shot my badger,' she burst out, tears welling.

Lilah could feel an answering hysteria. 'What?' was all she could repeat.

But Abigail had no intention of telling the story again. It had been bad enough trying to get her mother to listen quietly, without bleating about upsetting Gordon and getting them thrown out of the house. She couldn't hope for much understanding from the murderer's girlfriend.

They were inching their way towards the living room. Lilah wondered where Heather was, and why she hadn't come to see who was visiting at that time of night. 'Where's your mum?' she asked desperately. 'You're not here on your own, are you?'

Abigail made a scornful sound and pushed open the living room door. 'Mum, there's someone to see you.'

Lilah watched Heather O'Farrell lift her head and focus slowly on her face. She saw the lack of understanding. 'Hello, Mrs O'Farrell,' she said.

'You know me – I'm Gordon's girlfriend. We've seen each other once or twice. I gather there's been more trouble here today?'

The woman shook her head slowly. 'That was Abby's fault. Her badger got out and went up to the farmyard. Gordon shot it. You can't blame him. He didn't know it was hers.'

'That's awful,' Lilah sympathised readily. 'Horrible things seem to all happen at once, don't they?' she went on clumsily. 'Actually, I came to say how sorry I am about Sean.' She looked round for Abigail, but the girl wasn't there. Footsteps thumped up the stairs. 'She seems to have a way with animals,' Lilah went on. 'That looked like a wild rabbit.'

'Rabbits, hedgehogs, squirrels – her's a proper little Gerald Durrell.' Heather waved a vague hand towards the back wall of the room. 'But the badger was the favourite. Her be ever so upset about it.'

Lilah dimly understood how grief for the animal would get entwined with that for her father, the two losses adding up to more than double the initial sadness. 'I'm sure Gordon wouldn't have . . .' she stammered.

Heather interrupted. 'He've always been very strict about it, you see. He doesn't like anything cruel – the culling business isn't to his liking, or so Sean said. But he do believe the badgers bring the TB to the cows, so he never would have let her keep it, if he'd known. You can't blame him, really, for shooting it. 'Twas Abby broke the rules, and if she's made him furious now, that's an end to our chances of going on living here.'

'Can I sit down?' Lilah asked, trying to process this lengthy speech. 'Just for a few minutes?'

The woman tipped her chin at the other chair in the room. Lilah took it, and leant forward. 'I'm sure Gordon won't evict you – not until you can make other arrangements, anyway.'

'They think it's all in my mind, you know,' Heather said suddenly, with a slow uncurling of her hand that somehow managed to indicate her whole body and its wretched condition.

'Oh, I'm sure it's not,' Lilah said earnestly. 'What an unkind thing to think!'

'Sometimes . . .' Heather faltered, '. . . well, sometimes I do wonder. The doctors say there's naught they can find wrong with me, arthritis or some virus thing. The tests keep coming back normal. I got to wondering, really, what difference does it make?'

'I don't follow,' Lilah frowned.

'Hurts just as much, whatever the reason for it. I feel just as bad. But you don't want to hear about this.' She stared into Lilah's face. 'What did you come for?'

'I told you – to bring my condolences, and to

see if there was anything I could do to help.'

A look not far from dislike crossed Heather's features. 'Gordon's new girl then, are you? They get younger every time.' She laughed abrasively. 'I've seen a good few of them over the years.'

For the first time, Lilah realised that Heather was probably a good ten years younger than she looked; that she and Gordon had lived here on the farm together since they were in their early twenties. She had no intention of asking about Dunsworthy history, but she found herself wondering a hundred things at once; things that Heather O'Farrell was very likely to be able to tell her.

But she forced herself to stick with her original intention. 'I came, really, to ask you whether you had any idea who might have killed Sean,' she plunged on. 'I mean, anyone he'd had a row with or who'd got some grudge against him. I expect the police have already asked you, but I know them. They don't give you time to think, and they never properly understand the way things are, do they?'

'Your dad were killed, up in Redstone?' Heather remembered. 'And you were going with that tall policeman till not so long ago.'

Lilah sighed; she'd hoped that someone who hardly ever left the house might have missed some of the local gossip. 'That's right,' she smiled sadly, hoping to keep the attention on her father's death, rather than her liaison with Den.

'Jilly told me. Her keeps me up with what's happening. Don't know where I'd be without Jilly. And they're letting him do the investigating here, then?' she went on slowly. 'Bit strange, isn't it? I should say that Gordon Hillcock might not be his most favourite man in the world. 'Twould make it hard to keep an open mind, that sort of thing.'

It was the first time anyone had stated the situation so baldly to Lilah. She resisted the sudden, unexpected urge to defend Den, to shout *He would never let anything affect his professional judgement*. In a moment it passed, and she narrowed her eyes in a kindred suspicion. 'That's what I thought,' she agreed. 'That's why I don't think it's a good idea to leave the investigation entirely to him.'

She watched Heather closely. The woman was like a passive white sheep, bleating about her misfortunes, cowering in the house, apparently trying to hasten to an early death for no good reason, just like a silly ewe. But Lilah needed Heather to talk to her, to give an account of Sean's life that had not yet been heard and which could explain the circumstances of his death. Lilah believed, on the basis of very little experience, that most husbands and wives knew each other through and through. She believed that even if one partner was keeping secrets, the other one was generally able to guess what those secrets were. 'So,' she encouraged, 'who do *you* think it could have been? Who could have hated Sean enough to kill him?'

The widow let her gaze fall away from Lilah's, in a motion of despair and futility. 'It's no good asking me,' she mumbled. 'I never knew what he was up to. You'd be better off asking one of his mates. Fred Page, maybe. Or Eliot from next door.'

Lilah paused, knowing care was required. 'I gather Eliot and Sean were pretty good friends?' she attempted.

Heather smiled tightly. 'You heard a bit more than that, shouldn't wonder.'

'Well . . .'

The widow sighed. 'Don't worry yourself – I knew Sean was fonder of Eliot than he were of me. It's sure to come out, now he's dead; things always do. Eliot's nice enough, and he'll be sorry at what's happened to Sean, if he's heard, as I dare say he will've done by this time. I thought of calling him, but . . .'

'You don't think maybe they'd fallen out? That Eliot could have been the one—?'

Heather shook her head with a watery smile. 'There only be one person who'd fall out with

Sean bad enough to kill him,' she said with impressive certainty. 'And I dare say you think you know him inside out by this time. What is it – three months? And you madly in love with him and his clever ways with women.'

Lilah's insides lurched and acid welled up into her throat. She choked on her sudden bewilderment. 'How . . . ?' she tried to say.

A flash of pity showed in the older woman's eyes. 'You and me, we're just two in a long line,' she said gently. 'And you may not believe me when I say I still have only to look at him for my blood to start hammering. Even now, with me like this, and never a man's hand on me for fifteen years and more. Gordon Hillcock's a devil and it were a bad day for you when he noticed you.'

The acid threatened to sear her gullet. It was as if Heather's melodramatic words were burning her from the inside, as she let them enter her ears and soul. 'No – it isn't true!' she spluttered. 'He *loves* me. There's never been anyone before that he's felt like this about. He said so. We're absolutely right together.'

Heather cast a brief glance at the ceiling, appealing silently for confirmation of her position. 'Well, don't say I never warned you,' she said. Her expression softened into a kindness that Lilah found even harder to endure. 'I don't blame you,' Heather added. 'You'll never find another man to give you what Gordon can give a girl. It's as if he was born with the gift of knowing what we like. And no one can say he's wasted it, either.' For all her illness and lack of colour or energy, the woman's cheeks glowed for a moment at what could only be remembered bliss. 'The Hillcocks and the O'Farrells have lived side by side for near twenty years,' she said in a dreamy tone. 'And between them, they've given me just about everything I've got now, good and bad both. Everything.'

Lilah was angry and embarrassed. And frightened. 'Well,' she said hurriedly, 'I'd better go now. Thanks for talking to me.' She scrambled up and started for the door. 'I hope things will work out all right for you.'

Standing on the bottom stair was the girl, the rabbit still in her arms, relaxed and accepting.

'Isn't that a wild one?' asked Lilah, hoping to calm her hammering heart.

Abigail nodded. 'Found him a month or so back, out in the road. Just shocked and scared, nothing broken. We're good mates now.'

The hall light fell on her face, catching her chubby cheeks and generous mouth in such a way as to make Lilah forget all about the rabbit. *No*, she cried silently. *Don't let that be true*. But it was too late. Heather's disclosures had already told her: Abigail O'Farrell had to be Gordon

Hillcock's daughter. And regardless of the realities she knew were common to close-knit families living together in a remote community, the police were bound to find this new detail highly significant. To the stereotypical, mealy-mouthed, unimaginative police mind, this might be just what they needed to prove to themselves that Gordon killed Sean.

CHAPTER FOURTEEN

Friday dawned very much milder than the previous days had been, and although cloudy, it seemed inclined to be dry. Den woke from a long, deep sleep with a sense that something was about to happen, after the inconsequential drifting of the previous day. Some piece of evidence would be discovered; a witness would materialise; even a confession made. He whistled as he shaved, and then treated himself to two rashers of fried bacon, filling the flat with one of life's most delightful smells.

The police station seemed subdued, almost idle, when he walked in. No phones were ringing, nobody was shouting in the holding cells. He was struck once more at the lack of impact made by the death of Sean O'Farrell. It might have given Forensics plenty of work to do, but the CID team seemed to be finding it well within their comfort zone.

DI Hemsley had called the briefing for nine-thirty and Den went to the meeting room a few minutes early. It smelt of stale cigarettes and garlic. The latter seemed to emanate from Young Mike, who was sitting alertly close to the whiteboard like an overeager schoolboy. 'Phew!' Den protested. 'What've you been eating?'

Mike flushed. 'Had a curry last night,' he admitted. 'Why? Can you smell it?'

'Just a bit,' Den grinned. 'They must have gone overboard on the garlic.'

'Sorry. Let's hope I don't have to interview anybody this morning.'

'If you do, my advice would be to keep your distance. They'll have you for intimidation, otherwise.'

Jane Nugent made it into the room twenty seconds before Danny charged in carrying a box file, which he dropped carelessly onto the table beside the whiteboard. 'Phew!' he expostulated. 'Who's been eating garlic?'

Young Mike waved his pencil gently in admission.

'Have a thought for your public, Smithson, eh? There's people round here still think garlic's fit for nothing but scaring off vampires.'

Everyone grinned obediently, Den thinking it was probably true, and wondering just where Mike got his over-spiced curry. Was it possible the lad had cooked it himself?

'Right – to work,' Danny continued. 'There's been a development. Some nice kind anonymous individual has written us a letter.' He picked up a white envelope from the top of the file and brandished it. 'Came through the letterbox last night, as far as we can tell. No fingerprints. Done on a standard inkjet printer. Let me read it to you.' He looked directly at Den, who began to feel distinctly agitated.

'*If you want to know who killed O'Farrell, you should talk to the Watson family. Ask them just how friendly Matthew was with him and why Sam had reason to loathe him. But it's Mrs Watson you should pay special attention to.* That's it. Cooper, you interviewed Mrs Watson, didn't you? Who might Matthew and Sam be?'

'Her son and daughter,' Den supplied.

'So this doesn't mean much to you?'

Den shook his head slowly, as he tried to think. 'Sam Watson was at the Limediggers on Wednesday. She's part of an animal rights or conservation group. They all seemed to have a down on O'Farrell in a vague sort of way. Nothing specific.'

'So this might not be just malicious nonsense?' Hemsley flapped the letter.

Den frowned. 'It's a classic try-on, isn't it, sir? I mean, if the writer really had any evidence against the Watsons, they'd spell it out. This is so vague, it's worse than useless. What are we supposed to do about it?'

'Confront these kids, for a start. Let them think we've come up with something that throws suspicion onto them. You know the way it works, Cooper. This might be very valuable.' He lowered his square head, looking reprovingly down his nose at Den. 'Open mind, remember. At all times.'

Den remained mulish. 'But who—?' he began.

'Never mind who, for the moment. It could be someone close to the Watson family, who doesn't want to be labelled as a Judas, but has seen or heard something they think we should know about. Someone who works with one of them; someone they regard as a friend. It's not always easy in these country communities to bear witness against your friends. Think about it – if they give us direct information and we make use of it, they risk being identified as the source, simply because there's such a limited number of people to choose from. Sometimes a hint is the best they dare offer. Understand?'

Den kept his head down.

‘Right. So there’s quite a few pointers to the Watson family. Thanks to Nugent,’ he nodded at Jane, who smiled self-effacingly, ‘we’ve got things more or less worked out as far as family ties are concerned. All these youngsters are pairing up as you might expect, and the assumption has to be that most of them know each other’s parents as well. The Watson daughter, now, is involved with a certain Jeremy Page and his dad was O’Farrell’s mate. I think we can all see that this gives us a clear link between the Watsons and the O’Farrells, apart from the milk recording angle. And the girl’s choice of boyfriend might make her mother very upset, because the Pages don’t have a good image locally. I take it she hasn’t made any mention of it?’ Danny raised his eyebrows at Den, who shook his head. ‘I’m just asking myself whether we might have a trigger here. Something that’s made O’Farrell even more objectionable to Mrs Watson than his nastiness to his cows. And it occurs to me that a woman who gets to meet all these farmers on their own turf, so to speak, seeing them at work, listening to them rabbiting on, letting their tongues run away with them because they hardly ever see anybody to talk to – well, she feels like she could be a pretty central element in the puzzle to me. Add to that the fact that she was at Dunsworthy when our man was slaughtered – and I’m wondering why we haven’t had her in here undergoing the third degree, instead of a cosy chat over coffee two days ago?'

The knowledge that Hemsley was counting Deirdre as a viable suspect was unwelcome to Den. Damn it, he'd *liked* Deirdre Watson, almost as much as he'd liked Ted Speedwell. Hemsley went on, 'I want both of you – Cooper and Smithson – to go back to the Watson place, and to speak to the youngsters. How old are they, by the way?'

'The girl's around eighteen, and I don't know about the boy. Younger, if he's still at home, presumably.' Den spoke flatly, feeling as if something which had been within his grasp was rushing away from him in entirely the wrong direction. His anxiety blurred into annoyance, laced with a thread of panic; he clenched his teeth, determined that his feelings should not show.

'Right. Well, be gentle but firm. I want details of every meeting they've had with O'Farrell in the past few months; every word they've spoken to him, everything they know and think about him. I suggest you keep them absolutely separate, and do it as a twosome. Not one with the boy and one with the girl. There's a whiff of conspiracy starting to come off this.'

'Not as strong as the garlic, though,' quipped Nugent, leaning forward as if to remind the others of her presence. Danny snorted and turned his attention to her, as she'd intended.

'Nugent, it seems you might have more of a part to play in this case than we first thought.' He chewed his upper lip for a moment, in uncharacteristic uncertainty, before apparently taking a decision. 'Right,' he repeated. 'We'll spend the next ten minutes running over the forensic findings again, getting as full a picture as we can of how the victim died, where and when. There's nothing new – we'll just be refreshing our memories and weeding out any fanciful embellishments. Then I want Cooper and Smithson to get cracking on the Watson interviews, and Nugent – I'll see you on your own.'

Den felt sick. It had taken him half a minute to work out that Danny was planning to send Nugent to speak to Lilah, sparing Den's sensitivities in his own clumsy way, but in fact only adding to his discomfort. Lilah was, after all, a valid witness and it was no surprise that she should be embroiled in the murder inquiry. He expected that Hemsley would probably arrange a call on a few of Hillcock's previous girlfriends as well. But Lilah was obviously the most important one, and it was no surprise at all that Den would be debarred from interviewing her.

It felt all wrong. He should have insisted on withdrawing from the case from the start. Now he would inevitably be party to whatever Lilah had to say about Hillcock – what a good man he was; how murder was not in his nature; how she'd stake her life on his innocence; how much she loved him. His stomach swelled and he tasted his morning bacon, gone sour and fatty.

The briefing was soon concluded, though not quite as rapidly as Danny had predicted. Den managed to pull himself together enough to contribute the name of Eliot Speedwell as another individual who might be pertinent to the case, and should be interviewed pretty soon. The Inspector's face was grim as he concluded the meeting. 'It's not an easy one,' he said. 'The circumstantials all suggest it was Hillcock, a lot of the locals think it was him, and the forensics don't suggest anybody else. But there's no case against anyone – not yet, at least. Nothing that would stand the shadow of a chance in court. And you don't need me to tell you that this sort of inquiry is not fun. It feels like a waste of time and effort from the outset. But we're not giving up, not for a long time yet. People get careless, they think we've lost interest. Things start to settle down and go on as before. That's when we have to be at our keenest. We have to have ears and eyes everywhere. So I don't want you even thinking of giving up.' He fixed Den and Mike with a hard stare. 'Understand?'

'Yes, sir,' they chorused obligingly.

* * *

Jane Nugent was uncomfortable with her instructions from the DI. *This is extremely delicate*, he warned. *By rights, we should bring someone in from another area, but they tell me there isn't anybody available till Monday.* And he had gone on to explain that they couldn't ignore the possibility that Den was somehow more involved in the Dunsworthy murder than might first appear. *Of course, we know he didn't personally kill the bloke – he was here at the station all afternoon – but . . . well, you can work it out for yourself.*

Jane had known better than to protest. Inspector Hemsley had been struggling enough as it was, without her stating the obvious. Her task was to talk to Lilah Beardon, get her take on relations between Hillcock, O'Farrell and Speedwell, and as much background as possible on how Hillcock had come to steal her away from Detective Sergeant Den Cooper. 'We'd have to question her anyway,' Danny said. 'It's just that Cooper obviously isn't the person to do it.'

'He shouldn't be on this case, should he?' she blurted. 'It's . . . messy.'

Hemsley nodded. 'Didn't have a lot of choice,' he admitted. 'Manpower being what it is. We're running not much over half-strength, with Phil off sick all this time. I don't have to tell you that I trust Den implicitly. I don't believe for a minute that there's anything in this idea of him taking revenge on Hillcock. But the Super's asking us to bear it in mind, so there it is.'

'Funny way to take revenge,' she muttered. 'Why not just stick the fork in Hillcock himself?'

'Precisely. Which is why the idea's crazy. But see the girl for me, will you? Watch for reactions to names and don't be afraid to drop some hints about Cooper. It's what you do best, Nugent.'

'Yes, sir.'

The crucial one-to-one interview needed to be set up properly. A casual encounter in a farmyard, with people coming and going, was not her intention. At a loss for a moment, she tried to work out a strategy, sitting in her unmarked car in a layby a few miles from Dunsworthy, where she had initially decided to search for her quarry. She had tried phoning Lilah's home from the station and received no reply. The young woman's movements were unclear, although Den had provided some scanty notes at the outset, including everyone associated with Sean O'Farrell. *Still living officially at Redstone, but seems to spend a lot of time at Dunsworthy. Studying at Bicton, schedule at present unknown,* he had reported about his former girlfriend.

It was unprofessional to try to intercept her, Jane decided. And a waste of police time, into the bargain. Better by far to keep trying Redstone and request a proper interview there. With a sense of an unpleasant necessity postponed, she started the engine and headed back towards Okehampton.

If she had continued on her way to Dunsworthy, she could have observed a scene that involved two apparently minor players in the investigation.

In one of the workers' cottages, at eleven that morning, Eliot Speedwell was confronting his father. A subdued, hesitant, anguished exchange, but a confrontation for all that.

'Why didn't you *tell* me?' Eliot repeated. 'I only heard this morning, and then by accident. You *knew* I was his friend. You *knew* how upset I'd be.'

Ted stood beside the living room door, one hand holding it half open, his body leaning towards the passageway as if being pulled by an invisible thread. His son had been to the farmyard, located his father, and dragged him back to the house for a private talk. Anxious about the desertion of his duties, Ted was inattentive, his accent thickened by worry.

''Twas on telly,' he said. 'Us thought 'ee'd have seen it by now.'

'I hardly ever watch television,' Eliot snapped. 'I don't even know now if I've got the story right.'

''Tis best 'ee don't know too much. Us wanted 'ee to keep away, keep out of trouble. Sean's gone now and is never coming back again, like it or not.'

Eliot's lean face crumpled. Taller than his father, slender, looking younger than his thirty-two years, he leant heavily on the back of the old settee. 'It can't be true,' he whispered.

''Tis surprising how the shock wears off,' his father assured him. 'Seems a long time ago now, to us already. Heather . . .' He cut himself off with a frown, glancing yet again out into the passage.

'What? Heather's what?' Eliot prompted irritably.

Ted rubbed his chin, seemingly trying to keep his mouth shut. But the words emerged anyway. 'Her be doin' well,' he said weakly. 'No cause to worry about Heather.'

Eliot stared at him, eyes slightly bulging. 'Why in God's name should I worry about *Heather*?' he demanded. 'It never crossed my mind. Surely she's not pretending she ever loved him, or anything sick like that?'

Ted spluttered. 'Her be his *wife*,' he said.

Eliot let his head droop until his chin almost touched his chest. His shoulders shook slightly, his hands tight on the well-stuffed settee. Then he looked at his father again. 'Yes, I know,' he grated. 'Heather was his wife. And I was just his *friend* – who nobody even bothered to inform of his death.'

Ted had had enough. 'I be goin' back to work,' he said. 'Shouldn't be here, this time of day. You get back, too. There's be the sack for 'ee, if 'ee just walk off without a word. Sean O'Farrell's gone, and there's an end to it. Police coming and going, giving us all the willies. They be most likely wanting to know the reason why, if they catch 'ee hanging about the place looking like the world's gone scatt. 'Tis likely to upset your mother, and I won't have that. Get back to work and forget that bugger next door. Un never did 'ee no good, 'tis better off we'll all be without'n, see if I'm not right.'

Eliot did as he was told. His father went ahead of him to the door, and as he pulled it wide, another thought struck him. 'And clear up that midden out front,' he ordered. 'Been here too long as 'tis. Don't know what us be thinking of, letting you dump it all here.'

Eliot swept the untidiness with a chastened gaze. 'I forgot all about it,' he confessed. 'I'll take one of the bikes with me now, in the back of the car. The rest's just junk. I don't know why I ever thought I wanted it.'

'Thank Christ for that!' Ted rejoiced.

His son frowned, and started to explain. 'It's just . . . moving house . . .' he faltered. 'I didn't know . . .'

'Don't fret, son,' said Ted. 'You've had a bad time of it, but now's the moment to set it all behind you. Make a new start, find yourself a nice girl.'

Eliot stared at the wintry fields across the lane. 'You know, Dad – I might just do that,' he said.

'The Watson kids'll be at school,' Den remarked to Young Mike. 'Home around four, I'd guess. That leaves most of the day with not a lot to do. Any suggestions?'

'Lunch,' said Mike firmly. 'Didn't we say we'd check West Tavy out?'

'You mean the Six Bells?' Den was distracted, his thoughts sluggish; he couldn't immediately remember why they'd been interested in the pub at West Tavy.

'Right. If we get there early we can have a word with the landlord. Didn't the woman at the Limediggers tell you that Sean O'Farrell used to drink there?'

Den squeezed his eyes shut, trying to dispel images of Lilah confiding to Nugent the depths of her feelings for Hillcock. 'Good idea. Except it's barely eleven yet. Bit early for lunch.'

'We can go the long way.'

'Good idea,' sighed Den. 'Head for Bridestowe and then left. I always like that avenue of chestnuts, or whatever they are.'

'Not so fine in January,' said Mike, but took the road indicated, anyway.

Twenty minutes later, still uncomfortably early for lunch, they were approaching the tiny settlement of West Tavy. Tucked into the folds of the Devon countryside, on the edge of Dartmoor, it boasted panoramic views in one direction only. On all other sides it was sheltered by high hedges and tall trees, even in winter, with a sense of concealment and ancient ways at odds with modern laws and moralities.

As they got out of the car, Mike drew Den's attention to a group of four men in green body warmers, gathered in a gateway, holding equipment comprising canisters and rubber tubing. Three large black plastic sacks sat on the ground at their feet. 'What d'you think they're up to?' Mike wondered.

Den studied the group for a few moments. 'Ministry men,' he concluded. 'I'd say they were gassing badgers. Not very discreet, either. Clever timing, though – broad daylight on a weekday, when the protesters are all at work or college. Filthy business, all the same. Looks as if they've had a productive morning.' He nodded at the unmoving sacks.

'What are they hoping to gain?' Mike's gaze was riveted on the group, with the inescapable fascination that Den himself felt for professional killers. He knew they were pondering the question of whether it was right to cull wild animals, struggling with the inescapable dilemma between gut reaction and trust in the logic of officialdom. 'Can't be helped,' Den muttered, turning away. 'Let's hope it's a quick death for the poor things.'

The pub was cold and smoky; a sad-looking log fire had only recently been lit, and the wood must have been damp. The air smelt of stale beer and dust. 'Bit different from the Limediggers,' Mike observed in a low voice. There was no sign of anyone to serve them a drink.

Two other people were present: hard-looking men in their early thirties. One had long, lank hair tied in a greasy red bandanna, his face grooved like a much older man's. The other had a prickly, close-cropped scalp, and a scrubby beard. Den didn't think either of them were agricultural workers; they lacked that indefinably settled air, the look of endurance that he associated with men who worked all day with livestock.

'Any chance of a drink around here?' he said loudly.

'You want Beryl. She'll be back in a minute,' said the long-haired drinker.

'I see the cull's underway, then,' Den continued. 'Can't mistake those Ministry men out there.'

The two did not react other than with curt nods and a semi-shrug from the crop-headed one. Den concluded that they held no brief for badgers, or perhaps for any living creatures, humans included. It was tempting to stereotype them as mere louts, so morally bankrupt that any feelings of kindness or sympathy were utterly out of the question. But Den did not like to write people off so easily.

'People round here think the cull's okay, do they?' he pursued.

'More or less,' agreed Long Hair, evidently the talkative half of the pair.

'Because TB's such a problem in the dairy herds, right?'

'Right.'

A woman appeared behind the bar – faded blonde, weary-looking, wiping her hands on a grey tea towel. 'What're you having?' she asked, with no sign of curiosity or surprise at their appearance.

Den scanned the paucity of handles lined in front of the woman: two kinds of bitter, cider and Stella Artois. 'Pint of bitter, please,' he said cautiously. 'Any chance of food?'

'Ham sandwich, cheese sandwich – and there might be a bit of roast beef left. I can have a look if you like.'

Den looked at Mike, who unenthusiastically indicated a preference for Stella and a ham sandwich. Den decided to skip the food. Beryl produced the drinks and wandered away to see to the sandwich. There was no sign of anyone else on the premises; no distant clattering in a kitchen or footsteps overhead.

'She runs this place on her own, does she?' Den asked Long Hair and his friend.

'Lunchtime, yeah. Not much business this time o' year.'

'Sean O'Farrell drank here, didn't he?' Den made a firm assumption that the news of Sean's death was thoroughly spread by this time.

The slightest flicker of wariness was manifested: eyes narrowing, lips hardening. 'What if he did?'

'Must have been a shock to everyone who knew him.'

'There's few who'll be sorry.'

'What about you?'

Another shrug. Crop Head sniffed noisily, but Den didn't think the sound denoted grief. 'Do I take it you're not much bothered?'

'You the police?' Crop Head asked suddenly. 'Axing all these questions.'

'CID,' Den confirmed. 'Just looking for some background info on O'Farrell. What sort of bloke he was; who might not have liked him. The usual sort of thing.' He swigged his beer between phrases.

'Lived dangerously, did Sean,' Long Hair

muttered. 'Never cared much what people thought of him.'

'So who do you think killed him?' The question, direct and without warning, was intended to take them unawares.

'Gordon Hillcock, of course,' came the easy answer. 'If you're choosing between Hillcock and poor old Ted Speedwell, there's no contest. And who else would walk into Dunsworthy yard in broad daylight, just before milking?' The man guffawed cynically. 'Not much need for CID heavies on this one, I'd have thought.'

Den nodded amicably and eyed Mike as he gamely embarked on the thick sandwich made with dry white bread and slender slices of ham. 'Sounds as if you know all about it,' he observed.

'Saw it on the news,' said the man. 'And everyone with a sister between Exeter and Launceston knows Gordon Hillcock.'

From outside there was the sound of slamming car doors; Den moved to the window. The green-clad Ministry men were climbing into a Range Rover in the pub car park. The black sacks and gassing equipment were nowhere to be seen – evidently they'd been stashed in the back. He watched the men as they remained in the vehicle, passing packets and bottles to each other. 'Seems they don't rate the lunches here,' he muttered to nobody in particular.

Ten minutes later, both the Ministry Land Rover and the blue police car left the Six Bells. As Den and Mike drove out into the narrow country lane, following the Land Rover, a second vehicle appeared from the right. An elderly Metro, it hooted aggressively and seemed to be trying to intercept the Range Rover. If so, it failed.

'Why are they hooting?' wondered Mike.

'They're not really trying to catch them,' Den guessed. 'Just making their feelings known.'

The Ministry vehicle accelerated away as quickly as the winding lanes would permit. Den tried to see the occupants of the Metro. There were four of them, all apparently young. As the driver thrust it into gear and set it moving in pursuit of the Range Rover, Den recognised Sam Watson on the back seat.

CHAPTER FIFTEEN

'Guess we won't have to wait till after school now,' said Mike, when Den had told him who he'd recognised. They were conducting a somewhat jerky car chase. Ahead of them the Metro was still hooting aggressively at the Ministry Range Rover, which ignored them completely, driving frustratedly through the narrow country lanes.

'It'll be interesting when we reach the main road,' said Den.

In the event it was all over very quickly. The Ministry men evidently had their strategy honed to a fine art, and took an unexpected diversion up an even narrower lane on the left. The Metro almost overshot the turning and stalled. Den elected to wait until it got started again, still unsure as to whether the young driver had even noticed the car following close behind him. At the end of the new lane, a right turn, followed quickly by another left, took traffic out onto the Plymouth road. The Metro had no hope of catching up and Den and Mike watched the faltering reduction in speed as the pursuers realised they had lost their quarry.

'Best just follow them quietly,' Den decided. 'Don't want them doing anything silly.'

It didn't take long. Within ten minutes the Metro was pulling into the front driveway of a neat semi-detached house. Den was standing beside the car before all four had got out of it.

'Sam Watson?' he asked the girl from the back seat. 'You might remember me.'

Startled, she stared up at him, obviously wondering where he had come from, how and why. It took her several seconds to remember where she had last seen him. 'You're that detective that was in the Limediggers,' she said eventually. The others clustered round wordlessly, their faces pictures of anxiety, curiosity and bewilderment. Young Mike remained beside the police car, no more than a casual bystander, to all appearances. In reality, he was effectively blocking the exit to the driveway, in case somebody opted to make a dash for it.

'We'd like you to come with us,' Den told Sam calmly. 'We'll drive you home and ask a few questions there.'

'What – now?' Her head went jerkily round the circle of her friends, one by one, as if searching for elucidation as to what might be happening. 'But I need to be back at school—'

'She didn't do anything,' said the boy who had been on the back seat with her. 'She wasn't driving. Why are you picking on her?'

'This has nothing to do with what we've just observed,' Den told him. 'It was our good luck that we happened on you the way we did. Nobody's saying she did anything; we just want to ask her a few questions, to assist us with our enquiries.'

The boy frowned. 'More enquiries?' He scratched his neck and stared at the bare hedge bordering the front garden.

'That's right. Now Sam, if you're ready?'

'You don't have to go, Sam,' the boy urged. 'They can't make you.'

Den took out his notebook and pencil. 'While I'm here, I'd better make a note of your names,' he decided. 'Just in case. After all, you have just been trying to interfere with government business, if I'm not mistaken. Let's see if I've got this right. You must be Jeremy Page . . .'

The boy nodded grudgingly. Den went on.

'And you two are Susie Marchand and Paul Tyler, if I remember rightly?' He eyed the driver and the girl who had been in the front passenger seat. 'What happened to Davy Champion, then?'

Jeremy Page said nothing, but scowled blackly and Den became aware of a suppressed rage that had violence threaded through it. The boy's fists were clenched and his chin raised defiantly. Den recognised the type: a youngster accustomed to regular knocks to his adolescent pride, either from a domineering father or a peer group that scorned him. Den suspected the former. The terrier-like defiance gave it away: the boy was used to someone bigger than him throwing his weight about, so all he could effectively do was duck and yap and keep his spirit alive by a dogged refusal to cringe.

'Okay. Thanks very much,' Den said amiably. Ushering a wordless Sam into the back of the car with no ceremony, he told Mike to drive straight to the Watson house.

The interview with Sam took slightly over half an hour. Deirdre showed them into the living room, having expressed angry surprise that her daughter had bunked off school, and then ostentatiously left the threesome alone with a sharply-closed door between herself and them.

'Don't worry about this,' Den tried to reassure

the girl. 'It's just a minor avenue of investigation that we're exploring. You're not in any trouble, as far as I can see.'

She sat on the sofa at Den's command. He had scanned the room as they entered it and positioned Sam on the most comfortable seat, keen to put her at her ease. He and Mike took matching upholstered chairs, side by side, facing her. Mike had his notebook open and ready. She stared at them truculently.

'Can you tell us as much as possible about the badger-baiting business around here?' he invited. 'Including what you know about Sean O'Farrell. We're interested in facts *and* rumours, okay?'

'I don't know anything about Sean O'Farrell,' she said with a flat stare.

'But your friend Susie said he was one of the enemy. I take that to mean that you think he kills badgers illegally, perhaps along with other animals you want to protect. The woman in the bar on Wednesday told us that Sean didn't agree with the cull. I'm finding all this quite confusing, to be honest. Gordon Hillcock doesn't like it, either, as I understand it. You seem like a bit of an expert – why don't you explain it to me?'

Sam chewed the inside of her cheek and Den felt a rush of irritation at the involvement of surly schoolgirls in the investigation. As witnesses, they were very hard going.

'Come on, Sam,' he urged.

'Okay.' She raised an open hand to indicate she was sorting out her thoughts. After a pause, she began to speak. 'It's complicated, right? The cull is just a part of it. There's other groups working on that – taking the legal side and trying to stop it that way. They're proper professionals, but we're not like that. We just want to do our bit to save wildlife in this area. We're not *organised* or anything. We talk to people, mainly, try to make them see it from the animals' point of view. That's the future for conservation, you know.' Her eyes were beginning to shine with the conviction behind her words. 'It's no good just waving placards and sabotaging hunts and culls. It's got to go deeper than that. You've got to change people's minds.'

'And Sean O'Farrell?' Den prompted.

'He was on our blacklist,' she said uneasily.

'Oh?'

'We think he was involved in baiting and lamping. He wanted all the badgers in the area wiped out, and didn't think the cull would make a proper job of it. Plus Dunsworthy's outside the cull area anyway. So he set out to do it himself.'

'But his daughter's got a pet badger,' Young

Mike put in. 'How does he square that, then?'

'Has she really? How funny. Of course, he let Abby do whatever she liked. He felt guilty, I guess, because she has such a rubbish time with her mum. Who knows what he might have done to it in the end, anyway?'

'But you didn't like Sean's campaign?'

She shifted uneasily, pulling her feet up under her. 'He was one of the old sort – that's what we call them. People who don't think animals have any proper feelings, so it's okay to kill them if they're a nuisance. We want to get away from that sort of thinking.'

Den scratched his head with his pencil. 'I'm still not quite following,' he admitted. 'You said it was important to talk to people. Did you actually talk to Sean about it?'

She grinned, a surprisingly rueful, quirky expression, suggestive of a powerfully vivid memory. 'We tried,' she said. 'It ended up as a shouting match. It was with my mum, not me,' she added.

'When was this?'

'A couple of weeks before Christmas. It was a school bazaar thing. Very embarrassing, actually. Matthew was there, too. Anyway, Abigail O'Farrell was running a Year Ten raffle and the prize was this big stuffed badger. Abigail's dad started on about the cull and my mum heard him and told him he was an idiot. It didn't last very long, but they said some pretty strong things.'

'Such as?'

'Oh . . .' she inhaled deeply, gathering strength. 'Mr O'Farrell said the only good badger was a dead badger, or a stuffed one, and Abigail went very red. One of her classmates told him he should respect animals' rights, and that set him off. He said it was all one big jungle out there and you had to kill anything that threatened your livelihood, or you were bound to go to the dogs. Then Mum joined in. She told Sean he should learn some sense and that people like him weren't qualified to speak about such things. That was when—' The girl paused, clenching her jaw.

'When what?' Den prompted.

'Well . . . I wasn't sure what he meant, but he said something like, "You're a fine one to talk with your mucky ways." And he sorted of *leered* at her. It was really horrible; it made us all feel dirty.'

'What did your mum do?'

'She went very pale and didn't say another thing. As if she was *scared* of him. He had this *vicious* look on his face, as if he really hated her. It only lasted a couple of minutes, but it was a bit of a shock. I mean – she does the recording at Dunsworthy – she's not meant to fall out with them.'

'Did you know that Abigail keeps a pet badger? Before Mike here mentioned it?'

She shook her head. 'Brave girl,' she remarked.

'And her father fed it for her when she stayed overnight at her boyfriend's.'

'Nah!' she protested. 'Don't give me that.'

'That's what her mother claims.'

Sam hesitated. 'As I say, he'd have done just about anything for Abby. If it was locked up properly, he might have thought it was okay.'

'So is your mum involved with the animal rights thing?'

For the first time in the interview, the girl seemed agitated. 'She doesn't talk to me about it,' she stammered.

'But—?'

'But nothing. It's only that she gets upset when she sees anybody being cruel to animals. She gives money to CWF—'

'Which is?'

'Compassion in World Farming.'

'And everyone seems to agree that Sean O'Farrell was cruel to animals,' Den said.

'Right. Like Susie says, he's one of the enemy.'

'Did Matthew know him?'

'Matt? No, not at all. He was just somebody's dad, as far as Matt was concerned.'

The interview drifted to a close after that. It was half past two and Sam pointed out to them that they'd made her miss a Psychology lesson. 'What am I supposed to say?' she asked, with a bold look at Den. 'Sorry, Miss – I was helping the police with their enquiries?'

'Den smiled non-committally. 'I'm sure you'll think of something,' he said.

Den and Mike adjourned to the car for a debriefing. 'What do you think?' Den asked carefully.

'O'Farrell had something on Mrs Watson. Something "mucky".'

'Right,' agreed Den thoughtfully. 'Sounds a bit strong, don't you think?'

''Specially in a public place.'

'She didn't tell me about it when I saw her on Wednesday.' His head was humming with disquiet. 'Seems to me that Deirdre Watson had nothing but contempt for O'Farrell. And wouldn't you say it's easier to kill someone you utterly despise?'

'Like Sean with badgers, you mean?' Mike offered ironically, one eyebrow raised. 'I didn't really get that impression from Sam. More that her mother was frightened of him, and didn't know what he might do.'

Den acknowledged the point. 'But the way he

was killed – isn't that how you'd kill a rat? Just hurl a fork at it. Exterminating vermin.'

'Women don't kill vermin,' Mike said, only half joking. 'They call in a Council operative or get their husbands to do it.'

'This is getting fanciful,' Den objected.

'No, it's useful,' Mike contradicted. 'It gives us a feel for the frame of mind of the killer. For why someone might want Sean dead.'

'O'Farrell was on those kids' blacklist. He was seen as the enemy. And yet he was a good dad to Abigail, a good husband to that drippy wife. And a reliable herdsman.'

'But you're right – he does sound like a rat to me,' Mike realised. 'Rats have families – but they're completely self-interested. They make other creatures recoil. Isn't that what we're picking up, that everyone except his wife and daughter recoiled from him? For whatever reason.'

'There's that friend, Eliot Speedwell. We ought to go and see him this evening, and get his side of the picture. He also knocked about with Fred Page.'

'He's not likely to tell us anything.'

The car phone rang. 'Hemsley,' Den predicted correctly, as he lifted it from its cradle.

'Any progress?' the Inspector asked.

'We've spoken to the Watson girl. She gave us

a few things to think about,' Den summarised. 'The boy's due home at four, so we're waiting for him. Though I've no idea what we'll say to him. We haven't got anything to link him with O'Farrell, apart from the anonymous letter. Sam says he never knew the man.'

Hemsley was silent for a moment. 'Forget him for now,' he ordered. 'It was probably just malicious gossip, as you said. There must be more important people for you to see.'

'Right, sir,' said Den, with some relief. 'By the way, the uniforms have been round all the local farmers, haven't they? Asking if they saw anything unusual or know of any reason why the man should be attacked?'

'They have,' the DI confirmed. 'Not a sniff of anything suspicious, or I'd have told you.'

'We thought we should see Eliot Speedwell as soon as he gets back from work. And, sir, there was a little incident earlier today you should know about.' And Den told the Inspector all about their encounter with the group of youngsters and the Ministry men. He told it in careful detail, repeating the names of the animal group members and pointing out the network that seemed to link them to each other and to Dunsworthy. It took almost ten minutes, with Young Mike chipping in.

'Get yourselves back here and file a report,'

Hemsley ordered. 'Then grab some tea and toast before you go to see young Mr Speedwell.'

'Right, sir,' said Den.

It was three o'clock before WDC Nugent caught up with Lilah. The girl finally answered the phone at Redstone and Nugent requested her to stay there until she arrived, which she did, eventually, via deep Devon lanes.

Lilah's manner was edgy, which was hardly surprising. 'I can see I'm in a funny sort of situation here,' she said at the outset. 'Neither fish nor fowl, you might say.'

'You're well placed to get an overview of how things have been at Dunsworthy,' Nugent suggested.

Lilah breathed a short satirical laugh. 'Not really,' she corrected. 'The truth is I spend most of my time there in the house. In Gordon's bedroom, actually.' Her tone was deliberately provocative.

Jane smiled thinly. *Lucky old you*, she thought. 'So how much did you see of Sean O'Farrell?'

Lilah wrinkled her nose and cast her eyes upwards. 'I'd say I spoke to him no more than five times in total. Saw him around, of course.'

'And how did Mr Hillcock feel about him?'

'I don't think he gave him very much thought at all. They've worked together for most of their lives, just getting on with it. They were very different characters. Gordon's clever, sensitive. Sean seemed a bit thick. Rather a shallow sort of person – I never saw any sign that he cared about anything much. Although he did have a sly sort of look to him, I suppose. He'd never look me in the eye. Maybe he didn't like women.'

'There seem to be various rumours going around concerning him.'

'You mean the badger baiting?' Lilah became more animated. 'Yes, I heard that. Filthy business. It would match his character, though. The way he seems to have been with the cows, getting his kicks from an animal's suffering. I don't think he had the brains to imagine how another creature was feeling.'

'Right,' said Jane slowly. 'And what about his family?'

Lilah tossed her head in a quick display of contempt. 'The wife's been out of it for years. Abigail seems to have a bit more about her, though.'

'You know Mrs O'Farrell, do you?'

'I went to see her last night, to offer my condolences.'

Playing at being Lady of the Manor, Jane surmised. 'That was nice of you,' she said.

'I think Abigail's connected with the animal

rights people,' Lilah offered casually. 'All the local kids seem to be into it these days, don't they? She's going out with Gary Champion and his brother Davy is one of the main organisers. He'd know all about Sean and the badger baiting, from Abby.'

Jane pursed her lips doubtfully. 'Doesn't seem that relevant,' she judged.

Lilah looked her in the face, eyes narrowing. 'Well, I think it is. I think your answer is in there somewhere – with the animal rights people, I mean. They believe in direct action, don't they? And I think you should remember that there were two people at least in the yard on Tuesday afternoon. Three, with Ted, though nobody seems to be taking much notice of him.'

Nugent had been carefully briefed. 'Why did you drive your tractor over the police tape?' she asked suddenly.

Lilah laughed, a single high note. 'Oh, wasn't that awful of me! I got the gears muddled up. It's different from the tractor we used to have here, and I never drove that very much anyway. I'm a hopeless novice, quite honestly. It's lucky I didn't hit one of the cows. Mrs Watson was there – she'll tell you what a mess I was making of it.'

'Did you know Mrs Watson before this week?'

'Never seen her, as far as I can remember. We

had a milk recorder for years, of course, but it wasn't her. I know Sam by sight, that's all.'

'Ted Speedwell,' Nugent changed tack again. 'What can you tell me about him?'

'He seems quite a sweet old chap. Doesn't say boo to a goose, just gets on with the work. Never heard of him falling out with anybody. Except Eliot, of course.'

'Eliot?'

'His son. This is just gossip, but people are talking about him being gay. That's why he was thrown out of the Army. But the interesting thing is, he was extremely matey with Sean. I think there's an obvious inference to draw there.'

'You're suggesting a homosexual relationship between the two of them?'

Lilah widened her eyes. 'I suppose I am,' she said innocently.

'Which would mean O'Farrell was gay as well?'

'It would explain their friendship. Funnily enough, young Matthew Watson's apparently gay as well, according to one or two of my brother's friends.'

'Matthew, son of Deirdre Watson?'

'The very same. He's only sixteen, but he's one of those boys that people notice. Good at drama, had a big part in the school play at Christmas.'

'Hang on,' Jane interrupted. 'This is just more gossip, isn't it?'

'That's how it is around here. All these people go to the same school, so they all know each other. The catchment area's enormous.'

Nugent observed a sudden cloud pass across Lilah's face, a flinch as if at a painful thought. She concentrated hard on the implications. 'It sounds as if you're suggesting something fairly nasty to do with two adults and an underage boy. Are you serious about it?'

'Sixteen isn't underage, is it?'

'That depends.'

Lilah wriggled. 'I said it was all gossip. But it would link Sean to Deirdre Watson – and she was there when he was killed.' She looked up, almost eagerly. 'Don't forget I went out with Den for nearly three years. I got used to making sense of apparently random connections, listening to him talking about his work.'

'Ah yes,' murmured Nugent. 'I was hoping we'd get around to Den.'

'I realise it can't have gone unnoticed that I think it's wrong to have him on this case at all. He's going to be very happy if Gordon gets done for murder.'

'But you think it was just a sort of coincidence, do you, that there should be a murder on a farm where you spend most of your time?'

Lilah frowned. 'What do you mean? It is a coincidence as far as Den is concerned, of course.' She blinked rapidly, her jaw tightening. 'Surely you're not suggesting . . . Christ! Is *that* why you've come to talk to me? That's utterly ludicrous.'

Nugent said nothing, sitting motionless, watching closely.

'You think Den might somehow have set this all up, in some totally sick and devious plot to incriminate Gordon?' She laughed disbelievingly. 'That's crazy. Den would *never* do anything like that. It wouldn't even occur to him. Den's as straight as they come, surely you know that? Besides, it would have to be the daftest possible way to wreak revenge . . .' She threw herself back in the chair in exasperation.

'So why object to him being on the case?'

Lilah looked cornered. 'Well . . . because he's human; because he hates Gordon. Even without meaning to, he's likely to be selective about the way he investigates the whole thing. There's a world of difference between setting something up, and taking the opportunity to capitalise on it after the event.'

'It sounds to me as if you've still got some feeling for him.'

'Of course I've still got some feeling for him. We were *engaged*.'

'But Hillcock's got something that Den hasn't?'

'You're implying I'm a gold-digger, after his farm?' Lilah giggled at the idea. 'I've already got a farm, thank you very much. Besides, I always promised myself I'd never take up with a farmer. It's a mug's game.'

'So what happened?'

'So it's not the farm. It's just him – Gordon. I fell in love with him. It happens.'

'So they tell me,' Nugent nodded, a little bleakly. 'Well, thanks for talking to me. I think that's all for now.'

Nugent hurried back to the station, mulling over the implications of Lilah's statement. Mostly it felt like a desperate attempt to find a scapegoat for the crime she knew her boyfriend must have committed. She had been randomly slinging mud in all directions. But underneath all that, there was an uncomfortably solid thread of logic. Lilah had conjured a network of passions and wounded feelings that might quite credibly have led to Deirdre Watson hurling herself at Sean O'Farrell for what she believed him to be doing to her precious young son. And then there was the animal rights angle . . . which could also lead indirectly to Deirdre Watson.

Oh well, she concluded, as she swung her car

out of the homeward stream of traffic and into the quieter street containing the police station, *It's not down to me to judge who's right and who's wrong.*

She encountered Den and Mike in the canteen and followed them to a table, where she gave them a severely edited version of her interview with Lilah. 'Sorry I had to do that, Den,' she said. 'But there was no way around it.'

'No problem,' he assured her, his face tight and pinched. 'Just give us the bits you think we need to know.'

'She claims – wait for it – Sean O'Farrell was gay and having it off with Eliot Speedwell, and young Matthew Watson, the milk recorder's son, is that way inclined as well and might have got himself involved with them. At least, that was what she implied. She's got no hard facts whatsoever.'

'Did you believe her?' Mike stared incredulously at Jane. 'Sean O'Farrell *gay*?'

'It does make things look a bit dodgy for Mrs Watson,' Nugent pressed on. 'If it's true and she knew about it, she'd be furious with O'Farrell.'

'We're going to see Eliot Speedwell tonight,' said Den calmly. 'We'll have to hope he sets us right, won't we?'

'What about young Matthew? Have you seen him yet?' Nugent asked.

'Not until after we've spoken to Speedwell,' Den said. 'If this is all a story, we'd be in deep shit making that sort of suggestion to the boy – in front of his mother, most likely.'

Jane Nugent sipped her tea and nodded slowly.

CHAPTER SIXTEEN

Den and Mike were both quite taken with Eliot Speedwell and his pretty little house, which had apparently once been a two-bedroomed artisan's cottage. Tall and slim, unlike his gnomish father, Eliot had a self-deprecating air.

'We understand you were a close friend of Sean O'Farrell?' Den opened, without much preamble. Eliot nodded, his pain well hidden but not invisible. 'His death must have been a shock.'

'Of course it was. More so because I only heard about it this morning.'

'Really? That suggests you weren't in especially close touch?'

'And that you never watch the local news on TV,' added Mike.

'Both true, more or less. I tackled my father about it earlier today. He should have been the one to tell me. I still can't understand why he didn't.'

'Slipped his mind, I suppose,' said Den. 'Or he expected you'd hear from somebody else.'

'Silly old bugger,' said Eliot, with a hint of fondness mixed into the anger.

Den asked if they could all sit down around the table at one end of the kitchen. Everything was small and neat, the space used intelligently. Eliot's offer of coffee was declined.

'You can probably imagine what we're up against,' Den began. 'We have to try and build up a picture of what this man was like, from an assortment of descriptions and comments from people who knew him. And just when you think there's something coming into focus, a whole new viewpoint turns up that throws it all out of shape again. For example, we have one picture of a man who was good to his invalid wife, sympathetic to his daughter, conscientious at work. But we've also had people telling us he was brutal, shallow, secretive. The young animal rights campaigners call him the enemy. As his friend, we wondered whether you've got anything to add?'

'People are complicated,' Eliot offered. 'What more can I say?'

'I'm sure that's true,' Den agreed. 'But when

a man is murdered with considerable brutality, in his place of work, *complicated* doesn't quite cover it. Wouldn't you agree? It looks as if someone was driven to extreme rage and acted on it.'

'You're telling me the killer was somebody who knew Sean?'

'Oh yes, I think so. Although we shouldn't entirely rule out a crazed drug addict, I suppose. Let loose on the community perhaps, and found himself wandering down a country lane to Dunsworthy Farm?' Den spoke ironically, deliberately trying to provoke a reaction.

'Not many of them around in January,' Eliot conceded. 'Might get a few in August.'

'Where were you on Tuesday afternoon, between one and four o'clock?'

'At work. In the pasty factory. I'm in personnel. About ten people can vouch for me.'

'When did you last see Sean?'

The answer came promptly, with scarcely a second's thought. 'Sunday afternoon.'

'Where was that?'

'Here.'

'When did you last visit Dunsworthy? Before today, I mean.'

'Christmas Day.'

'What time did you go there today? Weren't you at work?'

'About ten-thirty. I took the morning off. I couldn't have gone in, the state I was in. Three days before I heard he was dead. My oldest friend! So much for a close community!'

'How did you hear?'

'I saw it in the paper. I get it delivered on a Friday.'

'Weren't they talking about it at the factory?'

'I realise now that they were, yes. Just odd references, without any names. Nobody there would know I was Sean's friend. I didn't take any notice.'

'What did your father say when you tackled him?'

'Nothing much. Sean was murdered and the police were investigating, obviously. I wondered a bit why you'd not been to see me sooner. Looks as if I was completely out of the loop, doesn't it.'

'Your father was on the farm at the time of Sean's death, of course. Did he approve of your friendship with him?'

'Approve? I'm thirty-two years old, Sergeant. I can choose my own friends, without my father's permission. In any case, we grew up together, pretty much. We were more like brothers than friends.'

Den took a breath. 'Mr Speedwell, there has been a suggestion that you and Mr O'Farrell were more than just good friends, if you take my meaning. Assuming this to be true – or at least to be the general perception – what would your father's reaction be to that?'

Eliot stared unblinkingly at Den for half a minute. 'What?' he said finally. 'I don't understand what you mean.'

'You and Sean O'Farrell weren't lovers?'

Eliot exploded into a raucous laugh; a much bigger noise than he looked capable of making. 'Sean, *gay*?' he spluttered. 'My God, that's a good one.'

Den found that he didn't particularly mind feeling foolish. 'It's not true, then?'

'It most definitely is *not* true,' Speedwell assured him. 'Nothing could be further from the truth, in fact.'

'Meaning?'

'Meaning that Sean never had any sex drive of any sort. Something happened in his childhood – he never told me the details. Scared him off the whole business.'

'Was he impotent?'

'Put crudely, I should think he was. Except it never came to the point of him trying, as far as I could tell. Drove poor Heather crazy, of course, even though he tried to make up for it, looking after her so well.'

Den tried to keep his eye on the ball. 'So – forgive me, but you do seem an unlikely pair of friends. From what we've gathered about Mr O'Farrell . . . well . . .'

Eliot spread his hands. 'We were young together. I learnt a lot from him in those early years; stuff like self-sufficiency and when to keep your mouth shut. I was always rather a loner, shy and awkward. A misfit. Then I joined the Army, like a fool, and it almost destroyed me. I crawled home with a breakdown. Sean was next door, and was really good to me. Told me I was well out of it. I kept the friendship going out of gratitude, I suppose.'

'And you? Are *you* gay?'

Speedwell took a long breath. 'I thought I might be,' he said. 'I experimented – went to a gay club in Plymouth a couple of times. Sounds pathetic, doesn't it? At my age, I really should know at least that much about myself. I've always found it really hard to form relationships with women. None of them matched up to my mother, who is utterly sweet and good and kind and patient and all that sort of thing. But just lately I've started to get things straight. New house, new job last year, and maybe if I'm lucky, a new girlfriend. Someone who'll give me what I need.'

Den knew enough about psychology to doubt whether such a specification would bear fruit. He saw Speedwell as spoilt by the self-sacrificing mother, forever greedy for attention, giving nothing in return. He wanted to offer bland assurances and leave. But there was more to be asked.

'And why was Sean here on Sunday?'

'To borrow money,' came the prompt reply. 'He's done it before.'

'Did you give it to him?'

Eliot shook his head. 'I told him I'd had enough of his silly schemes. Most of them were on the wrong side of the law.' The man sounded careless of his own liability in having financed shady dealings. *Or fundamentally weak, more likely*, thought Den.

'What kind of schemes?'

'Oh, buying and selling. Nothing fancy. Scrap metal, unregistered animals, bits of scruffy land. None of it ever worked out to his advantage. I got involved a few times – helped him over a few of the practicalities.' Den remembered the jumbled accumulation of objects on the Speedwells' front lawn, and mentally ticked off that small anomaly. It had niggled at him that neither Ted nor Jilly seemed likely to be responsible for such a mess. Seemingly, Eliot had invited Sean to use it as storage, rather than his own premises.

'But you did lend him money on other occasions?'

'Now and then, yes. Never very much. It

was easier to give it to him than listen to all the bravado about how it was going to make us both rich this time.'

'Tell me, Mr Speedwell – did you actually *like* Sean O'Farrell?'

Eliot slowly shook his head, an ironic twist on his lips. 'No, Sergeant, I can't honestly say I did. Not for the last few years, anyway. I shouldn't think *anybody* really liked poor old Sean. Not deep down.'

The interview ended swiftly and Mike closed his notebook with a firm snap. Outside, Den said, 'That's it for today. We were right to leave young Matthew alone. If you're lucky, you won't be needed again till Monday, but I've a feeling Hemsley's going to send me back to Dunsworthy tomorrow. It's all coming down to the way O'Farrell treated his animals, as I see it. Somewhere on that farm, there must be more to learn.'

'Have fun,' said Mike.

As predicted, Hemsley detailed Den to go back to the farm on Saturday morning.

'But Hillcock won't be there,' he remembered. 'Not if he sticks to his plan. That's why he swapped milking with Sean. He wanted to go to some meeting or other.'

'So who'll do today's milking?' Hemsley asked.

'Probably a relief person. They've had time to organise that by now. Or maybe he'll fit it all in himself.'

'So talk to Speedwell, and the womenfolk. Maybe it's best if Hillcock is away, come to think of it. They'll talk more freely with him out of the way.'

Leaving it until ten o'clock, Den drove the winding route to Dunsworthy again, pondering on how repetitive murder inquiries tended to be. Innumerable visits to the scene of the crime; interviews with the same dwindling group of witnesses or suspects; going over and over the same forensic reports, like sifting through the same bran tub, handful by handful, on the off-chance that some forgotten little clue had been left sitting at the bottom.

He found the farmyard almost empty of vehicles; only the car shared by Claudia and Mary Hillcock sat under the corrugated tin roof of the makeshift garage that stood to one side of the house. No sign of Lilah's Astra, which came as some relief. And Den began yet another search for Ted Speedwell, discovering even more permutations of doors and gates and openings amongst the interconnected buildings than he remembered from before.

He looked into two of the cavernous cowsheds, then headed for the door of a third, smaller, one.

He savoured the atmosphere of the place: there was a timelessness about it that struck him. Some of the items hanging on the walls, sitting on rickety shelves or propped in corners, had clearly been there undisturbed for decades. Dust had become so thick that it formed a near-solid tissue, grey-brown, crumbly, all-pervasive. It would be obvious to a careful scrutiny which objects had been moved within the past few months. Even a relatively modern farm like Dunsworthy, with its vast buildings, was not qualitatively different from the more traditional Redstone, where Lilah had grown up. It was a world entirely at odds with urban life, where animal hair and cobwebs were instantly dusted and vacuumed into oblivion. With a sigh, Den acknowledged his envy of those who were born into such a habitat. Even in January, with the hostile weather conspiring with the forces of consumerism and health hysteria to annihilate the entire farming industry, he thought he would cheerfully exchange it for his safe, tidy little flat. He might even have been persuaded to change his career with the police for that of a farmer – if things had gone differently with Lilah.

He heard the car engine, but didn't show himself. He waited to see whether it was someone on farm business, whether Speedwell would manifest himself to deal with it. When no voices were heard, he ventured out of the shed from a doorway that did not open onto the yard. His former fiancée came striding round the corner and almost bumped into him.

Her presence, within easy touching distance, made his skin feel raw and exposed. If she wanted to, she could rake her nails down his chest or cheek; for a moment it seemed to him that that was what she would indeed do.

'Why are you back here?' she demanded. 'Sneaking round like a thief. If you want to speak to Gordon, why don't you go and knock on the door like a civilised person?'

'I'm looking for Ted Speedwell, as it happens,' he retorted coldly. The memory of her furious treatment of him on Wednesday revived him. Her aggression now made much less impression on him. It felt forced and unconvincing.

She said nothing for a long moment. 'Is Ted a suspect now?' she finally asked.

'I'm not at liberty to reveal any details of our investigation,' he said stiffly, hating himself and her in equal measure.

'Pardon me for asking,' she mimicked, with exaggerated pomposity. He hoped desperately that the situation they were in would bring back to her at least some echoes of their first farmyard encounter, on the morning her father had died, and Den had been kind and protective and instantly concerned. How was it possible that she did not remember it? He was welded to the ground, paralysed by her dogged hostility, unable to move until she released him.

'You know,' she said, in a milder tone, 'it wasn't anybody on this farm who killed Sean. You won't get anywhere until you wake up to that fact. Sean was involved in a lot of nasty business, with some nasty people. I know you won't take my word for it – you'll think I'm just trying to protect Gordon. But ask the milk recorder and her kids. Ask Fred Page. Though if you send a policeman to see him, they'd best go in disguise.'

He couldn't let it pass. 'Lilah – did you send an anonymous letter to the police station about Mrs Watson and her family? And what on earth were you trying to do, suggesting to Nugent that Sean and Eliot were gay lovers? It was pretty imaginative, I'll give you that, but completely irresponsible and stupid, as well.'

Her face told him a lot: discomfort, cunning, a delayed denial, all spiced with satisfaction at having got to him. 'I was just passing on the local gossip,' she said self-righteously. 'And of course I didn't send any anonymous letters. Why, what's been going on?'

'I told you as much as I can. I don't believe you about the letter. Now, where do you think Ted might be?'

She ignored his question, standing obstinately

in her thick quilted jacket and black wellington boots. He was almost sure she'd sent the letter about Deirdre and her family. What sort of desperation had driven her to do that? It could only be the prospect of losing Hillcock that was motivating her to go to such extreme lengths. She must really care about him. But how could she?

Looking at her, Den felt as if the gods were deliberately playing with him, bringing together such an unlikely couple as Lilah and Hillcock, just to teach him that he should never take anything for granted. But if he would never understand what had made her fall for Hillcock, it was all too easy to grasp what had prompted the farmer's behaviour. He was close to forty and must be facing his last chance of finding a wife. It wasn't unusual for farmers to retain bachelor status for longer than most men, but after forty, they became much too set in their ways. They didn't want the upheaval. With Granny Hillcock in her last few years or months, there'd be a nice big room in the house for a new wife to spread herself in, and perhaps use for a nursery before long. And a girl who knew about farming, educated, cheerful, robust – a girl such as Lilah – was now, as always, quite perfect for the purpose.

The waste of it, the sheer unnecessary stupidity of her thinking herself in love with a man so transparently on the lookout for a suitable mate, made Den want to scream. And he still wondered how in the world Hillcock had done it.

'Speedwell?' he prompted, unable to bear any further contemplation of her.

'I've only just arrived,' she said. 'Your guess is as good as mine. Look—' she burst out before he could continue his search '—won't you just tell me how it's going? What do the forensic findings say?'

'You *know* I can't.'

She squeezed her eyes shut for a moment, and he knew with complete certainty that after all, she was unable to dispel the memories of their shared discussions of his previous murder investigations. He knew then that Lilah would never really forget him, even if she lived to be as old as Granny Hillcock. Those three years they'd spent together would always count for something. She was always going to hear a little voice whispering *Den* when anything happened to bring her into contact with the police. It was a very small consolation.

'So you're helping out here, are you? Doing some of Sean's work?' He was trying to return to a safer footing. 'Busy time, I imagine.'

She smiled crookedly and he cursed himself. *What a bloody waste*, he repeated to himself, thinking of what they'd had and what they'd lost.

* * *

He found Ted tinkering with a piece of machinery in a rickety open-fronted shed, down a steep track leading away from the main farm buildings. The sound of a motor starting up and sporadic hammering had drawn him to investigate, and he stood quietly watching the man for a few minutes, trying to assess his eligibility as a murder suspect.

There had been no good or valid reasons for dismissing Speedwell from his calculations, and yet he found it quite impossible to imagine this small, unassuming man deliberately lunging into another human being with a sharp metal implement. There was something about him that literally made the idea unthinkable.

Speedwell had the hazy morning light on him as he bent over a blue-painted machine that Den thought he recognised as a power harrow. It had numerous metal teeth mounted on a frame about ten feet in length, with a complicated tower arrangement sitting on top; this was the focus of Ted's attention. The implement was connected up to a tractor, which was noisily chugging, making it easy to approach without being heard. No longer hammering, Ted was now poking the innards delicately – and presumably dangerously – with a long screwdriver. Den had to walk right up to him before the man became aware of his presence.

Ted looked up slowly, with no trace of alarm

or guilt. 'Oh, 'tis you,' he said calmly, his voice skilfully pitched to be audible above the engine. 'How'd you find me?'

'I heard the motor and the hammering,' Den shouted. 'Can we go outside?'

Speedwell ignored the suggestion, peering again into the bowels of the machine. Den had to try a less direct approach. 'That looks a fine piece of equipment. Is it new?'

'Got it last year,' Speedwell agreed. 'Something's come loose down here, seems like. Not been working proper for a while now.'

'Don't they come with a guarantee?'

The man shrugged. 'Not worth the paper it's written on. Quicker to do it us-selves.' He looked curiously at Den. 'Got more questions for me, then?' He went to the tractor and manipulated the throttle, reducing the noise, but not turning it off completely. 'There – 'ee can hear better now,' he said. 'No need to go outside.'

Den glanced around. It seemed he was destined to have all his conversations with the farmhand in inappropriate surroundings. The building was ramshackle at best, perhaps used originally for storing hay or sheltering animals. It now housed two tractors; several large black rubber buckets stacked tidily and covered with a liberal coating of reddish-brown dust; a big metal barrel standing on one end and streaked down the sides with oil; and a chaotic assortment of tools associated with the maintenance of mechanical implements. It was divided into two sections, the further one closed off by a door. The corrugated iron roof was sound, but there were gaps in the walls where more corrugated sheets had been nailed up as patches. The front was open, impossible to secure. 'Never get anything nicked from in here?' he asked idly.

Speedwell shook his head impatiently, as if the idea was fanciful. 'Can't see anyone coming down here to thieve a few tools,' he elaborated, obviously thinking the police habitually nursed the most unreasonable of suspicions.

Den moved to the silent second tractor and leant against a big black tyre. He folded his arms and tried for a relaxed demeanour.

'Just tell me one more time where you were on Tuesday, and whether you saw anything out of the ordinary,' he invited. 'And whether you've remembered anything else you should tell me.'

'What sort o' thing?' Speedwell continued to poke the harrow with his screwdriver.

'Perhaps I should tell you that we spoke to your son yesterday,' Den prompted. 'It was a few days before we discovered that Eliot and Sean were friends. It seems a bit strange that you didn't tell us that when we saw you on Wednesday.'

Distaste carved grooves around Speedwell's

mouth. 'We didn't think of it,' he said curtly.

'They seem to have shared in a few schemes over the years. Sean borrowing money from your son for various ventures – scrap metal and that sort of thing. How did you feel about that?'

Ted shrugged. 'Nothing to do wi' us. Us kept our noses out of it.' The simple honesty of this appealed to Den. He felt a strong urge to accept the man's words at face value, and go home for the rest of the weekend. He might have done it, if events had not conspired against him.

Once more he went over the same tedious ground. 'Just tell me again exactly where you were on Tuesday afternoon.'

Speedwell sighed and worked his lips as if about to spit. 'Up to Top Linhay, far end of the farm. Maybe half a mile off.'

'Did anyone see you there?'

The man shook his head. 'Who'd be up there?'

'And you stayed until it started to get dark?'

'Aye. Close to four, must have been.'

Den cocked his head and leant back against the tyre. 'Not much of an alibi, is it? Seeing there are no witnesses.'

'Didn't know I would want one, did I? Be 'ee telling me I should take some bloke everywhere with me, so's I can prove everything I've done?'

Den scratched an eyebrow. 'Good point,' he said. 'Perhaps we can leave it there . . .'

Speedwell wasn't listening. He'd managed to prod something significant inside his machine, and suddenly crowed in triumph. Carefully, he extracted a small metal ring. 'Got it! There's the little sod's been causing all the trouble.' He placed the rogue component in his pocket and moved to turn off the tractor engine. The familiar sudden silence was tangible.

The two men were standing on either side of the harrow, Den preparing to terminate his interview. Simultaneously they both heard a weak animal bleat from the closed-off half of the shed. They both frowned and looked towards the door.

'What was that?' asked Den.

'Search me,' returned Speedwell, already moving to investigate. 'Sounded like a calf.'

The door was padlocked shut, with an unobtrusive chain wound round a wooden post. Speedwell tugged at it and then shifted a few inches sideways to peer through a small hole in the panelling. 'Jesus Christ!' he gasped and began tugging harder at the chain. Den went to help him, quickly realising that the weakest spot was the door itself.

'Here,' he said. 'Get one of those tools – something long and strong.'

Ted came back with a long-handled sledgehammer, but did not hand it to Den. 'Stand back,' he ordered, and swung it clumsily at the door. The wood cracked but did not give until he dealt it a second blow and the panel to which the chain was attached gave way. Den yanked it open and the two men stood shoulder-to-shoulder, peering into the murky interior.

Ted had already seen what lay inside. Seven young calves were stretched out on the floor with the barest scattering of filthy straw beneath them. A sour smell of distress and suffering rose from them. All but one had their necks extended, mouths open, tongues protruding, eyes staring. The exception was hunched miserably, head turned into its flank like a baby fawn.

Speedwell bent over each in turn, lifting the heads and letting them flop back. 'Six dead and one with only minutes to go,' he pronounced.

Den was baffled. 'But . . .' he stammered. 'I mean . . . Why?'

Speedwell straightened and moved back to the doorway. 'Us've never kept calves in here,' he said slowly. ''Tis certain the boss don't know they're here. Poor little buggers've starved to death, look. Gasping out for something to drink.' His features crumpled and Den thought he was going to weep. The acute cruelty of it was only slowly getting through to him as he tried to make sense of the discovery.

'Wouldn't anyone have heard them?' he

demanded. 'Wouldn't they have bawled day and night?'

Ted dashed a hand across his eyes and sniffed noisily. He nodded. 'They'd have bawled,' he agreed. 'But 'tis a fair way to the yard, and with all the fuss over Sean, comings and goings . . . besides, there's other calves in the barn. Us'd think it was them.'

'But these would have sounded much further away.'

Ted shrugged helplessly. 'Us don't come down here much in winter. Help me with this little chap.' He went back to the surviving calf. 'Might save him if we're quick.'

Den had carried calves before, for Lilah, but they had been skinny little Jerseys, light and easy. This was a much bigger specimen with a heavy head and long sinuous body. It was also skeletally thin and terminally weak. He lifted it into his arms while Speedwell led the way back to the yard. 'How old would you say it is?' he asked.

'Six, eight weeks,' Ted guessed. 'Could be more. The winter calving started back a while now.' He was almost trotting back to the main buildings. ''Tis Sean's doing,' he decided. 'Keeping them down there, all secret. Some business he had going. Must have helped himself to milk from the tank for 'em. Cheeky bastard.'

'I still don't see . . .' Den floundered.

'Wait till Boss hears about this,' Ted said darkly. 'Poor little buggers. Boss hates cruelty. Always on at Sean to give a thought to how the beasts be feeling.' He pointed Den to the shed where Gordon had shot the badger, and told him to set the calf down. Rapidly he collected milk from the bulk tank and mixed it with a dash of hot water from a tap close by. 'Lucky tid'n tanker day, or there'd be no milk for'n.' It was a protracted, messy business, trying to get sustenance into the pathetic creature. Patiently Ted offered the milk in a bucket, but the animal was too weak to stand and the milk risked being spilt as he tried to tip it towards the dehydrated mouth. Den watched helplessly, while trying to keep part of his mind on his original reason for being there.

'A lot of people have been telling me Sean was cruel,' he said. 'You think this was definitely his doing?'

'Thoughtless, more than cruel,' Ted panted. He was scooping handfuls of milk into the calf's mouth, which was having better results. It swallowed painfully and emitted unhappy bleats. A lot of the milk was going onto the man's trousers.

'But he was good to his wife,' Den prompted.

'True enough. You'd think he'd be the same with the beasts, but 'twas as if he never saw they'd got feelings.'

Den could see no further purpose to remaining. 'Good luck with the calf,' he said awkwardly. 'It's a terrible thing to have happened.' A thought struck him. This level of neglect represented an obvious breach of the law. He should make a report of it. Reluctantly he waited for Speedwell to finish. Before he did so, Lilah appeared.

'What's going on?' she asked. 'Where did that calf come from?'

Den explained it to her, keeping it brief. She leant over the sick calf and smacked an angry hand against a vertical post. 'It's sure to die,' she said. 'Look at it! And where's the ear-tag? Were the others the same?'

Den turned to Speedwell, wondering whether he had noticed such a detail. 'Not a tag among 'em,' he said.

'Were they all bulls? How could they have been missed? How old are they?'

'Thirty calvings since end of October,' Ted summarised. 'Sean was meant to shoot all the bulls and take 'em to the hunt kennels. Easy enough to keep a few back.'

'The bloody swine! Gordon's going to be furious when he finds out. Poor little things, it's bad enough without this.'

Ted nodded dourly.

'If he wasn't already dead—' Lilah said, before catching herself.

Gordon would kill him, Den supplied silently. 'There's been a crime committed here,' he said formally. 'I'll have to file a report.'

'Then file it,' his ex-fiancée said. 'For all the good it'll do. The calves died because Sean died. He was feeding them, raising them for veal, probably. He'll have had some crony in Exeter or Plymouth who'd take them off his hands and sell them on.'

'Sounds a bad business to me,' Den said. The image of the dead calves floated before his eyes. He remembered the other dead calves, shot through the head and piled in the Dunsworthy yard. Was there any chance that Sean had been trying to save the lives of a few doomed youngsters? Had he thought he could rescue them and give them at least some sort of life? To judge by Lilah's reaction, this seemed unlikely – it was just some illegal scam that had nothing to do with the welfare of the beasts. 'Does this sort of thing happen a lot?' he asked her.

She sighed impatiently. 'It's the first time I've come across it personally. But the facts make it pretty obvious. Without ear-tags, they're illegal. The calves down in that barn were officially dead at birth. And it can only have been Sean keeping them there. Gordon would never have let them starve, if he'd known about them. There was a terrible run of bull calves, right through

November and into December, with another three last week. Sean must have seen a chance to make some money out of them. Or thought he did.'

It had been a gruelling morning, with the disturbing discovery likely to haunt him for some time. Casting around for a ray of light in this dark place, Den's eyes fell on the soft-faced Ted, cradling the sickly calf. *If Ted Speedwell killed Sean O'Farrell, I'll eat Granny Hillcock*, he thought passionately. The idea cheered him and he forced a swing into his walk as he went back to his car and coiled himself into the driving seat.

CHAPTER SEVENTEEN

Gordon put in an appearance at the meeting on Saturday morning because he'd said he would. Although he had asked Sean to swap milkings to make it easier for him to attend, it was actually going to be possible to do both, if he got a move on. This, he acknowledged wryly to himself, was what Sean had insisted all along.

'Why can't you do the milking first?' the herdsman had demanded. 'They won't start before ten-thirty, and you can easily get away from here in time for that.'

'Because I don't want to do three hours' work beforehand. I don't want to rush the washing down, change my clothes and then get my head straight enough to concentrate on what they're saying. What difference does it make to you anyway?'

Sean's answer to that had been vague and inarticulate.

Most of the local farmers had made the effort to attend. They'd hired a room at the White Hart in Okehampton, with coffee and lunch laid on, and a speaker from the NFU brought in – though nobody was too sure how that might turn out if things got militant.

Gordon had done the morning milking, washed everything down, changed his clothes and assembled his thoughts in plenty of time to be amongst the first to arrive. He took a seat in the middle of a row not far from the back of the room. He braced himself for the looks he would get as people recognised him and remembered the news stories from local TV and radio over the past few days. *The Western Morning News* had carried a story about Sean's death and the weekly papers had made much of it at the end of the week. Gordon had no illusions as to how notorious he had become and how ambivalent many of his neighbours' reactions were going to be.

Tom Beasley was the first to approach him, taking the adjacent seat to Gordon's. 'Heard about the trouble you've been having,' he said flatly. 'Must be hard, with everything else that's going on.'

Gordon nodded. 'That's the way of it, but we have to keep going. This thing is too important to miss.'

Tom shook his head sceptically. 'Can't see any good coming of it. What can us do? Storm Westminster with a herd of bullocks?'

'It's what they'd do in France.'

'They don't care so much for their beasts in France. Us'd be too bothered about they hurtin' themselves in the traffic.'

Gordon laughed his agreement. 'True,' he chuckled. 'And the media would crucify us if anything happened to a cow.' He tapped a copy of the local paper on the seat next to him. 'If they mention *Cold Comfort Farm* again, I'll not be responsible. Why can't they take us seriously for a change?'

Beasley laughed sourly. 'Us be nothing more than a setting for kids' stories and telly sitcoms,' he agreed. ''Tis enough to make men weep.'

'Can't go on, all the same,' said Gordon grimly. 'Milk money dropping again this month, no sign of any shift in lamb or pig prices, either.'

Beasley took up the refrain with weary familiarity. 'My missus says us'd be better off breeding pedigree dogs for city folk than this. Her sister's friend just paid five hundred quid for a golden retriever. Say nine or ten in a litter, two litters a year – you could live on that.'

Gordon snorted. 'You have to think bigger than that, Tom. Keep four or five bitches, advertise in America – you'd clear twenty thousand a year, no problem. And no need to go out in the rain, either.'

'Sell stock and machinery, and let the fields go back to nature.'

'You get a grant for that. Not just set-aside, but special conservation areas for wildlife. You with that bit of river, too. You'd get more for otters and Christ knows what.'

The conversation was a well-worn one, laced with bewildered irony arising from the knowledge that, crazy as it might sound, their hypothesising was actually based in reality. There really would be more money in breeding lapdogs or letting their land lie undisturbed. Or in offering livery services to middle-class children with ponies. Or in renting out fields for paintballing games or historical re-enactment groups. Anything would be more lucrative than traditional agriculture. This awareness ensured that the farmers in the room carried with them a strong sense of alienation from their lifelong assumption: that they were of some importance to the fabric of society. The denigration of their way of life had not been subtle, especially in recent years. Nothing was now impossible and they sat with their heads drawn down between their shoulders awaiting whatever further extraordinary blows might rain down on them.

The meeting was opened: a local activist made an impassioned speech, stating the obvious. The NFU man strove to tread a middle path, throwing all possible blame onto Brussels and not the national government. Individual farmers got up and told their individual stories, often heartbreaking in their accounts of expenditure exceeding income, month after month and perfectly good cows costing more to keep than they could ever hope to bring in with their milk.

Gordon said nothing, but he was glad he'd come. He was amongst peers, men who shared his lifestyle and who had no difficulty in understanding what was important. If they thought he'd murdered Sean O'Farrell, they weren't losing any sleep over it, and they certainly weren't going to break ranks and try to ostracise him for it. It was as if they'd nodded an acknowledgement of Sean's death, with fleeting regret, concern, puzzlement, and then moved on. They lived for the here and now. This, anyway, was how Gordon Hillcock chose to see it. At the end of the meeting he voted for a petition calling for special urgent recognition of the situation, to be handed in at Downing Street, with renewed efforts to get serious media coverage. But a picture came into his mind of Arthur Scargill and his distraught miners in the eighties, and he knew it was all futile.

He got home in the early afternoon, after a pleasant lunch with his colleagues, feeling for the first time that life just might settle back into the old groove, in spite of Sean's death. His mother and sister were at home, and Lilah's Astra was in the yard, although she was nowhere to be seen.

'Where is she?' he asked his sister.

'There's been something going on outside,' Mary told him. 'It's just one bloody thing after another these days.'

'Why? What happened?'

'I really couldn't say. Apart from that wretched badger the other night, I've been doing a very good job of staying out of the action. I promise you, that's how I prefer it.'

Gordon's mood took a nose dive. 'But where's Lilah?' he asked again.

'I told you,' Mary shouted at him. 'I have no idea.'

'And you don't bloody care a toss, either, do you?' he shouted back. 'The whole place could burn down and you'd just stand there making cakes and taking no fucking notice.'

She faced him squarely. 'Why the hell should I care? I've got no stake in the farm. All it is to me is a great black hole swallowing up practically everything I earn – and for what? The whole thing's finished, can't you see? Didn't they tell you that at your meeting this morning? We've got two years at most, the way things are going. Everybody knows it, why can't you admit it? Without Sean, it'll probably be less.'

Gordon's eyes bulged. His younger sister had always known how to enrage him, how to press the button that ran straight to his nerve endings. One of the very few people in the world who wouldn't be afraid to confront him with unsavoury truths, she always chose her moment unerringly.

'What the hell difference would Sean have made?' he blustered. 'There's about five hundred redundant herdsmen out there, all looking for work. I just have to snap my fingers and any one of them would start work tomorrow.'

'So why haven't you?'

He sneered in her face. 'That question's too stupid to bother answering.'

'Hey, you two – what's all this about?' Their mother was in the living room doorway, the usual detached expression on her face. Both her offspring had learnt decades ago that it was useless to appeal to her in such circumstances for protection or arbitration. 'Sort it out for yourselves,' was her usual line.

'Nothing,' Gordon muttered, and went into the kitchen, intending to make himself a cup of tea. The oak table was stained with spills from the past forty years, the grain embedded with grey streaks. He traced a finger along the decorative edging groove, as he'd done since early boyhood, sulky and defensive now as he had so often been then.

'Gordon thinks I ought to take more interest in the farm,' Mary said. 'He doesn't think it's enough that I pour almost all my money into the place.'

Before Claudia could make any attempt at a conciliatory reply, the back door banged and Lilah came in through the scullery. She was wearing thick socks on her feet, and unzipped her jacket as the family watched her.

'Gordon,' she said. 'I didn't know you were back. Did they tell you what's been going on here?' She looked round the three faces, eagerness and self-importance making her seem impossibly young to them all.

Gordon shook his head.

'Den came back to speak to Ted, and they found a lot of dead calves down in the tractor shed. Sean must have been keeping them for himself – a little sideline. No ear-tags, of course.' She paused, suddenly aware of the prickly silence in the room. 'We told him there was no way you could have known about them,' she faltered.

Gordon got slowly to his feet. 'Dead calves? Where did they come from?'

'They must have been yours. All those bulls, born in November, remember? He must have pretended to shoot them and kept them on stolen milk, locked away. When he died, they all starved. Except one. Ted's trying to save it, but it's pretty far gone.'

Mary was the first to notice Gordon's mounting rage. Even she, his brave sister, took a small step away from him.

'And that police boyfriend of yours saw them?'

Lilah refused to be baited. 'Yes, he did.'

'So now I've got another reason to have wanted Sean out of the way. Didn't that occur to you?'

She gazed at him in bewilderment. 'But you didn't know about it. If you had, you'd have made him get rid of them, or tag them, wouldn't you? Nobody in their right mind could think you'd kill him just for that.'

Without further warning, Gordon brought his fist down on the table with such force that the extending flap screeched against its sliding mechanism and a plate at the other end crashed to the ground. Claudia gave a cry of alarm and Lilah went white. 'You'll frighten Granny if you do that,' said Mary calmly. 'Pull yourself together, for heaven's sake.'

'Can you blame me?' he demanded. 'With all this going on, it's one bloody thing after another.'

From upstairs, they heard Granny Hillcock knocking on the floor with a stick. 'There – I told you,' said Mary. 'You can jolly well go up to her and explain. And don't come back until you're in a better mood.'

With no further argument, Gordon did as she ordered. The three women breathed sighs of relief at his departure. Lilah attempted a giggle. 'He's just like my father used to be,' she said. 'I guess that's farmers for you.'

Mary glowered at her. 'I can't think what you see in him. All he does is throw his weight about. Great big bully.'

'He's not,' said Claudia softly. 'He's being pushed too far by this business with Sean. It must be terrible knowing you're under suspicion for such a thing. You shouldn't needle him, Mary. It isn't fair.'

'Since when was anything around here *fair?*' Mary demanded; nobody made any effort to reply.

Gordon came back within ten minutes and Lilah went to him, as if drawn by a magnet. He sat in a wide carver's chair and she leant against him, inhaling the strong smell of his skin and hair. The presence of his mother and sister mattered little to her in these moments. Gordon raised his head and put his arm tightly round her waist. She met his gaze steadily, seeking to rekindle the sexual passion that had been so strong between them only days before. She put out a hand to grasp his and then let him draw it to his cheek in an old-fashioned gesture of intimacy. Her whole body throbbed at his touch. She cupped his jaw in her palm, rubbing the scratchy stubble. Gordon only shaved every two or three days and his abrasive chin was highly sensual. His blue eyes, deep-set beneath arched brows, were fixed on hers. But the knowledge of the events of the past days lay between them. Lilah imagined she knew the circles his thoughts were whirling around in, the guesses and suspicions that preoccupied him. *Does she really think I did it? Will people think we did it together? Will anything ever be the same again?*

'Come on, you two,' Mary chided them, clearly embarrassed. 'Let's have none of that.'

'You sound like an old maiden aunt,' Gordon told her, looking around Lilah at his sister. 'Go get yourself a boyfriend, why don't you? Maybe that'd loosen you up a bit.'

The unkindness, following so quickly on his noisy violence, disturbed Lilah and she withdrew from him. *He's just upset about the calves*, she assured herself. *He isn't usually like this.*

'I don't need loosening up, thanks very much,'

Mary responded tightly. After a moment's clattering at the sink, she wiped her hands roughly on a towel hanging over the Aga and left the room, her face averted awkwardly. Claudia remained in her own chair for a moment, and then slowly got up.

'I'd better get some notes written up,' she murmured. 'Can't sit here all day.'

Lilah and Gordon let the door close behind Claudia before indulging in a long, hungry kiss. Lilah felt the split between mind and body as a painful conflict. *If only we could leave it all to our bodies*, she lamented to herself. Instead, she spoke her mind. 'You've made Mary cry,' she said. 'What did you do that for?'

'She always was a cry-baby.'

'Well, I'm glad I never had a big brother, if this is what they're like. Poor Mary, with you still on at her, at her age.'

'She knows what she can do about it.'

'Except she can't, because you need her money to keep this place running,' Lilah rashly reminded him. The scowl that greeted her words made her heart thump painfully, for two or three fearful beats. But she stiffened her spine and resolved not to be afraid of him, just as she'd done with her father. This was the man she had chosen, and everything was going to be all right. She faced him steadily. 'It's the same for everybody these days. Farming isn't self-sustaining for anyone. It's bound to get better, though. It goes in cycles. We did history of agriculture last term, and you should hear what it was like in the 1880s!'

'It's a bloody mess at the moment,' he agreed, relaxing into a more familiar gloom. 'But never mind that. Come here.' He tightened his arm, drawing her closer, and she moved irresistibly into his embrace. After a moment she sat on his lap in a conjunction they often adopted. Gordon had substantial thighs and a broad chest. Lilah was slight and fitted his contours very neatly. She closed her mind against a sudden image of Den, ten inches taller than her, wrapping himself around her in a very different way.

'What happens next with the police?' she asked him suddenly.

He drew back his head to focus on her face, eyebrows raised. 'We don't have to talk about that, do we?'

'We do,' she insisted. 'What do you think'll happen?'

'If they think they can find enough evidence to bring a charge against me, I'll probably be held in custody until it comes to trial. That would be months.' He shivered and leant his head on her shoulder. 'And that'd be the end of this place.'

'That should be part of your defence,' she said

eagerly. 'You'd have to be crazy to risk wrecking everything here in a moment of anger.'

He huffed a cynical laugh. 'I don't think murderers often consider the consequences of what they do. It's a pretty stupid career move, whoever you are.'

'They won't charge you,' she assured him. 'It's only Den being so jealous that's got you listed as chief suspect. If they had more manpower, he'd never have been allowed on the case at all. It's quite unprofessional, as it is.' She thought a moment. 'But he's not going to invent evidence, however jealous he is. So I suppose it doesn't really matter in the long run.'

'Poor old Den.' Gordon smiled strangely. 'He must hate my guts. I know I would in his place.'

Lilah wriggled. 'These things happen,' she said softly.

Briskly he pushed her off his lap and patted her bottom. 'Come on. Ma's right, there's work to be done. Ted's not supposed to be doing anything today, and I left him all the yard work when I went off to that meeting. I'll have to make up for it this afternoon, before milking.'

'Do you want me to stick around? I don't have to be anywhere.'

'Are you staying the night, then?'

'If I'm invited,' she said primly. For invitation, she received another deep kiss, his tongue thrusting thick and solid into her mouth, his hands large on her back. As he let her go, he cupped one breast, holding it tight for a moment, hurting and inflaming her in equal measure.

Den wrote up his report on the dead calves after a snatched lunch. He tried to get a grasp of the suspected scheme that Lilah had described, wondering just how Sean could have hoped to get away with it or indeed make any money out of it. With bull calves worth nothing, it seemed an odd sort of scam to be operating, but he assumed there must be *some* expectation of profit. Although not acquainted with market prices for veal or beef, he supposed that a bullock of a year or so in age, reared on rich Devon grass, would fetch a few hundred pounds. Given that there'd be no need to buy fodder for it, this would be clear profit and no doubt worth the risk involved in keeping such animals hidden from sight.

'But why not be upfront about it?' he wondered aloud, talking to the pad in front of him. 'Would anybody have stopped him, if he'd asked Gordon for some milk and a shed to keep them in?'

'Talking to yourself?' Danny Hemsley put his head around the office door.

'Look at this,' Den invited him, showing him the report.

'I bet Hillcock would have made him pay for

them,' he said, after reading it quickly and asking a couple of questions. 'But you're right – it seems a funny sort of trick to pull, right on the boss's doorstep. Surely he never meant to keep them until they were grown up? How would he hide them?'

'Beyond me,' Den admitted. 'And whatever he thought he was doing, the poor little beasts died a very nasty death.'

The DI examined a stubby fingernail, thoughtfully, clearly not satisfied that the matter could be dropped. 'How would you say this fitted with O'Farrell's murder?' he asked.

Den shook his head slowly in defeat. 'I can't see that it does. Only if Hillcock knew what he was doing, and was so disgusted by it, it drove him to homicide. But if he had known, he would have fed the calves after Sean was dead, so he can't have known. And if he didn't know, it can't possibly be a motive for the killing.'

'What if someone else knew about it?'

'Ted Speedwell, you mean? I'd swear by all that's holy he had no idea.'

'Not necessarily him. There's all those women around the place. Four of them, if you don't count the old granny. Five if you count the girlfriend.'

'I can't make it fit, whichever way you look at it. How could keeping illegal bobby calves have any connection with O'Farrell's death?'

'I don't *know*,' said the DI in exasperation. 'But I think you should do everything you can to find out. There might be something you've missed. This case is going to slip through our fingers at this rate. I can feel it – these local farm crimes are always messy. Things are hardly ever what they seem, and even if they are, it's the devil's own job to prove it. If we went by your gut feelings and brought Hillcock in and charged him, he'd get off. You know that, don't you?'

'Yes, sir,' said Den.

Lilah was in bed before Gordon, waiting with naked openness for his attentions, committed in every cell to whatever sensations he chose to inflict on her. Despite the slight awkwardness arising from the presence in the house of Claudia and Mary, Lilah felt no embarrassment in sleeping in Gordon's bed. It was a generous queen-sized double, abandoned by Claudia when widowed and it made for luxurious sexual activity. The thick mattress was unfashionably soft, and the many woollen blankets took all the sting out of winter nights in an underheated house.

Gordon always slept naked, his broad, hairy body giving off heat which drew Lilah to him even in her sleep. She curled up against him, loving the round fuzzy contours of his belly. He was liberally covered all over with hair – arms, legs, back, as well as chest and stomach. Even his pubic hair was thick and bushy. Much of it was beginning to turn grey, while some remained dark brown, giving him a mottled appearance that she had labelled 'brindle' – the multi-coloured hue of some dogs. To lay her hands on Gordon's naked body – which never seemed really naked because of the hair – was a simple but powerful pleasure for her.

He had silvery puckered scars under the hair on his stomach, which she had found on the first time in bed together. 'What happened here?' she had asked in concern.

'Oh, just some childhood thing,' he replied airily. 'They removed my spleen. It all settled down in no time. I never even think of it.'

'But . . .' She'd tried to remember what role the spleen played, what the implications might be of not having one. Gordon had put his large hand across her mouth.

'I was fourteen,' he said. 'And I've never missed it. Don't I seem healthy to you?'

He did, of course, and she obediently thrust the whole thing from her mind.

He was sixteen years older than she was, an age gap almost exactly the same as that between her own parents. Gordon had a past; he could remember things from long before she was born, and he had the compelling power of the mature man. Gordon Hillcock's body was the thing that mattered most in the world to her. It was like having a secret source of wonderful food, or like having a million pounds hidden away in a hollow tree. She could go and tap into this joyous elixir any time she liked.

Unless Gordon was in prison, of course.

CHAPTER EIGHTEEN

Deirdre Watson had a tendency to dislike Sundays, whatever the season. In winter they were especially unsatisfactory. Moving restlessly around the house, she was aware of how dusty and cobwebby much of it was, and how untidy from the residue of Christmas. Pine needles from the tree were still scattered on the living room carpet and screwed-up wrapping paper that had missed the Boxing Day collection lay behind chairs and in odd corners. Dabs of Blu-tack on the ceiling showed where Sam and Matthew had fixed the decorations, and not scraped it off properly when they took them down again. The open fireplace was choked with ash under the grate, and there were nutshells underfoot on the hearthrug.

'This place is a mess,' she announced to nobody in particular.

She received no reply. Robin was reading the sports section of the Sunday paper and Matthew had all his attention on the kung fu game he was involved in on his Play Station. At least, Deirdre guessed it was kung fu. People seemed to be kicking each other a lot and turning backward somersaults. As far as she could tell, Matthew played this same game about five hundred times a day.

Tension in the household was high since the police had interviewed Sam. Her daughter had told her nothing of what had been said, but she was subdued and irritable afterwards, going up to her bedroom and firmly shutting the door. This had made Deirdre resentful. In fact, more than mere resentment burnt in her breast. She was desperate to know what Sam had been asked and how she had replied. 'It's all wrong,' she had repeated. 'I've got a right to know what they think. This is a *murder* inquiry.'

'That's right, Mum,' Sam had snapped back. 'Exciting, isn't it.'

'Don't be so cheeky,' Robin had warned his daughter, before lapsing back into a silence that Deirdre judged to be sheer cowardice.

Sam had gone out immediately after lunch, taking her mother's car and refusing to say when she'd be back. 'I can't stand any more of your prying into something that's none of your business,' was her parting shot.

None of my business? Deirdre had repeated to herself. *When I detested Sean O'Farrell so violently and made little secret of the fact? When that policeman is bound to think I'm in some conspiracy with Gordon?*

Matthew's head was pushed forward, his gaze unwavering on the screen in front of him. Deirdre watched him, savouring the long lashes, the curly hair. He'd always been a handsome boy; as a baby he'd been far more beautiful than his sister. People had made the predictable comments: *Such looks, wasted on a boy. He'll have all the girls after him when he's older.* He'd never caused her or Robin any serious anxiety, until recently. Now, suddenly, he seemed to be unbearably vulnerable, prey to forces and proclivities that she perceived as wholly malign. Her arms twitched with the desire to clutch him to her protectively. Silently she prayed that the danger had passed.

She sighed noisily and Matthew glanced up at her. 'What's the matter, Mum?'

'Oh – just Sundayitis. You know how I hate Sundays.'

She stood close to him, where he knelt on the carpet, the game console in front of him. 'The only things I can think of to do are boring old housework. It's all right for you men, with your papers and games.'

'You can play if you like,' he offered with a grin. 'You can be Mighty Magnus – he always wins.'

She was tempted. After all, why not? But she'd watched enough to know that two minutes would be the limit of her attention span. 'No thanks,' she declined. 'It's not really my thing.'

'Okay,' he accepted easily. Another rush of fear for him engulfed her. He was always so easy, so accommodating, not wanting to hurt anybody's feelings. She wanted to tell him to stop being so nice, to stand up for himself and be a bit more . . . well, *manly*.

It had to all be her fault. She'd let him play with dolls and dress in girls' clothes when he was small. She and Robin had encouraged him never to fight his way out of difficulties, but to negotiate and compromise. They'd been happy with his obvious awareness of how other people were feeling, his willingness to hug and touch at an age where most boys avoided physical contact. Now it seemed it was backfiring on them.

Robin discarded the newspaper abruptly. 'These dark afternoons are enough to depress anybody. Roll on spring, I say. We should all hibernate like bears and skip January altogether.'

Deirdre managed a laugh. 'It won't last for ever, I suppose. I'll go and make us some tea, shall I?'

'Good idea,' Robin approved.

Den missed Lilah most forcibly on Sundays. On this one, with a murder inquiry rapidly running into the sand and nobody sympathetic to talk to about it, he was feeling profoundly sorry for himself.

Danny Hemsley had been right to chastise him for failing to keep his mind open from the very outset of the case. From here on, as the investigation started to go cold and desk work on the forensics became the default focus of attention, he was resolved on a renewed and detailed exploration of any and every possible candidate for prosecution.

Doodling on a sheet of paper, he compulsively listed names. *Ted Speedwell, Eliot Speedwell, Heather O'Farrell, Abigail O'Farrell, Jilly Speedwell, Deirdre Watson, Sam Watson, Claudia Hillcock, Mary Hillcock*. Then he crossed them all out again, one by one. Either they had excellent alibis or they just didn't make credible murderers. Even though he had first-hand experience of unlikely killers – people you could never imagine would do such a thing – once the story was laid out logically, it was plain to see how the situation had arisen. He saw very little prospect that this same reasoning would apply to the Dunsworthy murder.

Ted Speedwell had to be the first person to consider. He couldn't prove his whereabouts and his fingerprints were all over the murder weapon. If he were to be charged now, the case for the prosecution would be almost as good as that against Hillcock – which is to say they would both be hopelessly weak. It would never reach the courts. Den found himself feeling rather glad about that: the idea of Ted in prison made him shudder. Even Hillcock, proud and independent, accustomed to taking control of his own life and organising his own time as he saw fit, would probably not survive a long sentence other than as a mental and physical wreck. It gave Den pause to think about it. Did he hate the man enough to want that to happen to him?

One day, Den knew, he would let slip just what his real feelings were towards custodial punishments for criminals. With every month that passed, his ambivalence became more acute, despite his stern self-admonishments. A year and a half earlier he had begun attending Quaker Meetings every five or six weeks, and had slowly become aware of their thinking on the subject of prison. They didn't like it. They believed it to be counter-productive, barbaric and wasteful. It cost the state ridiculous sums of money and turned out people who were simply more determined and skilful miscreants than before, as well as addicted to drugs. Den could not argue with any of this. *But it's my job*, he insisted to himself. *I'm paid to locate and capture lawbreakers, and when they're caught they get sent to prison. What happens after that is none of my business.*

Murderers, of course, were different. They'd put themselves beyond the pale and nobody – not even Quakers – would seriously suggest they should not be sent to prison; people had to be protected against their violent impulses. It was a commonplace that those prisoners serving time for murder were the most interesting. They often made constructive use of their time inside, and even sometimes showed remorse. So why was he getting himself in a stew over Gordon Hillcock all of a sudden?

He returned to his list. Deirdre Watson had aroused Hemsley's interest largely thanks to the anonymous note, which Den suspected had come from Lilah. The report on the interview with Sam Watson had highlighted the issue of badger culling, lamping and baiting, as well as other sorts of animal exploitation. How or even *whether* these concerned Mrs Watson was still unresolved, apart from her membership of Compassion in World Farming. Den couldn't see her as a killer, try as he might. Hemsley had reminded him of his own comments on how calm she had been at the scene of the murder, and how shocked Hillcock was by contrast – and still Den was not convinced.

Lilah's inflation of the rumour that Matthew Watson was gay and prey to Sean and Eliot had already been discounted as troublemaking.

He nibbled his pencil and then circled *Jilly Speedwell* on his list. She had freely admitted to having been at home at the relevant time on Tuesday afternoon. She could have gone up to the yard unobserved, and got into conversation with Sean. If something he'd said had enraged her, she might have snatched up the fork and thrust it at him – twice. Then she would have had time to get back to her cottage, wash herself and her clothes, calm down and be sipping tea when Ted came in from wherever he'd been before darkness fell.

A familiar sense gripped him of being in possession of only the most scattered fragments of the complete picture. It wasn't only that he was missing something that had been pushed under his nose, it was that some facts were so completely absent that he couldn't hope to understand how these people all fitted together. Police detectives were handicapped more or less by definition. Even knowing the right questions to ask, focusing in on hard evidence and using past experience to assess probabilities, it all came down in the end to lucky breaks. Some crisis or tragedy from the distant past might surface to explain the passions that made no sense otherwise. Or, more likely, they would not surface, and the whole thing would crumble into a condition of stalemate for lack of this crucial comprehension.

Lucky breaks did happen, of course, quite frequently. People became careless or they cracked under the strain of the fear of discovery. Information filtered in from suspicious friends and relatives. Or the killer was forced to commit further crimes in an effort to remain safe from detection. Or, less often, Forensics finally unearthed incontrovertible evidence. But even apparently rock-solid physical evidence tended to fall apart when attacked by skilful defence lawyers.

There was no human blood on Hillcock's clothes, or on Speedwell's. The marks and fluids in the yard had told a story of a swift and violent attack, followed by the dying victim's dragging himself, or possibly being dragged, into the barn. The stark scenario explained nothing.

In gathering gloom, both actual and spiritual, Den concluded that the case was definitely sliding out of their grasp. It wasn't going to end in a successful prosecution of the person responsible for Sean O'Farrell's death. The thought of returning to Dunsworthy to ask more questions of Jilly Speedwell or Claudia Hillcock or the others struck him as futile. It didn't matter that Sean had been cruel to animals. It didn't matter that he was inconsistent by nature – kind to his wife, patient with his daughter, yet disliked and mistrusted by just about everyone else who knew him. Most people were inconsistent once you started to delve into their personalities. Even if everyone who knew him had wished him dead, there was still almost nothing that comprised a viable line of enquiry.

Moodily, he tossed his notebook onto the chair beside him and got up to make himself some cheese on toast. It was still only five o'clock and there was nothing watchable on telly. He'd always thought it pathetic when people claimed to have nothing to do; it could only mean an empty head and an empty life. Now it had happened to him. The evening stretched blank and boring; the wind was getting up outside, and nobody he could think of would welcome a phone call or visit. Nobody, if he was honest, that he wanted to see or speak to, anyway.

Nobody, that is, except Lilah Beardon.

Despite his reluctance, Den returned to Dunsworthy on Monday morning, in time to catch Jilly Speedwell before she went to her job at the school. She answered his knock quickly, her frizzy hair seeming to stand out horizontally from her head, her fleshy shoulders and forearms filling the bright blue sweatshirt she was wearing. She sparked with impatience.

'I'm sorry,' he said. 'Just a few more questions, if you don't mind.'

'Waste of good time and money,' she asserted. 'Everybody knows who 'twas who did that to Sean, without all this circus.'

'Oh?'

''Tis plain as can be. Gordon Hillcock's temper has got the better of'n before now. And Sean never knew when to keep un's mouth shut, dozy sod. Wouldn' take much these days, with milk prices so bad and calves being shot, and the whole place falling round our heads, for it to lead to this.'

'You're telling me that you believe Gordon Hillcock murdered Sean O'Farrell?' Den said formally. 'Have you any evidence that this is what happened?'

'*Evidence!*' she scoffed. 'Us never saw it happen, more's the pity. But 'tis right, all the same. But 'ee won't get a confession out of'n. Not like on the telly, where the chap breaks down and tells the whole story. This be real life, and real life is messy. Sean's dead and his wife as weak as a rabbit and his girl going off with some boy like an alleycat. An' us stuck here with a man who could kill my Ted any time 'un likes. So pampered he is, by that houseful of women.' She stopped abruptly, clamping her lips together, as if belatedly aware of saying too much.

Den took a deep, careful breath, acutely conscious of the web of history and emotion that he couldn't hope to fully disentangle. Conscious, too, that Mrs Speedwell was echoing many of his own thoughts of the previous afternoon. 'Perhaps I could come in?' he suggested.

'I leave for work at half past,' she warned him.

'I won't take long.'

'Can't tell 'ee any more than I said already.'

'I'd just like to go through it again. We've got the picture a bit clearer now, the sort of man Mr O'Farrell was, how people felt about him . . .'

'Talked to Eliot, did 'ee?'

'He didn't tell you?'

'Wouldn't want to worry us. Not that we'd worry, really. Us knows he's done nothing wrong.'

'But he was Sean O'Farrell's friend?'

She smiled thinly. 'Funny pair, you be thinking.'

'Hard to see what they had in common, maybe.'

'Plenty they had in common,' she flashed. 'Growing up together all those years, like brothers at one time.'

A missing jigsaw piece suddenly became apparent. 'When exactly did Sean come here?'

'Born right here,' she said. 'His mum and dad had the cottage, and Old Man O'Farrell before them. Sean's granddad, he was.' She let her gaze wander to the untidy garden beyond the window. 'None of them made old bones, in that family. Least of all Sean,' she added with a grimace. 'What be poor Heather a'gwayne to do now?'

'And Abigail? Does she talk to you? She seems a rather lonely girl.'

'Abby be fine, with her beasts and that boyfriend. 'Tis Heather's the worry.'

'How did Abby get on with her father?'

Jilly smiled again and Den could see a revelation coming. 'Do 'ee mean her father – or Sean?'

Two years earlier, Den would have quivered with excitement at the implication. He would have snatched at the fact of a child fathered outside the marriage. But now he knew better. If Jilly Speedwell was in on the secret, it was likely to be a leaky one.

'I meant Sean,' he said coolly. 'But if you have information about the girl's parentage, I'd be happy to hear it.'

She kept her eyes on the garden, speaking slowly. 'Funny the way time changes things. Heather was a lovely young thing, outside all day, singing and laughing. Must've been high summer when she fell pregnant with Abby. Us knew it could never have been Sean – more like a brother than a husband to her. Happy enough, seemingly, and he took the little one as his own.'

'So . . . ?'

'Us all believed 'twas Gordon's.'

How dim-witted Den felt he'd been, not to see it coming. Who else, after all, could it have been? A roll in the summer hayfields, the young master and wife of the impotent herdsman, starved of physical affection and doubtless happy to have her own baby. An image of the scene, with Lilah's face and body in place of Heather's, filled his mind. Sixteen years or so had done little to change Gordon Hillcock: even in the grey stretches of January he was at it, indulging his appetites on young women who by rights belonged to somebody else.

He lost all will to continue the interview and took his leave a few minutes later, unable to shake himself free of thoughts of Lilah. He had little doubt that she was intent on protecting Gordon Hillcock from prosecution for murder – or that she had every chance of success. She had three months' start on the police; she knew his temperament and at least some of the background of Dunsworthy and its residents. He wondered how far she would go. Would she merely content herself with attempting to obliterate any indicators of Hillcock's guilt, gossiping to police officers and sending anonymous letters? He didn't think Lilah fully understood how widespread was the belief in Gordon's guilt. Mrs Speedwell had had no hesitation in fingering him as the killer. Try as he might, Den could find little consolation in this.

His interview reports were getting scrappier by the day, despite the flurry of new leads that had been made following the arrival of the anonymous note about the Watsons. Danny Hemsley wasn't slow to point this out when Den returned to the station. 'It's worrying me, Cooper, I don't mind telling you. How about we start a new tack? Find the unanswered questions, right?'

'Unanswered questions,' echoed Den, dully.

'Points of contention, things a defence lawyer would home in on. Like, why did O'Farrell struggle into the barn when he only had seconds to live?'

'I thought we'd covered that one, sir. He was trying to get to the phone in the office. It's the quickest way.'

'Tunnel vision, Cooper. Throw some more guesses at me.'

Den obliged, forcing his thoughts into lateral directions. 'He wanted to get to Hillcock and the recorder. One or both of them. He was trying to get away from somebody in the yard. He was afraid of being trampled by the cows. He had something in the barn or office or parlour that he absolutely had to get to before he died. He was cold. Quite frankly, sir, I can't see we're ever going to know for sure.'

'It helps, though, don't you see? It gets us inside the scene.' Hemsley jotted down Den's answers. 'For instance, this first one assumes that milking had already started, or was just about to start. But if that was so, the cows would already be standing around the yard, more or less filling it to capacity. Wouldn't it make a major disturbance if the attack happened in the middle of a great herd of cattle? Doesn't that have a bearing on the time it happened? Wouldn't you say it had to be before the cows were brought out of their stalls and into the yard?'

'Not necessarily,' Den argued. 'If two people were fighting in the yard with them, they'd just back away and clear a space.'

'Would they? Are you sure?'

'They would if one of them was O'Farrell,' Den said confidently. 'They were scared of him.'

'Says who?'

'Mrs Watson, Mrs Hillcock, Mary. Even Granny Hillcock said he was a nasty sod – though we can't be sure she's got the right man.'

'What about Hillcock?'

Den thought back to the milking session he'd

observed. 'They're a bit nervy with him, too, but it looked as if he could gentle them if he tried. I guess O'Farrell ruined their trust in people generally.'

'So whoever went into the yard, they'd shy away?'

'I'd say so, yes.'

'Which I imagine – as I said before – would make quite a commotion. Clattering feet, a few raised voices, that sort of thing.'

'Raised bovine voices, you mean, sir?' The picture conjured by the DI's words was accurate from Den's own rather limited experience. A herd of a hundred cows in a confined space, trying to avoid a fracas in their midst, would be difficult to ignore.

'So if an outsider killed Sean in the yard, with the cows, during milking, Hillcock and Mrs Watson would almost certainly have noticed something going on. And unless they're in a conspiracy together, it seems that this was not the case. Therefore, O'Farrell died before milking started, which was just after three.'

'And that would put Mrs Speedwell in the clear,' Den realised. 'She didn't get home till quarter to. Hardly time to get up to the yard and do the deed.'

'But it leaves *Mr* Speedwell very much in the picture.'

Den sighed wearily.

'There's another unanswered question,' Hemsley pressed on. 'Why didn't the attacker make any effort to hide the body?'

'We've been over that as well, sir. Assuming we're right that it wasn't dragged into the barn, then it seems most likely that the killer didn't realise what he'd done. And if it had been dragged or carried, the attacker would have got blood all over him, as well as needing to be pretty strong. As I see it, Sean was left in the yard to sort himself out and consider his evil ways.'

'Or the killer was interrupted?'

'Could be,' Den agreed.

'The weapon. Thrown down in a barn across the main yard from where the attack took place. How did it get there? Run that past me, will you?'

'There's a gate at the end of the railings, just before the biggest of the cowsheds, that opens onto the main yard. The attacker would have opened it, gone through, closed it behind him, crossed the yard and tossed the fork in through the first doorway he came to.'

'Passing on his way cars and possibly people in the yard.'

'Only Mrs Watson's car. And if she saw him, she wouldn't think anything strange of him carrying a fork from one side of the yard to another. But she would have been in the office anyway, so there wasn't much risk of her seeing him.'

'Why bother to do that? Why not just leave the thing lying in the yard?'

'Habit. A tidy mind,' Den suggested. 'Or – obviously – nobody would leave a sharp tool where cows were going to be milling about in a few minutes' time. It would be second nature to put it somewhere safe. Ted was going to need it next day for the silage. He was having trouble without it, after Forensics brought it in as evidence.'

'Why not clean the blood off it first?'

'In too much of a hurry. Worried that somebody would notice – cleaning a fork isn't a very normal activity unless it's part of a wholesale exercise where you do all the tools together. Perhaps he meant to go back and do it later, when nobody was about.'

'None of this sounds like Mrs Watson, does it?' Hemsley concluded. 'That's what you're wanting me to think, right?'

Den took a deep breath. 'Okay, say it *was* her. She could have met Sean in the smaller cow shed, started a row with him there, snatched up the fork and chased or followed him into the gathering yard, lunged at him with the sharp end and then taken the fork across the big yard, because she'd have the same instinctive reasons for not leaving it lying around.'

'Do we know where the fork was normally kept? Where would it have been to start with?'

Den had to think about this. 'Not in the shed where we found it, that's for sure,' he concluded. 'We asked Hillcock, didn't we? What did he say?'

'Cooper,' said the DI warningly. 'You have to be on top of that sort of detail.'

'By the silage pit,' Den remembered. 'There's a corner where you can stand things like that. I saw it when we went to see Speedwell in the yard. That would be the obvious place.'

'And how far is that from the gathering yard?'

'Ten or twelve yards. He'd collect the silage in the scoop on front of the tractor, and tip it over for the cows to reach. Then he picks up bits that had dropped in the wrong place, with that fork. It's difficult to explain,' he tailed off.

'But it would be in easy reach, and might possibly have been left closer to the gathering yard than you think?'

Den nodded uncertainly. 'But there'd be no reason for Mrs Watson to be out there. She only goes into the office and the milking parlour.'

'Maybe she needed to have a pee. I don't expect there's an outside privy?'

'Not that I've noticed,' said Den.

'So she'd creep into a corner of one of the

sheds or barns for that, don't you think? Then if O'Farrell saw her, he might have said something he shouldn't and she went for him.'

Den frowned sceptically, unable to find much in that idea to persuade him. They played with a few more hypotheses, putting layers of detail onto two or three alternative scenarios, until Hemsley called a halt.

'Enough,' he said. 'Now what about these badgers? Rumour has it that O'Farrell indulged in baiting and/or lamping, that much seems certain. And yet at the same time he allowed his daughter to keep a pet one in the back garden. So what was going on?'

Den had little difficulty with this one. 'People kill rabbits, but keep tame ones,' he pointed out. 'It might not be logical, but it's not unusual. And I get the impression that young Abigail could have pretty much anything she wanted. Plus it was one in the eye for the boss. Sean would probably have liked that.'

'But aren't badgers meant to be spreading TB like wildfire amongst dairy cattle? Wouldn't O'Farrell have to be crazy to let one live on the farm like that?'

'So long as Hillcock didn't know, and it never got near the cows, he'd be okay with it. Hillcock never went down to the cottages, and certainly not into their back gardens. Mrs O'Farrell made a special point of telling me that.'

'Why didn't he?'

'I don't know. No need to, I guess. He phoned them from the house or his mobile if he had anything urgent to say.'

'Hmm.'

'There's one funny thing, though. The Speedwell front garden is full of junk, which was part of a dodgy scrap metal scheme that Sean and Eliot were into. You'd expect Hillcock to have something to say about that. It's a real eyesore.'

'Not relevant,' Danny dismissed. 'Now – the big one. Sean's sex life, or lack of it. What does this say about his relations with his wife? Especially given this new stuff about the girl being Hillcock's?'

Den trod carefully. 'All I can come up with is that it wouldn't be likely to sweeten things between O'Farrell and Hillcock.'

'But why would it come to a crisis now, after all these years?'

'Danny!' Den burst out. 'It keeps coming back to Hillcock. Can't you see that?'

'Don't call me Danny,' said Hemsley automatically.

'Sorry,' said Den, frustrated, feeling more than ready to terminate the session and make himself a large mug of coffee. 'Did we just get anywhere, do you think?'

'I'm not sure we did,' Hemsley scanned the

notes without much sign of hope. 'But it never hurts to get the facts aired one more time. Especially when we're almost a week into the investigation and have bugger all to show for it.'

'I'll go and get some coffee,' said Den.

Abigail O'Farrell felt swamped. She rode the bus to school that Monday in a seat by herself, her face pressed against the cold glass, her eyes fixed on the muddy verges speeding past below her. It was her favourite thinking time, when she went over old memories, or dreamt about the future. Since last Tuesday she'd had more than enough to think about: the way people were behaving, the changes that she was going to have to face. Everyone had guilty secrets, even if they pretended they hadn't. She herself certainly had secrets – and not just the one she said she would keep on Gary's behalf. He had trusted her enough to show her the puckered purple scar on his foreskin, the result of catching his willy in the zip of his jeans when he was eight. 'Will it stop you from having sex properly?' she'd asked in an awed voice.

'Hope not,' he said, with a mixture of pride and brave endurance that she found deeply lovable. 'I'm lucky it didn't have to be removed altogether.'

Well, it was a leaky sort of secret, that one.

Gary's mum had told loads of other mothers about it, and there were people at school who could remember it happening. The exciting part was that Gary had let her have a look at it, and it did help her not to think about the much bigger secret; the one that nobody else but her knew about. The one that might change everybody's mind about her dad, even if he was dead and there was loads of sympathy for Mum and her, being left on their own after a horrible murder. Everyone knew how kind Dad had been, making sure Mum was okay – doing all the shopping and cleaning, as well as his job which sometimes took him ten hours a day, as he never tired of saying. Even if he was sometimes a bit hard on the cows – and she'd seen some of that herself when she was younger – and if he had some fairly unpleasant friends like Fred Page, who looked at you as if he wanted to do something disgusting to you – well, they all thought Dad must be okay because he was such a good husband and father.

She hadn't wanted to find him. She hadn't been following him or spying or anything. She'd just been minding her own business, last summer holidays, looking for somewhere shady to sit with her Game Boy, because Mum was driving her mad in the house. She'd gone to her pets' area, where she could watch the rabbits and other animals all getting on so nicely in their big cages that Dad had made for them. There was a copse of trees behind the cottages, down in a bit of a dip with a brook running through it. When she was little, Abigail used to spend hours down here on her own, paddling in the water and making dams and mud pies. She regarded it as almost her own private property, Dad should have known that. He shouldn't have been there at all, never mind doing what he was doing.

It had been horrible, the awful sounds and the dreadful violence of it. After that she hadn't been able to feel the same about him, even though he'd been her same old dad around the house. She knew something was different, even when she managed to push it out of her mind.

But she had never wanted him dead. He hadn't deserved that – *nobody* deserved that. Even though she could already see that he wouldn't really be missed, not even by her mum, and that without him there was a new sort of relief – still there was no way anyone should have killed him like that. She wanted to see him dead in his coffin and give him the special secret letter she'd written to him, and that she carried round with her, terrified that somebody might read it if she let it out of her sight. She wanted him to know that she knew what he had done, but it wasn't going to be any use because what she really wanted was her *old* dad back, from before last summer. The dad she remembered when she was little, who played and sang with her and laughed at the things she said and took her round the farm with him, talking about how lucky they were to live in the country where there was space to be free and nobody on your back all the time telling you what to do. The dad who let her keep a collection of stray animals, even though Gordon would have a fit if he knew about the badger.

Dad hadn't always been rough with the cows, either. Only if one seemed to deliberately go against him did he lose his temper and punch it with his hard fist, or pull its tail up until it really hurt. Abigail knew that must be agony – the cow would moan and try to get away. Once a new heifer, brought in for the first time for milking, collapsed when Dad twisted her tail like that. Abby was twelve then and she never went back to watch the milking again, from that day on. She had trudged back to the cottage crying at the cruelty of it.

And now he'd been dead for nearly a week and already she could hardly remember his face. She had a horrible scary feeling that he had been a stranger who'd just happened to live in the same house as her. Gradually over the past few years he had become more and more unknowable. Even before the thing in the copse, she had felt a yawning gulf opening between them and she had let it happen without doing anything to stop it. Parents, she had concluded, were only for when you were little and helpless. After that they were useless, and you had to find other people to love and talk to and share your secrets with.

Like Gary. They'd been going out together for a year now, and she knew it was one of those great romances that last for a lifetime. They'd get married when she was seventeen or eighteen and they'd always tell each other everything and he would be the best dad in the world, as well as a sweet lover and a fantastic friend.

She might even tell him one day what she'd seen Dad doing with Eliot Speedwell in the copse.

CHAPTER NINETEEN

Lilah was feeling a lot less optimistic and powerful than she had a few days ago. Den knew she'd sent that letter; her whole gay triangle scenario, ludicrous now she thought about it, had crumbled to nothing almost before it started. Her only hope was that enough seeds of suspicion had been sown for Deirdre Watson to remain under police scrutiny. Lilah still thought Deirdre was a credible suspect. Maybe the woman had found out about Sean's illegal calves – after all, it was part of her job to keep track of them all, with a proper ear-tag number for every single animal. Maybe she had tackled him about it and it led to a fight, with the recorder grabbing Ted's fork.

And then there was the badger baiting. Nobody

seemed to doubt that Sean had been involved in that and Deirdre Watson definitely wouldn't have had any stomach for that sort of thing. Nor would Davy Champion and his animals rights group. There was still hope, Lilah concluded. Just.

After a few more phone calls to old acquaintances, Lilah had discovered that Jeremy Page had apparently taken extreme offence at his girlfriend's being the object of police interest, and shouted his mouth off in the pub about it on Saturday night.

'I'm going to see Gordon again tonight,' she told her mother. 'I don't expect I'll be back till later in the week. I'll take a few clothes and shampoo, so I can go direct from there to college. Okay?'

Miranda nodded doubtfully. 'Looks as if I'm going to have to get used to living here on my own,' she said.

'Maybe it's time to think about selling the place,' Lilah said for the hundredth time.

'I'll wait for prices to pick up,' came the routine rejoinder.

'Which they're never going to do. They're already umpteen per cent lower than when Daddy died.'

'A blip. People are always going to want land. Besides, I'm not in any hurry. I quite fancy another summer here without the cows. I'd never find anywhere as nice as this.'

'It's nice everywhere in the summer. But it's not my problem. You do what you want.'

'Right,' agreed Miranda peaceably.

Outside, the Redstone farm buildings were decaying, rain and wind finding the weak spots; nettles and brambles growing up the sides of barns and sheds. Both the Beardon women knew that anyone buying the property now would probably raze everything but the house itself to the ground and start afresh with stables and looseboxes, or acres of glasshouses, and the whole character of the place would change beyond recognition. Neither was in any hurry for that to happen.

'Gordon's probably sorted out a relief milker by now,' Lilah said. 'He's been talking about it for days.'

'You don't think he'll use this as an excuse to get out of milk? Everybody else seems to be selling their herds.'

'Shush!' said Lilah with mock ferocity. 'Don't ever say that in his hearing. He'd rather die than sell his cows. They're descended from the ones his father bought a million years ago. He might get sick of milking them, but he's fantastically proud of them, all the same. He thinks he's going to buck the trend and be the last dairy farmer in Devon, the way he talks.' She frowned. 'Though he hasn't been quite so sure of himself these past few weeks.'

Miranda sighed. 'These men and their cows! Oh well – good luck to him, I say. I must admit he's been clever, combining old-fashioned tradition with modern methods. Reminds me of somebody.'

'Daddy, you mean. I had noticed, you know.'

'Well, they do say everybody marries their mother. Looks as if you're the exception.'

Lilah flushed. 'Nobody mentioned marriage,' she said, fearful of tempting fate.

Den was itching to bring Hillcock in for more questions. *Let me put it to you, Mr Hillcock, that you killed your herdsman last Tuesday. You drove a heavy fork into his body, twice. Why did you do that, sir?* He wanted to watch the man's face as he observed Den's certainty of his guilt.

He made his feelings known to the DI. 'What exactly do you want to ask him?' Hemsley enquired.

Den gave him a diluted version.

'Wouldn't do any good,' the Inspector opined. 'He's told us his story and he'll stick to it. He's not stupid; he knows we haven't got anything firm enough to warrant charging him. All he has to do is watch himself, and live with himself, and he's safe. If you bring him in and start bullying him, you'll just strengthen his resolve. Assuming he's the one, of course. Which I'm still quite inclined to doubt.'

'So what do we do now, then?'

'More interviews with the people lower down the list. Firm up some more of the detail. You didn't fool me about that fork, for one thing. I want sworn evidence that it was always next to the silage. Go and see the O'Farrell girl again, if you can do it delicately. Kids notice things, overhear conversations . . . get her on her own. She might have things she'd like to tell you, but not in front of her mum.' Den refrained from mentioning that there were draconian rules about interviewing underage girls, and that anything she might say would comprise inadmissable evidence. He knew all too well that there was a mile-wide gulf between the rules and what actually took place.

Abigail seemed paler than before, when he caught up with her. She had the defiant air that typified the modern teenager; self-sufficient youngsters, accustomed to their mothers being out all day at work, and yet over-protected and supervised by teachers and childminders to within an inch of their lives. Abigail was an exception to this pattern, with her invalid mother, and father only a shout away, but she had managed to conform to the general appearance.

Den sat in his car and watched the girl walk a few yards from the bus stop, towards the cottage. Already it was getting dark, Abigail's face white in the fading light.

He got out to meet her, trying to make it look like a coincidence that he was there at all. 'Hi,' he said. 'Fancy seeing you! Had a good day?'

She dipped her chin wordlessly, but her eyes were on his and he thought he detected a flash of hope in them. Either that or something very nearly as positive. She certainly didn't seem sorry to see him.

'Are you in a hurry or could we sit and chat in the car for a minute?'

She followed him without protest and they got into the front seats. 'Haven't you arrested Gordon yet?' she demanded. 'He killed again on Thursday, you know. He's a bastard!'

Den shifted sideways, his long legs folded uncomfortably under the steering wheel. He could see the likeness to Hillcock, now he knew of her parentage, in the way her eyes were set deep in her skull and the jawline bowed out at the lower edges. But if Jilly Speedwell had kept quiet, would he ever have noticed? 'What happened on Thursday?' he asked. 'Nobody reported anything to us.'

She laughed sarcastically. 'They wouldn't, would they? Not when thousands of badgers are being killed all across Devon.'

'Gordon Hillcock killed a badger?'

'Not *a* badger. *My* badger.' Tears welled up in her eyes. 'He shot him.'

Den was genuinely saddened. 'Oh no – not the one we fed for you the other night?'

She nodded. 'Bodgy. He got out.'

Den's stomach lurched. 'We didn't leave his cage unlocked, did we? Me and Mike?'

She shook her head. 'Lucky for you, no. It was me. I was doing them in a rush, after school. He was clever, you know. If you didn't push the stick right in, he could wriggle it out again and open the door.'

'Did Gordon know it was yours?'

'He says he didn't. Dad told me to keep it secret. Gordon thinks badgers carry TB, so he's stupid as well as a bastard. Even if he doesn't agree with the cull. A cow can't catch TB from a badger just by being in the same field as a badger – even if that badger has got it. It's passed by droplets in the breath. You'd have to be about a millimetre away from it for ten minutes to stand any chance of catching anything from it. They're all idiots, the government and MAFF and all those stupid scientists. And they're criminals. It's genocide.'

'What did your dad think about it? Did he agree with the boss?'

She turned her face away abruptly. 'Sort of,' she muttered.

'Abigail, I shouldn't really be here with you. It's not the proper way to do an interview, but I thought you might prefer to talk to me without your mum listening. You can get out and go, any time you feel like it – okay? I'm trusting you as much as you're trusting me. Do you understand?'

'Course I do. I know about girls shouting rape. I won't do that. It's stupid.'

'Good. So tell me a bit more about your dad and what you first thought when you heard someone had killed him.'

'I obviously hadn't been *expecting* it, but somehow I wasn't surprised.' She looked at him with big eyes. The gathering darkness blurred the detail, making it somehow safer to talk. 'You know about Fergus?' she said suddenly.

'The dog. Yes.'

'Dad poisoned him.'

'Are you sure?'

'I saw him mixing the stuff and putting it in some dog food. I tried to pretend to myself it was something else – medicine maybe, or vitamins, something that wouldn't hurt him – but I always knew really. You know how you can fool yourself over things?' She threw him a brief sideways glance. 'Do you know what I mean?'

'I think so,' he said slowly. 'Sometimes things are too horrible to seem real.'

'Right,' she agreed forcefully. 'Like the time . . .' she paused.

'I'm listening,' he murmured. 'The time—?'

'I saw him in the copse, with Mr Page's dog, Brewster. Another man was there, too. And another dog – a smaller one. He was making them fight, even though the little dog hadn't got a chance. I wanted to make him stop them, but his face – he was *loving* it. He was all, you know, red and grinning. It was like a different person. I pretended it *was* a different person. You know – possessed. I thought an evil demon had got inside him, making him do it. And I don't know where the little dog came from. I'd never seen it before. I think it must have died.' She wiped a hand across her nose. 'Why are men so horrible?' she asked with a whimper.

'I don't think I can answer that,' breathed Den. 'Who was the other man?'

She bit her lip. 'I don't know. He was walking away when I saw him. I think he was upset. His hand was over his face, like this.' She put her fingers over her eyes.

They were silent for a moment, before Abigail spoke again. 'It's worse, being on a farm. Farms are killing places. Cows, sheep, rats, badgers, dogs, calves – the poor little calves . . .' she faltered. 'Even Dad was upset about them.' Den blinked before remembering the dead bull calves in the yard the first evening he'd come to Dunsworthy.

'And now people,' he offered.

'It isn't much different,' she confided. 'I'm as sad about Bodgy as I am about Dad. Is that terrible of me?'

Den paused. 'You know, sometimes two sadnesses can get muddled up,' he said thoughtfully. 'Remember when Princess Diana died and everybody started crying about it, even though they never even knew her? Well, I think that's probably because they all had someone they really did love who'd died or gone away, and they had that sadness stored up inside them. So when the news was all about the tragic princess, with the flowers and the prayers and everything, that worked as a sort of unplugging – it opened up the feelings they'd already got inside them. Does that make any sense?'

'Not a lot,' she admitted. 'Or not the way you think. I was already sad about Dad before he died. Because I couldn't love him any more.'

Den made no comment. She looked up at him in the near darkness. 'Last night I dreamt he was still alive,' she whispered. 'And when I woke up and remembered, I was *glad*. That's the truth. I'm glad he's dead.'

You and everyone else, thought Den.

It wasn't until he was driving back to the

station that he remembered the gun. Hillcock's gun was still securely in police custody, waiting for such time as it might be deemed safe to return it to its owner. So how had he managed to shoot the badger?

The final encounter with the DI that day was brief, but shocking. Den's report on the Sam Watson interview was on the desk. 'I think we have to bring Deirdre Watson in first thing tomorrow,' the Inspector said. 'There's too much against her now; at least as much as we had against Hillcock when we brought *him* in. She's got to give us some answers in a formal interview.'

Den was struggling not to show his feelings. He clenched his fists in his jacket pockets. 'You're not arresting her?'

'Not yet, no.'

'But *everyone* thinks it was Hillcock.'

'Take it easy,' Hemsley advised. 'Trust me, okay?'

Den's shoulders slumped. 'I'll see you in the morning, then,' he said.

On Tuesday morning, Den and the DI interviewed Deirdre together. There was no doubting that she was nervous; much more nervous, in fact, than she had been in the aftermath of finding Sean's body. Den was struck by how much she had changed in a week.

'As you might expect,' Hemsley began, 'we've uncovered a lot of information about Mr O'Farrell and the people who knew him, in the course of our investigation. In a number of instances, your name, or that of one of your children, has been mentioned. All we'd like to establish this morning is just how this comes about.' He spoke softly, both hands on the table in front of him, no trace of anger or accusation in his tone. Deirdre sat on the edge of the chair, elbows tight against her sides, breathing in shallow gasps. She nodded rapidly, to indicate her willingness to cooperate.

'We understand that O'Farrell was consistently inhumane to the animals on the farm,' he said.

Deirdre twisted her hands together. 'I can see you think I have reason to object to Sean's activities,' she said. 'And I admit I didn't tell the sergeant everything when he came to question me last week.'

'Could you tell us now – honestly – what your feelings towards Sean O'Farrell were?'

'He sickened me.'

'And from what I hear, you're not easily sickened?' Hemsley suggested.

'That's true.'

'But this was different?'

She directed her gaze at him, ignoring Den. She knew where the real power lay. 'Yes, it's different,' she agreed. 'Last month, he had five newly-calved heifers to milk. They were all terrified of him – wouldn't come into the parlour, wouldn't stand still for him. And he just flipped. He hurt them as much as he could without leaving marks.'

'With you there as a witness? Wasn't there some trouble a few years ago, where you reported him for the same sort of thing?'

She nodded. 'That's it, you see. Nothing changed when I complained before, so he thought he was safe. He thought I'd got used to it – which I had, up to a point.' She fell silent for a moment. 'But I didn't kill him,' she added, almost inconsequentially. 'If I'd been going to, I'd have done it there in the parlour, last month.'

Hemsley swerved onto another tack. 'Did Sean know your son Matthew?'

Her eyes widened. 'Not that I know of. Matthew knows Abigail slightly. They go to the same school. Why?'

'Just a hunch. We picked up some comments about O'Farrell inviting locals to badger baiting sessions. We wondered . . .'

'Matthew would *never* do that!' she shouted. 'He's the softest, gentlest boy in the world. There's *no way* . . .'

'Okay,' Hemsley placated her. 'You just never quite know with boys, do you? No parents can be sure to keep tabs on them, or guess what they might get up to.'

'Not Matthew,' she insisted. Then her expression changed. 'Although I *have* been a bit worried about him. It's got nothing to do with Sean, though.'

'You're certain of that?'

She sagged. 'I am now, but I wasn't to start with. Sam got me started, saying there was talk about Eliot Speedwell being gay and going to places in Plymouth. Matthew's been trying to tell us for ages that he's . . . that way. We've been keeping very cool and calm about it, but suddenly it all seemed to be closing in. There are so many predatory men around and he'd be sure to get terribly hurt. I knew Eliot was friendly with Sean. He talked about him during milking sometimes. But it was only a few months ago – when I heard the rumours – I wondered if the two of them were . . . although I don't think Sean was really the type. It all seemed rather silly when I really stopped to think about it.'

'But not before you'd imagined the sickening Sean trying something with your son?'

'Something like that,' she admitted. 'I knew it was stupid, of course. I just panicked for a little while. I never thought I could be at all homophobic, but when it's your own son, and he's only sixteen . . .'

'I know,' said Hemsley softly.

She sniffed sharply and gained more control

of herself. 'Well, that's about all there is to it.'

'Not quite. Your encounter with Sean at the school bazaar, when he said something about your "mucky ways". What was all that about?'

She flushed deep red and twisted in her chair. 'That's extremely embarrassing,' she mumbled, 'and completely irrelevant.'

'Please tell me.'

'He meant the time I desperately needed a pee, during milking one afternoon. It was Sean doing it that day. They haven't got a loo outside, and I'd never ask to use the one in the house, so I made some excuse about needing more sample pots and dashed out to one of the sheds and just peed on the floor. It's not so unusual, really. But the swine followed me and totally freaked out. He went green in the face and said I was disgusting. It was all very unpleasant, but I decided it was some hang-up of his, and not my problem. Most men would just laugh it off, or be ashamed of having seen me. Sean acted as if I'd done something utterly unspeakable.'

Hemsley and Den said nothing and avoided each other's glance, each recalling their theory involving a very similar incident. The DI jotted a few notes on his pad. Deirdre's nervousness increased and she clearly felt she should say more. 'It's not as if I *ever* wished him dead. Of course not. But you said there were other things on your list. Badgers and other animals. Well, I have heard rumours about Sean and badger baiting, but not until after he died. Tom Beasley – he said something about it. And of course, Sean upset a lot of people, his own daughter amongst them, with the things he did.' She prattled on, scarcely drawing breath; Den could hardly bear it.

Hemsley held up a hand. 'It won't do, I'm afraid,' he said. 'And although I will have some further questions for you, I must first give you the usual caution. I'm sorry to tell you, Mrs Watson, that you are under arrest . . .'

CHAPTER TWENTY

'It does fit, Den,' said Young Mike, aware of Den's outrage, as were the whole team. 'Remember how she was when we arrived at the scene. No sign of any hysterics or squeamishness. She even had some blood on her hand.'

'But—' Den could hardly speak. '*Evidence!*' he exploded. 'There's nothing *at all* that amounts to a case against her.'

Hemsley pursed his lips and said nothing. Jane Nugent jumped in to ease the tension. 'Reminds me of that poem by Ted Hughes,' she remarked. 'The one about nasty beasties at the bottom of the pretty pond. I forget the title.'

Miserably, Den jerked his head at Mike and got to his feet. The Inspector was making a ghastly mistake and Den didn't want to see more of it than he had to. There were times, he grumbled to himself, when the job stank.

Gordon Hillcock was feeding the sick calf that had been found by Ted and Den, patiently cupping his hand into a bucket of warm milk, reminding it of a skill it must have possessed for weeks. He thought it was getting slightly stronger as the days wore on. He'd ask Mary to take over, if she'd condescend to set foot in one of the farm buildings for once. Ted was going to be fully occupied filling in for Sean in the yardwork. He'd already been given the job of burying the dead calves, despite the hard ground. 'Just get them out of my sight,' he ordered. 'I've seen enough death for one week.'

If it hadn't been for that policeman witnessing the whole business, he'd have made up an identity for the surviving calf – giving one of his cows a twin birth instead of a singleton. As it was, he supposed he'd be questioned and investigated because of what bloody Sean had been doing. There'd be reports and warnings and even the risk of a fine. It probably wouldn't matter to the RSPCA or whoever chose to prosecute, whether or not the man really responsible was dead. It was a sickening mess and Gordon just wished it could all be over and done with. The business with Abigail and the badger had merely added to his troubles. How Sean could have allowed her to keep the creature defied comprehension. The man was impossible, anyone could see that.

As he crossed the yard from the calfpen to the big shed, intending to rouse the cows for the afternoon milking, he heard a familiar tapping on an upstairs window in the house behind him. He turned and waved. Granny Hillcock often rapped on the glass if she saw him from her window. *She'll break it one day,* he thought to himself, not for the first time. The image of the old lady bleeding to death from such an ironic accident brought a thin smile to his lips. Granny Hillcock was a permanent fixture at Dunsworthy: she'd been there for almost eighty years, a length of time impossible to comprehend. She'd milked twenty-five cows by hand, night and morning, reared pigs and lambs and ducks and geese, and invariably had a book to read in the few minutes of rest after dinner, which was always served promptly at noon. She'd given birth to three children in her thirties and lost two of them to diphtheria. The disease had come unexpectedly to this sparsely-populated area of Devon.

'I ought never to have been such a fool,' she said, whenever she told the terrible story. 'Letting them die like that, with their throats closed up and the little faces turning blue.'

Gordon's father, Norman, had been her sole surviving infant, her eldest, and she spoilt him mercilessly, as if to compensate. Not satisfied with coddling him, she'd then transferred her attentions to Gordon, her son's firstborn, when he came along. When Norman died at sixty-nine, she had grieved as if he'd been another child lost as a result of her own carelessness. That death had tipped her into unavoidable old age, at ninety-five, and she had retreated to her room, venturing out very little since.

But Gordon never doubted her abiding powers. She could see and hear and think almost as well as ever. He was going to have to go up and have one of their long chats very soon now. He'd been putting it off since the events of Tuesday, not knowing how he'd explain Sean's death to her. After that visit from the police detective, she'd be wondering what was going on. It hadn't escaped his notice that she'd been watching from her window for longer than usual, tapping and waving, and sometimes gesticulating as if she had something urgent to say.

The cows were warm and comfortable in the vast shed, in no hurry to get up and stand outside in the chilly yard, waiting their turn to be milked. There were some who seemed to understand that the sooner they presented themselves in the parlour, the sooner they could get back to the nice dry straw, and who jostled their way to the front accordingly. Others – especially those with stiff legs – saw no reason to hurry. The ones approaching the end of their lactation received only small quantities of food during milking, and thus lacked much incentive to show up. It would be well over two hours before that last batch emerged from being milked and that was a long time to stand in the yard. But there was no alternative to making every last one of them get up and assemble outside, so he could pull the big gate closed behind them.

The milk recorder had never quite got the hang of all the different systems that farmers and their herdsmen used for separating and directing the cows, and she often marvelled aloud at how complicated it could be. Some farms divided the herd into two or three groups, sending them out into three separate yards, with manipulation of various gates. Gordon had tried to explain, to show why it was inexpedient to bring them out a few at a time. Far better to get the whole lot into the gathering yard, whatever the weather. 'Sean would never stand for the messing about that would involve,' he said, to her suggestion that the later beasts be allowed to have a lie-in.

Without Sean, Gordon was going to need a relief milker very soon. He should have done it before now, but he'd let it slide, on the grounds that Lilah would always take a turn if he asked her to.

Thinking about Lilah was a practice that Gordon tried to keep to a minimum. She was the brightest girlfriend he'd ever had: eager and young and ready for anything. She was also naïve and trusting, believing everything he told her. She was malleable and cooperative. She aroused feelings in him that he hadn't expected to experience ever again. He was close to forty, for God's sake. How could he possibly think he deserved such a girl?

And how could he expect her to settle for a chap like him?

By Tuesday midday, the news of Deirdre Watson's arrest had begun to spread. She had been kept in custody overnight, pending further questioning in the morning, and was permitted two phone calls, accordingly. She rejected the offer of a state-funded solicitor and made a single call to her husband.

Robin was stunned to the point of paralysis. Deirdre had to speak slowly and loudly, giving him no more than the basic facts. 'They're keeping me in tonight,' she said, hearing herself and thinking how it sounded as if she was in hospital, not a police cell. 'You'd better tell the kids the truth.'

'But you didn't kill him,' Robin spluttered. 'Did you?'

'Of course I didn't,' she said sharply. 'I don't believe you said that.'

'But . . . I mean, it's all a mistake then?'

'More or less. Look, Rob, I don't think there's anything you can really do for now. Just stay calm. It'll work out all right. Trust me.'

She asked him to let Carol know that she might not be able to do the next day's recording. 'Tell her I'm ill,' she said.

She marvelled briefly at her own restored calm. When other people flapped, she turned to ice, coolly doing whatever she had to. It had always got her into trouble, even as a child. There was that time when the dog had got run over and she had walked into the road and scooped up the mangled body without a hint of emotion. She'd been seven.

Robin called Carol, who all too easily got the truth out of him. Carol phoned Bob Parsons, who happened to be a close friend of hers, as well as due for recording the following day. Robin told Sam and Matthew, and Sam phoned Jeremy Page and Susie Marchand. Most of them phoned one or two others and by that evening Eliot Speedwell had heard the news and driven to Dunsworthy to talk to his parents. Ted ran up to the big house to make sure the Hillcocks had heard – which they hadn't. Jilly went next door to check whether Heather knew – which she did, because Abigail's Gary had told them.

Everyone was stunned. Some laughed scornfully; some narrowed their eyes and said they'd always thought that Watson woman was peculiar. Some flatly refused to believe it. 'Just a stupid rumour,' they said. 'Everyone knows 'twas Hillcock as done it.'

The one person who had not heard of Deirdre's arrest by that evening was, surprisingly, Lilah Beardon. And she was going to learn of it very soon, because she was on her way back to Dunsworthy.

The peculiar atmosphere in the kitchen made her heart lurch. Something else must have happened. She scanned the three faces for clues as to what it must be. 'What?' she demanded.

'You've not heard, then?' Gordon smiled at her, triumph on his lips. In his eyes, though, there was something darker. His eyes held no spark of humour or compassion.

'What?' she said again. Mary, sitting at the table writing on a sheet of paper, made a small *huff* of impatience. Claudia, in her usual chair beside the Aga with a cat in her lap and a radio mumbling close to her ear, took pity. 'Tell her, Gordon, for heaven's sake.'

‘They’ve arrested Deirdre Watson for the murder of Sean O’Farrell.’ He parodied the formality, turning himself into a newscaster for the occasion.

Lilah’s heart jumped again, this time in relief. She felt the fear roll away from her and her mouth stretched in a big daft grin. ‘Are you sure?’ she checked. ‘It’s not just a wild rumour?’

‘Sounds pretty sure,’ he confirmed. ‘They’re holding her in custody. You must be the last person in Devon to know about it.’

‘Oh!’ She raised her arms, preparatory to flinging them round him. ‘That’s wonderful!’

Gordon brought his hands up, fending her off. As she launched herself at him, he caught her by the ribs and held her at arm’s length. ‘Steady on,’ he cautioned. ‘Don’t go mad.’

She was jarred by his tone, made to feel silly and childish. ‘But aren’t you glad? I *knew* it must have been her. It all pointed that way. But I didn’t think the penny would drop this quickly. The police must be brighter than I’ve given them credit for. Oh, I bet Den’s feeling sick.’ She wriggled loose from Gordon’s hold, aware that she’d have done better not to mention Den’s name.

‘I imagine he wanted it to be me,’ Gordon said tightly.

‘He’s never pretended to like you.’

‘That’s not the same thing, is it?’ said Mary

angrily. 'There is such a thing as justice.'

'Of course there is,' Lilah laughed. 'And this proves it. It's all come right, after all.'

Claudia spoke from her chair. 'You know what this reminds me of? When there's been a child killed, or someone's wife or husband. And there's a trial and a person is convicted. Afterwards, the relatives of the victim all cluster in front of the TV cameras and say how happy they are. I always think, how can they possibly be *happy*? How can it help them, whether somebody's shut up for years as a punishment? It doesn't bring the dead person back again.'

Lilah turned to stare at her. 'They want to know the person who ruined their lives has been dealt with. Surely you must understand that, doing the work you do? They feel glad that the whole thing has become a bit less meaningless. Everybody likes there to be a proper end to the story. But anyway, this is nothing at all like that. This is about Gordon's innocence, Gordon being free. Nobody here is pretending to be very sorry that Sean's dead, as far as I can see.'

Claudia nodded acknowledgement of an argument deserving of respect, making a clear choice to overlook the rudeness in the middle of Lilah's speech. 'But in real life, stories never do have neat and tidy endings.'

'This one does,' Lilah said defiantly.

Claudia sighed. 'I don't think so,' she murmured. 'And even if it does look like a tidy ending, the beginning was terribly messy.'

'Come on, Ma!' Gordon protested. 'We don't want to bring all that up now.'

'I expect we'll have to, sooner or later,' said his mother.

Jilly Speedwell was torn in two directions. Ted had turned to jelly when he got back from telling the Hillcocks the news. He confessed to his wife that he had been terrified that Eliot was responsible. 'I know 'tis daft,' he said. 'He even had witnesses at work to say he was there all afternoon. I just couldn't help feeling . . .'

'I know,' she soothed. 'I was scared they'd think it was you. But all's right now.' Her words were a brave attempt at calming them both, but she remained jittery and nervous. 'I'll go and see to Heather,' she decided, having spent very few minutes imparting the news next door, while Ted went up to the farmhouse. Now she felt obliged to minister to both neighbour and husband at once.

Ted showed no sign of having heard her. 'But *why?*' he demanded. 'Why would the recorder kill Sean? There be no sense to it, woman.'

'Must be right, though. She was here that day. Must've done it before milking started. Gordon in the house with his papers, or the office. You in the Dutch barn. Her and Sean out in the yard.' She shuddered. 'Cold-hearted bitch.'

'Will they prove it, you think? Blood on her clothes maybe?'

Jilly shrugged. The excitement was doing strange things to her insides, making them all quivery. The idea that a *woman* could drive a fork into someone's undefended body was somehow thrilling. Liberating. She came close to wondering why she hadn't done it herself to the slimy worm that had been Sean O'Farrell, with his shifty eyes and nasty ways with animals.

She turned back to Ted, sitting so small in his chair. No, she wouldn't bother going back to see Heather. Why should she? Heather had made no effort to stop Sean's tricks. She'd opted out with her stupid illness, leaving the way clear for the man to do as he liked. 'Us'll be fine now,' she repeated. 'Gordon'll find a new herdsman, and things'll go on as always. We can forget that bugger Sean O'Farrell now.'

Early on Wednesday morning, with rain slanting down outside, blown by a vicious east wind, Deirdre Watson was brought yet again into the interview room for more questioning. As before, DI Hemsley and DS Cooper were present.

'We didn't cover everything yet, did we?' the

DI began. 'You might say we got sidetracked. But now we know who had good reason to kill Sean O'Farrell, it would help to fill in some of the gaps.'

'I did not kill him,' said Deirdre. Her eyes were bright, her hair well brushed. She seemed quite undaunted after a night in a cell. 'I can't understand how you've made such a mistake, but honestly, you've got the whole thing wrong.'

Hemsley proceeded as if she hadn't spoken. Den noted the flicker of alarm in the woman's eyes at this deliberate shutting-out. It was an old technique, unkind and unfair, in Den's view. 'So you don't approve of badger baiting?' the Inspector said softly.

'Of course I don't. Who does? It's sick, what they do. You should hear my daughter on the subject . . .'

'Oh? That's right – she campaigns for animals, doesn't she?'

'Very much so. There's nothing wrong with that. They don't break the law. But those youngsters are passionate about it. They'd kill anybody they caught baiting badgers or fighting dogs.'

Danny Hemsley cocked his head provokingly, letting her hear her own words again. 'Surely not literally?' he said. 'My information is that young Samantha is seeing a lot of a certain Jeremy Page.

And you may or may not know that Jeremy's dad, Fred, owns a rather unpleasant pooch by the name of Brewster, who comes to our notice at regular intervals. Now, Fred and Sean were pals, by all accounts. Funny how you get all these connections in a country area, isn't it? Everybody knowing everybody – and most of their business.'

'If Sam likes Jeremy, you can be sure he's nothing like his father. There is no way in the world that boy would be involved in baiting.'

Hemsley glanced at a sheet of notes in front of him. 'But you don't like Mr Page senior, do you?'

Deirdre didn't reply. The DI went on, 'Because I've got a quote here from someone we spoke to last week: "The Pages are just bloody gypsies with their savage dogs and vicious ways." Do you remember saying that? You ought to, because it's a quote from that same school bazaar at Christmas time where you had your little run-in with Sean O'Farrell. Quite a hot-headed lady, aren't you, Mrs Watson?'

She sighed, but showed little sign of losing her composure. 'Sometimes I lose my temper,' she nodded. 'But I don't really see . . .'

'What interests me – among other things – is how relations were between you and Sam once she started going out with Jeremy.'

'I didn't know for a while, and I've hardly seen her since I found out. She's old enough to make her own decisions. I can't say it bothers me particularly.'

'You trust her judgement?'

'Yes I do.'

'Really? You don't think she took up with him just to get at you?'

Deirdre laughed scornfully. 'Absolutely not. She would never be so petty. We have a perfectly normal relationship. If she has a grievance, she'll tell me about it to my face. She knows I say things I don't mean sometimes. I shouldn't have been so rude about the Pages, I realise now. Jeremy is nothing like his father.'

Hemsley used his pencil to add a little tick to the sheet of paper in front of him. 'Now, let's go back to badger baiting. It wasn't just these past few days you picked up the rumours about that, was it? You've known for a long time that O'Farrell and his mates were doing it. Just as you've known about those bobby calves he was keeping without their ear-tags.'

Her cheeks reddened. 'I guessed something was going on,' she muttered. 'You can shoot one or two calves a week and get the hunt to take them for the hounds, but there were nine or ten born at the beginning of November, most of them bulls, and I did wonder exactly what had happened to them. But it's not my business to challenge what the farmers tell me. I just log it all onto the computer.'

Danny nodded, unsmiling. 'So, Mrs Watson – could you tell me now of anything else you were aware of concerning Sean O'Farrell?'

She shook her head confidently. 'There isn't anything else. At least, I've already told you all I know. The attack by the Alsatian; his sick wife; his family background – I told your sergeant all that.' She flipped a hand at Den, suggesting he produce his notes as confirmation.

'Do you think Sean poisoned the Alsation?'

She glanced at Den hesitantly, before muttering, 'Yes, I expect he did. But I haven't got any proof.'

'So what makes you think he did it?'

'The dog humiliated him and Gordon made no attempt to punish it. When it died, I just assumed . . . it would be too much of a coincidence otherwise.'

'Sean O'Farrell was a pretty unpleasant character all round, it seems. So you felt you were doing the place a service by killing him. Maybe it was very much spur of the moment. Maybe he'd slipped over in the muck and the fork was there beside him and you just saw the red mist – drove it into him before you really knew what you were doing.'

'I didn't kill him. I didn't touch him. I never even saw him that day.'

'So who did?'

'It must have been Gordon.' The words emerged reluctantly.

Den crossed and recrossed his legs, causing both the others to look at him. Hemsley gave him a warning stare.

'So despite Mr Hillcock's obvious shock and distress at the discovery of the body and his apparently normal behaviour throughout the milking up to that point, you're convinced of his guilt?'

'I don't see who else it could have been. Because it certainly wasn't me.'

'You like Gordon Hillcock, don't you? Have you ever had sex with him?'

She turned to Den, as if seeking salvation. 'Is he allowed to ask me that?' she demanded. 'What's that got to do with anything?'

'We'll take that as a yes, then,' said Hemsley sweetly. 'Don't worry, it isn't very likely to come out in court. Though I'm afraid I can't make any promises.'

'I'll deny it,' she said hotly. 'I *do* deny it. I absolutely have not been having sex with Gordon Hillcock. At least . . .'

'At least?'

'Not for more than twenty years,' she admitted sullenly. 'Before I married Robin.'

At last the police detective had what he wanted: a show of emotion and a definite flash of panic. Den pulled the lobe of one ear until it hurt. The job entailed treachery, he knew that. But he never got used to it.

'Mrs Watson, can you persuade me that you did not, on Tuesday last, take a heavy garden fork and attack Mr Sean O'Farrell with it?' He spoke with total seriousness. 'Because I am more and more certain in my mind that you did precisely that.'

Deirdre turned again to Den for rescue. Her face was now a pallid grey, her eyes drawn back in her head like an animal in pain. It was awful to see.

'Of course I didn't kill him,' she said huskily. 'This is intimidation,' she added, struggling for control. Both men could see that she was shaking and close to tears. 'I was just doing the *recording*,' she burst out, with a break in her voice. 'It's my *job*.'

Den was frozen in his chair, horrified at what his superior had done, but he had no choice but to trust his tactics.

'It was *Gordon*,' Deirdre shouted, slapping her hand on the table. 'I know it was Gordon. There was no one else. He hasn't told you it was me, has he? He wouldn't do a thing like that. Gordon and I are friends . . . and . . .' she wavered. 'It wasn't me,' she repeated.

Hemsley nodded calmly. 'I'm sorry to have

upset you. You can go back to your cell now. And I must persuade you to get a solicitor. Either one of your own choosing or someone we find for you. Your position is very serious; you'll need to take legal advice. Any application for bail will be listened to, but I can't say how it will be treated.'

Deirdre Watson looked ten years older than when she had come in. Den shuddered at the power of the police to shatter almost anybody's equilibrium. Not for the first time, he felt ashamed of this power. 'I'll take you,' he said.

'Now?' she asked in a pitiful voice.

'Yes, now,' he said. 'The Inspector hasn't got any more questions for you.'

She cast a look of pure loathing at Hemsley as she got to her feet, but she said nothing.

CHAPTER TWENTY-ONE

'I'm going to come inside you tonight,' Gordon murmured.

'No! Gordon, you can't. It's right in the middle of my cycle.' She stared at him in panic.

'It's okay,' he soothed, with an oddly distant smile that gave no glimpse of the man she thought she knew. 'Inside – but not so you can get pregnant. Think about it.'

Before she could understand, he had laid a gentle forefinger against her anus, tapping it rhythmically, a feather-light touch. Then he leant over and switched off the bedside light, plunging the room into thick darkness.

Lilah swallowed. He wasn't consulting her, he was simply announcing his intention. There was absolutely no room for resistance, and so the idea never got itself formed. This was Gordon, her lover! Anything he did was – had been – all right with her. The pressure against her flesh intensified and she let go. She detached her mind as if it were a balloon floating away. Go with the bodily sensation . . . Gordon had taught her that from the start. The surprise was that this hadn't happened before. He liked his sex varied and this was, presumably, just another variation.

There were few preliminaries. As it began, words spoke in her head. *Penetration*. She hadn't known properly what it meant until now. *Violation*. Intrusion into a dark, forbidden, secret place, pushing ruthlessly, then agonisingly withdrawn only to re-enter, tearing something more than delicate tissue.

She lay flattened into the mattress, her face in the pillow. She never thought to scream or whimper. She let herself become body and flesh, experiencing the wrongness until it turned, from one second to the next, into the greatest ecstasy. It was pain distilled, wickedness made easy. All you needed was a man with functioning genitals and anything was possible. She was being taken into another realm where there was total freedom. The word *Death* replaced the others. You could die doing this and it would be all right.

Behind her, invisible, the man was gasping.

His thrusts were still slow: she wouldn't be unduly damaged by his invasions, after all . . . but she knew what was happening. The sounds were entirely different from his orgasms so far. He was hurting himself, suffering . . . dying. All she felt was a wetness, but she could smell the unmistakable smell.

She knew afterwards. It was as if he had clearly informed her, with those three silent words. *Penetration, Violation, Death.* He had told her what he had done, by showing her what he was capable of.

She stayed there in bed with him, but she didn't sleep. She lay for an hour listening to his regular breathing, wondering about her future, fiercely keeping the lid on the panic that swirled inside her. When Gordon woke up abruptly at the end of the hour, she froze, pretending to be asleep.

He sat up in the dark room, pulling the blankets off her, as if forgetting she was there. Then he got out of bed and took the pile of clothes from the chair standing against the wall. Lilah wanted to ask him where he was going, what he was planning to do. He must be intending to get dressed in the bathroom, not wanting to put the light on and wake her completely.

It was midnight. She could see the digital clock glowing on his bedside table. She heard him go softly downstairs and out of the back door. *Death*. The word repeated in her mind, echoing and swelling as she fell into a half doze. It was a relief to have Gordon out of the bed. Her rational mind told her all was well, that he must have remembered something he'd left undone, and would be back soon. She wanted to be genuinely asleep when that happened.

A sound woke her at ten to one and she was instantly clear-headed. 'Oh God, he's gone out there to kill himself!' she muttered aloud. Why hadn't she thought of that before? It seemed glaringly obvious now. In his own oblique way, he had confessed to her his killing of Sean O'Farrell, and now he was unable to see a viable future for himself. Suicide surely seemed to be the only option left to him.

Desperately she scrambled out of the bed and into a disorganised assortment of clothes. What had the sound been that had woken her up? A cow, she thought, moaning, long and low. Did that have anything to do with Gordon, or was it just luck that she had heard it?

She quietly let herself out through the back door. A light was on in one of the barns. In icy trepidation she approached its open front. Long metal gates separated it from the yard and inside were the dry cows – those due to calve in the next few weeks. Gordon was in a far corner with one of the cows. 'Come on!' he hissed. 'For Christ's sake don't do this to me.' There was something clearly wrong with the animal: her head was down and she was uttering low moans.

Normally Lilah would have run forward unthinkingly and offered assistance. But now Gordon was too strange and frightening for her to act spontaneously with him. She was a child again, faced with a terrible adult situation that she was powerless to influence. He was working on the unborn calf, pushing and pulling and cursing. As she watched, Lilah saw the cow collapse until she was lying prone. Gordon rolled with her, still holding onto the calf, redoubling his efforts.

'Oh, God!' he shouted. 'Listen, will you?' He raised his eyes to a spot near the roof of the barn. 'If this calf dies, that's an end of it. The whole place can go to hell and I'll take what's coming. If it lives and it's a heifer, I'll know I'm meant to carry on.' It was a bizarre bargain with the Almighty, spoken with such intensity that Lilah had no doubt he would stick to it. Stealthily, terrified that he would hear her, she edged away.

She had to pass the storage shed where Gordon had shot the badger, on her way back to the house. Hanging from a beam in the roof was a rope. At the end of the rope was a well-tied noose, and upended immediately beneath it was a packing case.

The cow must be saved. Gordon must have heard her groans and gone to her aid, instead of carrying out his intention. Lilah forced herself back into the house, imagining the scene. As she crawled into the bed and pulled the blankets over her head, she really didn't know whether she wanted the calf to live or die.

She lay awake for another hour, arguing with herself. She ought to go and help with the calving; she ought to phone the vet. She should go home to Redstone and never have anything more to do with the Hillcocks. But her limbs refused to move. Everything was paralysed, waiting for Gordon's fate to be decided by the suffering animal outside. After a little while, it did not seem bizarre at all that he should couch his decision in such terms. The viability of the farm had already been hanging by a thread before Sean was killed. Gordon had accepted that his future was beyond his own control – why not let it rest on an accident of biology? It was not for her to interfere. Anything she elected to do would not affect the final outcome. She felt beyond misery or horror or rage. She was a farmer's child: she knew how puny human beings truly were.

Eventually she slept, a deep dream-wracked sleep from which she emerged at seven o'clock, aware that Gordon had not come back to bed. She sat up, instinctively looking out of the window for signs of daylight and sounds of a new working day. Faintly she heard the thrum of the milking machine and lay back for a moment, letting the first taut response ease up. Gordon was alive and milking the cows as usual. The world had not yet quite come to an end.

With all thoughts on hold, she got up and dressed. She moved carefully as if a glass of water were balanced on her head. She didn't want to do anything that might alter the course of events, from this point on. She only wanted to *know*. She wanted to understand the *why?* and the *how?* and the *what next?* But she wanted someone else to make the decisions, just as Gordon obviously did. The fate of a family was in the balance, but more heavily than that weighed the farm itself, the livestock and the machinery – the inexorable daily demands that Lilah knew so much about. The day they had sold the cows at Redstone had been as emotionally devastating as the day she'd found her father's body in the slurry pit. Nobody who hadn't gone through it could understand what it was like. And if Gordon was facing it now, then she knew she would have to be there at his side when it happened, whatever terrible thing he might have done.

Mary was at the breakfast table with a mug of coffee. Lilah met her eyes and exchanged a wordless acknowledgement that it was almost over; that this was quite possibly the last day before everything changed. 'You're up early,' Lilah said.

'I couldn't sleep.'

'Nor me.'

'I need to talk to Granny. She's the only person who can settle some questions I need answers to. Will you come up with me?'

'Now?'

Mary nodded. 'I've got an hour before I have to leave for school. And I can't let it go any longer.'

Lilah sighed. It wasn't what she had envisaged, but this was a time to let herself be led, wherever the awful final twists might take her. 'All right then,' she nodded.

Granny was awake, with the light on. Mary set down a mug of tea and bowl of porridge on the little table near the window. 'Come and have it here,' she invited. The old lady cooperated willingly as her granddaughter helped her out of bed and into the chair. 'Not so cold this morning,' Lilah said. Dawn was just breaking, the sky a yellowy-grey.

Within a minute or two, Granny was sitting by her window as usual, staring down towards the old shed where Ted and Den had found the dead calves. The outline of the two great oak trees made a pleasing winter picture against the lightening sky, with the big old shed nestled between them. 'You get a great view from up here, don't you?' said Mary.

''Tiz my window on the world,' agreed Granny. The presence of Lilah seemed barely to impinge on her.

'Um . . . Granny . . . Do you remember when Gordon and I were little? Well, I was little – Gordon was thirteen or so.'

'Noisy little tackers, both o' you.'

'Gordon was poorly, wasn't he? I don't remember it very well. I'd just started school, and when I got home one day, they'd rushed him to hospital and everyone was in an awful state. And he was gone for a long time. I never did really know what was happening. I remember him coming home, dreadfully pale and thin.'

The old woman's face seemed to shrivel, the multitudinous wrinkles carved deeper than ever. 'They died,' she whispered. 'My little Wendy and her baby brother, Jimmy. Both of 'em . . . just died. Faces all blue. I didn't know they could die as easy as that.'

'No, no, Granny. I didn't mean them. That was *ages* ago.' She paused to consider just how long ago it must have been. 'Nearly seventy years, it must be. I'm talking about after that. When Norman's boy was poorly. Your grandson, Gordon. They took him to hospital. You were there. I remember how worried you were.'

Granny had been nearly eighty, even then, Mary realised. What to her was a lifetime ago was to her grandmother just last week, and therefore less vivid than the formative traumas of her earlier years. But Mary persevered. Granny's wits were very much intact, if you just gave the cogs time to start grinding.

'Hospital!' Granny echoed. 'They been and made I go there once, and near let I vade away and die. And vur why? God knows!' She scowled fiercely. 'Lissen to I, will 'ee. Stay out of they 'ospitals.'

Another time, Mary would simply have leant back and let Granny's distinctive tones just wash over her, knowing she was hearing a dialect almost lost for ever, conveying memories from a different world, a different age. Granny was a treasure to be cherished. But when it came to specific information, she could be deeply frustrating.

'Did Gordon nearly die, too?' she persisted. 'Nobody ever mentioned it again. It's as if the whole thing became a dark family secret. I don't know how long he was away, but I know he had an operation.'

'Six months,' said Granny suddenly. 'From start to vinish, six months. Your poor mam was thin as a rake with the worry. The lad came home two, three times, but went back for more. Drugs, gamma rays . . .'

'Gamma rays?' Mary interrupted. 'You mean radiotherapy?'

Granny shook her head vacantly. 'He came right again. Quiet, mind, and zolit'ry for a bit. Never many friends. That little boy from the cottages used to follow 'un about, zame as 'ee did. Norm and Claudia zed us should try and put it all behind us. And 'tiz what us did.'

'But . . .' Mary's head was filling with questions that she couldn't hope that Granny would answer. How could Claudia, the counsellor, advocate repressing and denying such a critical event in their lives? Not just preventing Gordon from properly processing his experience, but shutting Mary out of it altogether, presumably hoping she would have no lasting memory of it. It seemed extraordinarily perverse and completely out of character. These events had taken place in the early seventies, when openness and honesty had surely been the rule of the day.

But perhaps not, in medical matters. Especially not if cancer was involved.

Granny had returned to her scrutiny of the world outside her window. 'There be old Speedwell,' she remarked. 'Zee? I always knows it be Ted, from the way 'un walks. Watch now.' Mary looked over the old woman's shoulder. Ted

Speedwell was walking from his cottage to the yard, his legs much more bandy from this vantage point than they appeared to someone on the same level. He hitched up one hip as he walked, which Mary had never noticed, either. It occurred to her that the joint must be stiff, and perhaps painful.

''Tiz always worse on a cold day,' Granny continued, reading her mind. ''Ee should'a zeen 'un that day – when was it? – when us had the frost. Poor ol' feller could barely walk, and I zeen 'un spend all day over to haybarn.' She pointed to the Dutch barn almost out of her field of vision, to the left. Ted happened to be walking past it as she spoke. Mary slowly scanned the whole picture. On the far right, Granny could see the big oaks with the shed between them. In the foreground, partially obscuring that shed, was the gathering yard where the cows waited to be milked every afternoon. The big cowshed itself was out of sight except for its roof. Directly in front of the window was the milking parlour, with the attached tank room and office, and the small barn where Sean's body had been found. Granny Hillcock certainly did have a window on the world.

Mary looked at the old woman thoughtfully. 'That was Tuesday last week – the day it was frosty. The day Sean was killed.'

'Poor ol' Ted, diddlin' around over to Dutch

barn all afternoon,' she repeated. 'I zeed 'un. Windin' up string, brushin' down vloor, movin' dusty ol' haybales about.'

Mary smiled at the unnecessary alibi, imagining a defence lawyer trying to persuade Granny to repeat it all in court. Lucky it wouldn't be required. Fortunately for Gordon, his grandmother would never reveal what, if anything, she'd seen him do that day.

Lilah stirred where she sat on the end of the bed. Mary threw her a swift look, which said, *Hang on. We're getting there.*

'Do you remember Heather? She came here nearly twenty years ago when she married Sean O'Farrell, the boy at the cottages. She had a baby girl later on.'

Granny smiled sentimentally at the mention of the baby. 'Not enough babbies on the place – not since my Wendy and Jimmy passed over. But there *was* a baby . . . same round cheeks, same eyes. I used to go and zee 'un. What did I care who might have sired her?'

Mary exhaled in relief. 'Heather's baby was a Hillcock! Is that what you mean?'

The old lady's eyes twinkled. ''Twas the corn harvest, a real hot zummer. The girl were mazed with the guilt of it, till I tell'd her she mustn't worry. Every woman needs a babby and that silly sod of a husband weren't never a-gwayne give her one. Never a need to say a word to Claudia.'

'You've got a wonderful memory, Granny. You're a wonderful woman. Isn't she?' she addressed Lilah, sitting frozen on the bed.

The girl nodded and forced a smile, but couldn't manage any words.

'Go home,' Mary advised, when they were downstairs again. 'There's nothing useful you can do. You being here is probably just prolonging the agony.'

Lilah shook her head. 'I don't think I can,' she mumbled. 'Though I can't face Gordon, either.'

'We'll tackle him this evening,' Mary resolved. 'Get it all out in the open.'

Lilah's insides turned to jelly. 'Okay,' she managed to whisper, wondering how any of them were going to get through the intervening day.

Gordon would be finishing off outside within the next half hour, and coming in for his breakfast – assuming all the usual routines applied. Lilah knew she hadn't the courage to face him, had nothing coherent to say to him. But neither could she remove herself from the scene entirely. There seemed to be only one option left and she got her coat and walked out, heading for the road. She would spend all day walking round the fields, if necessary, waiting for something to happen.

Her thoughts were unfocused, no longer

trying to find another person to blame for Sean's murder. The actions and conclusions of the police seemed irrelevant now, impossibly far behind the reality of what was happening. They worked on a different plane, where facts outweighed emotions and there was always an eye on the legal convolutions ahead. None of that mattered to Lilah now. She couldn't even contemplate the implications for her own future, beyond the terror she felt at the imminent confrontation with Gordon. In her mind he loomed like a massive barrage balloon, his face close to hers, full of rage and pain and pleading. He was lost, that boy who'd been in hospital for six months with some sort of cancer and could surely never have been the same again afterwards? She knew enough about psychology and childhood trauma to understand that suppression of the experience had undermined and corrupted the whole Hillcock family for the past twenty-five years.

She grieved for that boy, who she had frequently glimpsed beneath the skin of the adult Gordon. She had been right to love him; right to defend him against other people's uncomprehending scorn. She had even seen, without realising it, the lurking death wish, the abiding suspicion that he should have died in his teens and that his survival was some kind of oversight. Granny had shone a light on this, and more, with her willing recollections. It had been as if she had just been waiting to be asked, all these years.

There was a light on in the O'Farrell house. As she approached the road, she saw the school bus arrive and pause, evidently to collect Abigail. Heather would be alone in the house, preparing to face another day. Some sense of sisterhood drew Lilah towards the light and the unlocked front door. She didn't even think to knock, but just pushed it open and walked in.

Heather was in the kitchen, washing up, standing straight-backed, her chin high. 'Hello,' said Lilah in a small voice.

Heather turned round smoothly, appearing neither surprised nor afraid. 'Yes?' she said, as if Lilah were a travelling salesman.

'Can I talk to you for a minute?'

'If you must. I was going out shopping. There's no food in the house, and I've had enough of sitting around, letting my life run down the drain.'

'You look a lot better.'

Heather laughed. 'Well, so I am. It's the relief, I expect.'

'Relief?'

'Knowing they've caught the one that killed Sean. Funny what a difference it makes.'

Lilah wished she could muster her thoughts and then keep them under control. She could barely remember how everyone had been reacting before the events of the night. She spoke hesitantly, groping for words. 'I was talking to old Mrs Hillcock just now. She remembers when you had Abby. She said she used to come and play with her.'

'Poor lady. She lost two of her own, you know. She never really got over it, after all these years.'

Lilah forced herself to think of Sean. Strangely he didn't seem important any more. 'When I came to see you before . . . you were trying to tell me that Sean wasn't Abby's father, weren't you?'

'Sean never could cope with sex,' Heather supplied readily. 'Didn't like anything to do with bodies. Touching, letting himself go. We only tried it a few times.'

'Did you mind?'

The woman's features drooped, returning her to the semi-invalid that Lilah recognised. 'It was the pretending, mainly. He forced me to pretend we were just like other couples. Said he'd leave if I told anybody. He couldn't stand the shame of it. And he said it wasn't unusual, lots of married people never had sex. And you get used to things,' she smiled wanly.

'Well it doesn't really matter now,' Lilah said. 'But please tell me, now it can't make any difference. Is Abigail Gordon's daughter?'

Heather leant heavily against the kitchen

worktop. 'All these secrets tumbling out,' she breathed. 'They say it happens when a person dies. It takes your breath away, it does really.'

'*Is* she?'

Heather shook her head, a teasing smile forming. 'No, Abby is not Gordon Hillcock's child,' she said. 'She's his sister.'

CHAPTER TWENTY-TWO

Mary Hillcock spent a distracted day at school, unable to focus on the work. 'Hey, Miss!' called Peter Stevens from Year Eight. 'My mum says your brother never killed that bloke after all. Is that right, Miss?'

She closed her eyes for three long seconds. 'I hope you never listen to idle gossip, Peter. It doesn't get you anywhere, mark my words.'

'But it was on the telly, Miss. Last week, local news. They said your brother had been taken in for questioning. That wasn't gossip, was it Miss? And last night they said a woman was likely going to be charged.'

'We're not discussing it now. I want you to do the exercises on page forty-six. I'm timing you, so I don't want anybody wasting any time. If you can't do a question, leave it out and I'll go through it with you afterwards.'

She sat back and gave her thoughts a moment's freedom. For the past week she'd gone over everything she knew about her brother, and tried to assess whether or not he was capable of murder. She had only reached a conclusion when the news came through of his innocence.

She didn't believe it. She had watched his face as Ted told him about Deirdre's arrest and listened to him telling Lilah the next day, and she had doubted him.

She remembered the anger he'd been capable of in his younger years. Over the weekend, she had looked back through her own girlhood diaries, reminding herself of how life had been for the Hillcocks at that time. The diaries were brief but they represented a daily record for seven years and through their pages she achieved something like total recall of certain scenes.

She remembered Gordon as a thin youth, barely half the size he was now. She remembered him being the object of their grandmother's adoration, while Claudia blew hot and cold, ignoring him at one moment, expressing acute anxiety about him the next. She remembered when Heather had arrived on the farm and how pretty she had been, with a shy, dimpled smile and cheerful, willing ways. She'd helped with the harvest, fed the calves, picked apples and made elderflower wine. It all felt like a long lost idyll now, in these dark winter days.

At last the school day ended and she set out for home, glad to have the use of the car for once, because Claudia wasn't working that day. She drove fast, hoping to be back soon after four, leaving time to think through what must be done. The coming storm was scary, but preferable to carrying on as they were. She and Claudia, and probably Lilah, were going to have to lock horns with Gordon and force him to face reality and admit the truth. Deirdre Watson was being charged with the murder of Sean O'Farrell and Mary for one needed to be completely convinced that this was a just conclusion to the inquiry. She needed her brother to assure her, with absolute sincerity, that he wasn't the one who should be in the prison cell. From the look of Lilah that morning, Mary believed she felt almost exactly the same.

But above all Mary wanted an end to the uncertainty over their future. Farming had been sickening her for a long time now: the exploitation, the grinding, inexorable demands of all those animals, the downward spiral into poverty and failure. When Gordon's dog, Fergus, had died in that horrible way, she had listened to his screams and wept, alone in her bedroom. She had cursed Sean, who everyone believed had poisoned the creature, and wished him a similar agony in return. She had other reasons, too, for hating Sean O'Farrell and regarding him as a loathsome piece of vermin inflicted on Dunsworthy by a malign fate.

Ten years ago, married to Mark Fordyce and quite contented with her life, Mary's equilibrium had been rocked by Sean O'Farrell. Befriending Mark, Sean had taken him along to one of the secret badger baiting sessions in a remote barn somewhere, initially, she supposed, as a sort of dare. Mark had been curious, and seduced by the forbidden mystery of it. From what she'd been able to glean, he'd actually quite enjoyed it. Eventually the shame nagged at him and he told his wife about it.

It would be too much to claim that this alone had broken up their marriage. But Mark changed, in her eyes, overnight. She didn't think she could live with a man who came home sweating and lustful thanks to his presence at a scene of primitive depravity. He knew well enough that it was a horrible thing they did, and yet he couldn't stop. He tried, once, to explain it to her.

'It hooks into something old and deep, that's almost disappeared from the way we live now. There's bullfighting still left, and that's about it.

It's on some other level of being; the animals are doing it *for us*, in some way. We're so civilised and cerebral, it's like being half asleep all the time. Teeth and blood and pain – they're fantastically *real* by comparison.'

She had listened and even half understood, but she couldn't accept. She'd spent all her life trying to get to grips with blood and pain, with sheep dying at lambing time and dogs getting tangled up with lethal farm implements. She knew that world existed and that there was no escape from it – but she couldn't go on living with a man who sought it out for a thrill.

So when someone killed Sean O'Farrell, with plenty of pain and blood in the process, she had not been sorry. At first she had harboured a secret satisfaction that justice had been done. Only slowly, as the bald truth crystallised in her mind, did she find herself unable to go on sharing a house with the person she strongly suspected had done the deed she might have performed herself if she'd had the courage.

Neither Lilah nor her car were anywhere to be seen when Mary arrived home. Claudia was in the sitting room, a log fire blazing, the cat on her shoulder. 'Had a good day?' Mary asked her. It was inconceivable that things could be as calm as they seemed.

Claudia appeared to be half asleep, looking up blearily at her daughter. 'I haven't seen Gordon all day,' she frowned. 'I don't think he came in for lunch. But he's milking as usual. All he ever does these days is milk the damned cows.'

'So where's he been since this morning?'

'I've no idea. That's what I'm saying.'

Mary recognised the note of detachment in her mother's voice. Claudia knew only too well that something was profoundly wrong, but she was still apparently hoping she could avoid facing it. Mary clenched a fist and banged it lightly on the arm of the chair. 'We're going to have to tackle him this evening,' she said firmly. 'It can't go on any longer. I expect Lilah will turn up soon and have her say as well.'

Claudia's eyes darted from one corner of the room to another, and the tendons of her neck showed prominent above the collar of her jumper. 'I don't know what you're talking about,' she said.

'You do, Mother. You most definitely do.'

Lilah came in at five-thirty, looking pale and cold. 'Where have you been?' Mary asked solicitously.

'I drove down the road a little way and fell asleep in the car in a lay-by.' She moved towards the fire as if unable to resist its allure. 'I just wanted the time to pass until you got home.'

'Not long now,' said Mary. She couldn't fail to notice that the girl was shaking, and she didn't think it was due to the cold.

They drank tea and found some dry fruitcake to nibble, but nobody felt hungry. Claudia made a poor show of reading. Mary drifted out to the kitchen and Lilah simply huddled close to the fire and let the time pass as it would.

When the slam of the back door finally ended their vigil, they waited like timid Victorian spinsters for their lord and master to come into the room.

Den had taken Thursday afternoon off, although Danny had asked him to drop into the station at five to cast his eye over the duty sheet for the following days. Den knew that the DI wanted to keep an eye on him through the climax of the Sean O'Farrell case, to ensure he didn't do anything to rock what felt like a very fragile boat.

The weather outside was improving and he wondered if he should go outside and enjoy it. Clear, sunny days in January were rare enough not to be wasted.

But he didn't really fancy it. His tall frame was familiar to all his neighbours and most of the shopkeepers in town. People would know the story of Lilah and Dunsworthy and there would be looks. Some would sympathise and some would disapprove. Either way, he didn't want it. The whole business had slipped messily through his fingers and he didn't want any reminders of it. Hillcock would go free, Lilah would marry him and get fat and matronly and complacent with a gaggle of little Hillcock babies around her feet. They'd joke about the way Den had tried to angle his investigation to make it seem that Gordon had killed his herdsman. He imagined that some of the jokes were already starting – and they wouldn't be confined to Dunsworthy, either.

But it was impossible to get the case out of his mind. Deirdre Watson was everything a murderer was not. Organised, focused, not at all the type to lose physical control, despite her intemperate words in public. Surely she would never launch a murderous attack in a farmyard without warning. And she was a woman. Den simply could not believe that a woman, however strong or angry, would kill in such a way. He couldn't think of any precedent. Deirdre was solid and mature. She'd raised two children and stuck with the same husband for twenty years. She wasn't addicted to drugs or alcohol or fast cars or guns. She was *decent*, for Christ's sake.

There was no way, *no way*, she had killed Sean O'Farrell. Was there?

Danny Hemsley said she had and he was fast putting together a case to prove it. The animal cruelty element was powerful, and after watching O'Farrell's insensitive treatment of the cows, it was just – *just* – possible to believe she had flipped. But Den couldn't credit it, and anyway Sean had not been milking that day.

In a last forlorn hope of proving Hemsley wrong, Den had spoken to Forensics again, before leaving the station, and had been told rather curtly that there was nothing more to say than was already in their report. Den had then had another look through the pathologist's findings, noticing the extraordinary comprehensiveness of it, as the post-mortem had taken Sean apart, inch by inch.

He forced himself to stop thinking about it. There were jobs around the flat to catch up on: a load of washing, some bills to pay, and he spent half an hour giving them his attention. But at the end of that time, it was still only three o'clock and the hours ahead stretched emptily. Inevitably Lilah came to mind again. Why was it that everything had gone so wrong for him since she left? It was as if all the laws of nature had been overturned. If she could leave him, then maybe Deirdre Watson could commit murder. Maybe Sean O'Farrell could torture cows in her presence and bait badgers for amusement and then boast about it. Maybe Gordon Hillcock could be a good hard-working farmer, with a long run of bad luck with women keeping him a bachelor for so many years. Maybe it was true love and he should wish Lilah every happiness. Maybe Den Cooper was the worst judge of character in the entire police force and he couldn't tell black from white, or murder from dodgy parking.

What he needed, and needed very badly, was a new woman. It was stupid to let month after month go by waiting for Lilah, who obviously was never going to come back to him. He tried to think who the possible candidates might be, out of all the women of his acquaintance. He'd grown up around here, gone to the local school, only left for the time it took to get his degree in Plymouth and complete his police training before coming right back again. Which meant he knew every likely female between twenty and thirty in the whole area.

One name floated up as he applied himself to the question: Alexis Cattermole. Nearly two years before, Alexis's sister had died, followed a few days later by the murder of her boyfriend. At the time, Den had been with Lilah and not susceptible to any other woman's appeal. But he had seen Alexis a few times since and noted how strong and cheerful she always looked. And somebody strong and cheerful was just what the doctor ordered.

He remembered the phone number, as he

remembered scores of others; he'd always been good with numbers – better than with words.

Alexis answered the phone and he felt a sudden clutch of panic. What in the world was she going to think of him?

'Hi!' he breezed. 'Den Cooper. Remember me?'

'Good God! Lilah's Den, you mean?'

'Um . . .'

'Oh, sorry. You split up, didn't you? I forgot, for the moment. Well, Den Cooper, what can I do for you?'

'To put it bluntly, I'm going mad here with nobody to talk to and I decided I need to get out. I don't suppose there's a chance in a million you're free this evening, are you?'

'You're asking me out? Why me, Den? I haven't seen you for ages. Must be eight or nine months.'

'Old times' sake?' he offered, with a self-effacing laugh. 'No, that's not really it. I promise not to mention Lilah. I'm not looking for a shoulder to cry on. Nothing heavy. I just thought it would be fun.'

'It's a great thought,' she conceded. 'The problem is, I'm seeing someone new and we're booked for the movies this evening.'

'Ah,' he sighed. 'Anybody I know?'

'I don't think so. He's quite new to the area –

a property developer, actually. The lowest of the low, to some people's minds. But we seem to get along quite well and I can't go on like this for ever. My biological time bomb is ticking, as they say.'

'Okay. I'm pleased for you. I hope it all works out. Give Martha my regards, and the rest of the family.'

'Thanks. I will.' He heard in her voice an echo of the shared misery and confusion that had followed her boyfriend's murder. It had been one of the saddest cases he'd worked on since joining the CID and he had no illusions as to the permanent damage it had caused.

Maybe, after all, going out with Alexis would have been a bad idea. He had forgotten she was a few years older than him. What he wanted was a younger girl. Someone fresh and funny, trusting and supportive. Someone pretty and bright and cheerful. Someone, in fact, just as Lilah had been, before she'd met bloody Gordon Hillcock.

He had one last try, when he presented himself in the DI's office promptly at five. 'I still don't get it,' he complained. 'You could have made just as good a case against Hillcock, and I'm not going to pretend I think you've got it right, because I'm damned sure you haven't.'

'Bear with me, Cooper, there's a good chap.

I'm doing this for you, if you did but know it.' The Inspector pressed his lips together tantalisingly and gave a fleeting wink. 'Trust me, my friend, okay? We're all working towards the same end here, whatever it looks like at the moment.'

Den stared at him, mind churning. 'Surely you're not using her as *bait*?' The realisation hit him smack between the eyes. Hemsley winked again, but said nothing. 'Good God, what'll the Super say if he finds out? Wasting all this money on the legal stuff . . .'

'All done in perfectly good faith, I promise you. There's a strong case against the woman: motive, means and opportunity. Circumstantial evidence. An unusual manner at the scene. Countless people have been charged on less than that. And I wouldn't call it bait, not at all. More of a face-saving exercise, thanks to your untidy love life, if you must know the truth of it.'

'But . . .' Den went cold as the implications dawned. Hemsley was playing a game that Den could never have guessed at. A ruthless game that was causing considerable misery to an innocent woman. 'But surely . . .' he tried again.

'Nothing more to be said. As far as you're concerned, Mrs Deirdre Watson killed Sean O'Farrell, and just for the record I for one would not be altogether gobsmacked to discover that she really did. Give her another couple of days and things might take a surprising turn.'

'You think she might confess?' Den's scepticism was close to a sneer.

Danny tapped the side of his nose and said nothing.

Lilah looked at Gordon's face and knew Mary's planned confrontation wasn't going to happen. It had all gone beyond that. She only needed to ask him one question: 'Did the calf die last night?'

He didn't even pretend surprise that she knew about his deal with destiny. 'It died,' he nodded. 'Nice little heifer, too. Choked to death before I could get it born.'

'Oh dear,' she said weakly.

'I've been arranging for a dispersal sale,' he said tonelessly. 'And a relief milker to tide us over until then. He starts tomorrow afternoon. Funny – it only took a couple of phone calls.' He sat down heavily on one end of the sofa. Lilah fixed her gaze on the thick socks he wore, unable to meet his eyes.

'Sale?' said Claudia in a high voice.

'What calf died?' demanded Mary, in counterpoint.

Gordon looked slowly at each in turn. 'You'll be all right,' he told them. 'You'll both have what you've been wanting for a long time – to be rid of this place. It'll all go to you, half each.'

Mary gave an inarticulate cry; Claudia put a hand to her throat. Lilah ignored them.

'So you'll be milking again in the morning,' she said. He nodded. 'We can go after that then. I can drive you.'

'Yes,' he smiled. 'You can drive me.'

They slept together again that night, but without making love. Gordon wept in his sleep, hot tears dripping onto Lilah's neck, where she clasped him close.

Afterwards, Den believed he had known what was coming, from the first split second he recognised her car as it drew up outside his flat. He'd been on the verge of leaving for work, stepping through his front door. *She always was good at timing,* he thought daftly, watching her walk round to the passenger door, waiting for Hillcock to emerge. He stood like a dazed bullock on the threshold of the slaughter house, knowing instinctively that something appalling was about to happen.

Wordlessly, Den led them up to his flat. In the main room, where Lilah and he had spent countless evenings before going to bed together, he arranged his visitors with slow formality.

'Gordon has something to tell you,' she said, looking at a point between the two men. 'We came here because I feel we owe it to you. We should of course be at the police station. It's completely against the rules.'

Den found himself wanting to skip the next part of the proceedings. He wanted to cut to the *Why?* and *How?* and *What the bloody hell were you thinking of?* It seemed somehow a gratuitous unkindness, like a stern father insisting on a confession, to force the man to utter the opening words.

Gordon seemed willing enough, however. He even smiled a little, as if finding something ironic in the situation. His words when they came felt rehearsed. 'I can't let you torture poor Deirdre any more,' he began. 'She and I go back a long way. I thought I could do it at first . . . that it was the perfect solution . . .' He looked at Lilah as if for courage. 'But for ever is a long time to live with this sort of thing.' He inhaled deeply. 'I killed Sean. I think you knew that all along.'

'Because of the badgers?' Den couldn't stop himself from asking, suddenly urgently needing to examine the reasons for the deed. Until now, he had concentrated entirely on establishing where the guilt lay. 'Because Sean was involved in baiting and lamping?' It sounded feeble in his own ears and Gordon's reaction made it more so.

'Of course not. What do I care about bloody badgers?' he scorned. 'Who'd murder somebody for that?'

Lilah made a faint sound, reminding them of her presence. Den felt cold. His thoughts cartwheeled, trying to grasp all the implications of what was happening.

'It was revenge,' she murmured. 'You know you always used to tell me, Den, how that was the most easily understood motive for murder? Explain it to him, Gordon,' she prompted.

Gordon looked at her with a frown. 'Revenge?' he asked her dully.

She faltered. 'Well, yes . . . sort of, at least.' To Den she was agonisingly vulnerable at that moment. Not a responsible citizen persuading her partner to confess his crime, but a young girl adrift in a greasy ocean of male motivations and obsessions.

Gordon heaved a tremendous sigh. 'No, I wouldn't call it revenge,' he judged. 'It was more a case of killing the messenger. He told me something I'd spent my whole life trying not to know.' He looked at Lilah. 'You still don't get it, do you, little one? I don't think you understand even now what it was all about.'

She started forward, insulted and yet still concerned to shield him. Den put his hand out to her, not connecting, but achieving his purpose. She subsided and crossed her arms tightly over her stomach.

Den wanted it all to be over with. He wanted

Hillcock tidied out of sight, leaving him to persuade Lilah that it had all been nothing more than a painful dream, an episode they could both file away as if it had never happened. It was going to be all right, he believed. Everything he'd wanted was actually coming true. He had to clench his jaw against the oncoming grin of triumph.

'Tell us then,' Lilah ordered Hillcock. 'You owe it to me, at least, to explain yourself.'

'Isn't it enough that I've admitted to it? You know about last night? Did you follow me?'

She met his gaze. 'You let everything hang on whether a calf lived or died.'

'Hang,' he repeated meaningfully. 'Yes.'

She grimaced and swallowed hard. Gordon sighed again. 'It took me most of the night; I thought I'd lose the cow as well, but she'll be all right, I think.'

'I wondered if I should call the vet.'

'The vet wouldn't have been any use.'

'No.'

Den kept silent, aware that they were speaking in code; that there were aspects and secrets that he might never be party to. It didn't matter now: he could afford to leave Hillcock some scraps.

Summoning reserves from somewhere, Lilah turned to Den. 'It was really about Abigail, I suppose,' she said. 'Gordon . . .' she prompted again.

'You're Abigail's father, aren't you?' Den said. 'She looks like you. And Sean found out – threatened to tell the girl, take her away, something like that. And you felt forced to kill him.'

'Close, Sergeant,' said Hillcock generously. 'In fact, up to that afternoon I thought the same thing myself. Heather and I had a bit of a fling at more or less the right time. As you say, the girl looks like me. Heather let me believe it. She got what she wanted, and told me never to speak of it. Sean would raise the kid as his own, and everything would be decent and respectable.' His face suggested bewilderment at the ways of this woman.

Den looked at Lilah. 'Is this news to you?'

She shook her head. 'I noticed how alike they are, a few days ago. I was quite sure Gordon must be her father. But then Mary took me up to Granny's room, and she told us a story that I finally realised explained that it couldn't be true. But I asked Heather before I worked it out, and she saved me the trouble.'

Den blinked. 'You've lost me. What does Granny Hillcock have to do with it?'

She flushed a painful shade of crimson and stared hard at the floor. 'Tell him,' said Gordon. 'It'll come better from you.'

'Gordon isn't anybody's father and isn't ever

going to be,' she mumbled. She looked at her lover. 'That's the message Sean gave you, is it? Your mother and sister and grandmother have all kept it from you, ever since you spent six months in hospital being treated for cancer. They wanted you to think Abigail was yours, so you'd believe you were a normal man.' She looked at Den. 'Being normal is important to Gordon.'

Gordon took up the story. 'It was my father. I imagine he put quite some pressure on her. I think my parents convinced themselves the kid really was mine, in the end.' His throat heaved with disgust. 'And Sean told me the whole thing, just splurging it out, there in the yard, because I said something about having kids with Lilah.'

The girl made an inarticulate sound of pain.

'You're the victim here,' Gordon said softly. 'But you've had a lucky escape.'

'Yes,' she nodded, with tears on her cheeks.

Den shivered. As he looked at Lilah, he found himself feeling nothing resembling love. Perversely, now that she seemed to be turning away from Hillcock, Den wasn't sure he wanted her after all.

Gordon grunted as if she'd punched him.

Den felt a surge of impatience with the whole sordid confession. 'That's enough,' he said. 'We'll all go to the station now and you can make a statement.'

But Hillcock and Lilah hadn't finished. 'She only visited me twice, in all those months,' he muttered. 'When I was having radiotherapy and my hair fell out. When Spike and Bobby and Jason all died, leaving me the only survivor out of the whole group, she wasn't there to help me. She wouldn't go and speak to the doctors when they asked her. It was always Granny and Dad, never my mother.'

In spite of himself, Den was hooked. 'What was wrong with you?'

'It was Granny who insisted on taking me to the doctor. I had a lump, right here.' He touched a point just below his collarbone. 'My mother said it would go away if we just ignored it.' He fingered the place reminiscently. 'I was thin and apathetic and didn't feel well. Granny took charge, and they said she'd saved my life. It was Hodgkins Disease – that's a sort of cancer than young boys are prone to.'

Den and Lilah shifted restlessly, but said nothing. 'I was in hospital in Bristol for nearly six months – though I went home a couple of times for a few days. That's a long way to go, if you're trying to run a farm. Granny and Dad came every weekend. Once they brought Mary. My mother came twice and cried the whole time. The nurses lost patience with her, because she made me cry as well. Anyway, the treatment in those days was massively aggressive. They removed my spleen and bombarded me with radiation. And I survived. I got completely better. They said it was a miracle. They must have told my parents that I was sterile as a result of the radiation, but they never said a word to me, and I never suspected. At least . . .' He looked at Lilah as if asking for forgiveness, or understanding.

'At least you did everything you could to hide it from yourself,' she supplied unemotionally. 'That explains quite a lot.' She flushed and looked away.

'So what about Sean?' Den asked, like any plodding policeman.

'No more to be said about him. He used me for his own purposes. He was a manipulator. Even Heather's illness suited him. He thought he could get away with anything. And then he taunted me, because he could see how in love with Lilah I was. It niggled him to see me happy. He couldn't resist bringing me down.'

'Was it such bad news, though?' Den persisted. 'Thousands of men are sterile.'

'Thousands of men don't have a prime Devon farm to hand on,' Hillcock spat back. 'But it wasn't just that. He *laughed* at me, deliberately trying to get a rise out of me. When I grabbed the fork, he laughed again. Still yammering away about my father and Heather and everything, when I knocked him down.'

'How come Mrs Watson didn't hear any of it from the office?'

Gordon shrugged. 'I thought she might, especially when he screamed. But the doors were shut and she was probably cursing that computer of hers. Then Sean got up . . .' He looked rather wildly at Den. 'I had no idea I'd hurt him enough to kill him. *He got up*, even after the second jab I gave him. Stood there looking down at himself, as if it was a little scratch. I left him there and went back to the house, chucking the fork in the shed as I passed. I washed my hands of him.'

'What did you think would happen? He'd have prosecuted you for GBH, at the very least.'

'I wasn't thinking about him. I was thinking about what he'd told me, and what it meant for Lilah, and the farm, and then there was the recording. I just got the milking done as usual. When I found him in the barn . . . dead . . . it was . . .' At last the man broke down, hands over his face, shoulders shaking.

Den watched with detachment, thinking back to the evening when he and Young Mike had first been called to Dunsworthy. 'You think he was trying to get to you? When he dragged himself into the barn? Was he heading for the parlour?'

'Of course he was. Always had to have the last word, did Sean.'

'He must have made a superhuman effort, with those injuries.'

Hillcock was plainly past caring. 'Okay,' said Den. 'We'll go now.'

'I'll stay here,' said Lilah, brooking no argument.

Deirdre was released and driven home in time for lunch. The sense of having been in hospital, rather than police custody, was still strong. Her legs wobbled like a post-operative patient and she couldn't face eating. She was weak and weepy and she no longer quite knew who she was.

People would know she had been seriously taken for a murderer. They would ask themselves how that could be. Some would sympathise, but in some confused minds she would always be guilty.

She felt rage at her treatment, but beneath that, pushing through like a prickly cactus, was fear. She knew now how treacherous the world could be.

After it was all over and Gordon had been taken into custody and Den was back in his flat, he found Lilah still curled in the same chair where he'd left her two hours earlier. He looked at her carefully. 'Are you okay?'

'No, of course I'm not,' came the muffled reply.

'You did the right thing, making him face the music.'

'I didn't make him. Nobody did. He decided for himself. He couldn't go on letting Deirdre take the blame for what he did.' She grimaced miserably. 'It was all my doing, putting you onto her the way I did.'

'You miscalculated,' Den nodded. 'Danny picked it up and ran with it. He knew she hadn't done it, all along.'

'What?'

'It was clever, you have to give him that. For one thing, it was a way of making sure nobody could say I was fixated on framing Hillcock. And it did bring the real killer out of the woodwork.' He smiled ruefully. 'I hadn't reckoned on him being that decent.'

'Who? Danny?'

'Hillcock of course. Not many people would care if the wrong person took the rap.'

'I think they would. I don't think anybody normal could live with something like that for long.'

'And Gordon is normal?'

'Don't,' she said quietly. She looked utterly defeated. 'We can't pretend Gordon never happened, you know.'

'Come here,' he said softly, going closer than he had dared so far. He bent over her and gathered her into his arms. Inside a voice was foolishly repeating a line from his distant schooldays. *But yet, the pity of it, Iago*. He didn't think he could find any better words to express his feelings.

THE COTSWOLD MYSTERIES